THE ONLY CATCH

JESS TURNER

THE ONLY CATCH

JESS TURNER

CITY OWL
PRESS

THE ONLY CATCH

CITY OWL PRESS
www.cityowlpress.com

Cover Design by MiblArt. All stock photos licensed appropriately.

Edited by Tee Tate.

For information on subsidiary rights, please contact the publisher at info@cityowlpress.com.

Print Edition ISBN: 978-1-64898-539-3

Digital Edition ISBN: 978-1-64898-540-9

Printed in the United States of America

For Josh, the main character in my favorite story.

Chapter One

For Chloe Foster, life both ended and began with the broken lock on the office door.

Earlier in the evening on that particular Friday, dinner service at Redbud was a meticulously controlled chaos. Chloe had been the executive chef for almost three years, and as *Food & Wine* had recently declared, the Chicago restaurant was having a moment. Reservations were booked for six months straight, the hostess phone ringing nonstop with hopeful pleas of anniversaries and date nights, marriage proposals and 50th birthdays.

Chloe was unaffected by the hype, the clamor for tables. She was unmoved by the fact that every Chicago magazine had declared her the "chef to watch" based on her vibrant, modern plates and almost religious devotion to local, seasonal ingredients. For her, it was always about getting food from the kitchen to the table with efficiency and flawlessness. She was a technician.

"One swordfish, two pork bellies, one ribeye mid-rare, one ribeye medium!"

Her expediting voice had taken practice. Too soft, and the sous chef and line cooks would think she was asking. Too loud, and it sounded like she was competing with other sounds in the kitchen.

She'd made it very clear that in her kitchen, her voice was the only sound that mattered.

"One citrus and fennel, two arugula, one chard!" Medium volume and always unwaveringly steady.

Servers were in and out, picking up plates at the pass. A flame raged a little too high, and a grill cook barely blinked while he used one hand to smother it with a pot lid, while the other hand sautéed tiny cubes of celeriac for the winter root hash. The kitchen was full of the sounds that Chloe loved most—the hiss of a steak hitting a cast-iron pan, the rhythmic chopping of tarragon and sage, bourbon being added to a reduction, and the *fwwwwoooomp* of the flame as it caught.

A server presented a steak to her. "Too rare."

The chef gently poked the top of the perfectly cooked meat with her middle finger, declaring it medium, just as it had been ordered.

"Re-fire steak!"

The diners were always right, even when they were wrong.

She used the corner of her towel to wipe a speck of clementine reduction from a plate of seared scallops, paper-thin slices of beets, and smoked pistachios. She pinched her tweezers to place a tiny tangle of baby pea shoots atop the dish. She sourced the greens from a grower who produced them in a rooftop greenhouse right here in the city.

Out of the corner of her eye, she saw David Newhouse enter the kitchen. With his coiffed hair and Prada suit, shirt slightly open at the neck, he always looked like he was headlining as "rich man" in a play and had been playing the part of the restaurant's owner since its inception. His wealth flowed from his wife, Lila Harris, but he carried himself as if it had always been his own. He had a clichéd obsession with luxury, which translated into pressure for Chloe to add more black truffles to the menu, more foie, more matsutake mushrooms. Recently, he'd tried to coax her to edit her scotch quail egg, the dish that had put both Chloe and Redbud on the map, and gild it with gold leaf. *Gold leaf!* She generally met these suggestions with a flash in her green eyes as she demanded that David concentrate on writing the checks and leave the cooking to her. He was trim, fit, and arrogant, way too tan for winter, almost trite in his sex appeal, and moved through the world with the confidence of someone who had never been asked to wait for anything.

They had been sleeping together for two years.

"Chef," David greeted her with a wide smile. Even his teeth were too white.

"Why is this plate still sitting here?" Chloe demanded, choosing to ignore him. "I sauced this two minutes ago. It should have hit the tablecloth three minutes ago, max!"

"Table eight keeps changing their mind about entrees after they've been ordered," a food runner replied.

"Well, congratulations to table eight! Get this damn plate off the pass then!" Chloe snapped.

David calmly cleared his throat and placed his hand lightly in the center of the chef's back.

"Can you take a minute to come out and meet someone?"

Chloe used the point of her tweezers to reposition a flake of Maldon salt atop a carefully formed oval of beef carpaccio. Her kitchen sometimes felt more like a lab—precise and sterile. This is what people wanted out of fine dining: tweezer food.

"David, we're really in the weeds in here. Can it wait?"

He responded by cocking his head to one side, his manicured brow arched.

"Fine." She sighed, smoothing the front of her chef coat. She tucked a strand of her short brown hair behind her ear, noting that it had grown too shaggy for her liking. When did people find time to get haircuts?

She followed David through the kitchen's swinging doors and out into the dimly lit dining room. She was always struck by how gorgeous it was, how perfect the temperature was, how the acoustics of the space were so thoughtfully designed that certain sounds were muted while others—like the clink of a champagne toast or the gentle peal of a woman's laughter—rang out softly. A young couple sat side-by-side, their backs to the exposed brick wall, their heads bent low over a shared dessert. The woman closed her eyes and tipped her head back at the first taste of raspberry elderflower panna cotta, a dish that Chloe had finally declared "right" only that morning. Another duo spoke softly to each other over flickering votives, ignoring their entrees completely as the man reached across the table and ran his fingertips across the woman's knuckles.

I don't care if you're on a first date or if he's about to propose. The raviolo needs to be eaten when it's hot! Chloe wanted to scold.

There were only fifteen tables in the small restaurant, all topped with pressed white linens and surrounded by modern, black, ladder-back chairs. Fifteen tables meant long wait lists, constantly filled reservations, and exclusivity—the basis of every restaurant The Harris Group owned.

David adjusted his pocket square and led her to the best table in the house, a two-top positioned against a floor-to-ceiling window, the perfect place to enjoy optimal people watching on Randolph Street. An actress whom Chloe recognized was seated across from a young politician who'd recently achieved notoriety for her fiercely outspoken behavior on the Senate floor. This is what restaurants like Redbud were great at—bringing together seemingly random combinations of people who met to discuss "projects" over their shared love of tweezer food. It was all designed for people who wanted to see and be seen, who would inspire other diners to tell their rich friends, "You'll never guess who I saw sharing a blood orange tart at Redbud!"

"I'd like you to meet the chef, Chloe Foster," David said, his hand still resting on her lower back.

David loved parading Chloe to the tables of VIPs, showing her off to them, showing them off to her. It was his very favorite thing, throwing open the doors to his manor like Gatsby and opening his arms as if to say, "This is mine, all mine, and aren't you lucky to be invited inside!"

When Chloe swiftly and gracefully excused herself, David exchanged air kisses with his guests and followed her through the swinging doors.

Everything on the line was running like the well-oiled machine Chloe had designed herself. Tickets were in order, Chloe's sous chef,

Steph, was expediting with confidence, and the plates looked flawless as they left the kitchen, one after another.

"Can I talk to you in the back for a minute?"

This time, David followed her, past the walk-in, through the dry storage, and into the tiny back office. Chloe locked the door with a brittle-sounding snap, and in less than a second, their mouths were on each other. David was an absolutely ravenous kisser. It was the thing that had surprised her the most the first time this had happened two years ago. He looked so proper, so refined, not a hair out of place, but when they were alone, his desire was almost desperate.

"We can't keep doing this," Chloe breathed, David's lips on her neck.

"Why not?" he replied, making quick work of unbuttoning her chef coat and groaning when she drew his lower lip between her teeth.

"Your wife," she offered as an image of icy, beautiful Lila flashed through her mind.

As they kissed, his hands in her hair, under her bra, his fingers sliding down the front of her pants, she wondered for a moment what David and Lila had been like when they'd first met, if they'd shared first dates over candlelight, moony-eyed as the food grew cold between them. Was their passion undeniable? Had they ever discussed children? Had either of them ever given up anything for the other?

"Hmmmm?" David responded, his mouth full of her.

"Your wife," she said again, her half-hearted resolve weakening when she felt his breath, hot in her ear.

"I promise you, the last thing she would notice is what I'm doing."

Chloe backed up against the desk, resisting the urge to sweep the papers onto the floor in cinematic fashion, and sat atop the stack of invoices that she would attend to in the morning. His mouth was everywhere—on her collarbone, her hip, her belly—until finally he was on the floor in front of her, her hands entwined in his hair.

And that's exactly how his wife found them when that lock on the door announced its failure with a sad little click. When Chloe would replay the scene over and over in the coming days, she would blame that broken lock for delivering the most humiliating moment of her life— the moment when she was looking directly into Lila's face for three full seconds while David's head was still buried between her thighs.

Chloe wasn't sure if the "no, no, no, no," that sounded in her ears had actually been spoken aloud or if it was simply a silent, echoed refrain in her own mind. She was, however, sure of what had flashed in Lila's eyes for the briefest of moments. She had seen a tiny flicker of what had looked like hurt, a barely-there twitch at the corner of her lipsticked mouth, before her tight frown had returned.

"Get up, David," Lila said in a voice so calm that Chloe shivered.

David flinched like someone had attacked him from behind, and in that second before he rose from the floor, he looked up to meet Chloe's eyes and she just knew that it—all of it—was over.

Somehow, she finished dinner service. When the final tickets came in, she excused herself from expediting and locked the staff washroom, where she avoided looking at her flushed cheeks and slightly swollen lips in the mottled mirror. She ran her hands under the water and clenched and unclenched her fists, trying to get some feeling back into her trembling fingers.

WHY? she screamed to herself.

David wasn't at all her type. And what was her type anymore? Her sixteen-hour workdays hardly left time for a dating life. But why on earth would she risk it all on *him*, a married man whom she didn't even like that much?

She wondered if Lila was still in the back room, if they had been negotiating, if David had begged, if he'd thought to defend Chloe in any way.

She exhaled slowly and clutched the sides of the small sink. She thought for a moment that if she could just squeeze her shoulders through the tiny window, she could roll out into the alleyway and start sprinting. She could leave the whole mess behind and open a burger shack on a beach somewhere.

"You OK?" Steph asked when the chef eventually returned to the kitchen. Her sous chef was looking at her with deep concern and something else, maybe pity, with a tinge of embarrassment.

"I'm fine," she responded too brightly, faking a half smile for Steph's benefit and summoning every ounce of energy to push her shoulders back. "I'll be fine."

Lila marched through the kitchen and out the side door, David trailing behind her, his head bowed. No one said a word. Whatever agreement the owners had reached about her future, it was painfully clear: this would be Chef Chloe Foster's last night at Redbud.

There was nothing more to do but collect her bag and jacket from the staff coatroom and pause to look around her kitchen one last time. She cleared her throat amidst the din of the breakdown routine, willing her voice to carry over the sound of the flat top being scraped, the counters being scrubbed, the racks of glasses being loaded into the sanitizer.

"Thank you, everyone," Chloe called out. The kitchen fell quiet immediately. "Thank you for...everything."

"Good night, chef!"

"Have a good one, chef!"

"See you tomorrow!"

Chloe held her breath as she walked through the chorus of farewells and see-you-laters from her unknowing team. She squared her shoulders again and willed her neck to support her head as she pushed through the side door to the alleyway. She didn't wait around to hear the words, "pack your knives and leave." She already knew.

It was only when she reached the sidewalk and the frigid Chicago air slapped her across the face with all the cruelty of February that she allowed herself to break down sobbing.

Chapter Two

She tried not to think about her restaurant, but still spent the next week thinking about how she was trying not to think about her restaurant.

She assumed Steph had taken the helm as executive chef, at least in the interim, and she really did want to be proud of her. Steph had been the first call she'd made when The Harris Group had offered her Redbud a year earlier. They'd worked together at a small Brasserie in New York shortly after graduating from their respective culinary schools. Because of her skills, focus, and the almost uncanny calm that she emanated in the kitchen, Chloe had been eager to work with her again. She was happy that a door had opened to her friend, who had worked so hard, even if that door was a result of Chloe's own garbage decisions.

Chloe picked up the phone to text her again and again: *Don't forget that the best tuna belly is available on Wednesdays only. Remember to pay the fruit man. Keep an eye on Jake, he's been lagging at sauté.* But she resisted. She knew she'd lost the right to advise, and through the numbness interspersed with pangs of regret, she couldn't stop asking herself, *what have I done?*

It took days to shake the muscle memory of her work at Redbud, to unclench her fists and realize that she didn't have to spend every waking minute running lists in her head, delegating, assigning, executing, expediting. She no longer had to get up before the sun to claim the freshest snapper at the fish market, no longer had to stand for eight, ten, sometimes twelve-hour stretches, stooped over cutting boards and plates as a white-hot pain settled into her aging knees.

She no longer had a reason to see David.

The fact that she didn't miss him didn't really surprise her. Their "relationship" was something she'd always left behind at work and didn't really consider again until he popped up in the kitchen every few days. Did she miss his hands, his mouth, the way he assessed her curves with an expression of wonder and hunger, how he made that sound into the side of her neck when she pressed him up against the cold wall of the walk-in? She didn't want to miss any of it.

Every time she replayed even a tiny snippet of their affair, she saw Lila and that look, that look that went from shocked to completely flat in the span of three seconds. She couldn't shake the way the other woman's eyes had filled ever-so-slightly, only to be erased with a series of rapid blinks and the return of her signature tight-lipped frown. Chloe quieted this stew of unwelcome thoughts by making an actual stew—a gumbo-inspired creation with a deep roux—which she promptly burned when she opted to scroll Netflix rather than adjust the burner. She opened the windows to allow the smoke to escape, and ordered more spicy Thai noodles from the place down the street.

She didn't leave her apartment for days, which left her feeling like a thirty-five-year-old cat lady without a cat.

One afternoon, she spent an entire hour examining her face in the bathroom mirror. She used both hands to push her cheeks back, lifting the outer corners of her eyes. She did an audit of every pore, every preview of what could be a wrinkle. She smoothed her short hair, still too shaggy, now cowlicked on one side from lying on the couch too much. She put on some dark lipstick and wiped it off.

"You're old," she said to her reflection.

And someone much younger has just been waiting to take your place, she thought with a dose of self-pity.

The week managed to feel like both a day and a month. She stayed up until the early hours of the morning, slept until noon, binged detective shows and peanut M&Ms, and wondered how life would feel if she never spoke to another human again.

On the seventh day, she called Julia.

Her sister was two years older and had been working in LA as a publicist for almost a decade. Her wife, Beth, was a stylist with a full roster of celebrity clients. Their glamorous, sun-drenched life was an entire world apart from the sweet childhood that Chloe and Julia had shared on their family's farm in Vermont. Julia was always regaling Chloe with stories of premieres and parties, the lunches and scandals of A-listers.

"Hey, sister!" she said warmly after the first ring. "What's up?"

"I messed up. Like really messed up," Chloe blurted without a pause.

"Tell me."

Chloe had heard Julia say the same two words countless times—to clients who had been pulled over for DUI in the Hollywood Hills, to actors caught partying a little too hard in strip clubs, to married costars caught, mid-embrace, between their trailers. There was never any judgment, no emotion in her sister's request, just a professional requirement for the full story.

Tell me.

And it all just poured out of Chloe. The way her work had been leaving her unfulfilled for a while and how the treadmill had been set to "sprint" for so long. How maybe she was done with tweezer food, how it didn't bring her joy anymore, even though she seemed to have an innate talent for it, and what did that say about her? She told her sister about the affair, the sneaking around, the broken lock, the look on Lila's face. She admitted that she'd started to wonder if her staff had suspected all along, if Steph had known. Her cheeks burned with humiliation at the thought. She confessed that she might never leave her apartment again. For a big city, Chicago was actually a pretty small town, and she was terrified that no one would hire her to be in charge ever again.

She told her sister how she had blown it all up.

Julia never said, "Oh, Chloe, a married man?" or "Oh, Chloe, after you worked so hard!" like so many older sisters would have. She just quietly absorbed Chloe's rush of words and asked calmly, "So, what are we going to do about it?"

"Well, Redbud is over."

"Yes, Redbud is definitely over. And I'll just ask you this one time, and I promise to accept whatever your answer is," Julia began. "Do you think we need to contact a lawyer?"

"Jesus, Julia, no. Definitely no," Chloe protested. "I wanted all of it. I made the first move, and I didn't even think about the fallout. I just...didn't care."

"Oh, Chloe."

There it was. The sympathy-disappointment cocktail.

"I have to find something else, obviously," Chloe said while assessing her apartment with its huge windows, restored herringbone floors, and modern kitchen. "It's not like it's cheap to live here. My takeout budget alone..."

"Of course you'll find something. You're Chloe Fucking Foster, remember? *Bon Appétit*? *Food & Wine*? You cook in a Michelin-starred restaurant! People wait six months for a table just to see what you'll do next!"

Chloe smiled despite herself. Her sister had always been her loudest champion.

"French Laundry, La Bernardin," Julia continued. "I mean, really? Do I have to read your resumé back to you?"

"I'm Chloe Fucking Foster," she murmured, suddenly feeling both hungry and tired.

"And if you decide to take a break from Chicago, I might have something for you."

"What kind of something?"

"I have a client who needs a personal chef, just for three—"

"No," Chloe interrupted.

"Let me at least give you the details!"

"Julia. No."

Chloe had known other chefs who had accepted similar offers, cooking for rich people in their private homes, and she'd heard the horror stories. Her friend from culinary school had turned down a chance to work the line at one of Jean-Georges Vongerichten's restaurants and instead took a high-paying job as a personal chef for a family in their Hamptons mansion. About a week in, she was packing school lunches and being treated like a nanny/cater waiter while witnessing the couple's marital indiscretions and getting bossed around by the children.

"Fine, but it could be great, just for—"

"No."

"OK, OK!" Julia laughed.

The sisters chatted for a few more minutes, and Julia revealed that she and Beth had just started the IVF process. She squealed when she confessed that they couldn't wait to be mothers. Julia told a story about a client who had been caught in a car with a prostitute, at first omitting names until her sister pressed her. They laughed when she finally revealed the very famous singer's identity, and Chloe didn't even know who it was. They said their goodbyes, and Julia reminded her sister to call their parents sometime soon.

A half hour on the phone with Julia, and Chloe felt lighter. Her sister was a fixer, a pep-talker, a soother.

"I'm Chloe Fucking Foster," she mumbled to her empty apartment, almost believing it.

She vowed to pull herself together and craft a plan the very next day. She would make some calls, charm some investors, and reach out to old contacts, as if David had never happened. She would walk into lunches and meetings with her head held high because her culinary pedigree would speak for itself. She would stop eating cereal straight from the box, and she would make eggs Benedict for breakfast. She'd get a haircut.

But for now, she sank back into the couch and curled her legs beneath her, desperate to finish the Irish lady-detective show she'd been devouring.

She could be Chloe Fucking Foster in the morning.

Chapter Three

The next morning, Chloe woke early and cleaned her entire apartment. She folded up the blankets that had been trying to claim a permanent home on her couch. She brought her many takeout containers and wine bottles downstairs to the recycling bins, and scrubbed the stovetop that had barely been used in a week, as if she were prepping for dinner service. She vacuumed the beautiful jewel-toned rug she'd shipped home from a trip to Morocco and fluffed the cushions on her modern, green velvet sectional.

She loved this apartment, loved its open concept and the insistent light that it let in, even in the dead of winter. She adored her Wicker Park neighborhood with its hipster scene and new money influence, and the coffee shops, bookstores, and refined little eateries that popped up around her every day. Mostly, she loved the way the place had held her in its arms for the last week.

But it was officially time to get out of the house.

She managed to sweet-talk her favorite salon into squeezing her in for a cut and color that afternoon. After two hours in the chair and her declaration of going "short-short this time," she practically skipped out of the salon, feeling like a chic, slightly tousled Audrey Hepburn. She ran her hand along the back of her freshly clipped hair and felt a new appreciation for the feeling of shedding something on her own terms.

Chloe had invited Steph for dinner that evening and was desperate to clear the air about everything that had happened. Also, she really wanted to make her friend some beautiful food.

She wandered the narrow aisles of her favorite neighborhood market, knocking a few ideas around. Soup? Roast chicken? Chili? No, Steph was a vegetarian, and meatless chilis were bullshit. When she meandered into the produce section and saw big baskets of lemons on display, she knew she had it—Cacio e pepe.

The first time she'd eaten it was when she was in Rome, her junior year of high school, as part of an exchange program. It was her first trip abroad, and her appetite for absolutely everything—from pasta to oxtail to gelato—had delighted her host family. Her host mother taught her to make the dish after Chloe had swooned over it at a restaurant, showing her how to grate fine clouds of pecorino and parmesan, how to always add more coarsely ground pepper, and then even more. *"Di più! Di più!"*

Chloe made her own version with an aggressive amount of lemon, and she always thought of it as her back-pocket "third date dish" if she cooked for someone at her apartment. Of course, her dates generally didn't reach that milestone because she rarely followed through. Who had time to date when they ran a restaurant? *Used* to run a restaurant. She hated the past tense of it all.

She grabbed a half dozen lemons—she would use the excess in her vodka tonics, depending on how the job search progressed this week—a box of bucatini, and the cheeses that she needed, adding a small round of camembert and a block of cave-aged cheddar for some pre-dinner snacking. She picked up a baguette from a local bakery along with a beautiful head of radicchio.

Walking back to her apartment through the swirling snow, Chloe felt almost cheerful. She was cooking dinner for her friend. They would eat and laugh and open a bottle of wine and hopefully redefine their friendship outside of the restaurant. She was going to tell Steph the truth about everything, and she was going to leave the rest of Redbud in her rearview mirror.

Yup, this is all going to be great, she thought, right before her phone buzzed in her coat pocket.

She knew before she even looked at the screen. David.

She waited until she was back at her apartment before listening to his voicemail.

"Chloe. We have to talk about what happened. I...I didn't want things to end like that. I think we need...maybe we can meet and discuss everything." He sounded shaken, unmoored. "Lila is just... she's out for blood. I'm staying at the Harbor Country house for a few days. Maybe you can...I don't know. But we do need to talk. Our lawyers have some questions about your contract. Call me soon, please."

Her contract. It wasn't that Chloe had forgotten about it, but she assumed that it would just go away in light of everything that had happened, that both Lila and David would *make* it go away. She realized that she would have to talk to him, or at least to his lawyers, at some point, but she couldn't bring herself to devote a speck of bandwidth to considering any of that right now. Right now, she had pasta to make.

When Steph arrived promptly at seven, the prep was done, the stockpot was boiling, and the cheeses had been artfully composed on a cutting board with assorted crackers and a bowl of buttery Castelvetrano olives. Chloe welcomed her friend inside, complimenting her on her outfit and wondering if she should go in for a hug. She assessed her own cropped gray sweater and high-waisted vintage Levi's, hoping she looked OK.

Why am I nervous?

"Wine?" Chloe offered, already serving two healthy pours of Pinot Noir.

"Please."

Steph curled her long legs beneath her on the couch, and Chloe realized that her friend had never been to her apartment before. Hardly anyone had been here, except for David, when they'd stumbled through the door at two a.m., after already beginning to remove each other's clothes in the hallway. She supposed she wasn't much for entertaining at home.

The two women chatted about the Chicago dining scene while Chloe busied herself with broiling the halved heads of radicchio until they started to blister and char. She mixed a vinaigrette of olive oil, aged balsamic, and honey to drizzle on top. Pasta was dropped into water, salads were plated, and wineglasses were topped off. Chloe drained the bucatini and tossed it in a sauté pan with butter, lemon zest, grated cheese, and heaps of coarse black pepper. Just as she'd been taught, she used a ladle of the starchy cooking water to move everything around in the pan. When the pasta hit the plates in a carefully composed tangle, and Chloe used the corner of her dish towel to wipe away a stray flake of pepper, Steph gave her a knowing smile.

"Always cheffing, right?"

Chloe shrugged with a grin and delivered their food to the table along with a bottle of Sancerre.

They quietly enjoyed their dinner for a few moments. Steph complimented Chloe on the lemon, the wine, and the dressing. When her friend tore a chunk from the baguette and used it to squeegee her plate, Chloe knew she'd done well.

Finally, Steph dabbed the corner of her mouth and set down her fork. Chloe held her breath.

"Chloe, what happened? I mean, I think I know what happened, but what happened?"

She exhaled slowly and peered at her friend over her wineglass. "I've been sleeping with David for about two years. I was restless. My dating life...I just didn't make time for anything else. And he was always there and...I don't know."

"And it just kind of happened?" Steph asked.

"I made it happen."

"But why him? He's such a...he's so arrogant. And married."

Chloe paused for a moment to consider her words, feeling a sort of resigned embarrassment. "There was just this chemistry. And we really clicked physically. And I never wanted more from him, and he never wanted more from me, and it was just this perfectly contained little thing."

"Until it wasn't."

"Until it wasn't," Chloe echoed.

The two women paused to refill their glasses.

"Did you know?" she asked, relieved to be free of the question she'd been obsessing over for the last week.

"I suspected, but I wasn't sure." Steph absently ran her finger around the top of her glass. "I didn't want it to be true."

Chloe nodded silently, desperate to think of what to say next.

The two women started speaking at the same time.

"I wish that—"

"So, what do you—"

"Sorry, go ahead," Chloe insisted, pouring each of them a splash of wine and watching as an errant drip landed on her friend's napkin, spreading like a bloodstain.

"So, what's next for you then?" Steph asked. "I'm sure there are a million restaurants knocking on your door."

"Well, I have a list of investors that I'll be calling tomorrow. I'll set up some meetings to talk concepts. I heard Annabella lost their executive chef, so maybe I'll look into that."

"Annabella is one of The Harris Group's restaurants now, remember?"

Chloe nearly missed the fleeting expression of pity that flickered in Steph's eyes.

"Oh, right. Well, it's a big city," Chloe said, even though it kind of wasn't.

She asked about Redbud, and Steph reported that things were going pretty smoothly. She'd moved Jake up from the line to be her sous chef, and he was really proving himself. Chloe nearly had to bite her napkin to stay quiet.

Jake isn't ready! She wanted to shriek. *Sabine before Jake, for sure.*

But it wasn't her place anymore. It quite literally wasn't her place anymore. Her friend was hardworking and smart, and she would have to figure it out on her own.

"Do you think...do you think you'll try to get it back?" Steph asked, her chin lifting slightly, her spine straight, as if she was squaring herself for battle.

"Try to get Redbud back? No. No, definitely not. I don't even want to cook like that anymore, with that fussy, fine dining mindset. I actually haven't for a while," Chloe insisted in a tone that was almost convincing. "And you're going to be great. Really, really great."

She wondered if that second *really* was too much.

"Well, you're going to be really, really great too!" Steph offered, once again looking as if she felt sorry for her.

After dishes of salted caramel gelato and two espressos each, the woman said their farewells at the door, hugging tightly.

"This was so nice! We should do this again soon," Steph said, zipping her down coat in preparation for the still-falling snow. "I'll host next time."

"Absolutely!" Chloe returned, counting the seconds until her closest friend was on the other side of the door.

It felt like goodbye.

After she'd locked up, she made the executive decision to ignore the dirty dishes and instead poured herself another glass of wine. The evening had gone well. Steph had loved the food, and it was a relief to share a bit of postmortem about Redbud, David, and Chloe's sudden exit. She stretched out her legs and lay back so she could stare through her giant living room window and admire the snow, spotlit by the streetlights. Had she been mistaken about that look of sympathetic embarrassment that had flashed across her friend's face?

She closed her eyes and let her heartache cover her like a blanket. Right before she dozed off, she found herself wondering just how many restaurants in the city Lila Harris actually did own.

Fifteen voicemails. Chloe had left fifteen voicemails with developers, investors, and fellow Chicago chefs, and not a single promising lead had come through. What was even happening? Why wasn't her phone buzzing with offers and invitations to lunch meetings? Wasn't she Chloe Fucking Foster?

She felt like she was chasing unrequited crushes all over the city.

She'd left two messages with Mattie Morrison, the young chef who had just won a James Beard award for her Lincoln Park farm-to-table restaurant. She'd been a Redbud regular and a Chloe Foster fan for years, but had responded only with a text offering,

Wish I could help!

Rory DaCosta, who'd told Chloe on at least ten occasions that she'd love to work with her, hadn't even returned her call.

After her emails had gone unanswered, Chloe eventually called Taylor Billings, the executive chef at Odette, in the middle of prep. She'd known Taylor in Northern California. They'd started at a small vineyard restaurant around the same time and had enjoyed each other as colleagues, advancing together and sharing the occasional cocktail after service.

"I'm sorry, Chloe. I can't," Taylor had half-whispered, the din of her busy kitchen a backdrop to her harried tone. "I'm sure you understand."

When Jenna Moran called back, and Chloe answered on the first ring, she didn't even care about the desperation her action suggested. Of all the chefs she'd reached out to, Jenna, a vocal advocate for female leadership in her kitchens, was the one she wanted to work with the most. She had four amazing restaurants. Chloe had recently enjoyed the best brunch of her life at L'oeuf, her West Loop café that boasted lines around the block, and her Brazilian place, Gostosa, seemed to be all that everyone in the city was talking about.

They'd set up a lunch meeting for that afternoon at a tapas bar, where Jenna was already seated when Chloe arrived. She looked as fierce as ever with her half-shaved head, multiple earrings, and slim-fitting black suit. The two women exchanged hellos and air-kissed each other's cheeks while Chloe thanked her for making time to meet.

"I hope you don't mind that I ordered for us already," Jenna said.

"Of course not," Chloe replied cheerfully, even though she obviously did.

Before their drinks arrived, Jenna cut swiftly to the chase.

"Look, Chloe, I respect you. A lot. It's why I wanted to meet with you today. I think you're brilliant."

Chloe tried to muster an expression that would look both humble and completely worthy of praise. She'd already arrogantly ranked Jenna's restaurants in terms of which kitchen she'd like to take over the most.

"But you have to know the power that Lila Harris has in this city," Jenna continued. "List the top twenty restaurants in Chicago. Lila has some involvement in every one of them, either because it's officially part of the Harris Group's holdings or because she's financed it. She has her hand in absolutely everything."

"I mean, I know The Harris Group is huge, but—"

"Chloe. Lila is the bank. *She's* the bank. She's financed all my restaurants, all your favorite places. And if she hasn't invested in your place, you don't want to piss her off because you might want her to invest in you someday. You see what I'm saying?"

All that Chloe could do was nod as their wine arrived, followed by a half dozen small plates of food. Braised pork cheek. Fire-roasted broccolini. Squid with jalapeño oil. Tiny manchego gougères. Chloe felt too sick to eat any of it as she considered the question she could barely stomach asking.

"So, what *are* you saying exactly? That I'm unemployable?" She pushed a fleck of mint around her plate with the tine of her fork, afraid she'd turn to stone if she met Jenna's eyes.

Jenna popped a gougère into her mouth and hummed her appreciation for the bite-sized puff. "What I'm saying is that Lila's reach is massive. She's everywhere. Her money is everywhere. And she knows exactly who to call."

Chloe fought back tears that were threatening the only coat of mascara she'd bothered to apply in over a week.

"And I think you're so talented and so cool. I really do," Jenna assured her as she sampled the pork. "And I would love for us to work together someday. I respect you, and I know what it's like to be a woman in this industry. But I have to tell you that you fucked the wrong person's husband."

Chloe continued to ignore the food and tried to absorb Jenna's words. Her training, her experience, her devoted study in some of the best restaurants in the world—none of that counted anymore? Lila may be the bank, but it was Chloe who had made Redbud what it was. It was Chloe and her meticulous attention to detail, her endless days, and her unwavering sacrifice of her personal life that had built Redbud from a concept to a raging success.

The delicate little cheese puff turned to paste in Chloe's throat as she remembered the look that had flickered across Lila's face–when their eyes had met in the back room.

Maybe you deserve everything that's happening here, she thought, twisting her napkin into a knot on her lap.

The rest of the lunch dragged on through a dozen more dishes and an equal number of awkward silences. Chloe tried to quiet the nagging voice in her head that whispered, *maybe you're not as good as you think you are. Maybe you never were.*

When the two chefs said their goodbyes, Jenna gently grabbed the top of Chloe's arm.

"Look. You know you messed up," she said. "But this isn't forever. Maybe get out of the city for a bit, you know?"

"Yeah, maybe," Chloe mumbled. "Thanks for lunch."

"Anytime, Chloe. You know I'm rooting for you."

Just not enough to have my back, Chloe thought sullenly as she returned to the windy sidewalk and trudged home through the cold.

It took another whole week of sending emails and making calls to prospective employers and investors in her pajamas before Chloe started to accept what was happening. She was being canceled. Rich and powerful Lila Harris, with her family money, her massive empire, and her womanizing husband, was ruining her prospects all over the city. And Chloe was the fool who had given it all up, who had handed Lila the keys to her life with her blessing to drive it all off a cliff. And for what? For David, a married man whom she didn't even care about beyond sex?

She didn't know what to do other than call him back.

"I was wondering if I'd hear from you again," he answered in his honeyed baritone.

Be calm, be cool. Take a breath, Chloe silently instructed herself.

"What the actual fuck, David?" she demanded in a way-too-loud-for-the-phone voice.

"I know, Chloe. I know. This isn't my doing. Lila just—"

"Lila just what? Lila just decided to destroy my career? Yeah, I've got that part. No one will hire me. I've got a goddamn scarlet letter on my chest, and every restaurant in the city wants absolutely nothing to do with me!"

"Chloe, you have to let her simmer down. Just give it a few months, you'll see," David said with that unnerving calm of his.

"A few months? I don't have a few months! I have rent."

"Well, surely you have savings..." David was starting to sound like he was losing interest in the conversation.

Chloe suddenly thought of the cartoons she used to watch with Julia, remembering a character whose ears would shoot steam when she was angry. Heat crept up her neck and into her face as she wondered if she was about to become that cartoon.

"Of course I have savings!" she snapped. "This isn't just about money. This is my career. It's what I do. I have to work. I don't know what to do with myself if I don't work."

Chloe hated what she was revealing to David. She'd never displayed any real emotion to him other than physical desire, and she didn't like the way she sounded—desperate and vulnerable.

"Regardless, your contract has been terminated," David said. "Every Harris Group contract is built the same. If there's a notable indiscretion, the right to terminate is ours. So, you don't have to worry about that part of things, OK?"

Chloe laughed bitterly. "A notable indiscretion. Is that what we were doing? Being notably indiscreet? Because you're making it sound like it was just me. Like you played no part in any of it."

"My lawyers advised me not to even contact you, Chloe."

"Fuck you, David," Chloe spat before hanging up. She regretted that she barely remembered the days of landlines, of heavy receivers that you could clang back into the cradle hard enough to rattle the rotary dialing wheel. Using an angry fingertip to tap a screen wasn't even remotely satisfying. Chloe grabbed the fuchsia silk throw pillow from her couch and screamed into it as loud as she could, hoping it had muffled things enough so her neighbors wouldn't think she was being brutally murdered.

After she returned the pillow to the end of her sectional and flopped against it, she called her sister.

"Julia, tell me more about that job."

Chapter Four

It's just three months, Chloe thought. As she was pulling her suitcases from the depths of her closet, she considered military boot camps, third trimesters, Weight Watchers. A woman could do anything for three months.

She would leave in the morning to start her new job as a live-in personal chef for Charlie Davis, one of Julia's biggest clients. She would prepare his meals, keep his refrigerator and cabinets stocked, and cook for any social gatherings he hosted. Chloe felt the position was about ten steps beneath her, but that depressing lunch with Jenna had helped her realize that maybe pressing pause on her life in the city could be a good thing. It could give her a chance to design a strategy for her next real job.

Admittedly, it had seemed like a much better idea when Chloe was operating under the assumption that she would be in LA for ninety days, shopping farmers' markets, correcting her pasty complexion, leaving her winter wear behind. But no, she was headed to Maine, to some small island where Charlie had a home overlooking the sea.

"Maine? Julia, Maine in the winter sounds worse than Chicago!" Chloe complained.

Julia had just shrugged and said cheerfully, "Pack your snow boots!"

"Pack your snow boots," Chloe muttered while she filled her suitcase with flannel pajamas and wool socks.

When she googled Charlie Davis, her first reaction to his photos was, "Oh yeah, that guy." She learned that he was a former teen heartthrob who had starred in a popular series of films about some kind of musical summer camp. He was twenty-four years old and had unruly dark hair, icy blue eyes that bordered on creepy, and a deep dimple in his left cheek. A few clicks down the rabbit hole revealed that there were entire Instagram accounts devoted to that dimple. The fangirls called him "fire" and "BF Goals" and they wrote weird narratives about being his girlfriend.

Her half-hearted sleuthing revealed some shots of him running, surfing, and playing football with some other bros on the beach. His general shirtlessness made it obvious that he spent a lot of time on his body and probably treated it like his job.

He looked like an asshole. That was fine. She didn't need to know him—just cook, stay out of the way, and leave in three months.

"If I have to do this ridiculous job, couldn't you have at least connected me with someone exciting?" Chloe pleaded to her sister on one of the many calls they shared in the week before her departure.

Julia snorted with laughter. "Like who?"

"I don't know! Like one of the cool musicians you rep, or Harrison Ford or something."

"Well, I don't work for Harrison Ford, so I have no idea if he's in need of a chef or not," Julia responded wryly. "And Charlie is a good guy, he's just...a little tricky sometimes."

Chloe was certainly no stranger to entitled rich people and their demands. She'd built an entire career on both cooking for them and working for them. She once left a job with a very high-profile chef after he'd shouted "idiot" at her in French one too many times during dinner prep. He'd looked at her with pity after she told him to go to hell, assuring her that there were a hundred other chefs lined up to take her place, but she had simply refused to go to sleep one more time with his enraged voice ringing in her ears.

"It will be fine, Chlo," her sister assured her. "Charlie just needs to get out of LA for a bit. And it's not like you're going to be sitting down to dinner with him. It's a big house, and you'll probably barely see him at all."

"What do you mean, get out of LA for a bit? Does this guy not have to work or something?"

"It's not that he doesn't have to work," Julia said slowly. "He's just not exactly...getting the offers he thinks he deserves."

"So, he's terrible at his job."

"No, but people aren't exactly lining up to hire him. Not for the stuff he wants anyway."

"So, he's been canceled?" Chloe guessed, wondering for a moment if she actually had something in common with the movie star after all.

"No," Julia protested. "He hasn't been canceled. He was just offered a big travel adventure series on Discovery. You know, one of those shows that's all about endurance, where people jump from helicopters, swim with sharks, and climb volcanoes and stuff?"

"What happened?"

"He's dragging his feet." Julia shrugged. "Despite his entire management team's pleas for him to take it. We all want a reset for him, after all the teen success and everything. But he's adamant about getting a big movie role, so the focus is on that right now."

Chloe twisted her face into a scowl. "I feel like I'm fourteen again, taking a babysitting job that I don't even want."

"I'm telling you, it's going to fly by," her sister assured her.

She sat on her suitcase to force the zipper shut, one last sweater stuffed in like a final protest.

Beyond packing and prepping her apartment for a three-month absence, Chloe had spent the last few days coordinating details with Charlie's assistant, who had booked her flight, her rental car, and her ferry reservations. Chloe had consented to a criminal background check, a credit check, and had signed extensive NDAs. It was all standard practice, she was assured.

She texted Steph to tell her about her plans. Her response was,

Good for you, girl! Take some time!

It left Chloe wondering if her friend was even more embarrassed for her than before. Next, she labored over a text to David, deleting and rethinking before finally settling on, *Leaving the city for a bit. Don't contact me again*. Before he had a moment to respond, she blocked his number, erased his contact, and deleted their long thread of texts. Done.

She gave her beautiful apartment an affectionate last look and made a quick run to her favorite bakery for a cortado and a kouignn amann, taking the long way home so she could savor her walk beneath the cloudless winter sky. While she ordered dinner, tried in vain to focus on her Netflix show's plot twists regarding the Irish detective, and hung up from yet another FaceTime with Julia, she repeated three words like an affirmation.

I'm really doing this.

It wasn't until she was unable to sleep the night before her departure, staring at the patterns that the streetlights cast through her bedroom window, that she found herself thinking, *why in the hell am I doing this?*

Her flight to Portland was uneventful, but as Chloe pulled into the ferry terminal parking lot in the tiny town of Craftsport and carefully parked her rental car in the line marked "reservations," she began to feel the panic in her chest swelling.

Why in the hell am I doing this?

The small ferry from the island was just arriving, and Chloe watched it dock between two barnacle-covered bumpers as cars began to slowly unload, one by one. She could hear the wind and noticed how the boat's workers hunched their shoulders forward and tucked their chins into their parkas as they waved to the departing passengers.

The small boatyard next to the dock was packed with all varieties of sailboats and other sea craft, propped up on stilts and covered in white plastic slipcovers.

Even the boats are wearing jackets, she thought.

When she worked up the courage to step out of her car, she was startled by the sharp clang of the metal clips striking the flagpole, rattling as the Maine state flag flapped noisily with every gust. It was a cold that put the lakeside Chicago winds to shame. It sliced immediately through the seams in her jacket, through the corduroys that had always felt like her "warm pants" before today.

And then she was hit with the smell. The foul stench of rancid sardines cut through the icy air with a force that you could almost taste. She wrapped her scarf around her face and tried not to inhale as she half ran to the terminal office.

As soon as she reached the counter, she couldn't help blurting out, "What on Earth is that horrible smell?" She really needed to work on her impulse control.

"It's just the fish cannery, hon," replied the woman behind the counter, barely looking up from her typing. Typing! On a typewriter!

In an effort to project some sense of politeness, Chloe tried to wipe the disgusted expression from her face.

"So, I have a reservation. To put my car on the ferry. I don't know if it's under my name or—"

"Chloe Foster? I've got ya right here, honey." The woman handed her two long yellow tickets.

"Is one of these a return ticket?"

"No, one ticket is for your car, one is for you. I was informed that you'd be on island for a few months, and we don't book returns that far in advance."

And that's when it hit her, even harder than the stink of all those dead fish. She was really doing this.

"Boat leaves in ten, got to be in your car in five, hon."

Caa. Got to be in ya caa in five.

The woman's accent made it sound like she was doing a comedy bit about salty New Englanders, but it didn't appear as if she was joking.

Chloe nodded her thanks and offered a thin smile. She made her way over to the wall-mounted map of Maine and traced her gloved finger up the coastline until she found Craftsport and then Deer Haven Island. She was literally headed out to sea.

As she was inching her car up the ferry ramp and handing over her ticket, she realized there really was no turning back, and with four cars lined up behind her, she couldn't have abandoned the plan if she tried. Wedges of wood were pushed under her tires with a force that made her jump, presumably to prevent vehicles from sliding into each other on the icy deck. When the engines roared to life and the boat bumped its way from the dock with a series of slow lurches, Chloe blinked back tears.

The truth was, she hadn't felt like herself since she'd left Redbud. She'd abandoned the routines that had become the center of her life, and now she didn't know whether to commend herself on going all in on this adventure or berate herself for the bad choices that had limited her options this severely.

And why hadn't she insisted on at least a phone meeting with Charlie Davis? Why hadn't she asked more questions? The only option was to not think about it too much for fear it would prompt her to jump overboard and swim to shore. Instead, she closed her eyes and leaned back into the headrest, trying not to focus on the slow, nauseating roll of the harbor.

The island began to show itself, its rough and rocky coastline rose up in craggy cliffs to meet an endless line of pines. Nestled between all those trees, in the spaces carved out to maximize the water views, were the most beautiful houses Chloe had ever seen. It was a showcase of weathered shingles, long gambrel roofs, and gracious covered porches. Some of the homes had paths that wound their way down the rocks, while others seemed impossibly perched on the cliffs, suspended above the rocky edges, forever looking out with no way down.

The biggest one was an enormous, shingled affair, with huge windows that looked out at the bay and four large dormers that rose from the roofline. A row of red painted rocking chairs lined the wide porch, and a long, elegant boat that looked like it was for rowing crew was tucked into an open shed at the water's edge. She knew immediately that this was Charlie Davis's house.

The ferry cut its engines and glided toward the dock, and Chloe marveled at how softly the big boat was eased into place, like a thread through a needle. The boat worker waved her off, and she crept forward, into a small parking lot lined with blocks of granite.

She pulled a creased piece of notebook paper from her tote bag and tried to smooth out the directions to the house, as she'd been assured that the mobile service was less than reliable on the island and the mapping app on her phone would likely be useless. She drove through the tiny stretch that appeared to be the town center, which consisted of a waterfront café that was closed for the season, an ice cream shop that was also closed for the season, a few little galleries, which were all closed, and a small stone library.

What in the world am I going to do here? She wondered, already missing the city that had always stayed open late for her, offering up its food trucks, bars, and bodegas when Chloe left the restaurant after midnight each night. *Where do people here even go?*

She realized immediately that this was a summer place, and that most of the rich people who owned homes on Deer Haven likely didn't visit in February. The lack of traffic on the winding island roads seemed to prove this theory correct. The few drivers who did pass her going the opposite direction waved as if they knew her. After the third time, she started waving back.

She drove by farmhouses with million-dollar views, over two short bridges, and past a boatyard with towering walls made of lobster traps before she reached Pine Point Road. She slowly made her way up the long gravel driveway until the trees opened to a snow-covered field and a gorgeous house with the ocean directly behind it. Her hunch had been correct. Charlie's was indeed the big house she'd admired from the ferry.

Before she was even out of the car, a petite, kind-faced woman who looked like a silver-haired Ina Garten was headed her way, hands outstretched to greet her.

"You must be Chloe! I'm Janey Higgins, the caretaker." The woman immediately pulled her into a hug. "Come in, come in, let's get you out of the cold."

Her Maine accent was strong, and she immediately reminded Chloe of her own mother, a nurturing woman who'd worked hard her entire life and didn't tolerate nonsense of any kind.

Chloe followed Janey into a large mudroom with a slate floor, black metal farmhouse pendant lights, and a wall of built-in cubbies painted in a warm grey-green. She hung her jacket on a hook and removed her booties, nearly moaning with ecstasy when her feet discovered the heated floor. She wondered for a moment if her toes would ever fully thaw from the boat ride.

Janey led Chloe on a tour through the rest of the house, first to the kitchen, with its dark soapstone countertops, fleet of high-end appliances, and the largest island she'd ever seen. Then the dining room that could easily seat twenty at the long, weathered farmhouse table. It was room after room of rustic antiques, coastal-inspired art, and overstuffed and elegant slipcovered furniture. Janey navigated her way down the basement stairs and revealed the wine cellar and the media room, which looked completely out of place with its modern reclining chairs, black walls, and massive projector screen. Next to that was a home gym, complete with a Peloton and all varieties of weights, a treadmill, and a rowing machine. Back up the stairs to the second floor, a dozen rooms branched off a long hallway.

Chloe tried not to remember the worst scenes from "The Shining" as the tour continued.

"How many bedrooms are there?"

"Fifteen," Janey responded. "This house has been in Charlie's family for almost a hundred years. His great-grandfather had it built for his great-grandmother as a wedding present. Generations of Davises have been coming out here for the better part of a century. Of course, now it's only Charlie, and he almost always comes out by himself, but I've been caretaking here since he was just a baby."

The flash of sadness that passed over Janey's face was quickly replaced by a sunny smile.

"Let's show you to your room. It's one of the smaller bedrooms, but I think it has the best view in the whole place."

Chloe appraised the spacious bedroom. Small? She'd been living in city apartments for too long if they thought this was small. She gasped when she saw the view. Windows stretched the length of one entire wall and looked out at the bay, where just a half hour earlier, she'd been on the ferry. A beautiful four-poster bed topped with plush white linens sat atop an antique Persian rug in shades of green and dark blue. It was the bed of romance novels, and Chloe found herself wondering who had slept here last, and for the hundred years before that. Janey opened the door to the attached bathroom, where a pearlescent clawfoot tub was positioned against another large window with a view of the harbor.

"Wow, this is beautiful. Which room is yours?"

"Oh, I don't stay here, honey. My house is on the other side of the island, near the boatyard."

"Does any other house staff stay?" Chloe asked, her stomach sinking.

"Only when there's an event, or when there are other guests, but that doesn't happen very often. Just mostly in the summer months when Charlie lends the house to friends."

"And Charlie?"

"Charlie stays in the main suite at the far end of the hall. He likes his privacy, and we wanted to be sure that you had the privacy you need as well."

What? It's going to be just the two of us in the house for three months, except for occasional but unlikely guests?

Chloe had just assumed she would be one of several people who would be staying on the property. Didn't rich people travel with a team? This entire thing had officially become weird, and Chloe wondered if it would be rude to shoo sweet Janey Higgins from her room so she could shout, "WHAT THE ACTUAL FUCK, JULIA?" into her phone.

She took a deep breath to steady herself.

"Does he always travel with a chef?"

"Well, his diet is really regimented."

Chloe murmured her agreement as if any of this made sense.

"Can we talk about what he likes?" she asked, pulling a small, black notebook from her bag and perching on the edge of the bed.

"He doesn't eat much..." Janey began. "Lots of chicken, breast only, never any skin. Lots of greens. Fish, but only steamed, no butter or oil or anything. Green juices. That kind of thing."

"OK..." Chloe's pencil was still poised above her notebook, because what could she actually even write about such a diet?

"He won't eat potatoes or pasta. Or really any white flour at all," Janey continued.

"So, gluten-free or completely no-carb?" Chloe had a terrible feeling about the menus in her future.

Janey's smile was clouded with pity. "I would just focus on the chicken breast and green juices, hon."

Kill me. Just kill me now.

They said their goodbyes in the kitchen, and Chloe got one more cookie-scented hug before Janey left, leaving her alone to call her sister.

"JULIA, WHAT THE ACTUAL FUCK?"

"Hi! Did you make it there OK? Is it beautiful?"

"You got me a job cooking for someone who doesn't eat! What am I even doing here?"

"Calm down, Chlo. I told you, I thought this would be a nice low-key gig for you. Give you some time to figure things out."

"Well, I'll have plenty of time for that, considering I'll barely be using the stove!" Chloe gestured dramatically to the grand kitchen, for the benefit of no one. "And this house is huge, and did you know it will just be Charlie and me here? No other staff?"

"Well, if the house is huge, does that really matter then? You'll have plenty of privacy," Julia pointed out. "Listen, Charlie is a total sweetheart. You'll probably barely see each other. And everyone out here eats like that, FYI."

Chloe remembered their last visit to Vermont together, when their mom had pronounced Julia, "California Skinny," and proceeded to offer her homemade jam and small crocks of butter at every meal. While Julia had jutting hipbones and a lithe frame, Chloe had the soft curves of someone who never passed up a crock of butter. She viewed Julia's obsessive spin classes, hot yoga, and trendy cleanses like a disorder, something that had never afflicted her until she'd moved to LA and started using words like "vegan-raw" and "juice fast."

"Well, I don't eat like that. And I don't cook like that," Chloe asserted. "And I'm thinking that maybe this was a huge mistake."

"Chlo, you've been there for ten minutes. Could you just give it a little time?"

"I can't do this, Jules. I need to figure something else out. Something that's not...this," she moaned, pining for her life in the city and wondering if she'd tried hard enough to make it work there.

"Please. Give it a week. Please."

Chloe opened the refrigerator and found it stocked with sparkling water, containers of protein powder, and more spinach than she usually kept on hand at the restaurant.

"Fine, but I'm going out to buy some real food that I can actually cook with."

Based on the directions that Janey had handwritten in her flawlessly slanted cursive, Chloe found her way to the small market at the center of the island. She was expecting to enter into a mecca of chips, hotdogs and cigarettes, and was thrilled to be greeted with bins overflowing with fresh produce, an aisle of gourmet condiments, and a gleaming seafood counter that ran across the back of the store.

She began to fill her basket with eggs, locally made oatmeal bread, and the most gorgeous purple carrots she'd ever seen. She picked up bunches of rainbow chard, chicken thighs, parsnips, and containers of yellow cherry tomatoes that were labeled "*greenhouse grown on island!*" She added pasta, two baguettes, and some heavy cream in a glass bottle.

No carbs? Only until he tastes my wild mushroom bread pudding, Chloe silently bragged.

After filling two baskets with staples, she made her way to the fish counter, where clams, oysters, and mussels were nestled into chipped ice like jewels in a Tiffany case.

"Hi, excuse me," she said to an impossibly tall, broad-shouldered man whose flannel-clad back was turned to her. He was stocking the lobster tank from a bucket at his feet. "What came in today?"

"All the lobster came in today. From my boat. Most of the fish is from this morning, all from local guys too."

The large flannel man turned to face Chloe, and it took everything she had to keep her expression impassive. He was quite literally the most gorgeous human she had ever seen up close. He looked about forty and had the lean, muscular build and sun-kissed skin of someone who'd spent his entire life working outside. His dirty blond hair was shaggy and a little too long, tucked behind his ears except for one unruly lock that fell across his forehead. Chloe bit her lip and fought the urge to brush it out of his eyes—those dark green, almost brown, eyes that crinkled at the corners and were fringed with sun-bleached lashes.

Jesus, Chloe, pull it together, she chided herself. *You've seen a man before.*

"So...is this your place?"

"No," he responded, skillfully sliding bands onto a lobster's claws and gently dropping the creature into the tank. "Catherine owns the market. I just supply the fish. I'm Ben."

He extended his hand, and when Chloe clasped it in her own, she was startled by how soft and cool it was.

"Chloe. I'm staying at the Davis house on Pine Point Road."

Jesus, Chloe. Just draw him a map in case he's a murderer.

"Oh, you're the chef!" he exclaimed with a megawatt smile, engaging each of his perfect laugh lines. "I heard Janey Higgins setting up a charge account for you the other day. She mentioned that you'd be on island soon."

"I'm the chef," she repeated like a dummy, unable to take her eyes from the edge of a tattoo that peeked from his rolled shirt sleeve.

He dropped the last of his lobsters into the tank, washed his hands, and finally tucked that stray golden lock behind his ear. For someone so tall, there was a surprising grace to the way he moved. As Chloe watched him roll down his sleeves and stack his buckets inside each other, she noticed how nothing he did seemed hurried. He even zipped his coat like he had all the time in the world.

"So, here's my card, Chef Chloe. Give me a call if you want anything special, right off the boat." His fingertips brushed hers, and she couldn't help but wonder how those soft, cool hands would feel on her lower back, her belly, cupping her bare shoulder.

"Sure, Ben." She glanced at the card before she pocketed it.

Libby Seafood Company.

Home of Chris Hemsworth, the Lobsterman, she thought.

She checked out at the single register, and as she was hauling her groceries back to the car, ducking against the cold, salty air that whipped across her cheeks, she found herself smiling for the first time since Chicago.

The sun was sinking fast, and by the time Chloe returned to Pine Point Road, the house was completely dark. She unpacked her groceries and poured herself a generous glass of Malbec. She wasn't sure what kind of access she had to that big wine cellar and made a mental note to ask Janey about it the next time they spoke. Did Charlie Davis drink wine? Likely too many calories.

She made a mushroom omelet for dinner, taking care to sauté the chanterelles in browned butter before adding them to her beaten eggs. She tore a hunk of bread from the baguette like a savage and ate at the banquette table that was built against the kitchen windows. She watched as the sun finished setting until it grew so dark outside that she was left staring at her own reflection in the glass. That utter inkiness, unpolluted by streetlights, reminded her of childhood on the farm, where the night sky had seemed infinite in its depth. After living in New York, San Francisco, and Chicago for the past decade and a half, she'd nearly forgotten what nighttime really looked like.

She texted her parents to let them know that she'd arrived safely. Then she sent a selfie to Steph, a shot of her holding up her large wineglass with that top-of-the-line, nearly unused kitchen as her backdrop.

She texted Julia.

Thinking I might just shack up with the wine cellar for the next three months.

She looked for Charlie Davis on social media, racking her brain for some of her passwords since it had been so long since she'd logged in herself. He was everywhere, in grainy photos taken on movie sets, in magazine shots of him looking serious at red carpet events. He was holding up his popcorn statue after winning an MTV Movie Award. He was starring in endless fangirl narratives about what it would be like to come home to him as a boyfriend/lover/husband at the end of the day. But there was nothing in his own voice, nothing authentic about his real life, no selfies of him with the Pacific at his back or his arm around his dog. Everything was observed from a distance, either from behind a professional lens or from what looked like a stalker's crouch in a nearby shrub.

"Here goes," she murmured, googling his name again, dedicated to learning something real about who this guy actually was.

She scrolled past the same paparazzi shots of him on the beach and leaving the gym that she'd already seen and eventually reached a photo of him climbing—or half falling, really—into a Tesla outside a Miami club. His hair was wildly disheveled, and his icy eyes were hidden behind a pair of dark Ray-Bans, but his mouth was curled into an undeniably sexy smirk. She zoomed in on his face and saw that he had a perfect, scarlet imprint of a lipsticked kiss on his cheek, which he appeared unapologetically pleased about.

Chloe rolled her eyes and continued investigating, finding photos of Charlie dancing in clubs in LA and Miami with leggy gazelles in barely-there dresses who she could only assume were models. In one of the pictures, which boasted the caption, *Life after Emma*, Charlie had his hands on a woman's hips as she raised her arms above her head amid a snowstorm of confetti being released from the ceiling. Chloe wasn't sure who Emma was, but at least there appeared to be life after her.

After finding more photos of the actor looking young and gorgeous while he had the time of his life, she skimmed an article about his last movie, a massive, critically-panned flop that had gone way over budget. The reviews declared the film "trite," "bloated," and "criminally long," some speculating that it could mean the end of his career if he didn't start making better choices about the projects he took on.

Despite what appeared to be a shared proclivity for carrying on with their bosses, would he think he could order her around? Would it take her more than a day to get him to eat real food? Was there any chance this arrangement could conceivably last for three whole months?

As she took in his glacial eyes, relentless dimple, and that ebony mop of hair, she wondered what she could possibly have in common with this person. She considered herself at twenty-four. She'd already cooked in Paris, Brazil, and Italy, passionately following the work where it led her. She'd just broken up with a dashing sommelier-in-training whose last name she couldn't for the life of her remember, and she was about to move to San Francisco to stage for a three-time James Beard winner. She was ravenous, desperate to fill herself up with every experience, every opportunity, hungry to make a name for herself. Now, focusing on Charlie Davis's expression, she couldn't help but think that he looked bored by all of it.

She texted Julia.

What have you gotten me into?

You mean your three-month paid vacation? You're welcome! ;-)

I did NOT ask enough questions about this thing.

It's all going to be OK.

She promised as Chloe shook her head, vowing to kill her sister the next time they saw each other.

Shifting her attention to Redbud's Instagram, she scrolled through a week's worth of posts, noticing that some of the dishes she'd designed looked just a little different now. The scallop was boasting a thin curl of purple radish on top, and the short rib appeared to be sauced with something new. She settled on a photo of Steph, looking gorgeous and powerful as she shook a sauté pan that held an impressive, yet controlled flame.

"Meet our new executive chef, Steph Lafleur," the caption boasted.

It was official. Chloe's capable right hand had stepped in to permanently take her place. Steph would carry on, building upon Chloe's years of work. She'd change things, reimagining dishes and systems in ways that would be completely outside of Chloe, all while the disgraced chef would remain banished, cast out to sea. She squinted at Steph's face, at the focus that was evidenced in the set of her jaw, and she felt a distinct and somewhat unpleasant pang. Steph deserved this. But Chloe couldn't shake the feeling that she'd been erased.

She was on an island, thirteen miles of ocean separating her from her real life.

She missed her staff, how the line cooks, dishwashers, bartenders, and hosts would each make a point of calling out to her when they arrived for their shifts. She missed cooking family meals with Steph, the two of them working side by side to prepare rustic, homey dishes of roasted vegetables and lamb meatballs, huge bowls of fresh tagliatelle, or stockpots of white bean chili. She missed cocktails after service and the morning menu planning sessions on the way to the market before the sun had risen.

She longed for the pace and purpose of it all and felt that hunger deep in her belly as she considered the vastness of Lila's kingdom. Thoughts of Lila became thoughts of David, and as much as she hated to admit it, she missed the thrill of their stolen moments, how they peppered her already frantic days with that added dose of fire.

It wasn't even nine o'clock when she dragged herself up to her room and took a heavenly soak in the giant tub. She could barely keep her eyes open as she put on her favorite sweats and slid into the cool, soft linens of the beautiful bed.

From the luxury of the high thread counts, she drowsily conducted some half-hearted career research, googling the most esteemed restaurants in the country and studying the faces of their executive chefs, searching for hints of discontentment in their eyes. She considered firing off an email to the headhunter who'd introduced herself at Redbud over a year ago, opting instead to scroll the open positions at the prestigious culinary school she'd attended. Feeling vividly nauseous at the prospect of teaching eighteen-year-olds the difference between a chiffonade and a julienne, she stuffed her phone beneath her pillow in grumpy disgust.

When she finally drifted off, she dreamt of boats navigating through an impossibly dense fog.

Chapter Five

Walking to the library had seemed like an amazing idea fifteen minutes earlier, when Chloe first stepped into the clear winter sunshine. She missed her walks to the restaurant, to her favorite bakery—missed having somewhere to go. But now the wind was blowing tiny ice crystals into her face and cutting through her leggings as if she wasn't wearing pants at all, and she already regretted it. She glanced at her phone. Four degrees. Too cold to even snow.

The entire outing had been born from desperation. She needed to get away from the house, from the complete solitude of deserted room after deserted room. Her hands had never been so idle, and it was officially starting to freak her out.

What do people even do if they aren't working?

When her arrival into the small, stone building was announced with an icy gust, the elderly librarian looked up from her romance novel and regarded Chloe with a mixture of disbelief and concern.

"Geez Louise, did you walk here, hon?"

Chloe nodded, removing her mittens and blowing on her frozen fingers. Her cheeks were bright red, and she could feel the stinging pinpricks of thaw all over her face.

"Oh, you must be the chef!" the old woman exclaimed with a kind smile, removing her reading glasses so they hung on a beaded chain around her neck.

Chloe was starting to realize that her arrival on the island was an event that had likely been discussed for weeks. The fact that she was working at the Davis house was known by everyone at the market, everyone at the post office, and now everyone at the library. So much for anonymity.

"Let me show you our cooking section," the librarian said, rising with a creak and limping toward an overfilled shelf bathed in natural light. "You know, this library used to be the old schoolhouse. Built in 1890."

Chloe nodded politely.

"They had to haul the stones to build it from a quarry up north. The ferry was a steam ship back then, and they were afraid the weight might sink it. It took dozens of trips."

More polite nodding.

"Well, I'll leave you to it, Chef," she said, giving Chloe's arm a good-hearted squeeze through her jacket. "I'm Lois, and you be sure to let me know if I can help you find anything at all. We have the internet here. That's our computer. The password is Lobster207."

She followed the librarian's crooked finger to an ancient desktop in the corner. She hadn't checked her email once since arriving—too busy Googling 'jobs for top chefs' and stalking Charlie Davis's portfolio. As the machine whirred to life, she realized she could have missed a vital message about a professional prospect. Maybe one of the chefs she'd contacted had responded with an offer, or at least a lead on something. Maybe one of her old connections in Napa had heard about her career implosion and had an opportunity to present her. But she had only three new messages, all from Lila Harris, all with the subject, "URGENT." She deleted them immediately, not daring to open what were guaranteed to be missives about wrongdoings and contracts, declarations of how the chef would "never work in this city again."

She just couldn't.

Her chest tight, she avoided all reminders of her career suicide by getting lost in the stacks for the next hour. She poured over multiple editions of homemade spiral bound volumes titled, "The Downeast Homemakers Cookbook," taking note of the many iterations of venison stew, all of which were listed as, "Ethel's Best Venison Stew" or "Lottie's Best Venison Stew." She laughed out loud at the page for "Maine Island Lobster Rolls" that featured only two ingredients: lobster and mayonnaise. The "recipe" went on to list celery, chives, lemon, parsley, all followed with the word "DON'T" in bold type.

She was studying a recipe for salt cod fritters when a deep and hushed voice hummed, "Well, hey, Chef Chloe."

She turned to find the lobsterman and his irresistibly crinkled grin standing behind her, his golden hair glowing from the light of the window as he held a battered copy of *East of Eden* in his large hands. She blinked, smiling before she could stop herself. Here she was, on an island for less than forty-eight hours and she'd nearly let herself forget about Ben Libby, who had been flirting with her at the market and who could get a job tomorrow as Charlie Hunnam's stunt double if lobsters suddenly became extinct.

"Looking to take the venison stew crown from Ethel?"

"I wouldn't dare go head-to-head with Ethel," Chloe responded.

"The Island ladies made that cookbook for years as a fundraiser for the school," Ben explained, gesturing to the tattered collection. "My mom is in one of them."

"Oh yeah? What was her specialty?" Chloe asked with genuine curiosity, always eager to talk food, even as she was struggling to take her eyes from Ben's height, his face, and that one lock of hair that refused to stay tucked behind his ear.

"Lobster potpie."

"Of course."

"You know, this library used to be the old schoolhouse," he said. "They had to bring all the stones from a quarry off island. They thought it was going to sink the ferry."

"Yeah, I think I heard that somewhere," Chloe replied, biting the lip that insisted on smiling whenever Golden Ben said anything.

Impulsively, she wondered how he would react if she leaned into him and pressed her mouth against his, if he would taste sweet or slightly salty like she hoped he would, if he would lead her to a hidden spot behind the history section, press her against the war memoirs and make out with her for the next hour. For the first time since they'd met, she searched for a wedding ring on his hand, and saw nothing but long fingers and bare, tanned skin. She tried not to consider the fact that this was their second conversation, and it had only now dawned on her to look.

"No fishing today?" Chloe asked.

"Nah, too cold. I just made deliveries and now I guess I have to tackle the paperwork in my office that I've been putting off all week."

Chloe took in the unhurried way he leaned against the bookshelf and narrowed her eyes. Was he one of those rare creatures without an obsessive drive for work, success, and more, more, more?

"The paperwork is the worst part of running a business," she affirmed. "All I ever wanted to do at my restaurant was cook, not sit at a desk."

As she strolled through the library with Ben Libby, she tried not to think of the other things she'd done at the desk in her small office at Redbud. He offered to carry her stack of cookbooks, but she clutched them to her chest, insisting she had it under control. As Lois stamped their books with a due date, Chloe doubted she'd still be on Deer Haven in two weeks' time.

"Ben, did you know this daredevil walked all the way here? In this cold? Why don't you give her a ride home?" The librarian suggested, winking conspiratorially at Chloe.

"Oh, that's OK, really," she protested, her newly thawed cheeks now beginning to burn. "I'm fine to walk back."

"I'm happy to do it," Ben replied, his lips curving upwards in a way that was so sexy, she feared for Lois's health.

Chloe reluctantly agreed, playfully frowning at the librarian, who wasn't even trying to hide her mischievous smirk.

As they bent their heads to the wind on the way to his pickup, her phone trilled with a text from Janey. Charlie's charter flight was officially confirmed. He'd arrive on Deer Haven the following day.

"Everything OK?" Ben asked, pulling out of the library's small gravel lot as Chloe continued to blink at her phone. She felt suddenly paralyzed by the reality of the movie star's arrival, overcome with a combination of anxiety and dread.

"Charlie Davis is getting in tomorrow, so I need to shop and get ready for him."

"Let's go shopping then. I'll stop at the market."

Chloe tried to keep her expression impassive in the face of Ben's enthusiasm. She did not shop well with others. Steph had been her right-hand chef, and she'd never once been invited to the sunrise trips to the fish market or to assess the new varieties of micro greens that her supplier was growing. She needed to be on her own to see, smell, and touch her ingredients. She wasn't seeking a collaborator, no matter how green his eyes looked as they awaited her response.

"Sure," she finally relented, softening as she took in his perfectly handsome face with its square jaw and stubbled cheeks. Why, no matter the venue, was he always backlit with the most impeccable golden light?

Her resolve fully melted away at the market, where they followed each other up and down the aisles as a seafood stew began to take shape in her head. Ben led her to the small produce section, where bins of purple, gold and pink potatoes lined the floor.

"These are all from Henry Allen's place," he explained, picking up a small tuber the color of an eggplant. "He works with mostly heirloom seeds. All organic. I grew up right next to his farm."

She selected a variety of what were hands-down the most gorgeous potatoes she'd ever seen as her phone vibrated in her pocket. Since leaving the house, she'd missed two calls from an unknown 708 number. It was a Chicago area code, and she wondered for a moment if David was attempting to contact her from a different phone. Ultimately deciding that it was likely just a Redbud supplier who hadn't updated their contact list, she shrugged and returned her phone to her jacket.

She followed Ben to the seafood counter, where he selected a scallop from the case and sliced off a thin piece, offering it to Chloe atop the knife. Without hesitating, she plucked it from the blade and popped it into her mouth, allowing the tender and luscious flesh to melt on her tongue. It tasted like the coast, like the cold sea air and the freshest salt. It was impossibly sweet. She hummed and wondered if it was too soon to accept the next bite directly from Ben's hand, allowing her lips to brush against his thumb as he offered her more.

Simmer down, Chloe, she told herself. *Don't make it weird.*

"It's almost a shame to cook them. I could eat them just like that forever."

"Well, let's get you some. And some of these," he asserted, gesturing to a dish of tiny, blush-colored bay shrimp.

Chloe wondered if they were on an accidental date or if Ben was just trying to upsell her on seafood. She realized that she didn't even care. She was just so happy to be out of the cold, surrounded by flawless ingredients—and a seemingly flawless man—as she considered the components of the perfect dish.

She was almost sorry when she was ready to check out. Ben reached for her overstuffed canvas totes, but she insisted she could handle them herself, slinging one over each of her shoulders. He leaned in front of her to open the passenger door of his truck, but she asserted that she had it under control, lifting the heavy bags onto the center of the bench seat and hoisting herself inside.

"You don't let anyone do anything for you, do you?" he teased, starting the engine with a rumble.

"I said yes to the ride, didn't I?"

Ben chuckled sweetly when Chloe asked if he needed the address, and she quickly realized that a man who lived on an island of three hundred likely knew where the movie star's house was. His truck bumped over frost heaves and potholes as he stretched his arm across the back of the seat, pointing out every home they passed. Some were nestled behind the pines, but still visible from the road. Others were at the top of long, wooded driveways, completely hidden. He had an anecdote for every single house.

"That's Donny Buck's place. He makes the best chili every year for Super Bowl. This is the Weymouth Farm. They just bought a winter place in the Caribbean somewhere. This is Cheryl Brown's folks' house. I fell out of that tree and broke my arm when I was a kid. I also had my first kiss behind that shed over there."

"You know everyone here."

"I've lived here my whole life."

Chloe tried to relate. After all, she was from a small town too, but it was different than growing up contained within the borders of an island. And she was only about thirteen when she started plotting her escape from Vermont, always sure she was destined for more.

Ben gently tapped his long fingers on the steering wheel to the rhythm of the ancient U2 song that thrummed softly from the speakers as they reached Pine Point Road far too soon. She didn't want to leave his truck just yet, and even though she had hours of cooking to do, she was so content just breathing in the woodsmoke and lemony scent of him as they drove in loops around the island.

"I'd offer to bring your bags inside for you..."

"I've got it," Chloe replied, removing the heap of groceries that sat as a buffer between them.

"I thought you'd say that."

They blinked at each other, both smiling somewhat dopily, the late morning sunshine beaming all around them.

"Thanks for the ride."

"Anytime, Chef Chloe," he replied, tucking his hair behind his ear, his eyes crinkling at the corners in a way that she already found herself craving.

He waited until she was at the door before he backed out of the driveway with a very cute wave.

Stepping inside the house, she found herself thrilled at the realization that something had finally *happened* on Deer Haven.

Chloe spent the next several hours in the company of an old friend—Julia Child's Beef Bourguignon. As she rendered bacon fat and dropped chunks of stew beef into the Dutch oven, she was flooded with memories of cooking the dish in culinary school. She and her roommate had pooled together all the cash they had to buy the wine and the meat, inspired to master the art of French cooking after seeing "Julie & Julia" at the two-dollar movie theater. As she poured in nearly the entire bottle of cabernet, newly liberated from Charlie Davis's wine cellar, she could practically hear her old friend Kaitlyn's high-pitched giggle.

What had happened to her old best friend? They'd just kind of lost track of each other when they went on their respective internships —Chloe at a renowned bistro in Paris, Kaitlyn somewhere on the coast of Spain. Forgetting about Kaitlyn was the first of many lessons about the friends you make in the kitchen. When you're working together, grinding it out every day, tasting from the same spoons and splitting bottles of wine, it feels like you've found your forever people. But then it just ends. You move up or move on. Your restaurant family fades away, and you find yourself struggling to even remember anyone's last name after it's over. And then you do it all over again at the next job.

Chloe sauteed onions in an unapologetic amount of butter and remembered how she'd reinvented this dish in the early days of Redbud, trading the beef for duck and even smoking her own duck bacon to replace the pork. She wondered if Charlie Davis would have preferred poultry over red meat, immediately dismissing the very concept that he wouldn't eat any of it. Janey couldn't possibly have been serious about the steamed chicken breast. No one *really* hired a chef like her to cook like that.

After Chloe shingled paper-thin slices of Yukon gold potatoes in tidy concentric ovals for a Dauphinois, she texted her sister.

Charlie's getting here tomorrow.

Julia responded almost immediately.

I just saw the email from his office,.

Do you always know where he is?

Chloe asked, wondering how that would feel, making your way through the world wearing a series of administrative tracking devices.

Of course. And FYI, he's always cranky after traveling.

Awesome. (Side eye emoji, eye roll emoji)

This is all going to be great. Easiest job you'll ever have.

Famous last words.

Later, she assessed the absurd volume of food she'd spent the entire afternoon preparing. Who was going to eat all of this? She imagined packing it up and bringing it to Ben Libby's door. She could probably find his house, but showing up with dinner for eight felt just unhinged enough to stop her.

She had a better idea and wrapped a dishtowel around the Dutch oven to secure the lid. Dressing for an Arctic expedition and ducking her head against the punishing wind, she loaded her car with the still steaming dishes and slowly drove down the snowy driveway.

Janey had left her home address and the phone number for every service offered on the island—like the chef might want to charter a whale watching boat for the day—and Chloe navigated her way easily. When she arrived, she found the caretaker bundled in insulated coveralls and a hat with earflaps, coaxing her chickens into the hen house for the night.

"Oh, hi, honey!" she called out. "What are you doing here so late?"

Chloe glanced at her watch. It was 4:45 p.m.

Janey lifted the cover of the Dutch oven. "Bob and I were just getting ready to heat up some soup for dinner, but this looks a whole lot better!"

"I just felt like making some old favorites. Fine tuning for when Charlie gets here."

"Oh, honey, he won't eat any of this. But I'm so grateful that you thought of us! You are just so sweet."

Chloe searched her files to try to remember if anyone, anywhere, at any point in her life had ever described her as "sweet" before, and she came up blank. There was something she liked about it when it came from Janey.

"Come on in and eat with us!" the old woman insisted. "We'd love to have you."

"Thank you so much, Janey, but I really can't. I have something in the oven back at the house," Chloe fibbed. "I just wanted to bring this over really quick."

The truth was, even though Chloe was attempting to "settle in" and "make the best of it," like her sister had demanded, she wasn't at all ready to immerse herself fully in the Deer Haven experience just yet. Despite the excess of free time she'd had on her hands, she hadn't even unpacked her suitcase, and the drawers of her dresser still sat empty, challenging her to commit.

"Well, another time for sure," Janey said warmly, her apple cheeks pink from the cold. "Oh, and Charlie's charter plane gets in around eight tomorrow night, so I'll pick him up at the airstrip and bring him to the house."

"OK...yes, OK," Chloe stammered. "I'll be ready for him."

Navigating the curves of Pine Point Road, Chloe was surprised to feel her stomach aflutter with nerves. Charlie Davis would soon be on the island, and she would be cooking for someone who didn't eat. Running through menus and dishes in her head, she assured herself that she could win him over. Afterall, it was what she'd been doing for her entire career as a chef—convincing people, getting them on her side with every bite.

"I'm Chloe Fucking Foster," she muttered as she half-stomped up the walkway and into the house.

She shed her layers in the mudroom, poured herself another glass of wine and settled into the too-soft couch, where she turned Ben's business card over and over in her hand.

Her cheeks grew warm as she considered unbuttoning her pajama top and sending him a selfie, looking as sexy as one can in green plaid flannel. She could take things from zero to sixty to make the next three months interesting. As her poorly constructed fire burned out prematurely, Chloe wondered again what people did to entertain themselves all alone in the middle of the ocean.

If she were in Chicago, she'd be in the thick of dinner service by now. She pictured Steph expediting with confidence, her team of chefs firing steaks and plating microgreens with a focused exactitude. The dining room would be full, Cami fielding phone calls and walk-ins at the hostess stand with grace, while Chloe was here preparing for bed, resolving to get a good night sleep before her new boss who was *not* Harrison Ford arrived the next day.

Settling into the warmth of her duvet, she wished she could at least program her dreams to deliver something good. Something about a fisherman who read Steinbeck and kissed her throat while she buried her fingers in his golden hair.

Chapter Six

Chloe spent the entire next day preparing for the movie star's arrival. She sautéed leeks, fennel, and shallots until they started to caramelize, her pan hissing as she doused them with crushed tomatoes. A container of shrimp shells from Ben was now bubbling into a rich seafood stock on the back burner.

As she lowered the heat and gently added the tender scallops to what would become a perfect stew, she found herself surprised by how much she enjoyed repeating a simple line in her head: *I think the lobsterman likes me*.

Her phone trilled with an incoming FaceTime, and she propped it against a bottle of heavy cream so her hands were free to continue working.

"Hey sister!" Julia called out, LA gridlock behind her.

"Is this a good idea, Jules? Your driving skills..."

Her sister was wearing ridiculously oversized sunglasses that had likely cost as much as a month's worth of Chicago rent, and her curly hair was piled atop her head in that perfectly coiffed yet sloppy way. The sun was setting outside Chloe's window, casting the harbor in streaks of fuchsia and lavender, which meant that in LA, Julia was probably heading back to the office after lunch with a client.

"I just wanted to check in on you and see how you're doing out there," she said. "You have everything you need?"

"I'm fine," Chloe assured her. "I'm not sure why I had to come early."

"That's just how his team wanted it done."

His team, Chloe thought. *In a matter of hours, I'll be living with someone who's accustomed to being serviced by a team.*

For the ten thousandth time, Chloe asked herself what she was doing with her life.

She pictured Charlie on the beach, with the models, partying late into the night with his entourage. She was beginning to wonder if Deer Haven was penance for Charlie, too—ordered rest, a rehab-by-the-sea, just like Julia had prescribed for her. She thought of David alone in his posh country house, drinking scotch and wearing an ascot or some shit, impervious to any real fallout from their affair.

While her sister chattered on about schedules and protocols, Chloe considered Ben Libby, just living his quiet life on Deer Haven, trapping lobsters and reading books while she had been killing herself in the city, blind to the notion that anything else could possibly exist beyond all of it.

"I met a sexy lobsterman," she blurted.

"Now we're getting somewhere!" Julia squealed. "Maybe you're going to have a great romance out there!"

"Maybe I don't want a great romance."

"Sure, you don't. Who would want that?" Chloe cringed as Julia leaned on her horn and released an impressive stream of expletives to a fellow driver. "So...there's one other thing."

She dropped a bay leaf and a few sprigs of thyme into some simmering cream and said she was listening.

"Have you seen Natter this morning?"

"I don't know what that is, so...no?"

"Natter? The gossip blog?" Julia exclaimed in obvious disbelief. "Their socials are huge! Their Insta has like ten million followers."

"OK, I believe you, but still no."

"Well...there's something about you on there today."

"Something about me? What? Why?" Chloe demanded.

"Don't freak out. Here, I'll send it to you."

Wiping her hands on her apron, Chloe clicked on the link and gasped when the headline flooded her screen.

Superstar Chef Flees Michelin Starred Restaurant Amid Scandal

"Julia, what is this?"

She continued reading. *Chloe Foster has abandoned her post as executive chef at her hot Chicago restaurant, Redbud, as rumors of sexual misconduct are swirling. It seems a long running affair with restaurateur David Newhouse has derailed the chef's—*

She couldn't read any further.

"Sexual misconduct? Jesus, they make it sound like I was some kind of predator or something! Can you make this go away?"

Julia checked her reflection in her rearview mirror and began to apply a coat of red gloss to her lips as horns honked on either side of her. "I like to think that I'm all powerful, but contrary to your apparent belief, I don't own the internet. I wish I could."

"Seriously, no one is going to want to come anywhere near me now."

"Chloe, listen, everyone knows that Natter is trash. Just gossip."

"All ten million followers know that?"

"It's going to be OK, you'll see," she assured her sister in the soothing voice that she reserved for clients in crisis. "Things need to blow up before they can blow over. In a couple days, no one will even remember this."

More like in a couple days, no one will remember me, Chloe thought sullenly.

She'd only read two sentences, but they were enough to make her feel defeated. The sex and David's name stung—but "abandoned her post" was what gutted her. Like she'd walked away from Redbud without a second thought, had taken off her apron and run without looking back. As if everything she'd built meant nothing. As if it had all been that easy.

"Chlo, I have to go," Julia said just as traffic appeared to be moving again in California. “Call you later, OK? I need more on this hot lobsterman!”

The sisters bid their farewells and Chloe found herself alone again in the now dark kitchen. She couldn’t help herself. She opened the article and read the rest of it.

It seems a long running affair with restaurateur David Newhouse has derailed the chef’s career and dashed her prospects at restaurants all over Chicago. One former colleague even went as far as describing the scandalized cook as “un-hirable.” Looks like this James Beard winner might need to cook up a new plan for her future. #youwantfrieswiththat?

“Fuck!” Chloe exclaimed, slamming her phone onto the counter just as the cream started to boil over on the stove, scorching and hissing as it streamed into the flame of the burner.

Someone from Redbud must have tipped off Natter, but she couldn’t figure out who or why. Was it Lila, attempting to cement her power position, to flex that upper hand and remind the world who was really in charge? Could it have been Steph, the only person who’d heard the confession directly from Chloe’s mouth? It could’ve been anyone. Secrets didn’t keep in a kitchen, and she hated herself for forgetting that.

She exhaled slowly and heated a second pint of cream, steeping it with the aromatics and parking herself in front of the burner this time.

I’m Chloe Fucking Foster.

She silently repeated her new mantra again and again, even as the lump in her throat refused to dissolve and the humiliated tears that had collected in her eyes threatened to spill over.

Her phone sounded with an incoming text from Janey.

> Hi, honey! Charlie’s charter is delayed. Don’t wait up. He won’t need anything tonight.

A rush of relief filled the chef as she rotated her shoulders, willing the knot of tension to release in her upper back. She wouldn’t have to greet a cranky movie star when he arrived after a long day of travel.

She could go to bed and likely have the whole morning to prepare for him. He would get a full night's sleep and they'd meet when he was well-rested and ready to give her a little more direction as to what he actually wanted from her.

She plodded up the stairs, feeling thoroughly annoyed for the first time rather than charmed by the symphony of creaks that followed her.

In bed, eyes back on her phone, Chloe wondered if Ben Libby was one of the ten million people who read Natter, if he'd scrolled through the mundane celebrity tidbits and landed on a story about a disgraced chef who'd "abandoned her post" amid rumors of misconduct.

She'd scrolled more in the last few days than in the last ten years, her feed now a painful parade of familiar faces. There was David Chang laughing and posing on the back of a shrimp boat in Louisiana, Christina Tosi braiding a rainbow of challah dough, Jenna Moran slicing ahi tuna with surgical precision. And there was Steph, her arm slung around Oprah's shoulder like an old friend, both grinning broadly from the Redbud kitchen.

I miss my work, Chloe thought, feeling that loss in her stomach like a hunger for something she wasn't sure how to satisfy.

Before she finally drifted off, she couldn't help but feel resentful at how the callouses on her hands were starting to soften, the spots she'd been actively hardening for almost twenty years nearly erased.

Forever a light sleeper, she was awakened only an hour later by quiet footsteps on the creaky stairs. She wasn't sure why, but her instinct was to quickly pull the blankets over her head until she heard the soft click of the door all the way at the other end of the long hallway.

Charlie Davis had finally arrived.

Chapter Seven

The next morning, Chloe woke before the sun. After hearing Charlie arrive, she'd found herself awake at 2:30 a.m., thinking about how thoroughly weird it was that she was just down the hall from a movie star, and how they would be cohabiting in this giant house for ninety days like a bad reality show—and why, why, why had she let Julia talk her into this?

Prep, execution, cleanup, she repeated like a poem, trying to convince herself that this was just like any other service.

She beat eggs and diced veggies for omelets, juiced grapefruits and blood oranges and was just sliding a tray of pecan sticky buns into the oven when the door to the mudroom opened and a blast of icy air followed.

Chloe stifled a gasp, realizing that all the internet sleuthing in the universe couldn't have prepared her for the man who had transported from the gossip sites and into the kitchen. Charlie Davis was taller than she expected, and even through his down vest and baggy sweats, she could tell that the pecan sticky buns had been a colossal waste of time. Then she noticed the dimple. That was the dimple that the girls wrote sonnets about, long adolescent haikus celebrating that little divot, which remained carved into his cheek even when he wasn't smiling.

Chloe had cooked for more than her fair share of famous people throughout her career. It was something that came with the territory of working at elite restaurants. She'd seen actors, writers, and politicians sitting at her tables over the years, and they used the sides of their spoons to crack their rosewater creme brûlées, just like everyone else. So it wasn't that she was awestruck by who Charlie was, it was the fact that he was standing five feet away from her and he was so completely breathtaking. It was like looking into the sun.

"Oh, hi! You're out. I mean you're already up and out," she stammered like a moron. "I thought you were still sleeping upstairs. I'm Chloe."

"Hi, Chloe. I'm Charlie," he said in a voice like honey. "I get up early to run."

"Are you hungry? I can make you an omelet. I have peppers, prosciutto, mushrooms..."

He took off his hat and attempted to smooth his fashionably disheveled hair before padding over to her in his socks. "I don't eat the yolks."

"You don't eat the yolks?" Chloe swallowed hard and said the words, that as a chef, she hoped she would *never* have to say. "I can make you an egg white omelet."

He blinked at her, a small smile playing across his lips. His eyes were the coolest ice blue, rimmed with such impossibly long black lashes that they reminded Chloe of Pippa, the Siberian husky she had as a kid. They flickered briefly over her flushed cheeks, the lower lip that she was biting, the apron she'd hastily tied around her waist.

"Do you want to talk about menus for this week?" She managed.

"Maybe later." He grinned at her, dimple engaged, before turning his attention to his phone. "I'll just make a green smoothie after I shower."

And that, Chloe thought as she watched him walk away, *was how you combine the sexiest and least sexy words ever spoken into one sentence.*

He disappeared into another part of the house, leaving Chloe to wonder why the kitchen suddenly felt too hot, and why her voice had broken like a pubescent teenager when she'd asked him about meal planning.

She scolded herself for her own bravado in preparing that breakfast. Pastries? Prosciutto? Janey and Julia had both told her what he liked, but she'd remained convinced that *her* food would be enough to change his mind. She would make sure she wasn't in the kitchen at all when he returned to make his smoothie. She refused to be a chef whose primary responsibility was measuring protein powder into a $1,200 blender.

Restless, she bundled up in her down coat, snow boots—*damn you, Julia*—and carefully made her way down the rocky path toward the water, trying not to slip and crack her skull—not that Charlie would think to look for her before next week. The sky was steel gray and there was dampness in the air that suggested snow. She made it to the water's edge and stared out at the choppy sea, calculating the distance to the mainland and wondering if anyone had ever attempted the journey by the kind of kayak that was housed in the small shed behind her.

She dialed her parents, cursing the crackly and occasionally hollow sounding island reception she'd begun to expect.

"Are you OK, dear? Are things not working out there?" her mother asked before saying hello.

Chloe didn't know how to respond. Confessing to her mom would involve admitting the reason she'd run from Chicago, telling the truth about Redbud, owning up to the affair, the career suicide, all of it. They just weren't details she was interested in sharing with the woman who'd left a book about "your changing body" on Chloe's bed when she was twelve and had never mentioned it again.

"It's just weird here, Mom. He doesn't really eat."

"Of course he eats!"

"I mean he doesn't eat real food. He wouldn't eat breakfast except for some powdered stuff he put into a blender. I feel like I've forgotten how to do my job."

"Honey, come home."

"What?"

"Just come home for a bit. Forget about all that business there. I don't know what happened in Chicago, but if you felt like you had to leave, you could have just come home to the farm."

Chloe side-armed a flat rock and watched it skip over the rough water. She hadn't lived with her parents since she left for culinary school when she was seventeen. She'd visited many times of course, but moving back? Could she just do that? Rebound to the farm where her tall, green boots still sat in the mudroom, waiting for her to return to her chores? Could she just hide there, telling her mother how she liked her eggs every morning, starting tomato seedlings under the heat lamps in the greenhouse, driving that backfiring vintage tractor that her father refused to retire, furrowing rows for peas and beans?

She'd be antsy after a day.

"I can't come home, Mom. I've committed myself to be here." She whipped another rock into the sea, but rather than skating across the surface, it sunk with a resounding plop. "But I'll visit, I promise."

"Any time, dear. We'd love it. You can even bring your actor friend if you'd like!"

Chloe chuckled at the idea of Charlie throwing grain to the chickens and being served one of her mother's massive, boiled dinners.

"Mom, he's not my friend."

"Well, give it a day or two. You'll win him over and he'll be asking for seconds before you know it."

Chloe said goodbye with repeated promises to visit soon, shivering when she sat at the shore's edge. The cold immediately seeped through her jeans.

I'm Chloe Fucking Foster, she said to herself as she chucked one more rock into the water and watched it land with a satisfying splash.

She made her way up the perilous path toward the house, taking extra care on the rocks coated in a thin glaze of ice. When she reached the granite doorstep, she was greeted by a beat-up plastic bucket topped with a Post-it note.

Chef Chloe- Thought you would enjoy these. -Ben.

She slowly lifted the perforated lid to find a dozen crabs absently climbing over each other and tumbling weightlessly against the side of the bucket. Chloe felt a distinct heat rise up her cheeks, Charlie Davis and his blue eyes all but forgotten.

Back in the kitchen, she unearthed a massive stockpot from the back corner of the pantry. At the restaurant she would have steamed the crabs in beer with a dash of sherry vinegar, but here she used salted water only. It would have been a culinary felony not to allow something that fresh to sing on its own. When they cooled enough to handle, she picked the flesh from the claws and legs, careful to reserve the shells, which she would sauté in butter, shallots, and bay leaves to create another stock.

She stifled a moan when she sampled a tender piece of crab meat. It tasted like the ocean and cold beers at the beach at sundown. Ben had delivered summertime in the middle of February. It may have been the most romantic gesture any man had ever made.

He picked up on the second ring.

"Did you get my delivery?"

"I did. They're beautiful." Chloe cradled the phone against her shoulder while she stirred the stock.

"Well, I'm sure you'll make them even better. A lot of people just throw them back."

"I'll try to do them justice," she promised, realizing just then that when he was on his boat, braving the wind and pulling his traps, he'd been thinking of her.

Ben paused and a silence settled between them. She pictured him tucking that stray lock of golden hair behind his ear. Was she really getting turned on talking about crabs?

"So, I think you should let me cook something for you, Chef Chloe."

"Ok. Yes. That would be great. Yes."

Four yeses? Really?

"I'd love it," she admitted, desperate to regain a sense of cool. "Do you need me to bring anything?"

"Just your appetite."

"I always take that wherever I go."

"See you at seven. I can't wait."

She hung up and grinned like an absolute fool. She had a date. A date with a sexy lobsterman who wanted to cook for her. She paused to consider when she had last gone on a real date. Could it have been Mark? From an entire year ago? After Mark, dating had just seemed like this annoying task that she had to remind herself to do, a box to check to make her feel like a normal thirty-five-year-old woman. And it usually felt like more trouble than it was worth as long as she had David, who was always willing to come over late at night or follow her to a secret spot in the restaurant.

But now there was Ben, who had just declared his intentions with a bucket of crabs. In that moment, when she was remembering the sweet way he called her "Chef Chloe," and the tattoo that two separate times had almost revealed itself on his arm, the only thing she could think was that she hoped she didn't mess it all up. Also, that his house wasn't gross and he wasn't a murderer.

Charlie walked into the kitchen, wearing black sweats and a rumpled white T-shirt, looking like he'd just woken up from a nap.

She found herself thinking, *Oh, right. You*, as he stretched his arms above his head and revealed a glimpse of the taut stomach below his navel. *I'd nearly forgotten about you.*

"What am I smelling?" he asked, yawning and gazing at her with a sleepy smile.

"Crab. Just off the boat today. Do you eat crab?"

I know it sounds like carb, but it's really very different.

Charlie shrugged and plopped down at the banquette against the window. "As long as there's no butter," he finally replied, appearing fascinated by the ferry that was currently chugging its way across the harbor.

She studied Charlie while he studied the view and she realized how young he looked, younger even than his twenty-four years, with his unmarked skin and bright eyes. Her googling had taught her that he'd been famous since he was a kid, but she wondered how long he had been paying people to take care of him.

His phone vibrated in his hand, and he answered without looking at the screen, obviously waiting for whoever was calling.

"Hey, Bran."

Bran?

"No, I am...then try. Well, try harder!" He pushed his fingers into his eyes like he was either trying to ward off or give himself a migraine. "Look, there has to be something other than this kind of stuff."

He was getting agitated with whoever Bran was, and Chloe wondered if she should make a quiet exit to give him some privacy, but she was busy—mixing crab meat with lemon juice and slicing paper thin shavings of celery. It was a big house, and if Charlie wanted distance, he could relocate to any of the 347 rooms to get it.

"Just...just make it happen. Please." Charlie slid his phone across the table where it stopped at the very edge.

Chloe kept her head down and diced the gorgeous yellow tomatoes she'd picked up at the market, drizzling them with chili oil and a splash of balsamic, kosher salt, and a crack of fresh pepper. She dressed some arugula with olive oil and arranged it in a perfect mound on a plate. Then the tomatoes, avocado, and a generous portion of crabmeat on top. Another quick drizzle of olive oil and it resembled a dish she would have presented at Redbud.

She looked up to see Charlie staring at her, his eyes bright, that dimple completely engaged.

"You're really good at that," he said.

"Yeah. I am."

She placed the plate in front of him alongside a fork and a well-worn chambray napkin.

"It's beautiful," he said, casting his megawatt smile directly at her, prompting her cheeks to burn in a way she found irritating.

Chloe held her breath as he was about to take his first bite. It was a picture-perfect composition of tomato, avocado, and crab, and his fork was raised midway to his lips when his phone vibrated again.

He lowered his hand and answered it as she released a defeated exhale.

"Bran. What did they say?" He strode into the dining room, where he pleaded with his manager to "try again," "call someone else," and "make it happen." She heard him climb the grand, creaky staircase and close the door to his bedroom. His immaculate plate of food sat untouched, mocking her.

Why am I even here?

When he didn't return after a half hour, she slid his dinner into the refrigerator and mixed the rest of the ingredients in a bowl for herself, drizzling it with olive oil and sprinkling coarse salt on top. She poured a large glass of chardonnay from one of the bottles in the fridge and texted her sister.

He almost ate! 👀

Keep at it, Chlo. 🙏

👀, 👀, 👀

Later that night, after Chloe had blissed herself out with another soak in the giant bathtub, she padded down the stairs in her flannel pajamas to find Charlie's clean dinner plate drying in the dishrack. It had been a day full of victories after all.

Chapter Eight

Driving around the island the next morning, Chloe realized that when it came to Deer Haven real estate, wealth revealed itself in concentric circles. The grandest houses were at the edges, where the sea showed itself, unobstructed, from every porch, deck and most of the windows. These houses were likely only occupied for a few weeks each year. The average homes were positioned one layer closer to the center, where you could possibly get a glimpse of a cove or harbor beyond some trees, but you certainly couldn't access the water without walking across someone else's property. The smallest homes were right in the middle of the island, modest little ranches and farmhouses without even a hint of waterfront. It seemed like the rich had staked their claim on the entire ocean.

She remembered to wave at the two vehicles that passed in the opposite direction and noted that everyone seemed to have their own signature greeting. Some raised their hand in a sort of salute, some lifted a hand and nodded, some simply extended an index finger without letting go of the steering wheel. Chloe would have to work on her own wave. Finger guns? The Queen Elizabeth? Jazz hands? Her stomach dropped. She still had nearly three months to figure it out.

Back at the house, she saw she had another missed call from that same 708 phone number. Still no voicemail.

Janey's truck was parked in the driveway, and Chloe found herself looking forward to seeing her again. She dropped her canvas tote bags on the kitchen counter and followed the sound of Charlie's low laughter to the living room, where the two of them were sitting on those overstuffed sofas, deep in conversation.

"Hi, honey!" The caretaker jumped up to give her another one of her warm vanilla hugs, and Chloe couldn't help but lean into it.

"How are you settling in? Are you finding everything you need? Taking good care of our boy here?"

Our boy?

Chloe almost missed the way Charlie glanced up at her, smiling mischievously, his cool eyes twinkling.

"Sit, sit," Janey insisted, patting the space beside her.

Chloe obliged, sinking into the down cushions. Could this be any weirder? It felt like a blind date and all that Chloe wanted to do was get back into the kitchen, unpack her groceries, and start roasting the chickens sitting on the counter.

"I just loved the meal you brought us the other night," Janey said, leaning forward to place her hand on Chloe's jiggling knee. "It was like eating at a fancy restaurant in our own kitchen!"

"I'm so glad."

"You're lucky to have such an amazing chef here," Janey boasted, giving them each a pointed look that Chloe took to mean, *we really need this arrangement to work out, do you understand?* The caretaker squinted at Charlie expectantly, a look meant to function like a gentle elbow to the ribcage.

"So..." Chloe began, trying to think of something else to say to Charlie beneath the burn of Janey's keen gaze. "You work with my sister."

"Julia's awesome," he replied.

"She really is."

Wow. Brilliant banter.

"You two seem really different." He appraised Chloe as the corners of his mouth turned upwards.

Chloe shrugged. "Yeah, she looks like my dad. I'm the spitting image of my mom. Also, she doesn't eat enough. I'm sure you can trust a skinny publicist, but you must have heard that you can't trust a skinny chef."

Charlie's slow smile traveled up to his eyes. Chloe reluctantly admitted they were not so creepy in person. She pulled at the neck of her sweater and narrowed her gaze, trying to figure him out as he blinked back at her.

"I'd love to have you for supper, Chloe," Janey interrupted. "Nothing fancy, but I haven't had any complaints so far!"

Chloe had never received so many invitations in a twenty-four-hour period. She assured Janey that dinner sounded wonderful.

"You're going to be on island for a little while, and I'd be happy to help you get the lay of the land," the caretaker offered, turning to gently squeeze Charlie's arm. "And you can come too!"

Charlie affectionately leaned into Janey, and Chloe felt obligated to ask, "Anything else?" before excusing herself to the kitchen.

While she was stuffing the chickens with halved lemons, garlic cloves, and bunches of fresh thyme, she wondered if she could get through the next three months without being in the same room with Charlie Davis. She wasn't a woman who harbored crushes, who was prone to overheated giddiness when a man smiled impishly with his full, flushed lips, sparkling blue eyes and devastating dimple, reducing her to wondering how it would feel to watch him slowly pull his sweatshirt over his head as the fire crackled behind—

NOPE! No. Simmer down, Chloe, she interrupted herself before the image could fully unfold.

This all just felt too close—being in someone's house, surrounded by their history, seeing them before, after, and in between each meal. She longed for the simplicity of knowing that the diners would leave, that service would eventually be over. Chloe silenced the voice echoing in the back of her mind, the one that assured her that none of this was going to end well, and willed her mind to drift to dinner with Ben that evening. *He* was cooking for *her*. She wondered if she should bring one of the roasted chickens just in case.

Janey and Charlie appeared in the kitchen to say their goodbyes. She hugged him, and he rested his cheek on the top of her head.

"Be good," she said before turning to Chloe. "And make sure this one eats. He's too skinny."

Charlie rolled his eyes like a teenager, but he was smiling, dimple in full effect. He seemed to glow in the kind light of Janey's motherly affection and Chloe wondered for a moment about his own parents. Janey had mentioned that first day that it was "just him now."

As the caretaker was leaving, she said, "Oh, and Chloe, the wine cellar is all yours. Please enjoy anything you'd like, OK?"

More beautiful words had never been spoken. Chloe had been dipping into the collection all week, but it was nice to finally get permission.

As Chloe showered the chickens with paprika and more black pepper, working the spices under the skin with her fingertips, Charlie craned his neck to observe her work.

"Does that ever gross you out?" he asked, hands shoved into the pockets of his sweats.

She considered all the things she'd done throughout her career that he would have found far more unappealing than raw chicken skin. She could tell him about the mountains of bone marrow she'd scraped, the duck tongues she'd roasted, the fish guts, the offal, or the hundreds of lobsters she'd murdered over the years—not by dropping them into boiling water but by driving the tip of her chef's knife unapologetically through their heads.

"No, this doesn't gross me out. If you're going to eat something, you can't be afraid of touching it. It's all part of it. What we cook is giving itself to us. I want to honor it by taking the best care of it that I can, you know?"

Charlie nodded. "I've eaten at your restaurant. It was amazing."

"Really? At Redbud?"

"I was in Chicago for the World Series last year. My friends got us a table by shamelessly dropping my name." Charlie shrugged. "I saw you. You came out of the kitchen at one point. Your hair might have been a little longer, but I think it was you."

Chloe brought her hand to the back of her pixie cut and lowered it quickly, hoping for some reason that he didn't notice.

She cleared her throat. "What did you have?"

"Pork belly. A potato tart thing. Some kind of salty caramel cake with nuts in it."

She gasped, fixed her mouth in mock horror, and pretended to clutch a string of pearls around her neck.

Charlie chuckled in that low way of his. "I know. It was before I started working with my new trainer. When I was allowed to eat carbs and sugar."

"The good old days?" Chloe teased.

"He's worked with tons of actors who were getting ready for Marvel movies," he replied, almost defensively.

Chloe stifled an eye roll and began to peel butternut squash with practiced speed. She sautéed leeks, carrots, and celery in a small stockpot, noticing that Charlie didn't seem in any hurry to leave her to her work. She pivoted to her cutting board and used the side of her chef's knife to crack the skins from cloves of garlic. In seconds they were minced and tossed into the pan with the other vegetables, followed by the squash. She added two quarts of very overpriced vegetable stock and turned up the heat to let everything come to a gentle simmer.

"Now what?" Charlie asked, his eyes bright and curious.

She swallowed hard and tried not to look at him. "Now I let the vegetables cook down so I can puree the soup."

"And then?" Charlie smiled expectantly, and Chloe began to understand the Instagram accounts and weird social media fan fiction. She hated admitting how intoxicating it felt when he looked at her like that.

She felt a small rivulet of sweat run down her lower back and settle into the waistband of her underwear. She cleared her throat softly and lifted the pot lid, trying to collect herself while he awaited her answer.

"And then I toast some cashews with curry spices and a little chili oil and sprinkle them on top before serving it," she managed.

He nodded and continued to observe while Chloe washed her

knife, dried it thoroughly, and returned it to her knife roll just like she'd done ten million times before. *Is he just going to stand here?* she wondered. It wasn't that it was unpleasant, it was just weird having an audience of one who was looking at her with his almost turquoise eyes like he was completely riveted with everything she was doing. Like he was starving.

"It's kind of like acting," he offered, searching her face and waiting for her to agree.

What is? Pretending like my thighs aren't on absolute fire right now because you're still looking at me like that? Yes, it's truly the performance of a lifetime.

"The recipe is the script. And then it's all about practice, asking yourself if it's a situation where you can improvise. It takes discipline. And if you want to be good, you really, really have to give a shit. About every tiny detail. Because at the end of the day, your job is to please people. Or...I don't know," he said, color rising to his cheeks. "I probably sound stupid."

"No...it is. I mean, you don't," she stammered.

Charlie was now beside her at the stove, inexplicably stirring the soup with a wooden spoon, making slow figure eights in the simmering liquid. His arm kept brushing against hers, and she didn't pull back. Rather she held her breath each time it happened, waiting for his touch again.

"I think I'll go for a run," he finally said, breaking the thick and strange silence between them.

He strode from the room to do whatever it was that people did to prepare for running in fifteen-degree weather, and Chloe finished the soup, using the spaceship of a blender to grind it into a velvety puree. She wiped her damp forehead on her sleeve and frowned, thinking, *what even was that?*

Had they been having a moment before he'd bound from the kitchen, or was that just part of the Charlie Davis magic? Chloe shook her head to break the spell and finished her work, writing a careful note about reheating the soup, as if a person needed detailed instruction on the use of a saucepan and a burner.

She selected the trashiest sounding romance novel from the bookshelf and brought it up to her bed, where she spent the next several hours skipping ahead to the most scandalously smutty parts when the plot started to drag.

She texted Julia.

Things are weird here.

Tell me…

I don't know. I'm getting to know Charlie a little.

He's a sweetie, right?

She wondered if she should tell her sister how they'd begun to look at each other, how she was beginning to understand the folklore surrounding that dimple.

Not sure yet.

This is going to be a good three months, I promise.

Date tonight with the lobsterman. Will provide full report later.

Get it girl! 🔥🦞🔥

The sky began to darken, and Chloe watched through the window as the ferry silently chugged across the bay, its lights flickering to life. She wondered what Charlie was doing and tried not to think of him down in the basement gym, sweating and grunting.

She took her time in the bathtub, filling it and refilling it with hot water so many times her cheeks and belly were pink and flushed when she finally dried off. She dug through her suitcases and labored over what to wear, scolding herself for not bothering to unpack yet. She ultimately settled on high-waisted jeans and a wide-necked black sweater that slid off her shoulder, exposing both her lacy bra strap and her best freckles. She tousled her short hair, sweeping her bangs to one side before applying mascara and a touch of burgundy lip stain. She felt sexy, casual, and effortlessly cool as she allowed herself to admire her reflection before her thoughts turned to what Ben was cooking. If he could even cook.

She waited downstairs in the kitchen until the headlights of the lobsterman's truck announced his arrival in the snow-packed driveway.

"Headed out?" Charlie asked, appearing from the dark of the dining room. He leaned against the doorframe, taking a large bite from an apple. He was objectively, astoundingly, disconcertingly good-looking.

She commanded herself to stop looking at his mouth.

"Yes, headed out," she responded with an attempt at breeziness. "The soup is in the fridge. Just reheat it on low. I also made you a salad with roasted chicken breast."

"I think I can handle that," Charlie and his dimple said.

"Well then...have a good night."

"You have a good night too, Chloe," he said with a knowing smirk.

She grabbed her coat and practically ran outside, where Ben was already making his way toward the house.

"Oh, hey!" he greeted her warmly. "I was going to come to the front door like a gentleman. I planned my knock and everything."

"Oh, that's OK," Chloe said, breathless from the cold air and the far-too-sexually-charged apple eating.

She paused to look up at Ben and his halo of gorgeous hair that shone golden even in the dark. She wondered if she'd stumbled upon some mythical island of beautiful men, if the universe actually rewarded those who did horrible things in the real world.

"I'm excited to cook for you. I hope I'm worthy." He gave her a big smile, his eyes crinkling at the corners as he tried to lean over to open the truck door.

"Don't worry, I've got it," Chloe said, pulling the door open herself and climbing onto the bench seat. "And I'm sure you'll be great."

The truck crunched down the driveway and Chloe stole a sidelong glance at her date, who was still smiling softly, his giant hands resting lightly on the steering wheel. He brushed that rogue lock of hair out of his eyes and said, "I've been looking forward to this all day."

"Me too," she responded, forcefully pushing thoughts of Charlie and his mouth out of her mind.

Chloe had never been very good at first dates. She hated small talk, and what was a typical first date other than a nonstop volley of small talk? It always felt awkward and forced, and she usually just wanted to skip ahead to the good parts, like in that romance novel she'd left on her bed, the binding nearly split with the strain of being splayed open.

They were soon turning up Ben's driveway, another long stretch of gravel canopied by pine trees. The truck bounced over a few potholes that the snowpack hadn't quite filled, and they both laughed as they were jostled toward each other.

"Here we are!" he cheerfully exclaimed, quickly jumping out to open Chloe's door for her. She beat him to it, exiting before he even had his hand on the handle. He really needed to learn that she preferred to open doors for herself.

His cottage was nestled among the trees, perched neatly at the edge of a small cliff. The moon's reflection announced the ocean just beyond it. The shingles were stained dark gray. The small window boxes were filled with evergreen boughs. Even in the dark, Chloe thought it looked like something from a storybook. He led her inside, where the open concept, gleaming pine floors, exposed ceiling beams, and soft, warm light made her think *hygge*. It was a word she'd only learned recently when discussing restaurant concepts with the interior designer from the Harris Group. Everything about it was cozy, lived in, and completely inviting.

"This is beautiful."

"Thanks," Ben replied, running a hand through his hair and tucking it behind his ear. "I've been working on it for a few years. It was pretty rough when my folks handed it over to me. They bought it in the seventies and lived here forever. They just left the island a few years ago to live with my sister in Portland. It's hard to get old here, you know?"

As if on cue, an arthritic looking golden retriever made his way down the stairs and lumbered over to Chloe. He sat at her feet and leaned his face against the side of her thigh, his watery brown eyes closing as she gently scratched behind his ear.

"And who's this?" she asked, laughing as the dog released a blissful groan.

"This is Jasper. He'll act like no one has ever pet him before. Right, old guy?"

Like a cat seeking affection, Jasper pushed his head into Chloe's hand as she stroked his ears. She smiled, remembering how hard she'd campaigned for a dog when she was a kid. When the farm next door had a litter of husky puppies a few weeks before her tenth birthday, it was all she could talk about. On the very morning that she graduated to double digits, her dad had come into the house holding what looked like a tiny baby wolf, just for her. Chloe had fallen in love the instant Pippa was placed in her arms, the very minute she let out that first little chirp of a bark. She could still recall her musky puppy smell and those eyes—light blue and rimmed in the darkest black. Chloe had immediately thought of those eyes the day she met Charlie.

And now here was sweet Jasper, tenderly offering his paw to her until she took it in her hand.

"OK, OK," Ben softly chided. "Let's not come on too strong for our guest here."

He pointed to the dog's bed near the woodstove and Jasper dutifully complied, turning slow circles on the round cushion before collapsing with a harrumph and immediately closing his eyes.

Ben crouched on one knee in front of the fire, pushing in a piece of wood that he had no doubt split himself, and Chloe took a moment to admire his broad shoulders. Everything about him looked so solid, his movements so assured.

"Are you hungry?" he asked, turning to face her.

"Always."

"Well, I already have a few things going, so I'll start pulling the rest of it together," he said, crossing the open space to the kitchen. "Beer? Wine?"

Chloe very rarely drank beer, but something about the sleepy heat of the wood stove, the aroma of what smelled like tomato sauce, and the way Ben was looking at her while he rolled up his shirt sleeves all worked together to convince her that cold beer straight from the bottle was the best idea anyone had ever come up with.

"Cheers, Chef Chloe. I'm so glad you're here." They clinked their bottles together and continued to make eye contact as they each took a long, slow sip.

"So, what are we making?" Chloe asked, finally breaking the spell.

"Well, *you're* not making anything because you're my guest. But *I'm* making lobster fra diavolo. And I baked some bread today."

Like a magician, he whipped a tea towel from two gorgeous baguettes that had been tucked beneath it.

What???

"You can cook."

"Were you expecting canned baked beans? I've lived alone for a long time. And I like to eat." He tucked the towel into the waistband of his pants and lit the burner under a stockpot of water. He added a small handful of kosher salt and began to chop parsley and some Calabrian chilis with an unhurried, deliberate rhythm.

I think I'm in love, Chloe thought, already feeling the effects of the beer as Ben added the peppers and a large heap of cooked lobster meat.

"Your lobsters?" she asked.

"Of course."

She relaxed into a chair at the rustic wood table—likely made of boards that the lobsterman had hand-planed after chopping the tree down himself. He sliced a thick piece of bread and slathered it with a generous smear of cultured butter and a sprinkle of salt before handing it to her. She moaned her appreciation and asked, "How did you learn to bake like this?"

He smiled over his shoulder. "I took a class."

"You took a class."

He shrugged and grinned again, ducking his head as he finished his work. He dished out two portions of spaghetti, making sure hers had the largest pieces of lobster on top. She could smell the heat from the chilis, and she felt giddy with the anticipation of digging into something so spicy. It did not disappoint. It was a perfect dish—the acidity from the tomatoes, the heat, the salt, none of it overpowering the sweetness of that beautiful lobster.

"This is amazing," Chloe said. "Really."

"Not too spicy?" he asked, his forked poised above his plate expectantly.

"Never."

They ate and drank for the next hour, sharing stories about their backgrounds and their childhoods. Chloe was surprised that she didn't get her usual antsy desire to fast forward through the conversation. She told him about her parents' farm, about Julia, and shared tales of all the kitchens she'd worked in throughout her career. He told her about his mom and dad, how he'd been fishing since he was a teenager, how he'd decided to stay in his childhood home to save the cottage from its formerly sagging roof and crumbling foundation.

"Have you had a chance to travel much?" she asked.

"Oh sure, here and there. But I've never stopped wanting to come home to this place, you know? I always knew I'd live here forever."

"But surely you've wanted to experience living in another place at some point," she insisted. "A year in Italy? Norway for a few months? You could fish in the Pacific Northwest and live in Portland?"

"I left for a year once," he shrugged. "I followed...someone. To Denver."

"And?" Chloe asked, noticing the cloud that passed across his handsome face as he paused before saying, "someone."

"And...it didn't really take."

"The 'someone' or the place?"

"Both."

"So, Deer Haven for life?"

"I guess so." He chuckled, the cloud once again lifted.

Chloe nodded like she understood, though the truth was that other than her childhood in Vermont, she'd never stayed anywhere for more than a few years. Her general pattern was to live somewhere for about eighteen months before she got that itchy feeling.

"How old are you?" she asked.

"Forty-one. How old are you?"

"Thirty-five." Chloe paused for a moment. "Ever been married?"

"Nope." Ben took a sip of his beer and rose from the table to get them each another.

"Why not?"

"Just haven't met my person yet, I guess," he answered matter-of-factly.

"No serious Deer Haven ladies?" she asked, wiggling her eyebrows and making him chuckle.

"Slim pickings as they say," he responded, peeling at the corner of the label on his bottle.

"I'm sure there have been a few..."

He paused to chew, conveniently buying some time with another sip of beer.

"There was Kate. She was a teacher here. She moved off island to teach at a private school. We were together for about two years. And Jessa. She moved to Boston. And then Lauren. We were on and off for a few years. She didn't want to stay here forever either. She was in the Peace Corps, so she traveled all over."

He tucked his hair behind his ear and Chloe considered the pattern that Ben was describing, the series of women who had all held bigger dreams than a seaside cottage on Deer Haven. In her experience, men who said they liked strong women soon found out that the drawback was that they couldn't be tamed, that the very quality that the guy found most appealing was often the thing that inspired the woman's departure.

"How about you?" He countered. "Ever been married?"

"Nope," she answered, following with her own long sip. Her mouth was on absolute fire from the chilis, but she found herself relishing the burn.

"Why not?"

"I guess it never really dawned on me—you know, as something I wanted. My job always filled me up so much. I never craved anything else."

"And you were happy? Working that much?"

A quick slideshow of career highlights flashed through her mind: working the line for the superstar chef who communicated only in rage-fueled shouts, learning how to fold tortellini with a beloved mentor in her tiny Bay Area trattoria, dispensing aerated camembert from a canister for a certain chef who valued style over substance and insisted on putting foams on absolutely everything, cooking at Redbud on opening night, sharing family meals with her staff.

"Yeah, I was happy," she finally responded. "Until I wasn't."

"And then you came here."

She raised her bottle toward Ben, and he met it softly with his own.

"So, what's it like working for the movie star?"

"I'm not sure yet," Chloe answered. "We don't really know each other and he's not that interested in food. So, I have a lot of free time on my hands."

Though we did have a very strange moment over a pot of soup, she resisted adding.

"You must have met him before, living here for so long. His family has been coming here for generations, I guess."

"I know who he is," Ben replied, coolly.

Chloe waited for him to continue, studying his face while he appeared to be biting his tongue.

"Do you miss the city?" he asked, obviously eager to change the subject.

Before she could answer, he set down a large piece of apple pie in front of her, still hot from the oven.

"I needed a break," she admitted through her first, blissful bite.

It was the first time that Chloe had spoken the words that her parents and Julia had been insisting upon for years. It felt kind of amazing to say it aloud, to admit that she'd needed to take some time away from her life in Chicago, to press pause on her sixteen-hour workdays, the mess with David, the critics, and the stress.

"I *really* needed a break."

Even better the second time.

The brief silence that settled between them was interrupted by Jasper, who sighed from beneath the table as he rested his chin on Chloe's knee.

"I think you have an admirer," Ben said with a chuckle.

"The feeling's mutual," she replied, her eyes bright as they met his.

They finished their dessert and Chloe found herself delighted in her level of tipsiness. She felt loose and warm, full and completely content. She walked over to Ben's extensive record collection—of course he listened to vinyl—and browsed the worn spines. His taste was eclectic. The White Stripes were nestled against Nina Simone, and next to that, Band of Horses, Miles Davis, and Johnny Cash. She pulled "Fine Line" by Harry Styles from the shelf and held it up to Ben questioningly.

He chuckled softly and shrugged. "Hey, 'Watermelon Sugar' is a good song, Chloe."

She laughed and returned it to his collection, then pulled "Magic Potion" by the Black Keys from its sleeve.

Ben stretched his arm across the back of the sofa and crossed his legs, looking completely and gracefully at ease in his tall body. She could feel his eyes on her as she gently dropped the needle. The bluesy grit of guitars filled the air. They smiled at each other and drank their beers, turning every now and then to gaze at the glass panel on the front of the wood stove and the fire that crackled just beyond it.

"I love this song," she murmured as "You're the One" hummed from the speakers. She closed her eyes and leaned her head against the cushion.

When she opened them, she could see Ben's tattoo just barely peeking out from the rolled cuff of his shirt, and she finally asked what it was, moving a little closer. He pushed his sleeve up his bicep and revealed a beautiful black and gray illustration of an octopus. Its long arms were wrapped around his upper arm and appeared to be swaying in the tide, moving with every one of his breaths, which seemed to be coming slightly faster as Chloe leaned in. Her sweater slid down her shoulder, exposing her freckled skin, glowing in the light of the fire.

"They're escape artists, you know," she said softly, noticing he was watching her lips as they formed the words.

He reached out his big hand and touched the back of Chloe's neck, leaning in until his mouth was on hers, soft, warm and curious. He tasted like beer and apple pie and she found herself hungry again, searching his mouth with her tongue. She buried both hands in the back of that golden hair, taking entire handfuls of it between her fingers. With one fluid motion, he lifted her by the waist, so she was straddling his lap, never detaching his lips from hers. She could feel him between her thighs as he kissed her neck, her throat, gently pulling her sweater down so he could brush his lips across her shoulder. She kissed him until she felt lightheaded. He reached his hand under her sweater, up her side, across her belly, before turning his attention to the button and zipper on her jeans.

"Is this OK?" he asked hoarsely.

She nodded and guided his hand down the front of her pants. His fingers found her and she pushed toward them, writhing against his palm while they explored each other's mouths. She came with a shudder, moaning into the side of his neck as he wrapped his arm around her back, pulling her closer. She stayed pressed to him for another few minutes, chest to chest, their hearts thudding against each other in an alternating rhythm. He kissed her again, deeply, less urgently than before, and she moved her hand to the front of his pants, where he was still hard between her legs.

"Mmmmm..." he hummed pleasurably. "Let's save something for next time."

Chloe settled into his side, Ben's arm around her shoulders. They stared at the fire, which was close to dying out, though Ben seemed in no hurry to rise from the couch to stoke it again. Chloe wondered if she had ever felt so satisfied in her entire life. A different kind of woman may have been bothered by Ben's tapping of the brakes, insecure that she wasn't desirable enough, wasn't sexy enough for this beautiful man, but Chloe felt nothing but sleepy contentment. She searched her memory to recall the last time someone had been so giving to her, someone who she wasn't in service to, someone who wanted absolutely nothing in return. Maybe never.

They stayed just like that until almost midnight—drinking, chatting, and playing records until they both started yawning and Ben offered to take her home. Chloe was truly sorry it was ending, the perfect first date she hadn't dared to dream possible. She kissed Ben softly, lingering in the warmth of his mouth as he ran his knuckles down the side of her cheek. Under a groggy, half drunken spell, she practically floated to the house, noting that he didn't start backing up until she was safely inside, his headlights making a path all the way to the door. She turned to raise her hand in a wave, and she could just make out his wide smile through the glare in the windshield as he waved back.

Getting ready for bed, she gazed at her swollen lips in the bathroom mirror. She pressed a fingertip to her mouth, remembering the feeling of Ben's tongue, of his teeth softly biting her lower lip. She hadn't kissed anyone like that since high school and her first thought was to text Julia to share all the hot details, since it was only just past nine in LA. She stopped, phone in hand, and decided to keep the night for herself just a bit longer.

Just before she flicked off her bedside lamp and settled into the smooth cool of her sheets, she poked her head from her room, glanced down the hallway, and noted the thin bar of light still shining beneath Charlie's bedroom door.

Chapter Nine

The next morning, Chloe slept late and was awakened by the sun streaming in through her window, reflecting off the bay. She stretched like a cat and indulged in a mental replay of the previous night's events, wondering if she'd met the world's only sexy, book-reading, bread-baking, single man, right here in the middle of the Atlantic Ocean.

Back in the kitchen, she heated the kettle for coffee and scooped grounds into the French press, grateful that Charlie wasn't around.

She texted Ben.

That was fun last night.

He responded immediately.

Do it again sometime soon?

I'd love that. Give my boyfriend Jasper a hug for me.

Ben answered with a thumbs up and Chloe wondered if it could really be that easy—if it could all be as uncomplicated as spicy pasta, cold beer from the bottle, and saying exactly what you meant all the time with no concern for pretext, context, or game playing.

Charlie broke her reverie by entering the kitchen, his tousled hair standing on end, his T-shirt sticking to his chest. He used the hem of his shirt to wipe his sweaty forehead, exposing the ripple of muscles on his stomach.

"Do you drink coffee?" she asked, trying to keep her eyes off his shoulders, his chest, his arms.

"Nah, I'm good, thanks. I'll make a smoothie in a bit."

"Would you like some eggs?"

He smiled and shook his head, then plopped down onto the banquet and started scrolling on his phone. Chloe busied herself with thinly slicing potatoes and onions and sautéing them in butter until they were brown and crispy. She beat four eggs and poured them on top, shaking her skillet to loosen everything. She grated some cheddar and quickly put a lid on the pan, turning the heat to low and allowing the eggs to puff up and cook through. As she was sliding it onto a plate and sprinkling the top with fresh chives, she noticed Charlie craning his neck to watch.

"That smells really good."

"Would you like some? We can split it. I made enough for two," she offered.

The fact that he was thinking about it so carefully still struck Chloe as thoroughly odd, even considering what she already knew about his restrictive eating habits.

"You know what? I'd love some," he said, his eyes bright.

Chloe had to bite her lower lip to keep from smiling as she cut the frittata in half. She watched him take his first bite and chew it slowly, sighing as if a little fat and carbohydrates had never tasted so good. She carried her plate into the dining room and ate while boats glided across the harbor, savoring the sound of his empty dish clattering into the sink.

He's eating, Jules!

You've got this, Chlo! Sexy Lobsterman update?

Chloe sent a single fire emoji 🔥, noting the undeniable deterioration of her own communication skills.

Details?

🔥🔥🔥

As she was texting, another missed call from the mystery 708 number lit up her screen. Still no message.

"God, the signal really is crap here," she muttered, tossing her phone onto the table, resolving to ignore the ghost reaching out to her from her old life. She told herself again that if it was a career prospect, the caller would have left a voicemail.

With a couple of hours to spare before dinner time, Chloe made a quick batch of chocolate chip cookies with pecans and dried cranberries, and started the dough for her favorite focaccia bread. While the dough proofed, she prepped the leeks, celery, and potatoes for crab chowder. Of course, Charlie's would be in a separate pot sans potatoes and cream, whereas hers would be made as the food gods had intended: full of fat and starch.

When Charlie entered the kitchen, he was on his phone, grinning, dimple in full force. "Bran! Yes! Send the script...OK, I will." He hung up and stared at Chloe in ecstatic disbelief. "HBO wants me for a limited series!"

When Chloe turned from the stove to give him her undivided attention, his eyes sparkled with excitement.

"This is the first time in a year that I've been considered for anything other than the asshole best friend in a low-budget rom-com."

He whooped and grinned, surprising her by coming in for an abrupt hug before lifting her off her feet and twirling her around.

"That's exciting!" Chloe assured him, wondering if she was showing the appropriate amount of enthusiasm for his victory.

"Want to hear the funny part?" he asked, looking at her

expectantly. "They want me to gain some weight for the role. They said fifteen to twenty pounds. Bran thinks this job could redefine my career. Make people finally see me in a different way."

Without a word, Chloe stacked four cookies, still warm from the oven, and handed them to Charlie, who was grinning like a kid who had just gotten everything he wanted for his birthday.

"What, now?" He laughed. "We're doing this?"

"No time like the present!" His use of the word "we" didn't go unnoticed by Chloe, who was already adding extra Yukon golds—carbs!—to the pan. She retrieved the glass bottle of heavy cream from the fridge and poured in the entire pint. Charlie laughed again and she scolded herself for liking it so much.

He ate his cookies and helped himself to two more while Chloe finished dinner, poking holes in her focaccia dough and sprinkling it with liberal amounts of coarse salt and thyme. She killed the heat under the stockpot and added what remained of Ben's crabmeat, stirring gently to preserve some of the larger chunks. She thinly sliced raw brussels sprouts and tossed them in a vinaigrette made of Dijon mustard and fresh tarragon. Charlie watched her every move, asking questions along the way. He appeared fascinated when she emulsified the dressing by shaking it in a small mason jar.

He was absolutely glowing, and when he looked at her, she couldn't help but surrender to the shallowest parts of herself, the parts that didn't really know him and didn't need to know him as long as he kept looking at her that way. She couldn't deny that the thrill of those lingering gazes was helping the long day on Deer Haven pass just a little more quickly.

"Do you want to eat here or in the dining room?" she inquired, ladling a generous portion of chowder into a bowl.

"No, here is fine," he answered, gesturing to the kitchen banquette. Like her, he enjoyed being up against the window, watching the lights cut through the darkness of the harbor. "You can join me, you know."

"Eat with you?" Chloe blurted out, nervous disbelief coloring the edges of her voice.

"Is that weird?"

"Um...it's a little weird, but it's OK."

The truth was, Chloe still thought their entire arrangement was thoroughly weird.

She sat across from him as they ate in companionable silence. He was making scandalous pleasure sounds with every bite, and she was desperately trying to come up with something to say.

"What's the story of this house?" she finally offered.

He daintily set his spoon beside his bowl and then brutishly swiped his linen napkin across his mouth. "Well. It's been here forever. Built by my family a long time ago. And it's always been our place to escape to. I've been coming here my whole life."

"Where did you grow up?"

"California. L.A."

"Julia told me that no one is really *from* L.A."

"Living proof right here!" Charlie and his dimple countered.

Chloe was unsure how to ask what she really wanted to ask, the question to which she suspected she already knew the answer.

"And your parents?"

Without looking up from his plate, Charlie said, "My parents died in a car accident. Right before I got my first movie."

"I can't imagine..."

"They were so supportive of me through everything. All the auditions, the rejections, but they never got to see me really make it."

"Oh, Charlie," she replied, her voice full of sadness. "Any brothers or sisters?"

"Nope, just me."

Just as Janey Higgins said on the first day—*just him.* Chloe thought of that poor sad boy, losing everything when he was so young, and still going on to dance on the lunch-room tables in those stupid movies, tossing his thick bangs and making the tweens swoon, beckoning the world with that dimple. Doing it all through that kind of grief must have been heartbreaking.

"They must be such a big part of why you like to come here." She stopped herself from reaching out to brush a crumb from his lower lip. Instead, she concentrated on her salad, sitting on her other hand to control herself.

"They loved it here. I always have, too. Sometimes I just feel like L.A. is crushing me, you know?"

Chloe nodded. She knew what it was like to feel utterly trapped in something that you didn't dare question. And she knew how it felt to be locked into a certain life, to be on a ride that was starting to make you a little sick, though it hadn't dawned on her to just get off.

"I can't go anywhere," he continued. "I can't even go for a run without the paparazzi following me. They just camp out at the gate. It was worse when Emma and I were together. They followed us everywhere."

The chef made a mental note to google "Charlie Davis girlfriends" as soon as they said goodnight.

"The whole scene...it just feels like too much sometimes," he said, glancing up at her through lowered lashes, inviting her to dig deeper.

"I can understand why Deer Haven would feel like an escape from all that. But I saw some pictures of you. With your friends. You looked like you were having a pretty good time."

"Didn't I?" he replied with a shrug.

She reached for the wine and offered Charlie a glass, finding herself shocked when he accepted. She delivered him a hefty pour and sank back into the seat across from him, close enough to touch his hair, to smell his shampoo when he bent his head to eat his salad.

He took a sip and stared at her with widened eyes before letting out a low chuckle. "I haven't had alcohol for over a year." He savored a long, slow drink. "So good!"

She laughed, and without really thinking, blurted out, "Yeah, what's up with the not eating thing anyway?"

"It's my trainer," he replied. "And I guess Bran too. I have to treat my body like my job. Diet, workouts, all of it."

"That sounds like my idea of hell," Chloe said. She could sense the telltale chardonnay flush creeping up her cheeks, making everything feel just a little too hot.

"And look at what good it did me! I haven't been offered a

worthwhile job in forever! No one takes me seriously. They think I'm stupid because I look like this. They also think I can't act, and sometimes I think maybe I can't. I don't know. Do you know how many times I've just wanted to eat a sausage and pepperoni pizza and drink a six-pack and just say, fuck it?"

Chloe nodded as if she could possibly understand, trying to deny the delicious shiver that raced up her spine when he cursed.

"The worst part," he continued, "is watching everyone else just move forward so easily, getting work, moving on. Cole Frasier has that huge series, and he didn't even really sing in the movies, he just lip synched to someone else's voice. All my work in the gym, all the diets and vocal training and everything else and the people most interested in me are still the people who just want to sell my photo to the gossip sites."

A part of Chloe couldn't help thinking that these weren't real problems—being *too* fit, *too* beautiful, having fans *too* interested in what you did and where you went. But then she remembered Charlie's face when he'd mentioned his parents, that look of utter anguish, and she found herself softening. Losing your whole family when you were still a teenager, trying to navigate your career, your relationships, your life completely on your own—she couldn't even imagine it.

It was impossible to think of her own career as something she'd truly achieved by herself. It was always the knowledge of the love, the safety net that her parents provided, that gave her permission to take risks. Even when everything went to shit at thirty-five years old, she could still consider going home to them.

"Why do you still want it?" she wondered aloud. "It all sounds pretty brutal."

"Because it's what I've always wanted. It never occurred to me to want anything else, you know?" he explained with a shrug.

Boy, did she know.

"Can I ask you something?" Chloe asked, running her finger around the top of her already half empty glass. "Why did you need me? I mean why did you need a chef here at all? Up until about an hour ago, it seemed like you would have been happy surviving on protein powder."

He bit his lip and gazed at her sheepishly. "Um, I didn't really. Need a chef, I mean," he confessed. "Julia convinced me that it would be a good idea. That I needed a break and you needed a break. She's always been so good to me, so I wanted to do something for her. She wanted to help you."

Chloe couldn't help but laugh, shaking her head. "Fucking Julia."

"Right?" Charlie responded. "Honestly, she scares me a little."

They squinted at the darkness beyond the window until Charlie finally spoke. "Why did you want to leave your restaurant?"

Chloe looked unflinchingly into the turquoise eyes across from her, not pausing for even a moment to consider her words. "I got caught with my boss in the back room. By his wife. Who owns the place."

She waited for some hint of judgment or shock to flash across Charlie's face but saw none.

"So, I didn't...want to leave, I mean. Or...I don't know. Maybe I did."

Why had that been so hard for her to say out loud until this moment? She hadn't even broached the subject with Ben the night before. It had taken her so long to just plainly lay out the facts.

I chose something. I got caught. These were the consequences.

"But why did you decide to leave the city?"

And abandon my post.

"Because I live my life not asking anyone for permission. And I messed up. And suddenly I felt like I had to beg for another chance," Chloe confessed. "And I don't ever want to beg. For anything."

Why am I telling him all of this?

She had to admit that he was surprisingly easy to talk to despite the Charlie Davis spell that left her feeling a little sweaty. She made a silent pact with herself to stay focused. They would be friends. She would cook for him. He would finally eat. She would save her salacious thoughts for her next date with Ben, and she would try to stop looking at Charlie's arms, his hands, his mouth. And in a couple of months, she would leave and go back to her real life in Chicago.

Then he suggested they open another bottle of wine.

Charlie went down to the cellar to retrieve "something red" per Chloe's less than explicit instruction, and she ducked into one of the house's many powder rooms. In the mirror, her green eyes were dark and a little wild. She ran a hand through her short, tousled hair and spoke to her own reflection in a whisper.

"This is your boss. You're a little buzzed. Be a friend but keep your shit together."

She noticed that she'd missed a text from Ben. It was a picture of a gorgeous loaf of ciabatta, presumably baked by the sexy lobsterman himself.

She hurriedly replied with a heart-eyed emoji. Her thoughts consumed by the fact that Charlie Davis was waiting for her on the other side of the door, and he was going to smile at her in that way that made people swoon. He knew exactly what he was doing.

"Keep it together," she hissed to the mirror again.

When she emerged from her bathroom pep talk, she discovered that he had moved their party of two into the living room. He'd opened what looked like some pretty old pinot noir and was working on dividing the entire bottle evenly between two large glasses.

"Stop, stop," she laughed. "Charlie, that's too much!"

He shrugged and grinned impishly while she chose a seat on the couch opposite him, the coffee table acting as an appropriate and essential buffer between them.

"Should I light a fire?" he asked, gesturing to the large stone fireplace.

"No!" She answered quickly and far too loudly, remembering the wood stove with Ben and the golden shadows it had cast on both of their skins. "I mean, I think the temperature is just right in here."

They worked on their overfilled glasses and chatted about their families. His father had been the wine collector, his mother the book collector who had filled the library shelves with everything from Kafka to Judith Krantz. She told him about the farm, how her own parents raised everything they ate, and how it had shaped her philosophy about food, fueling her passion for cooking. She made him laugh when she shared her best stories of life in a professional kitchen—the language, the debauchery, the things she'd seen and done. He talked about his new role, how he couldn't wait to read the whole script, how it sounded exactly like the kind of part he'd been trying to get for so long.

They were each about two-thirds through their wine when he pulled a small, battered joint from the pocket of his hoodie and held it up like a prize.

"What? Where is that from?" She giggled, silently scolding herself for getting drunk enough to giggle.

"Oh, I'd say about 2015. It's been hibernating in my dresser drawer since I was fourteen. What do you say, Chef? Should we fire it up?"

Surprised at the vaguely square way he was holding the joint, she asked, "Do you not smoke generally?"

"Not anymore. My trainer... he worries that I'll break my diet plan if I smoke weed."

"Break your diet plan? Oh no! What would happen then?" she asked with a teasing gasp.

"I might exercise poor judgement and eat a carb."

Chloe snorted at the absurdity of it all. "We need to go outside, though. I don't need Janey coming in here tomorrow and smelling anything."

They bundled up in their down coats and wool hats. It was freezing out on the porch, but everything was completely still, not even a hint of wind sweeping off the ocean in front of them. Charlie lit the joint and took a small puff at first, then a longer drag, the bright ember glowing orange in the darkness. He exhaled an enormous plume and erupted into a fit of coughs.

"Smooth, right?" she teased.

He nodded, laughing and wiping his eyes before passing it to her.

Chloe closed her lips around the wetness left by his mouth and held the smoke in her lungs for a few seconds before exhaling three perfect smoke rings into the icy air. "Still got it."

"Wow. I think you're my new hero," Charlie said with awe.

She executed a dainty bow and wandered to the porch railing, wondering what it would be like to wake up to the ocean every day. Charlie appeared by her side, and she indulged in one more small puff before handing the joint back. She was already feeling its effects powerfully on top of the gallon of wine she'd consumed.

"Why do you come here in the winter?" she asked, burying her chin into her coat in a futile attempt to stay warm.

"I didn't always. As a kid, I usually came here in the summer, when the sailing school was running. But now I like it better this time of year."

"My God, why?" she asked, a shiver traveling from her toes to her fingertips.

"Because no one else is here," he replied, challenging her to notice his dimple. "No one but us."

She watched her breath come in clouds, suspending itself in the frigid air for just a moment before disappearing. When she gave him a sidelong glance, she saw him shudder. His arm was pressed against hers, but she couldn't feel anything through their layers of wool and down.

"Chloe," he said huskily in that low voice of his that could easily drive her to do bad things.

No one but us.

"Yes."

"Let's go inside and eat a ton of those cookies."

She burst out laughing, and they returned to the warmth of the house, to the dim kitchen lit only by the stove's hood. They joked and teased each other and ate too much until she found herself craving the bliss of that big soft bed in her room with its cool sheets and excessive pillows.

"I need to go to sleep," she declared, yawning into her hand.

He nodded and followed her up the stairs, echoing each of the step's creaks and squeaks with a trail of his own right behind her.

They paused in the hallway, and she wondered what it would feel like to just kiss him, to allow herself to be pressed against the wall, his mouth on her neck, her leg wrapped around his waist like one of the racy heroines she'd been reading about in that tattered paperback. She cleared her throat, praying he couldn't see her heart trying to punch through her shirt.

"Well," she managed. "Good night."

"Sleep tight, Chloe," he purred, eyes heavy from their indulgences, dimple going strong.

They stared at each other in smiling silence for a full five seconds before Chloe turned and briskly strode to the end of the hall, walking far too fast to look cool. She shut her door with a gentle click and fell back onto her bed, on top of that cloud of blankets that were just waiting to cushion everything.

She replayed the evening's events, reassuring herself that she had acted appropriately. She didn't flirt, and they'd kept all their clothes on. Yes, she'd made a choice to get kind of wasted with the person who employed her. At least she had the good sense to know when to call it a night.

When the lights were off and she was nestled into her bed, she realized she hadn't thought about David, Lila, Steph or Redbud for the last couple hours, not since confessing her sins to Charlie. It was the longest she'd managed to go without cursing herself for everything that had happened in Chicago, and she had a feeling it had something to do with the movie star and the way he'd begun to shine his light on her.

It's fine, she told herself. *Distractions like Charlie were harmless. Everyone liked shiny new things to look at. He can be my drinking buddy, my dinner companion, my pal.*

But when she considered the way her gaze had lingered on his lips when they'd said goodnight, she found herself squeezing her eyes shut and thinking, *uh oh*.

Chapter Ten

Chloe woke up feeling like her skull was full of fireworks and regret. After barely swallowing three ibuprofens completely dry, she staggered to the bathroom and took a thirty-minute shower, swaying until the water started to run cold.

Last night was fine, just don't let it go any further, she ordered herself, the hangover throbbing in her temples.

She threw on black leggings and a hoodie, ran a hand through her hair, and called it a win. This was the best she was going to manage today. A glance down the hallway to Charlie's open door confirmed he was no longer in his room. As she tiptoed down those damn creaky stairs, she wondered if he was in the house at all.

In the kitchen, she brewed coffee and toasted a piece of baguette slathered generously with butter. She covered it with raspberry jam once she pulled it from the broiler. The sky outside was cloudless and blue, and as she squinted out at the day, she noticed a lone figure rowing gracefully across the harbor. A black beanie was pulled over his eyebrows, his breath coming in clouds. His movements were smooth and rhythmic, his shoulders and back visibly powerful even through his fleece layers. Chloe watched, entranced, as he glided across the water, arms pumping with the silent cadence of pistons on the world's most efficient machine.

As he disappeared around the curve of the cove, she called her sister. It was only 7:15 on the West Coast, but she was an early riser. Chloe knew she would pick up.

Birds chirped in the background when Julia answered cheerfully.

"Where are you—the Amazon?"

"Out on the patio. I just did my Pilates and now I'm enjoying my juice and returning emails out here." Julia laughed. "How's it going with Charlie?"

"Good? I think? Better." Chloe couldn't bring herself to tell her sister about the charge that had passed between them in the hallway the night before, so she focused her energy on being annoyed with Julia instead. "Hey, thanks for forcing this on him, by the way. You knew he didn't need a chef out here."

"I didn't force anything on anyone," Julia replied smoothly, pausing to draw something presumably full of kale through her straw. "He needed to be alone for a few months but he's terrible at being alone. You needed to be somewhere else to get your head together. And it's probably beautiful out there."

"It's cold."

"It's good for you."

"Says the person lounging on her sunny patio in the middle of winter," Chloe shot back.

Julia chuckled, and for a moment Chloe could only hear the birds twittering softly. "So seriously, are you getting along OK? I thought he could use someone to take care of him for a bit, and you can be surprisingly good at that."

"Gee, thanks."

"You know what I mean, Chlo! You would never describe yourself as nurturing, but you're great at taking care of people."

Chloe looked out at the water just as a flock of Canadian geese flew by in their perfectly choreographed V.

"Apparently I've been hired to fatten him up like a Thanksgiving turkey."

"He's up for a pretty big part. He hasn't had much work in the past couple years, so this could be a huge deal for him. And his team thinks he's going to get it."

"Well, based on his recent cookie consumption, I'm guessing he's feeling confident too." Her coffee had gone cold while she waited for Charlie to row back into view.

"So...how's the sexy lobsterman?"

She remembered Ben's bread photo from the night before, realizing he was trying to show her something delicious while she was busy talking herself out of misbehaving with Charlie.

"I think I kind of like him, Jules. But I don't know..."

"Just see where it goes," she said encouragingly, the briefness of Chloe's stay unspoken between them.

"So," her sister began. "Beth is pregnant."

"What? Oh, Julia, that's awesome! In your first round of IVF! That's so, so exciting!" Chloe hoped she sounded as thrilled as she felt. Her head was still fuzzy, and she needed something more to eat. "Have you told Mom and Dad?"

"Not yet. We want to tell them in person, and we were hoping you could make the trip to Vermont, too. Next week. We've already booked our flights."

"Well, I kind of have to be here, right? For Charlie?"

"Charlie's schedule is still getting finalized, but I think he'll be back in L.A. for a few days next week to meet with HBO. The timing is perfect."

Chloe imagined her parents' farm in the winter. Her dad would be just beginning to tap their maple trees—a process Chloe had always loved as a kid. She thought about her mom's baking—hot bread fresh from the wood cook stove, chicken pot pie, and chocolate brownies. She pictured the system of trails that wound through the woods on their sixty acres, how she and Julia had explored every inch of that land throughout their childhood.

"Text me the dates, OK? I'll be there."

The sisters chatted for a few more minutes before giddily getting to say, "See you next week!"

Julia and Beth were having a baby and Chloe would devote herself to the role of cool auntie. She could imagine standing in the kitchen, her little niece or nephew on a stool at her side, measuring flour, cracking eggs. She would teach them to make the best grilled cheese, the best hot chocolate, and those little cinnamon pinwheel cookies that her mom always made from the scraps of leftover pie crust. She would fly to L.A. for birthday parties and school breaks, her carry-on loaded with souvenirs from her travels and a wooden toy from that gorgeous little shop on Armitage Avenue that she always walked past. She would be amazing at it.

She wondered if she should tell Charlie her sister's news, but hesitated, realizing that even though Julia described her clients as "family," she might not actually want to share the inner workings of her life with them.

The sound of shoes stamping snow on the front step prompted Chloe to duck below the countertop as she pretended to search for something in the lower cabinets. Any attempt at hiding herself was defeated when a stack of pans collapsed deep inside the cupboard, announcing her presence with a thunderous crash.

"You OK down there?" Charlie asked.

She popped up from her crouch and had to steady herself from the dizzying effect of moving that fast with a hangover that large. She assessed his smooth cheeks and wide, clear eyes. She realized that was the difference between your twenties and your thirties. Charlie had risen at who knows what hour, likely splashed some cold water on his poreless face and immediately started exercising. Chloe had spent the better part of the morning contemplating throwing up in the shower.

"I saw you out there. Was it cold?"

He shrugged and grabbed an apple from the fruit bowl, biting into it with a resounding crunch.

"It's cold, but nice. Fresh air is the only thing that helps me on mornings like this." He smiled wryly, and tried to catch Chloe's eye, but she was purposely avoiding his face by burying her torso in the open refrigerator as if the eggs weren't in the same exact spot they always were.

"Are you hungry?" she asked from the depths of the crisper

drawer. *Or are you just here to make me question every decision I've made in the past month?*

"Uhhhh, sure."

Was it her imagination or did he sound vaguely wounded, like he'd attempted an inside joke and she'd rebuked his efforts?

"What would you like? Eggs, bacon? I can make you some pancakes?"

Charlie was staring at her so intently that it was impossible not to meet his eyes when she turned to await his response.

Don't even think about admiring his mouth on that apple. Again.

"I'll have what you're having, Chloe," he purred, challenging her to admire his wry grin.

What I wouldn't give for a time machine, she thought, still avoiding his gaze and wondering what she would do with the gift of a do-over. Would she pull the cookies from the oven and retire to bed before nine, or would she have just one more glass of cabernet and pull him toward her in the dim light of the upstairs hall, hooking her fingertips into his waistband and feeling his breath hot on the side of her neck as she—

Chloe. No.

She shook her head sharply, challenging the aftermath of the wine, and began cracking eggs. She laid out strips of bacon on a sheet pan and slid it into the cold oven, setting the temp to 425 and the timer to twenty minutes. She sliced thin pieces of sharp cheddar and filleted last night's focaccia.

When he asked what they were eating, and she finally met his eyes, she noticed he let out a relieved exhale. He didn't like it when she stopped paying attention to him.

"The greatest hangover sandwich of your life," Chloe responded, slathering the focaccia with butter and pressing it onto the griddle with a satisfying sizzle.

"I'm not really hungover." He chuckled.

"Then I'm eating this in honor of my own poor life choices."

Chloe dragged a wooden spoon through the soft curds of egg while she simultaneously wished that her head would stop pounding and Charlie would stop watching her. She assembled their sandwiches —grilled bread, eggs, avocado, sizzling bacon, and cheddar. She placed them under the broiler and, when the cheese was perfectly blistered, dotted each one with a healthy squirt of sriracha before covering them with their focaccia tops.

They slid into the banquette seats across from each other, and Chloe watched while Charlie took an enormous bite.

"You eat real food now," she said incredulously.

He finished chewing and smiled at her. "I talked to Bran this morning. HBO is pretty much a done deal. I'm headed to L.A. for a couple days next week. To finalize things and meet some people."

"Julia said you might be doing that."

Shit. Now he'll know that I've been talking about him.

"I don't know why I was so focused on movies! Limited series are obviously where it's at right now," he declared.

"Well, it sounds great," she offered, choking down a few bites of her breakfast and beginning to feel a bit better. "I'm thinking about taking off for a few days while you're gone. To visit my family in Vermont."

"Nice," he responded absently, fingers furiously texting someone.

Well, OK then, she thought. He really was moving beyond what had passed between them in the hallway the night before, and so was she.

Good. Great. Obviously for the best.

He felt like a stranger again—cool, detached, and unknowable— as they avoided each other's faces and focused their attention on their sandwiches and the view beyond the window. Just as Chloe was silently calculating the odds as to who would speak first, Charlie announced that he had to read a script and excused himself. Breakfast was officially over.

Thankful that her hangover seemed to be contained, she begun working on a big pot of tomato sauce, sautéing onions, garlic and fennel before dumping in the remains of last night's pinot and several cans of San Marzano tomatoes. She knocked the heat back to low and added salt, oregano, and crushed red pepper, allowing the sauce to simmer while she prepped everything else for lasagna. She hadn't made the dish in years. When you lived alone, lasagna just didn't make sense unless you were willing to eat it every day for two weeks. She'd make two pans—enough for Charlie to eat for a couple days and another to take to Ben.

As if on cue, her phone vibrated on the countertop beside her.

Can I take you out on the boat today, Chef Chloe?

Without hesitation, she texted back.

Yes, please!

She was genuinely excited to see her lobsterman again but escaping the weirdness that she'd helped cultivate in the Davis house was an undeniable bonus.

Chapter Eleven

A few hours, two finished lasagnas, and one short nap later, Chloe and Ben were headed to the dock. His long arm stretched across the bench seat of his pickup, his golden hair glowing in the early afternoon sunlight. He looked gorgeous in his flannel shirt, grey wool pants, and work boots. She glanced down at her own outfit of black leggings, a black down jacket, and tall black Hunter boots. You could take the girl out of the city and all that.

Jasper rode between them, upright and beaming, his panting dog breath filling the truck. When Ben turned into the marina and stopped, the old dog leapt from the truck, confidently trotting down the dock. He climbed carefully onto a boat, where he stood, tail wagging, waiting for them to catch up.

Ben's boat was navy blue with the words "Andrea May" painted in tidy block letters across the back. He reached out to assist her as she climbed aboard, and unlike the other times he'd tried to help her in and out of his truck, this time she accepted. The way the boat bobbed up and down, knocking against the dock with a nauseating rhythm, made it easy to place her hand inside of his much larger one, at least until she found her sea legs.

Once she was not-so-steadily standing on the small platform, she watched while Ben untethered from the dock, pushed off with his boot, and started the engine. The boat roared to life and Chloe had to stabilize herself on the side rail, even though they hadn't moved yet.

"You good? You OK?" he asked, smiling over his shoulder.

"All good!" she called back, her stomach still unsettled from the last remnants of her hangover, as he gracefully guided the boat around few other vessels anchored throughout the harbor.

It looked like the only boats that remained were the fishing boats, as the sailboats and cabin cruisers of the rich had long since been pulled from the water, stored safely at the boatyard near Janey Higgins' house. Chloe sat down on a small bench, turned her face from the punishing wind, and watched Ben steer, his broad shoulders squared toward the stern. Jasper appeared to be living his best life, front legs up on the bench opposite her, his ears pushed back, and his tongue cheerfully lolling as they picked up speed.

The pine trees and rocky shores of the island passed by and she saw Charlie's house, staring down at them with its wide porch, those big windows reflecting the sky. Ben waved at another fisherman who was pulling what seemed like miles of rope before reaching his trap, full of lobsters and woven with seaweed. He maneuvered around a bend to a sheltered cove, where he cut the engine and turned to face her.

"Hi," he said.

"Hi."

He retrieved a thermos from a small cabinet near his knees and poured them each a cup of steaming lemon tea. Never a tea drinker before, Chloe considered herself converted at that moment, when the shock of hot liquid hit her very cold mouth and instantly warmed its way through her body.

"Who's Andrea May?" she asked, wrapping her hands around her cup.

"My mom. This was my father's boat. He always said he wished he could name a fleet of ships after her." Ben shrugged and smiled, glancing at Chloe as if to gauge her reaction toward the romance of it all.

Chloe marveled at Ben's height as he bent to kiss her, slowly and softly as the wind ruffled her short hair. She pulled his wool hat over his ears as she kissed him back, pressing her down clad body into the front of his.

"So, are we going to pull up some lobster traps?" she asked when they pulled apart.

"I don't generally dress like this when I haul traps." He chuckled, gesturing to his soft coat and wool pants. "And I don't generally smell this good either!"

"You make a vital point," she responded, boldly burying her cold face into his chest, inhaling as he wrapped his arms around her.

"These are some of mine though." He pointed to a smattering of navy-blue buoys painted with three thin pink stripes, suspended atop the choppy water. "They're easy to spot this time of year."

She pulled her hood up, feeling the cold air rising from the water as the sun shone brightly in the cloudless sky. Ben looked, as always, completely comfortable, and hadn't even zipped the front of his jacket. This prompted Chloe to burrow deeper into his shirt as she wrapped her arms under his coat. When he ran his hands down her back and pulled her closer, it felt like they'd been there before. Being in Ben's arms wasn't dizzying in its newness the way sharing space with Charlie was. It felt utterly and disarmingly familiar, as time-honored as her work in the kitchen. It was muscle memory.

People always said they were "married to their work," but for Chloe it had always been more than a marriage. Her work had been a husband, a mistress, *and* a best friend—the thing that she gave herself to with devoted monogamy, the thing that consumed her with passion, and the thing she couldn't imagine herself living without. It had been everything. The idea that her obsession with it had deprived her of a pleasure as simple as wrapping her arms around a man in the middle of the afternoon made her feel unsteady, like she was standing on the deck of a small boat in choppy seas.

"You love it out here," she declared into his chest.

"I've spent my whole life on a boat."

"Have you ever thought about doing anything else?"

He lowered his chin to the top of her head and let it gently rest on her wind-tousled hair. "Honestly? No. I can't imagine anything this good. I don't have a boss. I'm outside every day. Look how beautiful it is here." He gestured to the ocean that surrounded them. "You know, when my back is killing me after baiting traps all day and I have to hobble from the truck to the house, it doesn't exactly feel like living the dream. But then I get up the next day and feel the sun on my face again."

Chloe nodded in deep understanding. She knew what it felt like to love your work while simultaneously feeling your body break down because of it. She was thirty-five with the knees of a seventy-year-old after her years of cooking on the line. Her job inspired her to drink too much and sleep too little. Running a kitchen was a frustrating, impossibly demanding, and often thankless pursuit. But even though she was starting to feel almost betrayed by all it had taken from her, she missed it so damn much.

Why did I run from the city like I was admitting defeat? she thought. *Why didn't I fight for Redbud, for something? And what am I doing in Charlie Davis's house? How did I allow any of this to happen?*

But then Ben tipped her chin upward and kissed her, this time with more urgency, his most unruly lock of hair falling across her own forehead.

"I want you to take me back to your house," she whispered into the side of his neck.

He smiled that slow grin and asked if she wanted to drive. She positioned herself at the helm while he stood at her back, his hands over hers and his body acting as a shield from the wind. The engine roared to life and Ben helped her maneuver out of the cove, across the open water, and toward the dock.

Back in the truck, he was smiling in that easy way of his, and she wished he would speed a little, maybe even forget to wave at the other cars on the road. They bounced up his long, gravel driveway, over the potholes and under the canopy of pines until they reached his cottage. He put his arm around her shoulders while they strolled to the door, and Chloe fought the urge to break into a full sprint while pulling him by the hand after her.

Does this man EVER hurry? she wondered, anxious to get into the house, into his bed.

Inside, he got the woodstove going, and after minutes that felt like hours, closed the glass door to the crackling flames. Jasper gratefully settled onto his fireside bed and Chloe allowed herself to linger in front of the stove, dropping to her knees to pet the sweet old dog and attempting to remove the chill that had settled into her bones. She was trying on Ben's leisurely pace like a borrowed coat. She was taking her time, seeing if it fit, even though she'd wanted to tear their clothes off before he'd even struck the match.

Ben offered her some wine, some tea, a snack, all of which she declined. She caught herself holding her breath as he made his way over to her, pulling her into his arms so she could rest her cheek against his chest. She ran her hands up his back and could feel every muscle, every breath through the fabric of his shirt. He kissed her slowly at first, his hands on the sides of her face.

She followed him to the second floor where his small bedroom was located. It was as tidy as the rest of the house and offered an unobstructed view of the ocean and the sun that was just beginning to set behind the trees. He was kissing her neck, and she had her hands entwined in that glorious head of hair when he lifted her sweatshirt over her head. She was happy she'd worn her favorite black mesh bra and found herself even happier when he brought his mouth to the fabric. She unbuttoned his shirt and pushed it off his shoulders, wishing she had the willpower to stop the clock for just a few moments, just long enough to appraise every inch of his torso—from his broad chest to his trim waist, each part of him lean and muscular.

When Ben dropped to his knees in front of her, Chloe didn't worry for a moment about the extra few pounds that had settled into her hips and belly since she'd stopped working at the restaurant. All she knew was her fingers in his golden hair, his broad hands on her hips, and the way it was all making her feel dizzy.

Then, like it was nothing, he lifted her up and was inside of her before they even fell back onto the bed. Her legs wrapped around his waist. He moved rhythmically, gently at first, his hipbone hitting her in just the right place until she eventually screamed her orgasm into the darkening room. She wrapped her legs around him again, locking her ankles and pushing him deeper inside of her until he shuddered and collapsed, his hair softly falling across her face.

They stayed like that for a few moments, catching their breath while the sun disappeared completely and his bedroom became nothing but shadows. He rolled onto his elbow, bending his head to kiss her freckled shoulder before pulling the soft and faded quilt over them both. She pressed her cold feet into him, and he received them between his warm calves.

I've found the perfect man, she thought, curling against him. *I had to travel to the middle of the goddamn Atlantic, but I've found the perfect man.*

"I love these freckles," he whispered, running his fingertip down the bridge of her nose.

"I always hated them as a kid," she confessed, closing her eyes when he brought his lips to her eyelids, her chin, her cheeks. "Back then I just wanted to look like everyone else."

"Terrible idea." He buried his face into the side of her neck and pulled her on top of him, tugging the blanket and covering her shoulders again.

Chloe rested her chin on Ben's chest so she was looking up at his face, at the light stubble on his chin and into his green eyes with their perfectly crinkled corners. She wondered if this was the moment where they were supposed to talk about what it all meant, where it was going, what was next. Should she remind him that she was only here for a short time, that she wasn't looking for anything serious? When he started running his fingertips down her spine, she was relieved to pass the time in ways other than discussing where things stood between them.

An hour later it was hunger that finally drew them from the bedroom, and they padded down the stairs together, Ben in his T-shirt and boxers, Chloe in his flannel shirt that reached nearly to her knees, a look taken from every romcom ever made. She boldly opened his refrigerator to assess their supplies and Ben stood next to her, his arm draped around her shoulder while he peered into the mostly empty shelves.

"Sorry," he said. "I'm overdue for a trip to the market, I guess."

"Do you have bread?" Chloe asked, prompting Ben to hold up the remaining half of the prizewinning loaf he'd shown off in his text. "Do you have cheese?"

Ben opened a drawer in his refrigerator and frowned. "Just American."

"Ben," Chloe responded in a very serious voice. "I don't want to live in a world in which we all act like American cheese isn't the greatest option for grilled cheese."

"I thought you might want something fancier," he chuckled.

"Never."

She snatched the cheese from his hand, tossing Jasper a small piece that he skillfully caught in the air. She turned on the heat under the well-seasoned cast iron skillet and added a generous pat of butter.

Ben tucked his disheveled hair back behind his ears and studied her, smiling. "You just make yourself right at home, don't you?"

"I've cooked in a lot of different kitchens." She shrugged, watching as the processed cheese began to liquify at the edges of their sandwiches.

"I like you making yourself at home here."

Chloe slid their sandwiches onto plates and tried to disregard how serious that sounded, and how nervous it made her. They ate their dinner standing in the kitchen, Ben declaring it the best grilled cheese he'd ever had. Chloe credited the bread and couldn't help but notice the pride on his face as he received the compliment.

"So, what's it really like to work for a famous person? To *live* with a famous person?"

"Charlie?" she asked, as if her roster of celebrity roommates was so long that his statement required clarity. She bought herself a few extra seconds by taking a slow sip of water. "He's fine. I mean, I'm just getting to know him and what he likes."

The memory of the heat that had started to build between her and the movie star flickered through her mind and she worked to push it away. She was in Ben's kitchen, in Ben's shirt, and he was beautiful and constantly looking at her like she was the most fascinating person in the world, like he couldn't wait to hear what she was going to say next. She willed herself to focus on what was in front of her.

"I used to see him down at the sailing school when he was a little kid. And I've had a few...run-ins with him over the years."

"What does that mean? Run-ins?"

"Once at the bar—

"Wait, stop," Chloe interrupted, a gravely serious expression taking over her face, her eyes wide and unblinking. "There's a *bar* here?"

"It's only open during the summer," Ben laughed. "In the old red barn near the ferry dock."

Chloe recalled seeing the "closed for the season" sign when she first got off the boat, one of many indicators that she'd made a certain kind of choice by agreeing to come to Deer Haven in the winter.

"So he was at the bar, with another guy, a friend of his," Ben continued. "Everyone said he was the kid from some teenage superhero show?"

Chloe shrugged, waiting for him to go on.

"So, I went in for a beer, and he and this other kid looked like they'd been there drinking for the better part of the day. And I'm not sure which one of them instigated it, but they started talking trash to some local guys and Charlie starts taking swings and I jump in to break it up. He caught me with his elbow right here." Ben pointed to his upper cheekbone. "I had a pretty nasty shiner for about a week."

"Wow. That doesn't sound like him," Chloe weakly replied.

"Well, he was really drunk. And like I said, I don't know who started it," Ben explained. "And then another time I found his boat."

"You found his boat?"

"He had this gorgeous Boston Whaler. I think it was his grandfather's. Beautifully restored, all mahogany."

Chloe shrugged again. She had no idea what a Boston Whaler was.

"He would joyride around in it when he was a teenager, stop wherever, and just leave it for days tied to other people's moorings. So, one morning I'm heading out to haul traps, and I see it half run aground in a little cove. It's all beat up. The bottom has been bashing against the rocks as the tide has come in and gone out again."

"Well, it sounds like he was just a kid."

"Yeah. Just another spoiled rich kid who was never taught to appreciate anything," he said, his expression darkening.

"I'm not sure that's fair," she replied, feeling suddenly protective of teenage Charlie and all that he'd lost.

"When I tracked him down and told him that I'd found it, he acted like he had no idea what I was even talking about. He barely looked at me. He just told me to go ahead and bring it to dock it at the marina. And then he handed me a hundred. Like I worked for him."

Chloe's stomach sank. It sounded like not all of Charlie's unsavory behavior was contained in L.A. and within the pages of those glossy tabloids and gossip sites. Some of it had clearly spilled over onto Deer Haven, following him out to sea like a bad habit that he couldn't quite shake.

She wanted to counter with, *that's not the Charlie Davis that I know*, but she decided to bite her lip as a silence settled between them.

"So sad what happened to his parents though," Ben finally said. "But I guess it hasn't held him back too much."

"Mmmm," she responded, remembering how Charlie's blue eyes had grown flat when he talked about his mom and dad, how they had looked almost electric when he talked about his new job.

"I just can't get used to the idea that you live there in that big house with him. Just the two of you."

Chloe blinked at him, trying to decipher the intent of his tone. Was she hearing notes of Jealous Boyfriend? She really hoped not, because pants or no pants, she would have no qualms about *abandoning her post* if that was the role he was playing. She decided to give him the benefit of the doubt and surrendered a small smile. She really did like him.

"Yeah, it's pretty weird," she replied. "But we mostly manage to stay out of each other's way. And I just think of it as just another job, you know?"

And I'd obviously never behave badly at my job.

"No, of course," he said. "I just mean I don't know how I'd ever feel like I could get comfortable, you know? Living where I work."

"It's not a big deal." She shrugged. "And it's only for a couple more months anyway."

"Right. Only for a couple more months."

She watched his muscles move under the thin fabric of his T-shirt as he attended to the dirty plates in the sink. She pressed herself against his back and wrapped her arms around his chest as she murmured, "But I'm here now," feeling his heartbeat quicken beneath her hands. He finally turned to kiss her deeply, his soapy fingers already working the buttons on her shirt. She couldn't keep her hands from his chest, his arms, his waist. She ran her fingertips down that beautiful tattoo on his arm, pressing her lips to the places where the ink was the darkest.

He pressed her back against the wide post that divided the kitchen and living room, using it to support her while he moved inside of her, leaving her to wonder if this had been his intention when he was renovating his house—sanding that cedar column to be so smooth that it would feel like velvet on her bare skin. His lips were on her freckled shoulder while she clutched him with her thighs, arms around his neck. She pushed his hair out of his eyes and looked into their green depths, focusing on where his dark pupils were surrounded by an almost golden ring. When he slowly lowered her so her bare feet were on the floor again, she worked to catch her breath as she wrapped his soft plaid shirt around her body.

Ben dressed slowly, grinning at her while he retrieved his hastily discarded T-shirt from the fruit bowl atop the counter.

She filled a mug with cold water from the tap and drank it as if she'd been lost in the desert for a week. "You're really good at that, you know," she said, returning to the sink for a refill.

"Well, you're really sexy, you know, Chef Chloe." He pressed his lips to the corner of her mouth and wrapped his arms around her. "You kind of drive me crazy."

After he stoked the fire, he sat beside her on the sofa, draping his arm around her shoulder and pulling her closer. She rested her head against the side of his chest, staring into the flames, feeling flushed, calm, and happy. She must have dozed off, and when she awoke with a start, she had that disoriented feeling of not knowing if she'd been asleep for seven hours or fifteen minutes. Bleary eyed, she sat up to find Ben reading a beat-up looking paperback.

"I fell asleep," she groggily declared, shifting her bent legs beneath Jasper, who had draped himself across her lower half like a blanket.

"I didn't want to wake you," he said, running his fingertip across her lower lip. "Did you know that you make a little humming sound in your sleep, not quite a snore, but kind of like an mmmmmmmm sound?"

"I've been told," she answered, stretching her arms above her head and glancing at the cover of his book. "*The Old Man and the Sea*? A little on the nose, don't you think?"

"Hey, it's the only book I could reach! You had me pinned!" He smiled and folded down the corner of the page before returning it to the small table next to the couch.

"I have to get back," she declared softly. "I don't want to, but I do."

"Or you could stay."

"I have to get back to *(don't say Charlie)* work. I have to prep for breakfast, and make sure he's all set on dinner."

They retrieved their clothes upstairs, and as Chloe pulled on her socks, she felt a distinct sadness. She looked longingly at the twisted sheets on Ben's bed and found herself wanting nothing more than to get between them again. She felt homesick suddenly, and she hadn't even left yet.

He held out her jacket, offering her a sleeve, and she gave him an exasperated look as if to say, *I can put on my own coat!* But as she slid each arm in and felt his lips press against the back of her neck, she found that she didn't mind his gentlemanly gesture as much as she thought she might.

Back in Charlie's driveway, she leaned across Jasper in the truck's cab and kissed Ben tenderly. His mouth tasted both sweet and salty and it was all that she could do to not just curl up on his lap and call it a night.

"You sure you don't want me to turn around? Go right back to my place?" He kissed the side of her neck and lightly closed his teeth on her earlobe. It was nearly enough to change her mind.

"No, I have to get back," she insisted.

"Next time then."

"Next time. I'm headed to my folks' place in Vermont for a couple days this week."

"Is it too early to say that I'll miss you? Is that weird?"

Ben's gaze searched her face while Chloe bit her bottom lip. She wondered again if she'd met the one person on earth who just said what he was thinking, what he was feeling. She kissed him again, lingering on his stubbled cheek.

"Oh wait! Wait right here!" She ran into the house and grabbed the second pan of lasagna from the refrigerator, where Charlie had been considerate enough to put it away. "I made you a lasagna."

"What? You were sitting on this all day when all I had to offer you was American cheese?" he teased, eyes in full crinkle mode.

Chloe shrugged and stood on her toes to give him a final kiss through the truck window.

"Bye. Goodbye, Jasper."

Inside, the house was as quiet as ever, Charlie nowhere to be seen. She flashed to what Ben told her about Charlie, and she wondered if she'd been right about him in the beginning. Maybe he wasn't the occasionally sweet, ever curious, sometimes confusingly aloof guy she'd been getting to know these past few days since she'd arrived on Deer Haven. Maybe Charlie was kind of an asshole.

After navigating the creaky staircase to discover the door open to his unlit bedroom, she headed to the basement. She found him in the home theater, wearing his uniform of sweatpants, a hoodie, and a black knit beanie, enjoying *The Notebook* on the massive projector screen.

"Oh, hey," he offered, pausing the movie when he finally noticed her.

"Hey. Did you eat?"

"I did. The lasagna was awesome. Thank you." His perfect chiseled face was lit only by the screen in the otherwise dark room.

"*The Notebook?*"

"Ryan Gosling's body looks amazing in this movie. We had the same trainer for a while."

Chloe didn't know whether to laugh, agree, or make a barfing sound, so she concentrated on neutralizing her expression completely.

"Did you want to watch?" he offered, that slow grin making its way across his face. "I'm only about a half hour in. I could restart it."

"That's OK, I've already seen it. And I have some stuff to do in the kitchen."

She wondered if she was imagining the look of disappointment that flashed in his eyes.

He glanced back at the screen. "So, you've met some friends here?" he said with what seemed like an attempt at nonchalance.

She thought about Ben on his knees in front of her in his bedroom, Ben holding up her leg while he kissed her against that cedar post, Ben biting her ear in the truck. "Yeah, I guess."

"I used to be friendly with some of the townies when I came here as a kid. Some of them were OK."

She narrowed her eyes through the darkness at him. Now that she'd heard Ben's retelling of their assorted "run-ins," she found herself thinking for the first time about the dynamic that must exist between Deer Haven's rich visitors and its year-round residents. Ben, Janey, Catherine from the market, Lois the librarian, they all had actual lives on the island, homes and families and day-to-day jobs. Visitors, even visitors like Charlie who had been coming to this house since he was born, were on a break from their real lives. Everyone surrounding them was there to delivery luxury and convenience during their short stays, to give them everything they wanted.

"Townies?" she blurted. "You sound like an asshole when you say that."

Charlie flinched and Chloe started thinking about how unfortunate it would be to get fired already, but she'd hated hearing

Ben's stories about the arrogant summer person who'd acted like he owned the place. She was already beginning to see the many faces of Charlie—the confident Charlie who barked orders at his "people" on the phone, the sweet and silly Charlie who drunkenly giggled his way through all the cookies, the Charlie who held her gaze for way too long—and realized it was like watching someone play different roles in different movies. It was officially starting to make her feel off kilter.

"I didn't mean it like that," he said quickly, employing his dimple to plead his contrition. "I'm sorry, I do sound like an asshole."

She shot him her best disapproving look as he held up his hands and laughed.

"I'm sorry! It was a dumb thing to say," he insisted. "What's your new friend's name?"

"Ben Libby."

"Well, you should invite Ben Libby to the house sometime. We can have drinks or something."

"So, are you leaving tomorrow?" Chloe asked, eager to change the subject. "I saw your suitcase."

"Yup, back to L.A. for a couple days. Meetings and final details to work out for HBO."

"That's great, Charlie. Really," she replied, clearing her throat to convincingly reset her tone. "When are you coming back?"

"Thursday."

"Me too."

She was struck by the tediously professional turn their conversation had taken, and it wasn't lost on her that this was the only kind of conversation they should be having, should have ever had. She shouldn't be smoking weed with him and telling her best bawdy kitchen stories. He shouldn't be inviting her to watch a movie—the fucking *Notebook* of all movies—and there certainly shouldn't be any heated moments in hallways or anywhere. She would cook the food, he would eat the food, and she would be paid for the job she'd been hired to do. Simple.

Charlie returned his attention to the oversized screen while Chloe returned to the kitchen, where she prepared some Danish pastry dough for the morning, placing the covered bowl into the refrigerator for its overnight rest. Feeling suddenly ravenous, she pulled out the lasagna and cut herself a corner piece, noticing with pride that the actor had polished off nearly a third of the dish already. She ate alone at her favorite spot at the banquette table, savoring the salty cheese, fatty sausage, and spicy tomato sauce, replaying the afternoon with Ben in her mind.

She closed her eyes and pictured his face when he removed her clothes and saw her curves, the fullness of her hips. He'd looked like he was hungry. She planned to enjoy her time in Vermont, but she also found herself looking forward to being back in his truck, rambling down that dirt road back to his house, back to his bed.

And Charlie? Charlie would just be a sparkly little blip at the edge of her memory. Someday she'd think back to their three months together and would find herself barely able to remember the line of his jaw, the exact icy blue of his eyes, the way her name sounded when it spilled from his mouth. *That would be that*, she thought as she finished her dinner, staring into the starless sky beyond the window.

Chapter Twelve

Charlie's flight was at noon out of Portland, which gave Chloe plenty of time to shape, fill, and bake the Danish before he departed. So much of cooking depended on a practiced instinct, but pastry was pure science. The leavening, the effects of water and steam, and the way you could change the structure of something with just the temperature of your hands had always intrigued her.

She was just easing the pastries into the oven, half of them filled with lemon curd, the other half with raspberry jam, when he joined her in the kitchen. He was wearing slim-fitting dark jeans and a black crewneck sweater that somehow made his eyes look even brighter. She willed herself to look away from his lean torso and the way the cashmere was hugging his chest and arms.

"Coffee?" she offered.

"I'm good, thanks."

He was in phone scrolling mode, barely looking up from his screen as he settled himself into the side of the banquette that Chloe had come to regard as his.

"Tea then? I can make you a smoothie?"

"Um, yeah, OK. A smoothie," he responded, never taking his eyes from his phone.

Chloe busied herself with adding bananas, frozen mango, and

what was left of a quart of strawberries to the blender. She scooped in some vanilla Greek yogurt—full fat!—and topped it off with almond milk and a healthy squirt of honey before turning the Rolls Royce of kitchen appliances to high. The fact that she'd ended up making Charlie Davis's smoothies after all wasn't lost on her. Her real life as one of the country's best chefs suddenly felt a million miles away.

She closed her eyes to the deafening pitch of the whirring motor while she thought, *this is how it was always supposed to be. Taking his breakfast order, baking the pastries, all at a safe distance.*

She was just pouring the smoothie when Janey Higgins came through the mudroom door.

"Good morning, good morning!"

Her naturally rosy cheeks were further flushed from the cold when she gave Charlie a hug, prompting him to yelp when she pressed her face against his.

"You're freezing!" he exclaimed, eyes lighting up, dimple fully engaged.

"Well, it's cold out there! I left the truck running. Charter flight leaves in twenty minutes." Janey glanced at Chloe and then at Charlie, her cheery presence filling some of the space between them. "How are you two getting on? Everything been good here?"

Charlie responded with a "Great!" just as Chloe said "Good," and the two exchanged a look that would have been funny if it wasn't so awkward—a look that made her feel like a teenager who had hastily hidden the bong behind a pillow when her mom walked in.

The timer announced the Danish, and Chloe was grateful to have a job as she watched Janey perch on the bench and put her arm around Charlie. The pastries were steaming hot, their filled centers molten as Chloe slid them off the baking sheet and onto a cooling rack. She dusted them with powdered sugar and watched as it instantly disappeared, melting into a glaze.

"Raspberry or lemon, Janey?"

"Raspberry please, dear."

"Charlie?" She looked at him expectantly, spatula poised midair.

"Both." He gave her a wide smile. Who was she to resist grinning back as she loaded his plate?

The amount of butter that the recipe required bordered on scandalous. Janey and Charlie murmured their appreciation as they took their first bites.

"Honey, tell me you've been letting her cook for you like this all week!" Janey said to the movie star, plucking an errant flake of pastry from the front of his sweater. "Chloe, this is delicious."

"So good, Chloe," he echoed, using the side of his thumb to wipe a tiny blob of lemon curd from his lower lip, making the room instantly feel too hot in that Charlie-Davis-broken-thermostat way that she was getting used to.

She ordered herself to think about Ben, to stop looking at Charlie's mouth as it closed over the warm pastry.

This isn't good for you, she reminded herself as he met her eyes and his dimple deepened. *Just because you always do this, it doesn't mean it's good for you.*

"We'd better get going, hon," Janey said, daintily wiping her mouth.

Chloe handed her a plate piled with pastries. "For you and your husband," she said, pressing the dish into the kindly woman's hand.

"Thanks, sweetheart! He'll love this."

"See you in a few days," Charlie said, raising his hand in a weird wave.

Chloe misread it as a high-five invitation and awkwardly tapped his palm.

What?

"Good luck with everything out there."

"Thanks. Have fun in Vermont. Tell Julia I'll miss her at Mori Sushi."

He smiled, and she wanted to touch her fingertips to that dimple. She wished she didn't want to, but she wanted to. He looked like he had something else to say, but he just grinned even wider as if he knew exactly what she was thinking.

And just like that, they were gone, Janey's truck leaving behind a cloud that hung against the pine trees in the cold air. Chloe felt her shoulders relax and found herself feeling profoundly relieved to be alone in the house again. For the next three days, she wouldn't have to worry about Charlie's meals or his dimple or the angle of his cheekbones. She wouldn't have to worry if that look in his eyes was meant for her or if it was just the natural state of his face. She sat down with her coffee and texted Ben.

Getting ready to leave in a few minutes. Just wanted to say bye!

Can't wait until you get back. I ate your lasagna for breakfast.

And?

It was perfect.

She thought about Ben's little house, how he'd assured her that he liked seeing her make herself at home there. She imagined woodstove fires and bread dough rising in that tiny kitchen, sleeping in on Sunday mornings after hot sex the night before, wearing nothing but his soft flannel shirts forever. She shook her head to dissolve her fantasy. This was not what she did—constructing mental romance novels in which a gorgeous man swept her off her feet and saved her from herself. This was all supposed to be just for fun!

What the hell is this island doing to me? she asked herself, aggressively dumping the remains of her coffee into the sink and rinsing her cup with the hottest water her hands could tolerate.

She showered and hastily packed, piling sweaters, wool socks, and jeans into her suitcase. She remembered the last time Julia had visited Vermont in March a few years earlier, when she'd shown up in the middle of mud season wearing Keds and a suede moto jacket, as if her entire childhood in the Northeast had been undone by a decade in L.A. She'd spent the weekend in her dad's barn coat and her mom's tall muck boots and had somehow managed to pull off a look that the sisters had laughingly declared "farmyard chic."

Chloe couldn't wait to spend some time with her family.

The ferry ride and five-hour drive passed quickly. Chloe attempted to listen to an audiobook she'd been looking forward to, but she found her mind wandering to Ben, and then to Charlie. She'd never felt so consumed by thoughts of men, and she couldn't say that she liked it. Miles passed, entire chapters unheard, as she remembered Ben's mouth on her belly, considering Charlie's lips as he bit into that apple.

The audiobook was eventually abandoned and Chloe blasted Sleater-Kinney instead, hopeful that the fuzzy guitars and post-feminist howls would help her return to the person she thought of as *herself*—the badass woman who ran one of the most successful restaurants in the city, who viewed men as a fun little indulgence, but never, *ever* a distraction from work.

She followed rivers and mountain roads the rest of the way, passing farms and more farms, driving through tiny towns that featured little more than a church and a gas station. She turned onto a winding, frost-heaved stretch of gravel that wove through canopies of maples, now gray and winter-bare. She slowed down on the last bend, remembering how she'd careened off the road at that exact spot the day she got her driver's license. She had underestimated the icy patches and thunked the front end of her Ford Escort into a snowbank while her mother pumped a non-existent brake on the floor of the passenger side. Her dad had towed her out with his tractor, revealing a series of dents in her bumper—the first of many.

The farm showed itself on the hill in front of her, the light-yellow farmhouse nestled in its snow-covered field, the barn anchoring it to the frozen earth. Chloe parked next to the mountain of snow that her father's plow had been creating for the last four months, confident that its remnants would persist through May. She stretched and took in the greenhouse with its curl of smoke streaming from the chimney pipe and the swags of thin rubber tubing connecting the dozens of maple trees in the grove at the edge of the field. Her dad would soon be consumed with sugaring. The chickens clucked absently as they pecked the snowy ground beneath the apple tree, polishing off what remained of their lunch of grain and compost. She headed toward the front door, already able to smell her mom's bread baking.

She was home.

Her mother threw her arms around her before Chloe had a chance to set her bag down, stopping her in the doorway with her tight, cookie-scented grip. It was a flurry of hugs and hellos, her dad appearing in the kitchen, looking grayer and slightly more stooped than the last time she'd visited, followed by Julia and Beth, who surrounded her on each side with a collective embrace.

"How was the drive?"

"Are you hungry?"

"I love that jacket, Chlo."

"We're so glad you're here."

Chloe hugged everyone back, feeling overwhelmed by the whirlwind of attention and overcome by the two feelings that always drew her back to this little sanctuary: warm and lucky.

"Geez, Mom, who else is coming?" she teased, taking in the sight of five pies cooling atop the kitchen island.

"You know your mother," her father lovingly interjected. "Always cooking for an army!" Her mom smiled and swatted him with a dishtowel.

"Plus she wants to 'put some meat on my bones,' according to our last three phone calls," Julia said wryly, placing her hands on her hips and striking an indignant pose in her wide-legged wool pants and fitted sweater.

"Well, you and that exercise cult! You're getting too skinny!"

"Mom!" Julia laughed, tossing her long strawberry blond curls to one side. "It's just *called* Soul Cycle. It's not a cult!"

"It sounds like a church to me. Now, who wants pie?"

"None for me, Sarah," Beth responded with a grimace, placing a hand on her belly, taut with the faintest hint of a bump. "My stomach is..."

Julia reached for Beth's hand and gazed at her wife with so much love in her eyes, rubbing the back of her neck gently. "This one is a warrior."

"I still can't believe I'm going to be a grandmother!" Their mother clasped her hands together and Chloe could almost see the movie playing inside her head: walking around the yard with the baby bundled against her chest, identifying every species of flower, pulling out that old step stool from the pantry and teaching them how to cut biscuits with an overturned water glass, showing their small hands how to slowly turn the crank on the food mill, their little eyes watching, mesmerized, as apples became sauce. This little one was already so lucky.

The family sat around the weathered wood table, laughing, chatting and enjoying their pie. It was a fairly typical occurrence for Chloe to be eating within ten minutes of arriving to her parents' house.

"Chloe, how's the island?" Beth asked, tilting her head to one side inquisitively, her long tassel earring brushing her shoulder.

"Oh, you know, still getting used to things out there, I guess," she responded through a mouthful of maple custard. "The house is beautiful."

"And how's Charlie doing out there?" Julia asked, her fork poised in the air. "He was kind of a mess before he left. Frustrated with the business. He needed a little break for sure."

"He was a mess?" Chloe asked, attempting to keep her tone disinterested.

"Well, you know how it is," Julia began, as if any of them other than Beth had the faintest idea of how it was. "Some of these actors get famous when they're so young. And then they want to do more serious things, but maybe they don't totally have what it takes for serious things, and no one wants to give them a real shot. No one wants to take a chance on that transition. And then add a pretty big flop to the mix, and suddenly the phone kind of stops ringing."

"But it sounds like things are looking up for him, right? With HBO?" Chloe asked.

"Yeah, definitely. He's got a good chance at getting it. Bran's acting like it's a done deal, but it's not. That's why he's back out there for these meetings. To win them over."

Chloe nodded and felt a sudden kinship with her movie star. She thought of her calls to investors in Chicago right after the David thing blew up, to her awkward lunch with Jenna Moran, to the dozen unreturned overtures to other chefs. Was the measure of true success in their respective careers reaching the point at which you no longer had to audition for rich people, when you weren't required to constantly, desperately, sing for your supper? Chloe had naively thought she was there until she'd found herself standing in the middle of the city, completely alone. At least Charlie had a team behind him.

"Are you making friends out there? Meeting anyone?" her mother asked.

Chloe flashed to Ben smiling over his shoulder while he steered his boat, Charlie laughing and passing her that stale joint, Ben's hopeful expression before her first bite of lobster fra diavolo. "Um, I guess? It's an island, so there's not a lot going on. Socially, I mean."

"I'm sure Chloe has managed to set a trap or two," Julia teased, wiggling her eyebrows and causing Beth to snort adorably, hiding her giggle behind her napkin. "Get it, Chlo? Traps?"

"Yeah, I get it," Chloe felt an inexplicable blush, regretting all the lobster and fire emojis she'd texted her sister. Desperate to divert the focus from her social life, she smacked her palms on her thighs and announced, "So! What are we doing today?"

"I have some work in the greenhouse to finish up," her father replied, wincing as he rose from the table and stretched his back.

"I'll help you out there, Dad," Chloe offered, leaving the others behind in the kitchen, where her mom had promised to teach Beth how to make biscuits, as if Julia would put a single carb into her body once they returned to LA.

Chloe followed her dad across the yard and toward the greenhouse, around the shingled chicken coop and the pole barn where he stored his tractors. She trudged through the snowy paths that had been worn down and tried not to focus on her father's crooked gait, the way his hips seemed perpetually shifted to one side, his right leg mostly unbending. He always said he would work until he died, and as much as Chloe couldn't bear to think about any of that, she couldn't ignore the fact that every time she came home, another piece of him seemed to have broken down just a bit more. It sometimes felt like seeing into her own future, watching herself stooped over the line at fifty, at sixty years old, still full of energy and great ideas while her knees screamed with arthritis, her back forever aching.

Inside the greenhouse, the air was toasty thanks to the small potbellied stove in the corner. Chloe inhaled the familiar aromas of soil and fertilizer, the scents of growth and rot that permeated everything within the clear plastic walls. Her father was starting the seeds for the lettuce mixes that would flourish in the greenhouse through the final weeks of winter and into the spring—arugula and bibb, along with tender baby leaves of light green and burgundy that Chloe would have killed for in her restaurant. Everything her dad grew was impossibly pristine. It was what had inspired her to expect excellence from all her produce suppliers over the years—the fact that she knew firsthand what could be achieved if you completely devoted yourself to the seeds.

She found herself assuming her usual stance on one side of the homemade work bench that ran nearly the entire length of the structure, her dad opposite her. He wordlessly placed flats of soil between them so they could make rows of holes with a wooden dowel and carefully drop the seeds inside. Chloe had spent countless Saturdays with her father in the exact same way, sometimes chatting and joking, sometimes quiet, planting these little specks, transplanting seedlings, watering, watering, *watering*. Later in the spring, if he could position the antenna just right, it would be the Red Sox on the radio, the same old broadcasters' voices announcing bunts and infield flies season after season.

They conducted their work in silence until her phone buzzed with an incoming call from that same unknown 708 number. She groaned and pressed decline, forcefully shoving her phone into the pocket of her jacket.

"Not going to get that?" Her father asked, his silver eyebrows raised.

"Nope." She shrugged, unwilling to invite an unwelcome reminder of her past into such a sacred space.

He kept his eyes focused on the dirt. "You know, your mother only bugs you about all that stuff because she worries about you."

"Worries about me? I'm fine."

"She knows that. She just wants you to settle somewhere. To be happy."

"I am happy, Dad."

Her father looked straight at her with his cloudy gray eyes, the skin around them weathered from countless seasons in the sun. He smiled in a way that seemed almost sad for her.

"Dad, I am," she insisted. "I'm just feeling...I don't know... untethered lately."

He nodded wisely, placing another tray of dirt between them. "Look, we know something happened with your restaurant. And you don't have to tell us what."

Phew.

"But if we can help in any way, you have to let us," he finished.

Chloe felt her throat constrict while her vision grew blurry with tears. All she could do was nod and try not to meet her father's kind eyes. If she did, she was afraid she wouldn't recover. She took a deep breath, managing a shakily stoic smile.

"OK, kid?" he asked.

"OK," she responded hoarsely, wanting to tell him that just being back here with them was helping, that walking into the warm embrace of her childhood home was therapy, even if it was coaxing out some of the emotions that she'd spent the last few weeks earnestly stuffing down. That was the disarming thing about family—they see right through the part you try to play.

"It's getting dark," her father said. "Should we go back in and see if your mother needs help with dinner or should we hide out here a bit longer?"

"Hide."

They both grinned the same crooked grin and continued with

their work in comfortable silence, making their little holes and dropping the seeds in, one by one.

Later that evening, Chloe found herself back in her childhood bed, her belly filled with her mom's chicken stew and yet another piece of pie. The sounds of shaking Yahtzee dice still rang in her ears. The tournament lasted over an hour, and Julia, emerging victorious as always, launched into a rendition of "We are the Champions" that inspired everyone to turn in for the night.

Chloe pulled the flannel sheets up to her chin and glanced at her phone: 9:25. A bona fide "late night" on the Foster Farm, and she was wide awake. She squinted through the shadows of her old room and was able to make out the worn spines of the Judy Bloom novels still holding court on her bookcase, the dozens of volumes of Sweet Valley Highs underlining them on the shelf below. Her favorite photo of her sister was still tucked into the corner of her vanity mirror, the edges now curling toward the center. In it, she and Julia were seven and nine years old with their arms slung around each other's shoulders, their faces painted like butterflies as they posed in front of the Ferris wheel at the Champlain Fair. It was right before her sister had insisted on riding the Scrambler three times in a row and then violently threw up her kettle corn into a trashcan. Chloe would take the photo with her, have it enlarged and framed—one for herself and one for Julia's next birthday.

She FaceTimed Ben, who appeared to be in bed too, a small lamp lighting his stubbled face, a paperback overturned atop his chest. He was wearing a worn white T-shirt and his octopus tattoo was dark against the skin of his upper arm.

"Hello there," he greeted her softly, tucking that perpetually stray lock behind his ear.

"I didn't wake you up?"

"Nah, just reading." He lifted the side of his mouth in a wry smile. "Well, maybe dozing a little, but mostly reading."

"*The Old Man and the Sea*?"

He lifted the cover to reveal an illustration of a tall ship careening on its side, its parchment-colored sails skimming the rough waters—"*Master and Commander.*"

Chloe smiled, the glow of her phone illuminating the smattering of freckles across her nose.

"How is it?" she asked.

"Not sure, I keep falling asleep." Ben closed the book and placed it beside him, in the space where Chloe was starting to wish she was curled against him. "How's Vermont?"

She settled back into her pillows and used her fingers to brush her bangs to the side. "Cold! But really good. It's so nice to see my family, to not worry about anything at all while I'm here, you know?"

"It's OK to want to be taken care of once in a while."

Chloe hissed out a dismissive little "tssssss" sound as Ben laughed and insisted he meant it.

"I think I just like it when someone makes my eggs for me in the morning," she teased, fully aware that being home with her parents was about so much more than that.

"I'll make you eggs in the morning. If you'll let me."

"You know, Wolfgang Puck won't hire a chef until they've made him an omelet. He thinks it distinguishes the real cooks from the hacks."

"Well, give me a chance to audition," he chuckled, bending his arm and tucking it behind his head, affording her an ideal view of his bicep.

She smiled, studying Ben's face—the faint lines near his eyes, the way his skin caught the golden light from his lamp. His lower lip always looked soft and full, begging to be bitten. She stared at his eyes, which went from green to golden to gray depending on the light.

"What are you doing in bed this early?" he asked.

"Everyone goes to sleep at like 8:30 around here!" She paused to pop in her wireless headphones so only she could hear Ben's low chuckle, the smooth edges of his deep voice. "The whole house has been dark for almost an hour. I didn't know what to do with myself."

"I can think of something you can do with yourself," he offered mischievously.

"Ben!" she gasped in a mock scandalized tone. "With my parents right down the hall?"

He smirked devilishly and Chloe squirmed beneath her blankets, suddenly very aware of the way the soft flannel felt against her bare legs as her hand crept across her belly. She sat up and pulled her T-shirt over her head, extending the arm that held her phone and affording Ben a grainy glimpse of her bare breasts in the darkened bedroom. He groaned softly and she thought she could hear his heart beating through the phone before realizing that it was her own pulse, fluttering against her earbuds. She propped her phone against the pillow at her side, freeing her hands, inviting him to look at her.

"See, now you're just torturing me," he breathed, gravel in his voice as he leaned his head against the headboard.

"What do you want me to do?" she whispered.

"You know what to do, Chloe."

The sound of her name on his tongue nearly brought everything to a crescendo right then, but she slowed herself down, focusing on Ben's face, his low words in her ears.

"Yes," she hummed, her breath catching in her throat.

She saw the muscles in his shoulder tense and shift. He pushed his hair from his forehead as she arched her body against her own hand, wishing he was in her room, wishing she was in his. She closed her eyes and pictured that smooth, wooden beam in his cottage, felt its worn velvet against her bare back. She could almost smell the wood smoke, could feel the motion of his boat as it skimmed across the waves. She allowed her phone to tumble from its propped position and settled face down into her duvet, where it remained until Ben finally released a guttural sigh.

When she looked at him again, she came like a thunderclap, low and rolling, finally exploding in the deafening crack that she'd been waiting for. She lay breathless and still, staring up at the ceiling and trying to collect herself before turning to her screen, where Ben was smiling sleepily back at her.

"Did you...?" she asked.

"Oh yeah. Did you?"

"Um, yeah. I'd say." She turned onto her side and pulled the blanket over her bare shoulder. "That was...surprising."

Ben laughed softly and stifled a yawn. "You make me..."

"Me too."

They said their goodnights in the dark before hanging up, 250 miles of highway, mountains and ocean between them. Feeling warm and content, she switched off her phone and fell asleep almost instantly.

Chapter Thirteen

The next morning Chloe woke with a start, forgetting where she was for a moment until she took in the achingly familiar sight of her old bedroom. She'd been dreaming about the

restaurant again. They were classic anxiety nightmares about forgetting to order food, then hiding in the back office where the door not only locked, but proceeded to lock her inside. She considered texting Steph to tell her about it, but she wasn't entirely confident as to where their relationship stood anymore. It hadn't gone unnoticed that her former sous chef hadn't reached out to her once with a question, concern, or single gripe.

I'm not in charge anymore, Chloe reminded herself, hesitant to appear desperate, like a hanger-on unwilling to let go. Then there was the Natter issue. She couldn't shake the idea that it might've been Steph. Maybe it wasn't a deliberate tip—just a casual conversation with another chef or a coworker. Maybe it had just slipped out. Chloe didn't want to believe that her friend would betray her, that they hadn't been good to each other after all.

Instead of dwelling on scandal, she turned her thoughts to Ben and their phone date the night before, as she remembered the way they'd whispered, how the whole thing had felt like a delicious secret. She loved how he made her feel—like her sexiest self, a ripe piece of fruit, the most interesting woman in the world. It was completely intoxicating.

She lifted her phone to find a text from him: a photo of the sun rising in shades of lavender behind the lobster boat, the edges of his long hair peeking out from beneath his hat.

Tell the Andrea May I say hello.

She typed a heart emoji and quickly thought better of it, sending a lobster instead.

Downstairs, breakfast had already been prepared, consumed, and cleaned up, which is how things went on the farm if you slept until eight. Her mom was punching down bread dough in a large ceramic bowl from the seventies, the same bowl that had hosted proofing after proofing since Chloe was a kid.

"Waffles over here, dear," she said, using her elbow to gesture to a platter piled high with the cold leftovers from breakfast.

Chloe didn't trouble herself with a plate, opting instead to smear a waffle with Irish butter and rhubarb jam and fold it in half like a taco, eating it standing up as she asked her mom where everyone was.

"Your dad's outside. He's tapping the last of the trees. It's going to warm up a lot by next week and the sap will be running." She covered her bowl of dough with a worn dishtowel reserved for exactly that purpose. "Julia and Beth are around here somewhere. I can't believe they were up so early, being on California time."

Chloe impulsively threw her arms around her mother, feeling the softness of her gray hair against her cheek. It had been a long time since she'd come home, and weird dreams aside, she was so happy to have woken up in Vermont.

Popping the last bit of breakfast into her mouth, she set out to find her sister, who was just where Chloe suspected she would be—sitting in her dad's chair in the corner of the living room, typing furiously on her laptop. Beth was on the couch, her own computer balanced atop her crossed legs.

"Isn't it still the middle of the night in L.A.?"

"Fashion doesn't sleep, Chloe," Beth responded wryly, rolling her eyes at herself and adjusting the neckline of her oversized sweater.

"What's your excuse for not being able to take a day off, Jules?"

"My excuse is having clients who go to house parties in the valley and do coke with randoms when literally every person around them is taking pictures with their phones." Julia's hair was pulled into a messy top knot and wisps of loose curls seemed intent on escaping while she angrily pecked her fingers across the keyboard. "Oh! And Charlie got HBO!"

Chloe felt a rush of pride as she began to plan a celebration meal for when they both returned to the island. She'd braise some short ribs in red wine and rosemary, make a buttery puree of celery root—could she get celery root on Deer Haven? Maybe parsnip then. She'd bake the fig tart she'd been thinking about, the one with the hazelnut cream and the miso caramel. They'd have a lovely, *casual* dinner at the table in the kitchen, and he wouldn't look at her in that way he'd been looking at her lately, like he was trying to figure her out.

Julia's phone buzzed. She groaned and started typing furiously, mumbling, "Oh great," with a grimace. Chloe wondered how anyone could be this agitated this early in the morning.

"Hey, let's go for a walk!" she suggested, barely eliciting acknowledgment from either woman.

"You guys!" She slowly closed her sister's laptop, nearly pinching her stubborn hands while Beth looked on with amusement.

"Julia, let's go," Beth insisted, prompting an indignant look from her wife before she reluctantly turned off her devices.

"Stella probably *could* use some fresh air," Julia finally relented.

"Stella?"

"We're pretty sure it's a girl," Beth said, resting her hand on her stomach.

"Isn't she just amazing?" Julia asked, her moony eyes cast on Beth, her question more a definitive statement.

"She is," Chloe responded sincerely, easily imagining her sister and her wife holding a perfect little baby Stella between them. She would have Julia's curly hair and Beth's dark eyes, and she would be a cooing, squirming little bundle wrapped in the Burberry baby blanket that Chloe had already picked out for them. They would all take turns fawning over the miracle of every blink and hiccup, marveling over how when she sneezed, she looked just like this cousin or that celebrity. As they pulled on their boots, Chloe smiled, deeply contented by the notion that her sister and sister-in-law were soon going to have everything they wanted.

"Are you crying?" Julia demanded, adjusting the middle finger on her cashmere glove.

"Shut up," Chloe replied, swiping her mitten across her eye.

After their mother bid them farewell with promises of BLTs on freshly baked bread when they returned, the three women piled into Julia's rental car and drove to their favorite walking trail. Once hosting the railroad tracks that wove throughout the area's mountains, marshes, and fields, the miles of paths had been the sisters' favorite place when they were kids. It's where they both learned to ride their bikes, where the training wheels had finally come off, and where Julia had attempted to rollerblade before determining that loose gravel and deep ravines were only working against her.

As teenagers, it's where they escaped their parents, to sneak an occasional cigarette and to talk about the adult-sized dreams that had felt so out of reach. In the summer, the path smelled of dairy farms and buzzed with bees that flocked to the wildflowers blooming along its edges. In the fall, it looked like it was on fire, the vibrant reds and oranges of the foliage appearing lit from within. Today it was quiet, the low whine of snowmobiles far in the distance, the snow packed hard underfoot.

They'd only been walking for about three minutes before Julia asked, "So, how's it *really* going there? Is it weird?"

"Yes, it's completely weird!" Chloe answered without hesitation. "He didn't eat at first and I didn't know what I was even doing there, you know, before it was revealed that you'd bamboozled us both."

Julia shrugged and held up her hands while Beth giggled and elbowed her gently in the side.

"And now I'm responsible for fattening him up, I guess?" Chloe continued. "It's *all* weird, being together in that big house, just the two of us. It's like I don't know the rules, you know?"

Other than the loosely defined, "don't sleep with your boss" rule, which I am trying very hard to follow.

"Don't worry so much about it, Chlo. He's happy with the way things are going."

"You talked to him about it?"

"The other day. He sounds like he needs very little when he's out there. He goes to the island so he can get away from everything, you know? But he's not great at being alone."

"He's dealt with some sad stuff, hasn't he?" Beth inquired.

"He's been through a lot," Chloe answered protectively.

They walked in silence for a few moments, Beth adjusting her sunglasses, Chloe kicking a small clump of dirty snow, Julia stealthily checking her phone by barely tilting it out of her coat pocket.

"He's *so* gorgeous," Beth finally said.

"Oh my god, it's like I can't even believe what I'm seeing," Chloe breathlessly confessed. "Like I can't look away! I want to but I can't! That dimple..."

"Simmer down, sister. Don't get any bad ideas," Julia laughed.

"Ugh, too late. I'm full of bad ideas every time I look at him."

Beth howled with laughter. "I told you! Didn't I tell you, Jules?"

"What about the sexy lobsterman?" Julia asked as they stepped aside to let a family of cross-country skiers pass by.

"Ben is...amazing," Chloe replied.

"Tell us!" Beth commanded. "We need details."

"Well, he's really tall. Huge hands. And he has this longish messy blond hair. He's beautiful and he has this sweet old dog who adores me. He loves the ocean. He bakes bread."

His mouth, that lip, his hands on my back, his mouth on my thigh, his voice whispering my name, Chloe thought to herself, feeling the heat rise from her neck, up into her cheeks, and down to other places.

"You're blushing!" Julia accused, pointing her perfectly manicured finger. "You're smitten! Besotted!"

"I'm not! I've known him for like a minute."

"Completely smitten," Julia said to Beth, as if Chloe wasn't there, walking between them.

"Where do you see this going with him?" Beth asked.

"I haven't really thought about it. I mean, I'm only there for a couple of months. I don't know, does it have to go anywhere?" She quickened her pace as if to flee from their line of questioning. "Also, it's an island. There's very little to do there, you know?"

"Well, you seem to be managing just fine," Beth teased.

The three of them chuckled and continued on the path, pausing as a rabbit hesitated, then crossed in front of them.

"And I'm not sure about Ben yet," Chloe admitted. "I think he might be kind of a..."

"What?"

"Kind of a townie?" She bristled at her own use of the word, the same word that had prompted her to curse at Charlie when he'd so arrogantly tossed it out.

She went on to explain how Ben had lived on the island for practically his entire life, how he didn't crave anything else, how he wasn't someone who wanted to travel, to have big adventures, how his life felt a little too contained. How he wasn't ever going to ask her to hang from the side of a helicopter while they flew over an active volcano together.

"Maybe he's just happy," Beth suggested.

"All I know is that you went from being a total non-dater to juggling two gorgeous men in the span of about a week." Julia shook her head with amused disbelief.

"I'm not 'juggling' anyone. And you're talking like I was living like a nun before," Chloe responded dryly. "You do remember why I left Chicago, right?"

"What I'm saying is that it's OK to admit that you like him, Chlo."

Even as Chloe protested, she couldn't deny that flutter, the one that she'd felt in her chest since Ben had left the bucket of crabs on the doorstep. As she brushed off their interrogation and tried to invalidate their joyful accusations with a shrug, she knew she was being dishonest. The truth was, she was starting to feel something opening up inside of her. She had certainly felt it in the dark with Ben the night before.

"It's been like a minute," she repeated weakly, in an attempt to close the book on such ridiculous notions.

"So what? I knew Beth was the one the very first time I saw her," Julia said, gazing at her wife.

"Aw, really? You did?" Beth replied, holding her clutched hands against her heart.

"You were wearing that yellow dress—"

"The Stella McCartney," Beth interjected.

"And we were at that stupid party in the Hills, remember? We were both trapped in boring conversations and our eyes locked across the room, and I just knew." Julia took her wife's gloved hand in her own. "I just *knew.*"

They walked in silence for the next few minutes, Julia and Beth still holding hands, Chloe with her own hands stuffed into the pockets of her down jacket. They heard the chickadees twittering in the bare branches, the crunch of their boots on the snowy path, and a stream gurgling deep in a ravine, its water just beginning to loosen around the ice-glazed rocks. The sun shone brightly on their faces and their breath came in clouds as they reversed direction and made their way back to the car.

Just as they reached the trail head, Julia turned to face Chloe, placing her hand on her sister's shoulder.

"Please don't close your mind to possibilities, Chlo. Promise me? There are so many possibilities. I'm not just talking about your lobsterman. I'm talking about your whole life."

Julia's earnest expression and self-help tone would have made Chloe burst out laughing if she didn't suddenly feel a lump in her throat. Their eyes locked, and Chloe saw the same shade of green flash with intensity in her sister's gaze.

"Just...promise me you won't let things get messy with Charlie," Julia pleaded.

"My god, Jules. He's like twelve. I'm not stupid."

Chloe wasn't accustomed to lying to her sister, but when the actor and the lobsterman took turns alternately flashing through her mind, she felt like the only sane strategy was to declare she didn't want things to go any further with Charlie. For both Julia's sake and her own.

"I know...it's just...it wouldn't end well with him. Promise?"

"OK," Chloe said softly. "I promise."

They drove back, singing along to old Alanis Morissette songs at top volume until they reached the farm, where their mother was waiting for them with BLTs on fresh bread, as promised.

The next two days passed in a contented blur of board games, family meals, and delightfully bad afternoon rom coms on cable. Chloe retired early each night and called Ben from her bed, the two of them whispering each other's names in the dark, discovering what was possible long distance. She padded downstairs in the morning for pancakes, and she drank her coffee with maple syrup in it, a habit she always fell back into when she was visiting her parents.

Julia and Beth were on their phones at the kitchen table, scrolling, frowning, pecking out missives before their own city had even woken up.

"Look who's fallen off the wagon again," Julia said in an irritated tone, turning her phone to her wife—but not before Chloe got a glimpse of a familiar physique.

"Is that Charlie?" Chloe asked.

"Mmmhmm...he's out with the She-Wolf again."

"Who looks amazing in that Saint Laurent jumpsuit!" Beth exclaimed, snatching the phone from Julia's hand and zooming in on the gorgeous woman with the impossibly shiny black hair at Charlie's side.

Chloe peered over Beth's shoulder. "Who's the She-Wolf?" she asked, hoping her tone signified indifference.

"Emma Marcone."

Chloe shook her head blankly, vaguely remembering how Charlie had mentioned Emma's name over his bowl of seafood chowder.

"From the camp movies? Charlie's ex?" She pulled up another photo of Emma, who was stunning with her perfect complexion and confident red-carpet stance.

"They've been on and off for years. He always lets her back in, and she destroys him every time. The last breakup was the worst because it wasn't until he saw the photos of her with her director while she was shooting in England that he realized she'd been cheating for months."

"Poor Charlie," Beth said, her face twisting into a frown.

"Three days back in L.A. and she's already sucked him in," Julia murmured, examining the paparazzi photos of them leaving a restaurant, hand in hand, ducking their heads against the flashbulbs.

Chloe left them to their phones before bounding upstairs and softly closing the door behind her. A quick search of Charlie's name brought up versions of the same photos. His expression was guarded in all of them, his dimple nowhere to be seen. Emma Marcone on the other hand—a long-legged goddess in her jumpsuit and killer heels—was smiling serenely in every shot, her elegant hand clasped tightly inside his. A search of her name brought up an impressive resume of films—period costumed pieces, romantic comedy leads, and a dystopian thriller that even Chloe had seen when it was all anyone could talk about during awards season. It seemed Emma's career had flourished while Charlie's had limped and stalled.

She wanted to discuss his successes and failures with Julia, to examine what had gone so wrong for him while they studied the photos of Emma clinging to his side, but she needed to leave if she was going to make the ferry back to Deer Haven.

As she placed her clothes into her suitcase, she quickly realized they'd already been laundered and neatly folded by her mother, who was likely packing up a bag of fresh eggs and loaves of Chloe's favorite cinnamon bread.

When they said goodbye, her parents squeezed her tightly, her dad's embrace slightly shaky but still strong, her mother pressing a kiss to her cheek.

"Don't be a stranger, kid," her father said.

"Did you get everything? Your boots? The bread?" her mother asked, even though she had already seen each item getting packed into Chloe's car.

"Stella can't wait to meet her Auntie Chloe," Beth declared, wrapping her willowy arms around her sister-in-law's shoulders.

Chloe hugged Julia last, holding on for a few beats longer than she usually did. They made pledges of trips to the West Coast and the Midwest, confirming a FaceTime for the upcoming weekend.

"Remember what I said, sister," Julia expressed before relaxing her embrace. "Remember what you promised."

"I know. I will."

Just as she often did on long car rides, Chloe devoted most of her drive to daydreaming about future restaurant concepts. She kicked around fine dining schemes for a bit before moving on to ideas like a soup restaurant, a food truck featuring tacos and homemade ice cream, a sandwich shop that also sells breads and small-batch condiments, and a pierogi stand. She knew she needed to start thinking about a *real* strategy, a *real* job when she returned to her *real* home in Chicago. Though she was looking forward to getting back to the island, she knew it wasn't real life, despite how real it felt on the phone with Ben for the past three nights.

She considered how long it would take for things back in the city to blow over, as Julia had predicted they eventually would. How long would it be before she could get back to the business of securing financing for her next great thing? How long would it be before everyone had forgotten the gossip about Redbud and how its executive chef had *abandoned her post* and sprinted from a scandal? A month? Two? Would she even have the clean slate she needed when her Deer Haven stint was over?

Chloe made a promise to herself: whatever came next it would be hers, and hers alone. If she took on a financier, she wouldn't be beholden to them when it came to concept. It would have to be her vision only, no investor looking over her shoulder while she composed plates, suggesting a garnish or insisting on gold leaf. She would demand they put that in the contracts.

Suddenly, she felt compelled to pitch some of her new ideas to Steph, to collect her friend's input, to get a sense of whether she'd be willing to leave Redbud and start something new. Together. And she wanted to ask if she knew anything about Natter.

"Hey, girl," Steph answered the phone. Her cheerful tone was tight, and Chloe couldn't help but think it sounded forced.

Chloe wanted to ask what she was planning, whether she'd remembered to contact the guy up north who supplied their spring ramps, and if the book was still jammed with reservations, but she bit her tongue.

"I'm just driving home from Vermont. I thought I'd call to say hi."

"That must have been nice. To see your family," she replied absently.

Chloe could hear the sounds of the kitchen behind Steph, and she considered asking if it was a bad time. Instead, she pressed on, hoping she could emerge on the other side of the awkwardness and feel natural chatting again.

"Are things good there? At the restaurant?"

"They are. Different, but good. Jake was a disaster as sous."

Chloe smiled empathetically for her friend, recalling the mistakes she'd made in the first kitchens she'd run, the errors in judgment, the blunders she'd never repeat.

"I've been there. And hey, you've gotta live and learn, right?" Chloe hoped her sentiment sounded as sincere as she'd intended and not condescending.

"You know David hasn't been back," Steph mentioned flatly.

"No?"

"I haven't seen him in here since that night. It's like he's been banished."

That night.

"Well, he messed up," Chloe said softly. "So did I."

"Have you been in touch with him?"

"No! God, no!" She exclaimed, guiding the car off the highway ramp and onto the long coastal route that would bring her all the way to Craftsport. "He called me in Chicago, but I haven't talked to him since I left the city."

"Lila found out that he'd been messing around with the chef at Birdie too."

"Zara Kelley? Really?" Chloe's tone remained even as she accepted the gossip in an altogether neutral way, noting that she felt absolutely nothing resembling hurt or betrayal at the depth of David's infidelity. "I guess I'm not surprised."

"Hey, I heard she's opening a food truck with Maya Rosen. They're looking for a third partner," Steph offered. "I told her to call you."

Chloe replied with a noncommittal, "huh, that's cool," while she was thinking Steph should be embarrassed to even mention such a project to her. It was the kind of thing she would have contemplated fifteen years earlier, but certainly not now. Steph was suggesting that Chloe was meant to—what—make grilled cheese sandwiches in the back of a glorified van? There was that rush of resentment again, even as Chloe wondered if they were both getting exactly what they deserved.

"So...I saw the thing on Natter. About you," Steph began. "It wasn't me, you know. I mean, you told me everything that night at your place, but I didn't say anything. To anyone."

Chloe exhaled with pure relief, in that single moment realizing just how much it had been bothering her whether Steph had been the one talking behind her back. That worry had hurt even more than the comments on the post that Chloe, in a moment of wine-fueled weakness, had gone back to read. They ranged from the innocuously judgmental "if you can't take the heat" to the outright cruel "total whore," and the worst of all: "guess we know how she made it to the top." Even though it still stung days later, the vitriol of strangers was nothing compared to the fear that her own friend had betrayed her.

"I knew it couldn't have been you."

Their silence stretched on for so long that Chloe wondered if they'd been disconnected.

"How are things out there, really?" Steph finally asked.

"This is just for now, not forever, you know?"

"Well, I'm sure your next place will be even better than this," Steph said generously. "Hey, Chloe, I have to run. The servers are here and I have to prep them on the new menu. Talk soon?"

Chloe said goodbye, suspecting it would be the last time they'd talk, and it filled her with a sadness that cut deeper than she thought it could. Without their shared work, there was no longer any glue to hold them together. The heartache of that realization simmered inside of Chloe for the next hundred miles.

She was still thinking about it when another "UNKNOWN" call lit up her screen—from a different number this time, but still with the 708-area code. Chloe barked her "hello," repeating herself twice in the face of the single bar of service, which would soon disappear completely as she drove up the coast. Hearing nothing on the other end, she grumpily tossed her phone onto the back seat, where it sat between her suitcase and a quart of maple syrup for the rest of the trip.

The boat ride was smooth and passed quickly, a far cry from the choppy seas and icy deck she'd endured the first time. The sky looked ominous when she made a quick stop at the market for dinner ingredients, slate gray clouds snubbing out the sun that had been shining so brightly when she'd left Vermont. She loaded her basket with groceries, assembling a meal plan while the teenager at the fish counter bagged up some fresh mussels for her. The market didn't have short ribs, but she still wanted to prepare something special for Charlie to celebrate his victory in L.A. She was selecting a butternut squash when Janey Higgins rounded the corner and spotted her.

"Hi, sweetheart!" the kindly woman exclaimed. "You're back! How was your visit with your family?"

"It was good—great, actually. I hadn't been home in a while."

"Our boy should be getting in at about 7:00 pm. I'm picking him up at the airfield and I'll bring him to the house."

Our boy.

Chloe really wished the caretaker would stop referring to Charlie like that.

"So you've been getting to know Ben Libby, it sounds like?" Janey's breezy tone suggested an attempt at nonchalance as she picked up a cantaloupe and added it to her basket.

"Geez, this really is a small island, isn't it?"

"Well, there's not a lot to talk about here, but when word gets out, it travels fast. I've known Ben his whole life. I went to school with his parents. Of course, they don't live here anymore, but they're good people. Ben too. We've all been waiting for him to find the right one."

"I don't know if I'm...we just met. I mean...the 'right one'—what does that even mean, you know?" Chloe stammered.

"I'm just saying that we all didn't know if he'd ever get over Lauren. And then, when he came back, and she moved to Timbuktu —or wherever—we still weren't sure."

She nodded, her silence encouraging Janey to continue.

"Don't get me wrong, we all *loved* Lauren. Smart and *so* beautiful. But she was never going to stay here. She was never going to fall in love with this place the way people do. We could all see that."

Chloe bit her lip to stop the flood of questions that threatened to rush out, inquiries that Janey would surely be able to answer.

How can a man as kind and sexy as Ben possibly be single?

Why hasn't he ever left the island, other than that one year?

How can a person not want more?

Just how serious was this thing with Lauren?

Janey had described Ben and his family as "good people." Would anyone think to describe her that way? Would she dare to describe herself that way?

"You getting enough for the house?" She lifted her chin toward Chloe's shopping basket. "Big storm coming in tomorrow. Sounds like a whopper. There's a backup generator, so if we lose power, you two should be fine."

You two.

Janey said goodbye with a quick hug and a promise that she was available if they needed anything. Chloe brought her supplies to the front counter, where the woman working the register was already talking about the massive Nor'easter that was on its way, chit chatting about fifty-mile winds and the foot of snow in the forecast. Chloe smiled knowingly. As a Vermonter and a Chicagoan, she was a veteran of harsh winters and felt arrogantly amused at how dramatically everyone was treating the storm.

The sky did look a little grayer when she pulled into Ben's driveway for an unannounced pitstop on her way back to the Davis House. He was in the yard, still in his rubbery overalls from the boat, stacking towers of empty lobster traps against the garage. His face broke out in a huge grin as soon as he saw her, the spark in his crinkly eyes visible even before Chloe had stopped the car.

"Hey stranger!" he called out, pushing his wool beanie toward the back of his head.

There was that embarrassing fluttering again.

"I just got back and wanted to stop by."

"I'm glad you did. I have to tell you something though...I smell terrible."

Chloe laughed and hugged him anyway, the essence of his uniquely *Ben* scent mingling with the salty sea air and the vague stink of lobster bait. He pressed his lips softly against hers and she buried her fingers beneath the warmth of his hat.

"Look at us, in real life, not just on a screen," he murmured, kissing her again. "Why don't you come inside and jump in the shower with me?"

Chloe groaned, fighting the urge to hibernate in Ben's sweet little house for the next week, wondering when the time would feel right to ask him some of the questions that had scrolled through her head as she chatted with Janey.

"I can't. I have to get back to the house and cook. I've been gone for three days, and Charlie will be getting back soon." She kissed him again, softly biting that irresistible lower lip of his. "I really, really wish I could."

"There's a big storm coming," he said, pressing his mouth to her throat.

"Oh, I've heard. It's the talk of the island. Along with the two of us, apparently."

"People here love to talk. All it takes is a truck in a driveway and you're headline news."

"Well, don't worry, because Janey Higgins approves," Chloe teased.

"Janey Higgins is basically in charge around here, so an endorsement from her really means something," Ben replied with a chuckle.

Chloe pressed her body against his, barely feeling the cold wind that was starting to pick up around them.

"I don't need anyone to endorse you, you know," she said.

He wrapped his long arms around her and pulled her closer, shielding her from the gust. With other men, affection had often made her feel trapped, as if she wanted to slip out of the bottom of an embrace like a wet bar of soap from clasped hands. Ben made it all feel so easy.

"How about just an hour?" he murmured into the side of her neck. "I'll take a quick shower and then we can hang out for a little while."

Chloe felt herself softening. "Well..."

"You said he isn't even back on island yet. Just an hour, three hours tops. Ten to twelve hours at the very most," Ben smiled.

"OK, one hour," she relented, taking his hand and leading him into the cottage, where the fire was already lit and Jasper was waiting for her at the door with his tail wagging.

He raced up the stairs toward the shower with almost comical speed, taking the steps two at a time as she curled up with the elderly golden retriever. When he returned to her only minutes later, his hair dripping, his skin freshly scrubbed, he took her hand and led her upstairs. Then he reverently peeled off her clothes. He smelled like shampoo and wood smoke as they whispered each other's names into the darkening room, reenacting everything they'd promised each other over the phone for the last three days.

As the sun set behind the window near his bed, casting the sky in every shade of pink, she listened to his breathing grow even as he drifted toward sleep. She really had to get back to the house and worried if she stayed in this bed any longer, she would allow entire days to pass—just the two of them under the quilt as the wind blew and the snow piled up outside. She slid from beneath the weight of his arm and quietly gathered her clothes.

"Mmmmm...don't go," he pleaded, his low voice muffled by the pillow and thick with the sleep of someone who had risen at four a.m.

She pressed her lips against his stubbled cheek and tiptoed down the stairs, checking her watch and hoping that Charlie hadn't gotten home yet. As Jasper snored on the couch where she'd left him, she decided to leave a note. She'd write something light and cute, like "Thanks for the sex," or "Have a nice Nor-easter."

She was rummaging through the old roll-top desk at the foot of the stairs, in search of a pen and a scrap of paper, when her fingers settled on a bound stack of letters pushed to the very back of a drawer. When she slowly pulled them out, it wasn't the volume of smudged and heavily stamped envelopes that surprised her most, but the fact that she continued to stare at them for the next minute, marveling at their weight, desperate to know what they said.

She flipped through them, the first few from Denver, then Brazil, then Costa Rica, then Haiti. They were all from Lauren Chase. Pausing to confirm that Ben wasn't approaching behind her, Chloe slipped a letter from its envelope and scanned it—then another, and another. Each one was a heartfelt expression of contrition, scrawled in a steady and measured cursive, peppered with phrases like, *I'll spend the rest of my life being sorry, I know we can never be together after everything that happened,* and *I understand why you can't forgive me.*

Their story started to become clearer as Chloe read on. *When you asked me to marry you, it was easy to say yes. In that moment, it was the only thing I wanted to say. And in that moment, I really did mean it. But I understand why you won't write me back.*

When she examined the places where Lauren's pen had started to run out of ink, it hit her. She was jealous. What had begun as passive curiosity had officially crossed over into something else entirely, and this first-time feeling was amplified when she noticed the postscript — *Take care of Jasper. I think he always loved you more than he loved me.* Her heart sank as she glanced at the old dog, curled into a coil by the woodstove.

There were three letters that remained unopened, still sealed in their envelopes, all postmarked in the last two months. Chloe felt almost feverish in her desire to see what was inside, wondering why Ben had hung on to them. Did he reread them sometimes, poring over Lauren's words in heartache, anger, or resignation? Did it still hurt? Why had he buried them in the depths of a drawer like a secret he was keeping from himself? And why hadn't he even opened the last few?

Chloe looked up quickly when Jasper grunted, and she searched his watery brown eyes for answers when he gazed up at her.

"I know, I know," she said softly, wrapping the rubber band around the stack and tucking it back where she'd found it. As she returned the letters to their hidden place, she spotted the corner of a photograph peeking out from beneath a pile of envelopes. She slid it out slowly and silently, and there they were: Ben and, presumably Lauren, in raincoats and Red Sox hats on the back of the Andrea May, smiling as if it all would last forever. She was tall and beautiful as she leaned into Ben's side, his arm slung across her shoulders. Chloe could see how naturally they seemed to just fit together.

She swallowed something unpleasant that was rising in the back of her throat, wondering if it was heartburn, indigestion, acid reflux from all the wine she'd been drinking lately, or something she should be much, much more worried about. Was she, Chloe Foster, boss of all things and general answerer to no one *scared*? Scared that something genuine was growing between the two of them and that if she screwed things up, the memory of the greedy chef who once came to Deer Haven would end up shoved in the back of an old desk like Lauren?

She drove along Pine Point Road's winding curves slowly, attempting to pep talk herself out of her feelings the entire way. She reminded herself to have fun, but not do anything stupid— like get attached.

Charlie's house was completely dark when she arrived with her suitcase and grocery bags.

"I'm home!" she shouted into the empty rooms, her own voice sounding hollow as it echoed back at her.

Pushing further thoughts of Ben, Lauren, and the letters aside, she efficiently prepared and chilled a short crust dough for a lemon tart, peeled and sliced the butternut squash for a gratin, and scrubbed mussels in the deep, commercial-style sink. She ran down to the basement and chose two bottles of white wine from the cellar, one for drinking and one for steaming the shellfish. She prepped and cooked for the next hour, slowly stirring lemon curd and whipping cream for the tart, frying sage leaves until they were golden and crispy, thinly slicing shallots, and assembling the gratin.

She was carving a seeded baguette into thick slices when the lights of Janey's truck beamed through the kitchen window. The caretaker's horn gave a friendly little farewell toot as Charlie came in through the mudroom. He looked exhausted, his eyes ringed with dark circles, his face shadowed with the day's beard growth. Even his hair looked flat.

He dropped his bags and stretched his arms above his head, revealing that taut stomach and the black band of his underwear peeking up from his pants. Chloe focused on the oven timer, pressing the buttons and inspiring a series of beeps with the concentration of someone entering a nuclear code.

"Welcome back. Long trip?" she asked, finally meeting his eyes.

"The longest. It smells amazing in here." His eyes were wide and hopeful while he waited for her to acknowledge his big news. "Did Julia tell you?"

"She did! Are you excited?"

He helped himself to a slice of baguette and smeared it with the softened butter that she was going to use to finish the broth for the mussels. "I'm just happy to have a chance to do something different. To prepare for something real, you know what I mean?"

"I know exactly what you mean."

"And I can eat! They still want me to put on twenty pounds. I have to change up all my weight training, amp up my calories in a big way."

She tried to imagine him with a little more fullness in his face, the angles softened a bit. "I can help you with that," Chloe assured him, smoothing the warm lemon curd into the pastry shell and sliding it into the refrigerator to chill.

Charlie grinned at her, activating that damn dimple and buttering another piece of bread. She averted her eyes again, thinking that he shouldn't be smiling at her like that, that she shouldn't be basking in it like it was the first sunshine of spring. She shouldn't be reveling in the knowledge that while Ben was tucked into his bed and the letters were tucked into their drawer, that smile was only for *her*.

She wondered if he'd slept with Emma while he was in L.A. Her curiosity wasn't jealous in its nature—more the detached interest of a scientist observing two ridiculously gorgeous animals in the wild. And despite her best efforts, she found herself wondering if maybe Ben *had* written back to Lauren, maybe even just once.

It doesn't matter, just like this ridiculous crush on Charlie Davis doesn't matter. Repeat it again because you really mean it, she silently commanded.

It was the same story she told herself when Charlie announced that he needed a shower before dinner and she tried not to consider his clothes on the bathroom floor while he fired up the steam setting.

He returned to the kitchen with wet hair and pink cheeks as Chloe finished the mussels in their bath of wine, garlic, parsley, and butter. They had all opened up in showy fashion, displaying their tender flesh and welcoming the herbaceous broth. She rubbed the baguette slices with a clove of garlic and pressed them onto a cast iron grill pan to char.

I will build a wall of garlic between us! She thought, pulling the gratin from the oven and instantly filling the kitchen with the aroma of shallots and sage.

Her mouth started to water. "Where would you like to eat?"

"Oh, we can just eat in here." He plopped onto the bench on his side of the banquette and looked at her expectantly, his blue eyes restored to their customary brightness.

We.

Chloe brushed her bangs to the side and gave him her most neutral close-lipped smile. She had hoped that he would take his meal into the dining room, leaving her to the kitchen to eat and clean up without the distraction of his smooth forearms resting on the table between them. Or maybe she could just toss out a cheerful "Goodnight!" and take her dinner up to her bedroom, enjoying her bowl of mussels while sitting cross-legged on the floor like a weirdo. But that *we* was a plea for company—a difficult-to-resist plea for company—and Chloe felt herself soften at the reality that had finally finished unfolding. Charlie Davis needed a friend, and maybe she did too.

She brought the food to the table, passing him the ladle so he could fill his bowl with mussels, maintaining that neutral smile when he served her instead. She used the outer tine of her fork to delicately detach the meat from the shells and watched through lowered lashes as he made like the French, placing the end of each shell between his lips and using his teeth to gently draw the flesh into his mouth. She pressed her knees together under the table and tried to focus on her own dinner, savoring the nutty tang of the gruyere in the squash gratin, appreciating how it played perfectly alongside the briny acidity of the broth.

"You're so good at this," he said, dunking bread into his bowl. "I feel like I should send Julia flowers or something."

The chef felt her face getting pink again and she took a gulp of wine as if that had ever helped a freckled complexion defeat the power of the blush. She could smell his soap from across the table—light, clean, and vaguely peppery.

You like Ben, she told herself. *Ben really likes you. You were this close to admitting that you're great together before you found those letters.*

She ordered herself to break the spell with Charlie, to stop looking at him when he kept looking at her, and to add more garlic.

"What's the best food you've ever eaten?" he asked abruptly, his expression open, his gaze laser-focused on hers. She realized how much she liked his undivided attention. And how much she shouldn't.

"Ummmm, best food I've ever eaten...OK, I was in Thailand. A little outside Bangkok. We got on these long, flat boats and explored this floating market. You just pull right up to the vendors, and they serve you right in your boat. I had this bowl of noodles, and it was...it was the spiciest, saltiest, sweetest thing I've ever tasted. Every flavor was aggressive, but they were all completely in balance. It had these tiny little shrimp that just melted in your mouth and thin, thin shavings of chili. And it's chaos all around you, tons of boats sliding in and out on every side, and it's steamy with heat and you just sit there with your bowl of noodles balanced on your knees, and...it was just perfect."

Chloe closed her eyes and could almost taste that tanginess, that spice. She could almost feel the trickle of sweat that ran between her shoulder blades as the humidity rose from the river and made her shirt stick to her skin for the entire trip. "And I think it cost about $1.50."

"Wow. What else?"

"My mom's bread," she responded without hesitation. "Hot from the oven. Just basic white bread, but she uses honey instead of sugar. I'd absolutely slather it with salted butter when it was still warm, and I'd eat it off a folded paper towel."

Charlie smiled sorrowfully. "My mom wasn't much of a cook, but she made really great popcorn."

"What made it so good?" Chloe asked, laying down her spoon and giving him her full attention.

"Well, she always popped it in a pan on the stove. And she melted the butter in another little pan until it was brown. What's that called?"

"Browned butter?" Chloe offered with a small, tender smile.

"Yeah," he chuckled. "So, the popcorn would get these little dark flecks on it from the browned butter, and it was just the best."

Chloe wanted to ask him more about his family, ask him if it was hard to be in this house now that his parents were gone, if it bothered him that his career had mostly happened after they had died. And she wanted to know what kind of oil his mother had used, as she was partial to popping in olive oil herself.

"It must be hard," she responded softly while both of them studied the flickering light of a boat in the harbor below.

"It's hard. I guess it's easier now that it's been a while. Those first couple of years, though..."

Chloe slowly nodded like she knew. But she didn't know. She couldn't.

"It makes you kind of hold onto people, you know? People who knew you before, people who you can pretend feel like family," he said.

"Well, you know what it's like to lose someone."

And you're looking for something familiar to cling to, like this old house, like Janey, like Emma, like your obsessive rituals, she thought sadly.

Charlie gave her a half smile as he wrung his napkin in his hands, twisting the worn chambray fabric into a tight coil. They sat in silence, the large bowl of empty mussel shells an island between them.

She quietly cleared her throat. "How about dessert?"

"Let's do it!"

He was bright-eyed Charlie again, dimple engaged, megawatt smile lighting up everything, but Chloe knew. She'd seen the suffering on his face, had heard it in that tiny break in his voice when he told her about the popcorn. There was more to Charlie than most of the world had seen, and Chloe couldn't deny that she felt special that he'd shown it to her for a few moments.

She served them each a large piece of lemon tart, which hadn't had time to fully set, but it didn't matter. He talked about Emma, how they were still kids when they got together, how their relationship had been on and off for years, how it was fraught with drama, jealousy, and explosive fights. He told her about the paparazzi's obsession with the two of them, how they were followed everywhere, photographed at Whole Foods so the gossip magazines could publish a story analyzing their body language, as if bending down to tie a shoelace was a clear indicator of emotional distance.

"I started to feel like I couldn't leave the house," he grumbled, his expression turning dark. "I felt like I couldn't even open the curtains because even with a gate, they have these big lenses that can just get everywhere. And they have drones! Drones with cameras on them! And they're not supposed to fly them over our houses, but they do."

Chloe shook her head, her chest tight with the weight of it. Her own sister was part of this world that Charlie was describing. Who wouldn't want to disappear to an island in the middle of the Atlantic after enduring all of that?

"And Emma hated that I felt that way, that I couldn't...that I couldn't play the game with more skill, I guess." He shrugged ruefully. "She loves her work so much and I guess her director was part of that. I don't know, she came back from London with a fucking British accent."

"It must have made you feel like you'd been left behind."

"It was the first shoot in two years that I hadn't followed her on. I would just go everywhere she went, just tag along wherever the work took *her*," he confessed. "I knew it was stupid, that it was getting in the way of my own career, because I was turning stuff down to spend three months in Fiji with her. My agent, my manager, they were all pissed because I kept passing. They warned me that if I didn't keep working, the offers would eventually dry up, but I don't know...I just couldn't find a way to...resist her."

She fought the urge to ask him about the photos of them leaving that restaurant in L.A., taken just a day earlier.

Charlie ran his hand through his hair and squinted out the window like he was up for a role as James Dean. "What about you?" he asked.

"What about me?"

"Do you have a...person? Back in Chicago."

"No. No one special, anyway," Chloe replied. "I mean, I've dated, of course, but I've never really found anyone worth sticking around for in Chicago."

Tell him about Ben, she thought. *Tell him that you met someone wonderful right here on Deer Haven—someone kind and safe, someone whose touch makes you dizzy. Tell him that those letters probably don't even mean anything at all. Tell him.*

But she didn't.

She couldn't help but notice that Ben didn't always cross her mind when Charlie was around and she frowned, thinking that the first few weeks of whatever this thing with the lobsterman was should be the time when you absolutely can't stop thinking about each other. She'd felt that in Vermont, but everything somehow felt different when Charlie was in the room. It was like he hijacked all her bandwidth, like he was a bright, flashing light that completely blew out everything else in her line of vision.

Don't be an idiot, Chloe, she said to herself a half hour later when she heard Charlie in the living room, crinkling newspaper and stacking logs for a fire. *Say goodnight. Go to bed.*

"Do you want to hang out for a bit?" he called to her.

Say goodnight. Go to bed.

"Chloe? Do you want to hang out for a bit?" he asked again, now leaning into the kitchen door, his hands on either side of the frame.

"I'm pretty beat, Charlie. I think I'm just going to finish in here and head upstairs. Long day, you know?"

"Yeah," he replied, a little sadly. "For me too, I guess."

He left the makings of the fire unlit in the fireplace while she wiped the counters, scoured the pans, and started the dishwasher. When Chloe made her rounds, turning off lamps and light switches throughout the house, she found him asleep on the living room couch, curled on his side, hands tucked against his chest. He looked nothing like the drunk, arrogant guy from the tabloid photos that dominated the internet, the ones where his eyes blazed and he appeared to be declaring his status as the King of the World with his entourage of bros and the model draped across his chest. He just looked sweet, sad, and really, really tired.

She studied the fine line of his nose, the angle of his jaw, the fringe of dark lashes against that perfect skin, then covered him with the wool throw blanket draped across the back of the sofa.

He didn't stir at all, exhausted after the miles he'd covered since that morning. Limbs feeling heavy, Chloe tiptoed up the creaky stairs to her room, where she found herself unable to fall asleep for the next several hours.

Chapter Fourteen

The storm woke her up just before dawn, when the resounding crash of waves striking the rocks prompted her to bolt upright in her bed. She confused the echoing blasts for thunder at first. Tiny pellets of ice were blowing sideways, pinging against the window in random rhythms, and when she rose to peer at the first light of the day, all she could see was the blurry haze of snow in the half-darkened sky. The storm had officially arrived, and Chloe returned to the warmth of her blankets, wishing she could sleep through the entire morning.

She languished in the bath, sleepily watching the snow swirl and build through the window, wondering if Charlie was up, wondering if Ben was up, wishing for a moment that she'd woken up in her own bed in Chicago. She'd stroll to Belle Toi for pastries and cappuccino, and then she'd walk to the restaurant for morning prep, working out menu details with Steph and Sabine.

But that wasn't her life anymore, she thought as she drained the tub. Steph was planning and executing at Redbud. Her fabulous apartment was sitting empty, collecting dust in her absence, and she was about to head downstairs to find out if Charlie Davis wanted his pancakes with blueberries or chocolate chips.

She dressed in black leggings and an oversized red sweater,

running her fingers through her choppy hair and not bothering with makeup. Charlie was already in the kitchen, in his house uniform of a hoodie and sweats.

"Coffee?" he offered, his voice still scratchy from sleep. "I made coffee. I mean, I tried to make coffee."

She smiled and accepted the mug he handed her, trying not to flinch at the bitter, lukewarm brew he served from the French press.

"Oh, God, this is bad. Is coffee always this bad?" he asked, wincing at his own first sip.

Chloe stifled a laugh and assured him it was just fine, while stealthily dumping the contents of her cup down the sink.

The snow outside was already piling up, now falling fast and relentlessly, gusts of wind creating whiteouts beyond every window.

"It looks terrible out there," Charlie murmured, leaning toward the large picture window with one knee on the banquette seat.

"Well, luckily, we have nowhere we need to go," Chloe responded with forced cheer as the reality hit that she and Charlie would be trapped in the house together for the next twenty-four hours. Alone.

They ate their breakfast mostly in silence, Charlie scrolling on his phone, Chloe thinking to text Ben.

You weathering the MEGASTORM?

All good here. I remembered to get groceries, library books, and beer, so I should be good for a while ;-)

All the storm essentials!

Have everything you need? I can bring you something. Headed out to plow in a bit.

Chloe refrained from cracking a joke involving the word plow and assured him that she was all set.

Or I can even pick you up...

I wish. Here for the foreseeable future. Have to make sure Charlie is fed.

Sounds like babysitting.

Feels like it too.

Chloe immediately regretted her snide comment, sensing it was a betrayal to Charlie in some way, who was innocently sitting across the table from her, hunched over his own phone.

Just say the word, and I'm there in five minutes ;-)

😊

Some part of her wanted to text, in all caps with five exclamation points, *I DON'T NEED TO BE RESCUED!!!!!* But Ben really was sweet, and she would love to be with him in his little cottage, sitting by the wood stove and watching the snow fall, having sex on his living room floor, taking a shower together. But she was at work—whatever that even meant anymore—and she still needed him to hear her when she said she didn't need to be taken care of.

He texted her a red heart, and she dropped her phone onto the table like it had burned her hand.

"You OK over there?" Charlie asked.

"All good," she responded too loudly, but she was really thinking it was *way* too soon in this thing with Ben to be casually tossing around love emojis.

She cleaned up the breakfast dishes and started some pizza dough, placing the bowl in the refrigerator so it could cold proof throughout the day. Charlie had disappeared to the basement, and she found herself happy to be free of him for a few hours. She curled up in the living room with another of his mother's trashy paperbacks, pausing every few pages to watch the snow blowing and rising outside the window. Janey called to check on them, the old woman affably chattering about windchill and likely power outages, explaining that this storm was such a "whopper" that all the ferries had been canceled, "and the ferries *never* get canceled," she said dramatically.

We're really stuck here, Chloe said to herself again, barely listening to Janey's chipper voice. *Charlie Davis the Movie Star and I are really stuck here.*

It all felt so ridiculous.

She thanked Janey warmly and returned to her book, allowing herself to nod off for a few moments, her neck tilted at an impossible angle as it dropped against the side of the wingback chair.

Charlie was in the living room when she woke up, and she quickly swiped her thumb across her lips to make sure she hadn't been drooling in her sleep. She stretched her arms over her head and watched him build a fire, finally making use of the crumpled newspapers and kindling he'd so hopefully arranged the night before.

"It's crazy out there," he declared, tilting his head toward the window. "I've never really seen a storm like this before."

"Well, I'm a winter pro. And my expert advice is to just stay inside until it stops 'blowing a gale' as Janey just said."

"It's a real nor'eastah sweethaht," Charlie responded affectionately, a pitch-perfect imitation of the caretaker's thick Maine accent.

"A wicked nor'eastah!" Chloe chimed in, prompting them both to chuckle.

They each stretched out on the two overstuffed sofas that faced each other, Chloe allowing the down cushions to swallow her, Charlie lying on the opposite couch, looking as peaceful as he did the night before when she'd pulled that soft blanket over his shoulder.

"This is the part when I start to get restless," he said softly. "You know what I mean?"

"I'm always at the part when I'm restless," she replied, surprising herself with her own candor.

"You? You seem so cool all the time, though."

"Ha. I'm not. Not at all."

"But you're such a...you're such a boss. You always look like you know exactly what you're doing."

"That's because you only see me when I'm working. You don't see me when I'm fucking it all up." Chloe glanced quickly at Charlie. "But I guess I do that at work sometimes too."

"I know how that feels. Believe me."

"Oh yeah? What's the worst thing you've ever done on a job?"

They rolled onto their sides so they were facing each other. Their eyes locked as Chloe waited for him to answer.

"Hmmm. The *worst* thing I've ever done on a job?"

"Was it when you threw a plate of chicken from your trailer?" she asked, referencing the gossip item she'd uncovered during her hasty Charlie Davis research project.

"I told them I didn't eat the skin," he growled before a grin spread across his face. "Kidding! That never happened."

"Phew," she laughed. "But seriously, the very worst thing."

"I was living at this big apartment complex in Burbank where a lot of kid actors are put up while they're shooting or being sent out on auditions," he began. "Some of them were with their parents, some with chaperones. But I was eighteen, and my parents had already... well, I was of age anyway, so it was just me and this other actor, Dylan Whitmer. We'd both auditioned for the Summer Camp movies, and I was sure he was going to get it over me. He was just...better. So anyway, we threw a huge party. Kegs, a DJ. It got really out of control, and we got busted. I managed to pin the whole thing on him."

"That's not that bad."

"I snuck out the bedroom window when the cops showed up."

"OK, that's kind of bad." Chloe giggled. "Dylan Whitmer. I've never heard of him."

"Exactly. After his agent had to pick him up at the police station, his parents pulled him from the running. They packed him up and brought him back to Iowa or wherever he was from. They didn't want Hollywood corrupting him any further. I've always felt bad about it."

"I'm sure it was just instinct. Run! It's the cops!"

"I definitely remember pausing in my open window for a second, totally thinking that Dylan getting caught could solve my problem."

"But you were just a kid."

"I guess. But I knew better," he admitted. "And I still think about it. That was the part that started everything for me. It was what made me. And when it was down to just the two of us, I knew it was either him or me, and I'd only get it if he was out of the mix. And now I'm getting ready to do an HBO series, and he's...nowhere."

"But don't you think if he had the passion to begin with, he would have found a way?" she asked, thinking of her own years of scraping and clawing her way to the top, of literally shouting to be heard in some of the kitchens she'd worked in, of all the burns and cuts she'd suffered in her pursuit to get better, to make it. She never would have given up. She loved it too much.

"Maybe," he shrugged. "I would have found a way."

"Me too."

He flipped onto his back, the only sound between them the fire's successful crackling in the fireplace.

"What about you?" he asked.

"What about me?"

"What's the worst thing you've ever done on a job?"

"Really?" She snorted. "Do we not remember how I ended up on Deer Haven?"

"I guess I don't really know the whole story. I mean, you don't have to tell me, though."

Chloe closed her eyes, concentrating on the heat spreading across her cheeks.

"Well, I told you, I was sleeping with my boss. Or more specifically, my boss's husband, David," she clarified, unwilling to dignify him with the title. "And getting caught meant I'd officially blown everything up. To be honest, I'm not sure yet if I'll ever bounce back from this."

Chloe's eyes welled up as she focused on the ceiling. She'd spent the last several weeks fully aware that she was currently serving out a sentence, but for the first time, the words, *I'm Chloe Fucking Foster*, were a barely audible refrain somewhere deep in her ears. For the first time, she really didn't know if her career *would* recover.

"What was so great about him?" Charlie asked softly.

"Honestly?" Chloe began, delicately wiping her nose on the sleeve of her sweater. "Nothing really. He was just...there. And I was... bored."

Just like I'm a little bored right now.

He asked more questions about what her friends in Chicago thought, if David's wife had ever confronted her, if she ever missed him, but she was tired of talking about it. She was tired of even thinking about it, exhausted with Deer Haven for demanding that she sit with her own mistakes for such great stretches of time.

She bit her lip, suddenly overcome with the desire to join him on his sofa, to stretch her body alongside his as the fire popped with sparks behind the screen.

He was doing it again, casting his spell and disarming her with his eyes, his dimple, his hand in his hair. This time, she didn't even have the wine to blame. She remembered how he'd compared cooking to acting. He was telling her, *I see you, and we're the same.* And as much as she didn't want to admit it, as she snuck a glance at his profile, she'd kind of liked that. Sometimes being around him felt like that first leap onto Ben's boat, of searching for her sea legs while also sort of enjoying that feeling of unsteadiness.

Their eyes locked over the coffee table, and he held her gaze for just a beat too long as he raised his dark eyebrows, challenging her to be the one to speak first. His mouth parted as if he was about to say something, but he released a slow exhale instead, biting the side of his lower lip and eventually grinning that million-dollar grin that dominated the Instagram fan pages. She wanted to ask him to stop doing that and also to never stop doing that.

Her phone buzzed, and she contorted herself atop the too-soft sofa to retrieve it from her back pocket. Ben.

> Right outside in the driveway. Plowed my way over to say hi.

Hadn't she told him she was working? She rolled ungracefully off the couch and onto the floor while Charlie laughed, and she cursed those damn down cushions.

By the time she reached the mudroom, Ben was at the door, ducking his head against the wind. She let him in quickly, a cruel gust sneaking in behind him as she curled her toes inside her wool socks. His cheeks looked raw, and there were tiny crystals of ice on the golden hair that had escaped his hat. She reached out and took a lock between her fingers, even though she was still annoyed he hadn't honored the boundary that she'd halfheartedly set.

"Hi," he said breathlessly, stamping his feet on the mat. "I was just driving by and thought I'd stop in. Make sure you were OK here." He leaned in to kiss her, his lips warm despite the plummeting temperature.

"I'm fine," she responded coolly, softening the edges of her tone and trying again. "I'm fine."

I told you I was fine before, she still wanted to say. *I'm not a damsel in distress. I'm a capable woman who happens to be marooned on an island in a snowstorm with a helpless movie star/man-child who's starting to make me crazy in about thirty different ways.*

"We're definitely going to lose power with that wind. You must have a generator here?" He removed his gloves and rubbed his hands together to warm them. Chloe thought about how she could take them inside her own hands, sandwich them in the warmth that the fireplace had provided, but she didn't.

"Janey says we do, so I assume that means we're all set."

"Want me to take a look?" he offered.

She considered inviting him in, even suggesting that he stay for pizza, for the night. She could lead him up to that sumptuous four-posted bed, and they could nest into the duvet as the storm raged outside. She could lay her cheek to his chest and work up the courage to ask about Lauren Chase, not admitting to her bout of snooping, but bringing up the topic of their respective exes in a way that felt casual, organic. But she hesitated. She had set a boundary, and he hadn't respected it. Even though he was sweet and only offering to help, he'd still come when she'd specifically told him not to. It was enough to give her that all-too-familiar itchy sweater feeling.

She was about to assure him yet again that she was fine when Charlie appeared behind her, opening the door that separated the kitchen from the mudroom.

"Oh, hey, man," he greeted with charming ease. "I'm Charlie."

Something flickered in Charlie's eyes as he took the lobsterman in; some spark of recognition likely related to the bad behaviors that Ben had outlined for Chloe.

Ben stepped forward to grasp Charlie's hand in his own, giving it a hearty shake. "Ben Libby."

She looked from Charlie's face and back to Ben's, marveling at the men who were busy taking up the small space. With his dark hair, light eyes, and fair skin, Charlie stood in stark contrast to Ben's sun-weathered complexion and dirty blond locks. Where Charlie's eyes flashed with that almost hypnotic iciness, Ben's were deeper, wiser, and edged with those beautiful creases created by season after season on the water. Ben was a few inches taller, and as he subtly drew back his shoulders, Chloe wondered if he was calculating the height difference himself.

"Great to meet you, man. Want to come in? Warm up for a bit?" Charlie offered.

Chloe held her breath, wondering if Ben was going to clarify that they'd met before. More than once.

"Nah, thanks. I have more plowing to do."

Ben's eyes searched her face, and Chloe smiled apologetically, uncomfortably aware of Charlie's presence behind her, making them appear very much like a *we* in their stocking feet and fireplace-flushed cheeks. She gave him a chaste kiss on the corner of his mouth, and the way he pulled her toward him felt vaguely possessive, like he was trying to say something to Charlie with the familiarity of their embrace. She didn't like it at all.

She wondered how it would feel if Charlie just showed up at Ben's house unannounced, if it would feel as much like *their* bubble had been popped as it did in this moment. It was like sitting between your wife and your mistress at a dinner party. But who was who?

"Call you later?" she offered, pressing her lips to Ben's as Charlie retreated inside.

"I hope so."

He plowed the driveway on his way out, quickly pushing the snow into careful banks before turning his truck around. Chloe watched him through the kitchen window, sighing softly, not completely sure if it was a sigh lamenting his departure or a sigh at his insistence on coming at all.

Charlie interrupted her musing. "You made friends here fast." He rattled a plate from the cabinet and served himself an absurdly large slice of lemon tart. "Are you that kind of person? Who makes friends everywhere they go?"

Chloe retrieved the bowl of whipped cream from the refrigerator and placed a dollop atop Charlie's dessert, frowning at how effortlessly they moved around each other in the kitchen. "Actually, no. Not at all."

I'm more the kind of person who works sixteen hours a day and goes home to bed. And I FaceTime Julia, and she asks me if I'm trying to meet anyone, and I say yes, even though the answer is obviously no because I never left time for anything outside of my job, except for David these past couple of years, but even that always felt tangled up with work.

"I'm not that good at...making time for it," she managed.

Charlie nodded thoughtfully, taking a large bite. "I'm too good at it."

"What does that mean?"

"It means I surround myself with people all the time. My team, my buddies, Emma, even when I know it's not always good for me to have her around. Then I freak out that I don't have any time to myself, and I come here, and I have too much time to myself, and I freak out about that."

Chloe didn't really know how to respond, so she busied herself with checking on the pizza dough, testing its response to her prodding fingertip. The windows rattled, the wind a whistle as it swept off the water and wound its way around the house.

"So, Ben Libby seems like more than a new friend," Charlie teased, running his fork through his whipped cream and smiling impishly, his dimple playing the role of his partner in mischief.

"He's...it's all really new." She bit her lip and stared into the open refrigerator, which was packed with food but somehow offered nothing she was craving. "He's sweet, and he seems really into me."

"Well, that all sounds terrible."

"No, it's just that I'm not used to this, you know? I don't really date much, and he's great, but he already seems like he wants more and—"

"And you don't like to be pinned down," Charlie stated matter-of-factly.

Chloe nodded weakly. Ben was objectively perfect, and when they were together, she was constantly surprised at how right it felt. But she couldn't help thinking that everything about Deer Haven was temporary, and beyond having fun, making food, and having sex, what was the point of any of it? Three months was the plan. Three months had always been the plan.

"Well, I think it's OK to not want to limit your options," Charlie said with a shrug.

She blinked at him and shrugged back, thinking that she probably didn't need life advice from a twenty-four-year-old who paid a team to manage his affairs. She had T-shirts older than him.

She gave up on foraging the fridge and made some toast instead, slathering a thick slice of her mom's bread with peanut butter. She reminded herself that this was the part of the conversation when you asked the other person about their own relationships, because that's what *friends* did.

"How about you? Are you looking for something serious?"

Charlie leaned his elbows on the soapstone island, getting closer to her.

"I thought I was. With Emma. But being with her isn't always good for me, you know?" He popped a grape from the fruit bowl into his mouth, and Chloe watched him roll it across his tongue for a second before biting into it. "I saw her when I was in L.A."

"And how was that?" She asked casually, not willing to reveal that the She-Wolf had been quite the topic of conversation in Vermont. She certainly didn't disclose that she'd taken the time to zoom in on their faces in those paparazzi photos and had been able to tell that Charlie was unhappy in every one of them.

"Fine, I guess. She's just so...different now. I don't know, maybe we just outgrew each other. Or she outgrew me."

"Well, you were both so young."

Why the hell am I acting like I have any idea what I'm talking about? My longest relationship was with David, and I was delusional to even consider that a relationship. My only example of monogamy was my marriage to my job, and I even succeeded in blowing that up, Chloe thought. *And now I have this beautiful man who brings me buckets of crabs and makes bread and likes to have phone sex, and I'm acting like I couldn't be bothered. What is wrong with me?*

If Charlie suspected that Chloe was out of her depth with her therapy skills, he didn't let on. He continued to gaze at her intently when she was talking, like she really knew things. It was a look that she could already feel herself seeking, craving, basking in, the groundwork for addiction already laid.

I need to get out of this house, she thought, desperately casting her eyes from the ice accumulating on the outside of the windows to the snow blowing in violent gusts over the harbor, and then back to Charlie, who was smiling like he was on to her.

I'm going to do something bad if I stay here with you.

The wind howled, and the lights flickered briefly but didn't cut out. They laughed nervously and peered out at the thickly falling snow that seemed intent on undoing Ben's careful plowing.

"Do you know how the generator works?" She asked, sensing the answer before she'd even finished the question.

"I literally don't even know where it is," he responded with another grin.

"Well, Janey said she would walk us through it if we lose power."

"Then I'm sure we can handle it. I'm obviously a very handy, capable person."

She laughed and shook her head. It was something of a relief to hear him making fun of himself that way, when he acted just goofy enough to let a bit of air out of the balloon of tension that was building between them.

When he asked if she'd like to watch a movie, she accepted with the condition that she could choose. She'd pick something completely unromantic. She would sit as far away from him as possible. She wondered if suggesting keeping the lights on would be taking it too far.

She chose *Goodfellas,* and Charlie responded with a disbelieving "REALLY?" before nodding with a reverent respect for her selection. They headed down to the media room, into separate recliners with a full arm's length of distance between them.

She insisted on pausing the film at the halfway mark so she could teach him how to make popcorn. Back in the kitchen, she pulled out a dented stockpot and showed him how to add olive oil and three kernels, igniting the flame and explaining that the three popped seeds would serve as an indicator that the oil was hot enough. Once they heard all three muffled pops strike the underside of the lid, she told him to add a cup of popcorn, to shake the pan until a concerto of pops sounded. They were standing close to each other, facing the stove, his shoulder occasionally bumping against hers as he slid the pan back and forth across the burner. She instructed him to open the lid just a crack to let some steam escape, and he did so gently, flinching when a tiny spatter of hot oil broke free.

"Now I'm going to teach you how to brown butter."

Charlie looked at her with such a grateful smile, her eyes filled with tears. She placed a half stick of butter into a small saucepan and showed him how to gently swirl it around, explaining that it would spit at him at first until it settled down and started to deepen in color. He leaned over the pan, watching carefully as the butter went from pale to golden to a dark caramel color.

"Now smell it," Chloe instructed.

"Smell it?"

"Smell the butter. Does it smell like toasted nuts?"

Charlie bent his head to the pan and inhaled. "It does."

"Then it's done."

Chloe drizzled the popcorn with the browned butter and tossed a generous pinch of kosher salt on top. She handed Charlie a dishtowel and showed him how to wrap it around the top of the lid and over the handles so he could shake the pan and evenly disperse everything. He shook it enthusiastically, but with an earnest crease of concentration between his eyebrows, and Chloe turned for a moment to hide her smile.

As soon as he took that first bite, she knew where she had taken him. It was Proust with the Madeleine, Bourdain telling the story of his first oyster, that movie about the rat where a single bite brings the restaurant critic back to his mother's kitchen in France. It was Chloe eating her mother's bread. That's when food lit her up the most, when it was a feeling, a memory. She flashed back to her days of torturing ingredients with stainless steel tweezers, laying a single microgreen atop a paper-thin slice of something, surrounding it with a basil foam. Had eating that austere food ever taken anyone anywhere? Made them feel anything?

"It tastes just like my mom's," Charlie said hoarsely, his eyes shining.

"Well, now you know how to make it anytime you want."

They held eye contact until it started to feel palpably awkward, before returning to the basement with their snack. She dozed off right before Karen flushes all the drugs down the toilet and woke when the end credits were rolling. She yawned and stretched, realizing that she'd just taken her second nap of the day, destroying any hope of falling asleep at a reasonable hour later that night.

"You were out," he declared, smiling at her far too tenderly.

"I'm hungry," she replied, anxious to leave their dimly lit bunker. "I'm headed up to start dinner, see what the storm is doing."

Then everything went completely dark.

"Shit, the power!" he exclaimed dramatically, which for some reason struck her in the moment as the funniest thing she'd ever heard.

"Use the flashlight on your phone," she said between giggles, bracing her hand on the wall of the blackened stairwell.

They both held up their phones, navigating the rest of the steps by narrow beams of bluish light. Back in the unlit living room, it took a moment for Chloe's eyes to adjust to the shapes of the furniture, illuminated only by the vague luster of the moon in the stormy sky.

"Charlie, look," she said, pointing to the large picture window.

Outside, the wind was blowing so violently that the snow appeared to be falling upward, rising from below and heading toward the sky. Without a view of the ground because of the way the house was perched at the edge of the cliff, she had the sensation that the house was untethered, floating in space, or sinking to the depths of the ocean, bubbles rising around it.

He stood beside her and squinted at the storm as she admired his profile, barely lit by the window. She suddenly wanted nothing more than to run her fingertip down his jawline, tracing its angles to his perfect chin, brushing across his lips before heading up the other side of his face. She wanted to grab his hair with both hands, to pull him toward her mouth. She could still smell his soap, and she ordered herself to *pull it together*, the three words that she silently repeated like a skipping record when she was in a room with him for too long. She held her right arm down with her left hand, not even remotely trusting her body to follow her own mantra.

I don't want to want this, she thought, picturing Ben and his wide smile, remembering the spicy pasta and the way the small of his back had felt beneath her fingers.

I don't want to want you, she silently repeated, allowing herself to look directly at Charlie's face, at the curve of his mouth and the hollow of his dimple.

He turned from the window and started building a fire, snapping her back to reality with the sound of his aggressive newspaper crumpling. She called Janey, who confirmed that the power was out on the entire island. The caretaker explained how to start the generator, how to hold in a red button for five seconds before flipping a yellow switch, advising her to conserve electricity for the rest of the evening, only turning on lights where they were needed, not running any appliances if she didn't have to. Chloe assured her that she got it, promising to call if there were any problems with the house during the night.

She retrieved two flashlights from a drawer in the pantry and tossed one to Charlie, who caught it gracefully.

"Here. You need to come downstairs to hold the light."

"Lead the way, boss!" he joked.

"OK, red button, yellow switch," she murmured, shining her flashlight onto the generator like she was investigating a crime scene.

She could sense him leaning over her, bending his body above her crouched position while he cast his own light. She could feel his breath on the back of her neck, behind her ear. She could smell that soap again and nearly dropped her flashlight when he leaned forward to reach over her shoulder, to the side of the machine where the controls were hidden behind a small panel. He flipped it open and she quickly pressed the button and hit the switch as Janey had instructed. The generator announced its awakening with a whir and the basement lights all came on at once.

They made the rounds through every room, switching off lights throughout the house. Chloe preheated the oven for dinner, grateful to have an actual job on which to focus.

Ben texted while she was browning crumbles of sausage in a cast iron skillet.

Power out on whole island. You OK there?

All good here! Got the generator going. 😉

She punctuated her text with a wink emoji, such an innocent little symbol considering she was still thinking about Charlie's exhale, and how it had moved the tiny hairs at the nape of her neck when he'd leaned over her.

Need anything?

All set here. Just making dinner...thank you though.

See you tomorrow?

Yes, please.

She really was looking forward to seeing Ben. Things just felt so calm when she was with him, when she barely thought about Charlie at all. She felt guilty for being annoyed with him earlier in the day and hoped that he hadn't picked up on her irritation. She would try harder.

Charlie came into the kitchen just as she was nudging the pizza dough wider with her fingertips, then gently stretching it on the tops of her knuckles. At home, she would have cooked her pizza on a baking stone, but she settled for a sheet pan brushed generously with olive oil.

"Pizza?" he asked excitedly, his eyes bright.

She smiled, remembering one of their first real conversations when he confessed his desire to be a "regular guy" when it came to food. Now there were no rules beyond overindulgence, and as she topped the dough with sauce, whole milk mozzarella, and copious amounts of sausage and pepperoni, she found herself wanting to please him, wanting to make him happy enough to engage the dimple to its fullest effect.

They opened an expensive-looking bottle of Cabernet that he recovered from the cellar and ate standing across from each other at the counter. She tried not to look at his lips, which were just starting to take on the color of the wine on the inside. They chatted amicably about their childhoods, Chloe telling him stories of Julia's misbehaving adolescent hijinks, Charlie talking about his travels all over Europe and South America when he was a kid. They ate the entire pizza, and she couldn't help but acknowledge that she'd now met two men whose appetites rivaled her own.

The storm raged on, and when they stood near the windows, they could hear the waves crashing thunderously on the rocks below. They opened another bottle of wine and abandoned the messy kitchen, retiring to the living room to stoke the fire again. He rummaged through the hall closet until he unearthed a tattered Scrabble box.

Just say goodnight and go to bed. Say that the wine has given you a headache, that you have cramps, that you promised to FaceTime your sister. Don't even make an excuse, just politely say goodnight and go to bed. You haven't fucked this up yet. It's not too late.

She studied his face while her internal monologue silently raged on.

Just go to bed.

Instead, she set up the board on the coffee table, taking advantage of the light from the fireplace. Charlie looked so happy as he settled onto the couch opposite her, his posture loose and easy.

"I have to warn you," he said, shaking the threadbare drawstring bag full of tiles. "I'm kind of a Scrabble master."

"Then I feel I should warn you, I made it to the state spelling bee three years in a row," she retorted with a grin.

"Care to make it interesting then?"

"I have a feeling I might not be able to compete if we're talking cash wagers here."

"How about a drinking game? Every time you play a word worth 25 points or more, I have to take a shot. And vice versa."

"What are we, in tenth grade?" Chloe asked, her stomach rolling with the prospect of taking shots from some dusty bottle they pulled from the liquor cabinet in the library room.

"OK," he chuckled. "How about truth or dare then? Every time one of us scores a 50-point bonus word, the other has to complete a dare."

"So now we're in middle school?" she teased.

"Well, we've established that we're bored!"

"How about every time one of us uses six letters or more in a turn, the other has to remove an article of clothing?"

Oops.

The wine had officially gone to her head, and as they often did, her self-imposed warning bells and her conscience's refrain of, *don't do it, Chloe,* had all grown just a little quieter.

"Deal," Charlie agreed, holding her gaze steadily.

She considered laughing it off, saying that she was just kidding, that she was trying to see where things with Ben might go in the short time that she was here, because Ben was *great, really, really great*, and she was barely even worrying about Lauren's letters because they probably didn't mean anything anyway.

Instead, she found herself smiling widely and replying, "Deal."

Besides, she was an aggressively defensive player, which had always made her sister furious. They would play for hours on Saturday afternoons, applying cutthroat strategies and stretching the rules of grammar, doing anything to defeat the other.

"You're going down, Davis," Chloe ribbed. "And get ready to be really cold."

"We'll see about that," he responded, smirking confidently and offering her the bag.

She laughed when she drew an "A" to earn the first turn, hiding her grin behind her hand when Charlie pulled a "Y." Her word took shape in her mind before she'd even placed her tiles in order on her rack. She confidently played TORNADO, earning herself a double-word score, a fifty-point bonus, and a playful groan from Charlie as he unzipped his hoodie and peeled it from his shoulders.

"I have all vowels!" he complained.

"Yeah, well, it's not easy to take down a master." She sipped her wine and curled her legs beneath her, trying to control her smug expression as she planned her next word.

Charlie played ADIEU off her D, prompting Chloe to wryly respond, "French? Really?"

"It's acceptable!" he argued with a grin.

"OK, but only because you're in so much trouble."

She deftly laid down ZENITHS, pluralizing TORNADO and landing on the triple word score.

"What have I gotten myself into?" he chuckled, taking a gulp of wine and removing his socks.

She refrained from telling him that when engaging in a bout of strip anything, everyone knew that each sock counted as an individual article of clothing, and instead sat back on the couch, watching him curl his toes into the rug. He played ZOOM on her Z, and she responded with a taunt of, "Oooh, so close, but not quite," before carefully laying down her tiles to form TRANSOM.

"Are you kidding me right now?"

"I never kid about Scrabble, Charlie," she said with mock seriousness, watching with wide eyes as he pulled his T-shirt over his head.

His body was gorgeous, of course. Each muscle was sculpted by professional trainers, and by days spent surfing and running on the beach. His smooth torso was already starting to look broader than it did two weeks ago. He was filling out as instructed, looking slightly bulkier thanks to the breads, pastries, and potatoes she had been feeding him.

What am I doing? she asked herself as her pulse quickened and Charlie arranged his tiles, a small smirk forming on his lips. She tried to blame her breathlessness on the wine, the candles, the storm, the fireplace, but she knew it was more than that.

He played DELIVER and met her stare triumphantly.

She bent to remove one of her socks and hesitated. She knew that every poorly considered choice in Chicago with David, the very act of accepting this job and boarding the ferry so many days ago, had led her directly to this moment—challenging Charlie Davis to take his clothes off.

This is the part where I should think of Ben, she told herself at first. But all that she could see was the rise and fall of Charlie's bare chest and the way he stared at her in the firelight, like he was hungry again.

This is the part where I should think of Ben, she silently repeated, straining to listen to that inner voice even as it became quieter and quieter, fading behind the sound of her own heartbeat.

She pictured the Lobsterman, warm in his cottage with Jasper at his side. Had he cooked dinner? Was he reading one of his library books now that the plowing was finished and the storm had cleared the vehicles from the roads? She saw him stoking the wood stove and then settling onto the couch with that worn stack of letters, and then she imagined just quietly closing the curtains on the thought of him altogether, pulling down the shades in the back of her mind so she could no longer see the places where he continued to linger.

Then, because she'd had thirty-five years of calculated surrender to her impulses, of taking what she wanted simply because she wanted it, her inner voice adjusted its messaging.

This is the part where I blow it all up.

Without speaking, Chloe stood and pulled her sweater over her head, tousling her short hair and steadily returning Charlie's stare. She stood still, not shifting, not crossing her arms over her chest, just allowing the fireplace to cast its glow across her belly and bare, freckled shoulders. She could see his breath quicken as he softly bit his lower lip. She felt powerful standing over him like that, beautiful in the light of the flames as the storm raged at his back. She watched his gaze absorb her bare throat and the swell of her breasts in her sheer blue bra. They smiled at each other slowly, and she wondered if he could see her heart thumping in her ribcage, the signature blush rising in her cheeks. His eyes looked glassy and wild in the dim light, and she liked him like that—breathing hard, looking at her.

She sat down slowly, sinking back into the too-soft cushions, but not before knocking into the coffee table with her knee and toppling both of their wine glasses. Cabernet splashed and flooded all evidence of her skillful wordplay, and she leapt to grab the glasses while Charlie used his discarded T-shirt to mop the spill.

"Shit!" she exclaimed, running to the kitchen for paper towels. She soaked up the wet streaks on the Scrabble board. Charlie's shirt had absorbed the bulk of the wine and now looked like it had been tie-dyed in magenta. "Oh no, did it get on the rug?"

"Don't worry. I promise you this isn't the first glass of wine that's been spilled in here."

They both leaned over the table, toward each other as they wiped, and she was suddenly very aware of her shirtlessness. He gazed openly and unapologetically at the way her breasts spilled from the top of her bra when she was bent forward. Their gazes met over the wine-soaked towels, and suddenly it was like some kind of magnetic force almost violently pulling them toward each other.

His lips were on hers, her hands were in his hair, and neither of them paid a moment of attention to the jostled coffee table and the glasses that had overturned once more, spilling their remaining contents onto the floor. Her tongue was in his mouth, their bare upper bodies pressed together as she felt the heat from his belly and the thudding of his heart. He moaned softly into her mouth when she pulled him closer with both hands as they continued to kiss hungrily. She wanted to devour him.

His mouth moved to her shoulder, his lips hot on her skin as she wriggled out of her leggings.

"I've wanted this since the beginning," he whispered, running his fingertip down her belly, causing her to gasp.

She pushed him back onto the couch and slowly pulled down his sweats, running her knuckles down his thighs, his calves, as he leaned his head against the back of the sofa. She stifled an ill-timed giggle at the ridiculousness of it all. Charlie Davis was sprawled out, looking like an underwear model with his abs and his boxer briefs, his skin luminous in the light of the fire, waiting to have sex with her.

He reached into the pocket of the hoodie that he'd shed and pulled out a condom. Chloe tipped her head to the side and gave him a half smile as he shrugged impishly.

"I guess I'm an optimist," he confessed, pulling down his underwear and deftly rolling it on.

Chloe gasped softly when she took in the sight of his fully unclothed body. She had never admired a man's nakedness so blatantly before, and as she ran her eyes up his muscular legs, his unabashed hardness, taut stomach, and finally up to his face, she got the distinct impression that he liked it. He was magnificent, and he knew it.

"Come here," he said throatily, reaching his hand for hers.

She straddled his lap, and he ran his fingers down the length of her back, from the nape of her neck down to the small clefts that framed her tailbone, as she rolled her hips. Then it was all hands and mouths and tongues and their moans echoing through that big house while the snow swirled outside and the fireplace started to dim. He pressed into her deeply, and it still wasn't enough. She wanted *more* of him, *all* of him, and she found herself whispering, "more," until that final shudder, when he murmured her name in hot breath against the side of her neck.

Her legs were wrapped around his waist when he started kissing her throat, her chest, brushing his lips across every inch of skin. He used his tongue, his lips, until she clutched his hair in her fists and screamed her pleasure into the dark room.

Hearts hammering, they stretched out together on the couch and wrapped their arms around each other. She pressed her mouth to his bare shoulder, and they sighed contentedly in unison, prompting them both to laugh.

He released a sleepy-sounding "mmmmm" before gently pulling her closer, her back pressed against his warm chest, his arm wrapped across her bare waist. She stared into the dying fire while she listened to his slow breathing. They were both wide awake and completely spent. She considered disentangling their limbs, putting on her sweater, using the bathroom, adding some wood to the fireplace, but she didn't. She just settled back into the heat of his body and let herself be swallowed by the cushions, trying her hardest to silence the clutter of questions about what it all meant.

Chapter Fifteen

Chloe yawned and smoothed her hair, making a futile attempt to tame the crown of cowlicks that had formed in the night. The power was back on, and outside the window, the sky was impossibly clear and blue, as if the storm that had battered the shingles and rattled the windows in their frames just hours before had been only a dream. On the coffee table, her screen lit up with two more missed calls from the mysterious 708 number. Both had come in during the storm, and she had zero interest in dealing with them.

There were two texts from Ben as well. They had arrived right around the time she was talking herself out of him by the light of the fire.

Sorry I just showed up like that.

I could tell it bothered you.

She pressed the heels of her palms into her eyes, regretting the wine, the Scrabble bonuses, the power outage, all of it. She wondered what she should say, if there was anything to say at all.

She groaned as she rose from the couch, wrapping the blanket around her still naked body and stretching out her stiff lower back. She nearly flinched when she caught a glimpse of her reflection in the mottled mirror above the mantel. With her wild hair, swollen lips, and dark circles surrounding her eyes, her first thought was, *that looks like a woman who makes bad choices.*

"Charlie?" she called out hoarsely.

Nothing.

She padded upstairs to the shower, all alone in the big house yet again. She guessed Charlie must have risen with the sun—maybe he'd gone out for a run, or slipped from the sofa in the middle of the night, leaving her for the comfort of his own bed.

She lathered her hair and pictured Ben in his kitchen, kneading dough, a towel slung over his strong shoulder, and she shook her head to try to erase the image. Would he be able to guess what had happened? Did it matter? It wasn't like they'd made promises to each other or anything. She told herself that this was dating—seeing different people, no vows, just fun—but she couldn't shake the feeling that she'd made a mess of things.

She imagined telling Julia what had happened, hearing the blasé tone that she would force into her own voice as she promised, *Oh, it's no big deal. The Lobsterman and I barely know each other. And he's obviously still hung up on his ex anyway.*

But the truth pulsed like a migraine at her temples. She'd helped herself to something without truly considering the consequences. Again.

As she scrubbed her face a little too hard, her skin stinging, she recalled a childhood visit to her grandmother's house when she'd found a box of chocolates in the cupboard, long forgotten since Valentine's Day. While her Gram was out running errands and Julia was busy poring over the celebrity gossip magazines that were always stacked high on the coffee table, Chloe had sneakily eaten the entire box. She'd even savored the sickening syrup inside the cherry cordial, sucking the cloying gel through a hole in the bottom before moving onto the vanilla nougat, which always tasted like nothing.

To conceal the evidence of her gluttony, she'd tossed the thin brown papers behind the refrigerator. The ancient appliance was constantly running, and as if on cue, the wrappers fluttered up from the back and landed at her grandmother's feet when she returned from her shopping. She called her a "bottomless pit," and Chloe spent the rest of the afternoon throwing up in the small 1970s bathroom with the bifold door, coming to terms with the reality that no ten-year-old stomach was designed to consume that much corn syrup and palm oil.

She found herself craving more chocolate the very next day.

The inevitability of sleeping with Charlie had felt a lot like that drugstore candy sampler. She just wanted it. She knew it wasn't good for her, that she'd possibly pay for it later, but that hunger, that craving for more, was too powerful to resist.

Once out of the shower, she texted Julia.

I had sex with Charlie last night.

There. Committed so plainly to a handful of characters on her screen, it wasn't emotion, it was just gossip. And since it was only four a.m. on the West Coast, it wasn't even a conversation. It was just an innocuous confession. She punctuated it with a shrug emoji, an attempt at the offhand ease that she was determined to project, an indifference she wished she actually felt.

She dressed quickly in a pair of soft, army green joggers and a cropped black sweater, swiping a thin coat of mascara onto her lashes and using her fingers to sweep her shaggy hair to one side. Back in the kitchen, she began cracking eggs after recovering a sixties-era waffle iron from the darkest corner of the pantry. As she melted butter and mixed her dry ingredients, she thought about Charlie's hands pressing into her hips and the way the words, "come here," had sounded coming from the back of his throat.

The disappointment she'd felt when she woke up alone on the couch surprised her. She thought, *who does that?* before quickly admitting that *she* did that. She'd done the same thing so many times over the years—slipping out on a sleeping Tinder date, making an excuse about an "early day" to her boyfriend of three weeks, telling David very frankly, "Get out, you have to go," because she wanted to sleep in her apartment alone. Owning up to her dejection about Charlie's absence was admitting that last night had meant something to her. She avoided these thoughts as she made the waffles, ladling batter onto the iron, watching the steam curl from the sides before stacking them high on a plate beside her.

Charlie came in through the mudroom door dressed all in black—his hoodie, sweats, and beanie all working to make his eyes look even lighter. Chloe's gaze was immediately drawn to his lips, those lips that had been all over her body just a few hours earlier.

"Expecting company?" he asked.

"What?"

"That's a lot of waffles."

She glanced down at the towering stack that threatened to topple at any moment. "Oh. I guess I wasn't paying attention." Her small laugh sounded almost nervous, and she cursed herself for not playing it cooler. "Do you want some?"

"Nah, I'm good. I had a shake," he said, pulling his phone from his pocket and opting to scroll instead of meeting her eyes. He took off his hat and ran his hand through his hair, causing it to stand on end in a way that made him look even younger than twenty-four.

My God, twenty-four.

"A shake isn't food," she insisted.

His smile was weak and missing his dimple, the opposite of last night. "It was a weight gain shake."

"Still not food," she mumbled, aggressively stabbing a waffle, placing it on her plate, and drenching it with her family's maple syrup.

Chloe went to the window and surveyed the driveway and yard, taking in the smooth, windblown snowdrifts that almost resembled dunes, the bright sunshine giving them the effect of being coated in glitter. It was like waking up on another planet.

"Where did you go? I mean, how is it out there?" Chloe corrected.

"I went for a run." Still not looking up from his phone. "Cold, but really quiet."

"Charlie, last night..." she began, directionless as to how she would finish her own sentence.

She hoped that he would be of some assistance, but he wasn't even listening, quite obviously texting someone else. He chuckled at whoever made his phone ping and tapped a text in return with a smirk.

"Charlie."

When he decided to look up at her, his expression was blank, his eyes settling not on her face, but somewhere just over her head.

"I think we should talk about what happened last night."

"I know," he said quickly. "It was a mistake. I don't usually do that, you know."

Do what? She wanted to ask. *Play strip Scrabble? Sneak away in the middle of the night? Sleep with the help?*

She swallowed hard, fighting against the flood of questions that threatened to spill from her mouth while she found herself unable to stop considering that one word. *Mistake.* She wanted to point out that he had seemed to enjoy it, that he'd certainly appeared enthusiastic about her bare skin, her body clenched so tightly around his.

"Well, I don't usually do that either," she insisted.

Oh, wait.

He returned his phone to his pocket and finally focused on her face, his expression not searching like it usually was, but just sort of dull.

"And I don't want to mess things up for you, you know? Or for me," he said with a shrug.

"Because I work for you," Chloe responded softly, the reality of their arrangement sinking in once again.

"Well...yeah. And we've become friends."

"Have we?"

"Haven't we?" he replied, a brief and injured look flashing across his face.

"Sure," she said curtly, placing the batter bowl and measuring cups into the sink with a clatter.

Charlie returned to his phone, and she gave him a moment to say something, but he was texting again.

"So, you're not going to eat these then?" She gestured to the ridiculous stack of waffles.

With one swift motion, she dumped the entire pile into the trash can before turning on her heel and stomping out of the kitchen.

She made it upstairs before she felt the prickling of tears behind her eyes. As everything in that beautiful bedroom became blurry with the kind of shame and embarrassment that she wasn't used to feeling, she couldn't help but think *Ben would have eaten the waffles. He would have fawned over how perfect they were, how cinnamon butter was an ingenious innovation, how I was amazing at everything, and sexy and interesting and wow—has maple syrup ever tasted this good?*

But she hadn't even texted Ben back, and Julia still hadn't responded to her confession. Chloe followed the shrug emoji to her sister with the words, *big mistake.*

Her phone rang instantly, and before the word hello had even cleared her lips, Julia blurted, "Oh, Chlo, why? Why? I told you not to get any bad ideas!"

"Good morning to you, too."

"Sex with Charlie? I mean, bad idea, sister."

She could picture Julia at that moment—her curly hair piled atop her head, sipping matcha in coordinating kimonos with Beth, likely putting her phone on speaker so she and her wife could dissect the finer points of the conversation after they hung up.

"It seemed like a good idea at the time," Chloe weakly replied, a verbal version of the shrug emoji. "Now he's just acting weird, and it's so awkward, and I feel like an idiot."

Julia sighed. "Give it a day or two. He's just...he's kind of a mess, Chlo. This thing with Emma, and he's just now emerging from a pretty big slump in his career. And he's just...Charlie."

"What does that mean?"

"It means he's an actor in L.A. He's a player in the way that everyone out here is. And he's young, you know?"

Chloe didn't like hearing her sister's excuses for Charlie's behavior. She didn't appreciate that Julia was talking like she valued her loyalties to Charlie the Client above Chloe the Sister. It surprised her how much it hurt.

"Got it," she said coolly.

"And what about the sexy lobsterman? I thought you liked him."

"I do! I do like him. But Jesus, Julia...Ben and I have known each other for like two weeks." She hesitated before continuing. "And anyway, I feel like there's still something between him and his ex."

"Do you actually believe that, or is it just something you're telling yourself?" Julia pressed.

"Does it matter?"

"It matters if you're just inventing reasons to run."

"I'm not inventing reasons," Chloe huffed. "He asked her to marry him. She said yes. His dog is her dog. And why would he keep all the letters unless he still loves her? Unless he just isn't ready to let her go?"

"Why are you letting that get in the way if this is all just for fun anyway?"

"I don't know, Jules. I don't know what I'm doing. With Ben, or with...anything."

Her sister paused before gently asking, "Do you think you'll tell him?"

"I don't know," she replied. "I don't want to. It was kind of nothing anyway, the thing with Charlie. This morning everything just felt...different."

Chloe could picture Julia nodding, concern furrowing her brow. "Besides, not everyone mates for life, you know," she continued.

Julia responded with a "pfffffft" sound, which Chloe could only assume either meant, *pfffffft—you should be so lucky to have what Beth and I have,* or, more likely, *pfffft—but you don't even try.*

"I just wanted you to take some time to figure yourself out while you're out there. I mean, the thing with David and your job and everything...I just wanted you to be on your own for a bit," Julia said.

"I've always been 'on my own,' Julia," Chloe spat out. "I'm good at it, remember?"

"Are you?"

"I'm not a fucking problem that you need to fix. Getting me out here, throwing me together with him? Why did you even bother?"

"Because for right now, things are over for you in Chicago. And that's on you, sister."

Chloe sullenly pulled a loose thread on the expensive-looking white duvet cover and watched as the tension caused a dozen tiny stitches to snap. She rolled to her side so she could gaze at the clear sky outside the window, scowling at the choppy sea gleaming beneath the sun, defiantly bright in the face of her sour mood.

"And honestly," Julia continued, "I thought both of you could really use a friend."

"It's just...what if I'm right back where I started?" Chloe wondered. "Just making the same crap mistakes, doomed to repeat the same bullshit again and again?"

"Since when do you not have power over this entire thing?" Julia scolded. "Jesus, Chlo. You want a different outcome? Make a different choice."

Chloe sniffled and yanked on another thread, powering through its taut resistance and finally snapping it. She'd considered her time on Deer Haven as a reluctant pressing of the pause button. She hadn't come all the way out to sea to move forward. She'd come to bide her time, to tick off the days on her mental calendar until the coast was clear to return to her real life. And it just wasn't working for her anymore.

"Time for a new plan," Julia asserted as if reading her sister's thoughts.

"Oh yeah? And what would that look like?"

"Well, I'm sure I could connect you with another client. If you wanted to try this private chef thing again—in a different way."

Chloe pictured herself cooking in another famous person's house, with their gluten-free, dairy-free, lean-protein proclivities. She imagined having to deal with an entire family, not just a single, devastatingly attractive man, and knew that she didn't want to navigate those kinds of complications.

"I know of at least two people who would love to take you on."

"No," Chloe flatly replied.

"Well, have you ever thought about teaching? I'm sure every culinary school in the world would fall all over themselves to add Chloe Foster to their staff."

"Jesus, Julia. I'm not going to be a culinary school instructor. I have a Michelin star," she hissed, unwilling to acknowledge the research she'd conducted her first night on Deer Haven.

"Then I guess it's your turn to come up with some amazing new ideas," her sister said pluckily.

"You know, you have this way of making me feel just a little bit worse?"

Julia released a sharp burst of laughter. "Well, it's like I always tell my clients: things usually have to get much worse before they can get better."

"Sage advice," Chloe responded, her tone sarcastic.

"Well, I'm very wise."

The two sisters sat in silence for a few seconds, Chloe holding the phone to her ear as she took in the craggy Maine coastline from her bed, Julia likely out on her patio, tipping her own freckled face to the California sun.

"And if you really want my wise advice, get out of the house for a bit," Julia said. "Do your job, cook the food, make sure everything's all squared away there, and go see that sexy lobsterman. Break the Charlie Davis spell."

Chloe hated admitting when her sister was right, especially when she had to admit that she was almost *always* right. Since they were kids, whether it was navigating a middle school squabble or strategizing a way to team up to defy their parents, Julia just knew what to do. It was likely why she was so good at her job, and most definitely why she was always Chloe's first call when everything felt like it was unraveling.

"I love you, Jules."

"Love you, Chlo. Get yourself out of that house, OK?"

They said goodbye, and Chloe stared at the ceiling for a bit longer, studying the wide shaft of light that shone through the curtains. She would do everything her sister had instructed her to do. She would call Ben. She would fill the oven and refrigerator with food for Charlie. She would make herself scarce for a few days. She would inform Charlie that the weekend belonged to her, because he was her boss and she was his chef and maybe a friend. She would calmly assert that they were on the same page, that the night before had been nothing more than a fun mistake that didn't need repeating. Period.

When she gazed out the window at the end of the hall and saw that Ben had come by again to plow the driveway, long before Chloe had woken up on the sofa and likely before the sun had risen, she felt a heaviness in her chest.

Fancy a houseguest for the weekend?

She texted him, an attempt to make things feel light again.

For sure. I'm out on the water now.

See you later today.

Can't wait.

Packing a bag for Ben's house was easy, and as she quickly filled her leather duffel with jeans, sweaters, and her laciest underthings, she started planning dishes for Charlie's weekend alone. Roasted carrots with feta and mint. Baked mac and cheese. Chocolate cake. She would have to cook through the afternoon before disappearing for three days, but she was really looking forward to the distance, especially after her behavior with the waffles.

Back in the kitchen, Charlie had attempted to make himself useful and had run what she could only assume was a dishcloth coated in waffle batter across the now streaked countertops. She cleaned up his attempt at cleaning up before heading to the market, where she gathered everything she needed for all the homey, calorie-laden meals she'd planned, turning her back on the lobster tank and choosing cod instead. Something about serving Charlie the fruits of Ben's labor felt off to her, and when she strode to the front register, overflowing shopping baskets looped over her aching arms, her sister's words rang in her ears.

You want a different outcome? Make a different choice.

As she hauled her canvas tote bags back to the car, she assured herself that she was finally doing something right. Getting over Charlie Davis could be fast and painless if she committed to it, because things between them weren't real. She knew that he was nothing more than a conveniently timed distraction, a bright and shiny object that had caught her eye for just a minute but could never actually sustain her attention.

She could look back on their night together as a super-hot moment in time that could never be repeated, and that would eventually feel alright. She would push away the thoughts of his mouth on her bare shoulder, of his hands pressing into her back, of her fingers in his hair, until the memories faded into the depths of her consciousness like all the boyfriends and hookups before him.

She would start over. She would focus on Ben. She would ask him kindly and directly about Lauren Chase.

That's the plan, she muttered, trying to believe it as she opened the door and kicked off her snowy boots. She heaved her grocery bags onto the counter and began to unpack, devising a work plan for everything she had to get done in the next few hours.

When a dainty, throat-clearing cough sounded behind her, she released a little shriek before turning around and finding the She-Wolf standing in the kitchen.

Chapter Sixteen

She was taller than Chloe had expected, and her makeup-free face naturally looked as if it had been washed with an Instagram filter designed to remove one's pores. She wore leather leggings, a taupe sweater, and buttery-looking suede boots that she hadn't troubled herself to take off in the mudroom. She extended a manicured hand and introduced herself with a slightly affected British accent.

"You must be the cook. I'm Emma."

Chloe accepted Emma's handshake, noting that the other woman's skin was impossibly soft and cool. They gripped each other's fingers as tightly as two CEOs making a deal over a boardroom table. As the She-Wolf's sharp eyes met her own, Chloe could tell immediately that she was formidable, despite the fragile feel of her bony hand.

"I'm Chloe. The *chef*."

"Lovely to meet you," Emma breezed, flashing a dazzling set of teeth, not bothering to acknowledge her semantical misstep.

"Oh, hey, you're back," Charlie said, joining them in the kitchen and standing partially behind Emma. "Look who decided to surprise me."

Chloe expected a wide-eyed look of helplessness, a frown of frustration, an eyeroll of exasperation, but his face was impassive.

"I just thought, I have a break in shooting, why not pop in on Charlie at his favorite place!" Emma tucked a stray, silky lock of black hair behind her ear. "I guess I just forgot how cold it gets here in the winter!"

Emma fondly glanced at Charlie through lowered lashes, and Chloe suddenly felt like an intruder.

This is why I didn't want to be a personal chef, she would snarkily text her sister later.

It was all just too intimate.

"Well, you missed the storm of the year," Charlie said a little too boisterously. "A real Nor'eastah!"

Chloe could feel him trying to catch her eye to celebrate their lame little inside joke, but she focused instead on putting away the groceries, silently opening and closing cabinet doors, and methodically packing the refrigerator with seafood and produce.

He cleared his throat softly, as if he was about to ask permission for something. "I'm going to take Emma out to explore. Do you want to come?"

"No, thanks. I have a lot to do here," she replied, noting that Emma had raised her beautifully shaped eyebrows at the invitation. "I'm headed out for the weekend. I'll make sure you both have lots of choices, and I'll be back on Sunday."

"Should we go over the menu?" Emma offered coolly.

"I've already shopped," Chloe replied with an equal amount of frostiness, looking directly at Emma's striking face. "And planned," she finished pointedly.

"I think Chloe has everything under control here," Charlie interrupted, his hand rubbing the back of his neck.

"Fine, then. Just don't let me forget to talk to you about gluten when we get back. And dairy. And refined sugars of any kind," Emma said.

"Great," Chloe replied flatly, fighting the urge to add a sarcastic, *can't wait!*

Charlie and Chloe's eyes finally locked, and they each offered the other a weak smile as Emma excused herself to freshen up what looked to be a perpetually fresh face. She made her way to the hallway powder room with the confidence of someone who knew the lay of the land, and Chloe realized that she had likely stayed in the house before.

"She just kind of showed up," Charlie said softly. "I didn't invite her. She just came." He ran his hand through his already tousled hair and looked at her pleadingly. "She always does this. I just...I feel like kind of an asshole."

Chloe realized that he was waiting to be comforted, to be assured. He needed to be told that having sex with your chef and then welcoming your maybe-girlfriend within a twelve-hour period was just fine. Normal, really. Just as normal and fine as sleeping with your boss and then immediately running away to hide at another man's house for the weekend.

"Charlie, we both know what happened last night...it was just the storm and the wine, and we just got caught up in all of it." She didn't say it to be generous; she said it because she needed it to be true.

"And the Scrabble," he responded, his dimple appearing despite the sadness of his half-smile.

"Yes, and the Scrabble," Chloe said softly, remembering his absolutely blazing eyes, the heat of the fire on her skin when she stood to remove her sweater. She swallowed hard and continued in the breeziest tone she could muster, "It's OK. Really. I'll cook a ton of food, I'll get out of your hair, and you'll have the place to yourselves."

"You're really leaving? For the whole weekend?"

"I think staying would be completely weird, considering... everything happening here right now."

Emma returned before Charlie could respond, her hair artfully arranged in a messy topknot. "Ready?" she asked, looking only at him.

"You might want to put on some different boots," Chloe suggested, casting her eyes toward Emma's suede-clad feet. "You know, snow and ice and everything."

Emma shrugged and returned her gaze defiantly. "I didn't bring another pair."

"You're welcome to borrow mine. They're the black Bogs in

there." She paused her chopping and gestured to the mudroom with the tip of her large chef's knife.

Emma responded by wrinkling her nose as if she'd been offered a toothbrush from the trash can, and Chloe was unsure if the disgust was on account of the unfashionable nature of the boots or the fact that they had previously been on her own feet.

"They're just boots, Emma. You should have brought something more practical," Charlie said.

"They probably won't even fit me," the She-Wolf murmured, closing the door on what remained of the conversation, to Chloe's relief.

Do your job, cook the food, make sure everything's all squared away there, and go see that sexy lobsterman, she repeated to herself while preparing the meals that would feed Charlie and Emma for the next two days. As she roasted carrots in olive oil and cloves of garlic, whisked a smooth béchamel for the mac and cheese, and prepped the fish for the chowder, she couldn't stop thinking about what had happened the night before. She frowned, wishing for a bout of amnesia as she rhythmically chopped dark and hearty kale leaves for a salad, creating perfect ribbons while willing herself to forget.

She was just setting the timer for the dark chocolate applesauce cake—her mom's prized recipe—when the Hollywood lovebirds returned from their outing.

"It smells amazing in here," Charlie declared, just as Emma said, "Is that cheese?" pointing in horror at the two pans of macaroni cooling on the counter.

"That is indeed a lot of cheese," Chloe confirmed. "I've also made salad, roasted vegetables, and fish chowder, but I steamed some cod on the side in case you wanted to skip the potatoes and cream."

"Lovely, then," Emma responded, turning her attention to her phone, a cue that Chloe took to mean, *that will be all.*

Charlie smiled apologetically, and Chloe ignored them both, concentrating her efforts on cleaning the kitchen until the timer sounded for the cake. She worked quickly and efficiently, loading the dishwasher, packaging food for the fridge, and counting the minutes until she could untie her apron and drive to Ben's, more than ready to be free of the Davis house for a few days.

The sun was just beginning to set behind the trees when Chloe finally left. She hadn't even made her way out of the driveway before her phone started ringing.

"Is Emma *there*?" Julia practically shrieked, not bothering to greet her sister.

"Oh, she's here. She showed up around noon. How did you know?"

"Her Insta. She posted a picture of the two of them with a bunch of snow and pine trees and shit behind them. Hashtag together again, hashtag winter wonderland."

"Was she wearing my boots?"

"What?"

"Nothing. Did you know she speaks in kind of a British accent? 'Lovely then. Lovely then,' like she's in Downton Abbey or something. Like I'm the downstairs help."

"Well..." Julia began.

"Well, what, Jules?" Chloe demanded, reminding herself to slow down on the snow-covered road. She pulled over to finish her conversation, since the last thing she needed was for Ben to have to come and tow her out of a snowbank.

"Well, you do work there. For Charlie, for the house. Not that you should ever be treated like anything less than the talented, amazing chef that you are," she added vehemently.

Silence swelled between them until Julia made another joke about lobstermen and setting traps and maybe something about clams that barely made sense, before they said goodbye.

Just as Chloe was about to pull back onto the road, her phone trilled again, the screen lighting up with the same 708 number from all the missed calls.

"Oh, for fuck's sake," she muttered, anxious to once and for all remove herself from whatever contact list she was still on so that she could focus on getting to the warmth of Ben's place.

"Chloe Foster?"

The second she heard the voice on the other end of the line, she felt breathless, like she'd managed to summon a ghost.

"This is Lila Harris," she said in her characteristically clipped tone. "I was starting to think you'd forgotten how to answer your phone. You leave the city, and you just stop reading your email?"

"I...um...Lila?" she stammered.

"I've been wanting to discuss something with you." Her affectation was curt and icy, and Chloe cursed the unusually crystal-clear connection that Deer Haven was currently delivering.

In what world would Lila Harris have something to discuss with her? Maybe she was going to sue her. Or scream at her for disrespecting her marriage. Or tell her that they all had chlamydia. In a daze, Chloe cut the engine and took a deep breath. She squared her shoulders and lifted her chin, assuming her best game face, her professional face. She told herself to be strong, that she was in charge, to remain steady, which was a tough sell as she shivered in her compact rental car in the middle of nowhere.

"I'm surprised to hear from you, Lila," she declared in the most confident, even tone she could muster.

"Well, yes, after what transpired at Redbud, I can understand why. But that's ancient history.

She could imagine the elegant woman waving her manicured hand as if shooing away a gnat, and she wanted to shout, *it's been four weeks!*

"Regardless," Lila continued, "I'd like you to come work for me again."

"Um...what? At Redbud? What?" It was the best Chloe could manage.

"Not Redbud. We just closed on a new space in Logan Square. We're beginning construction and would like you to be a part of building it."

"I don't...what? Why?"

"Because you're a brilliant chef," Lila fired back. "And you were discreet after everything with that bastard soon-to-be ex-husband of mine. But above all else, you're a brilliant chef."

She wondered for a moment if Lila was operating with an ulterior motive, if she was setting her up. Or did she think Chloe might still talk to a lawyer, frame it as a sexual misconduct suit against David, against the company?

"I'm not going to sue you, you know," she said flatly.

"Well, I should hope not," Lila responded brusquely. "We'll do a walk-through of the space, and we can discuss details. If you ever checked your email, you'd see that I sent you site plans, blueprints, and comps of the neighborhood."

"I know the neighborhood. It's my neighborhood."

"Fine, fine. Let's set up a meeting in two weeks."

"I'm in Maine right now. On an island."

"Well, charter a damn boat. I'll have my assistant call you back soon to confirm the day."

Chloe wasn't sure what to say, whether she should thank Lila or insist upon terms, if she should assure her that she was the chef for the job, or if she should just coolly say that she would think about it and leave the conversation with a vague sense of the upper hand. It didn't matter, because the mogul had already hung up, leaving Chloe shaking in her car, not because of the cold engine and the snowy road, but because she'd just been offered the keys to her old life.

She drove the remaining half mile in a daze. Lila had been trying to get in touch with her since her first couple of days on the island, to make her an offer, to invite her back. As she pulled into Ben's driveway, she shook her head in silent disbelief. If she'd answered that first call or if she hadn't deleted the unread emails, she would likely have been on the next ferry, departing before Charlie had even arrived. She wouldn't have come to this little cottage the first time Ben had invited her. She would've already been long gone, headed back toward Chicago, where she'd kind of remember that hot guy in the flannel shirt that she'd met at the market, eventually not really thinking about him at all.

Her chest swelled with affection as Ben ran out to help her with her bag. He appeared fresh from the shower, his wet hair curling around his ears, his breath coming in clouds as he wrapped his arms around her in the driveway. She leaned into him and inhaled his Ben scent, all soap and wood smoke and the coconut shampoo that she'd spotted at the edge of his bathtub during her last visit. She reminded herself that he wouldn't be able to tell that she'd slept with Charlie, that she'd fallen into an old pattern.

This weekend could be a reset—red button, yellow switch.

"Hi," he said, bending to kiss her softly.

"Hi," she exhaled, instantly light with the relief of being away from the house, from the job that was Charlie and Emma, from Lila's snippy voice on the phone.

Ben attempted to pull the small duffel from her shoulder, but she braced it with her hand, assuring him that she had it under control. Inside, the smell of cooking filled the small cottage, the wood stove glowed in the corner, and Billie Holiday crooned sleepily from the record player. She smiled at his mastery of mise en place, at his ability to prep the ingredients and set the stage. He took her coat and offered her a glass of wine, which, to her delight, he served in a small mason jar.

"Mmmmm," she hummed, allowing the flavors of smoke and berries to wash over her tongue. She followed him into the open kitchen. "What are we cooking?"

"Garlic mashed potatoes, a little salad, and I got some steaks from the Perkins Farm."

As he ignited the burner beneath a well-seasoned cast-iron skillet, she perched atop a kitchen stool, where she sat on her hands and willed herself not to take over. She sipped her wine and tried to enjoy herself, to focus only on the heat from the fire, the sleepy dog beside it, and the way Ben had slung a dishtowel over his broad shoulder, but her mind was racing. She tried to be present, to not sift through the hundreds of restaurant concepts that she'd daydreamed about for the past fifteen years, their menus and interiors flashing through her mind on a rapid loop.

Ben unwrapped two large ribeyes and patted them dry before

sprinkling them with ample amounts of coarse salt and cracked pepper. The meat was pressed onto the screaming hot pan, three minutes per side, before he placed a large pat of butter atop each steak and slid the skillet into the hot oven. It was exactly how she would have cooked them in her own kitchen.

"Are you sure you've never worked in a restaurant?"

"Nah, just cookbooks. And YouTube."

She slid her hand under the bottom of his shirt, tracing the thin trail of hair that started at his belly button and disappeared into his waistband. He turned to face her and kissed her slowly, placing his large hands on her cheeks.

She swallowed the secrets that had taken up residence in the back of her throat and vowed to look only ahead. At least for the rest of the weekend. Or until she mustered the courage to bring up Lila. And Lauren. And maybe Charlie.

"No distracting the cook," he whispered into her ear, sending a delicious shudder from the nape of her neck down the length of her spine.

"I wouldn't dream of it," Chloe replied, admiring the way Ben looked in his worn carpenter pants as he bent to peer into the oven.

She crossed her legs, pressing her thighs together and remembering everything about the last two times she'd come to this little house, how he'd pulled her onto his lap on the couch, how he'd undressed her in his bedroom, slowly peeling off her layers with reverence, as if in worship. Inexplicably, her thoughts turned to Charlie and Emma, and she wondered if they were eating any of the food she had spent all day preparing, if *they* were sinking into the too-soft sofa cushions together this time, if he was whispering *her* name like a prayer.

"How do you like your steak?" Ben interrupted, snapping her from her unproductive reverie.

"Bloody."

"Then dinner is done!" he declared, handing Jasper a bone. The old dog promptly stuffed it under his bed before collapsing on top of it with a contented grunt.

As Chloe cut into her meat with the ease of a hot knife slicing through butter, she practiced what she'd been working up to for the better part of the day.

I found your letters, she silently recited.

Tell me about Lauren, she could say.

So, I was snooping through your desk drawers a few days ago...

Did you and Lauren get Jasper together, or did he already belong to her when you met?

She then ran through the sentence that had been sprinting through her head since Lila's phone call.

I just got an offer...from someone I probably shouldn't trust.

But she couldn't seem to find the words for any of it, and before she could perfect her lines, she blurted out, "Where do you see yourself in three years?" It was the same question she asked every person who applied to work in her kitchen.

"I want to get married," he said plainly, setting down his fork and looking directly into her eyes.

"Is that a proposal?" She choked, attempting to laugh off his statement as she took another panicked gulp of wine.

"No, not a proposal," he chuckled, "But I just want to be direct. I'm forty-one. I want to settle down with someone. I want kids. Before I'm too old to lift them up to ride on my shoulders, you know?"

It seemed that Ben had been practicing a speech of his own, and she nodded like she understood, even when the voice in her head was absolutely screaming, *Abandon your post! Abandon your post!*

"How about you?" Ben asked. "Ever been close?"

"No, never." Chloe considered her words very carefully. "I'm not that good at sharing space with people."

"Well, you're kind of sharing space with someone now," Ben pointed out.

"Yeah, that's different," she insisted. "It's like we're staying at the same bed and breakfast or something. Except it's my job to make the breakfast."

And watch movies with him, and drink wine together, and play strip Scrabble and tell him my secrets and stare at his mouth when he eats and try not to obsess about what it could all possibly mean.

"If you could live anywhere, like *really* anywhere, where would you live?" Chloe asked, a desperate attempt to change the subject.

"Honestly? Here. On Deer Haven."

Chloe tried to neutralize the disappointment that she feared would take over her face if she stopped concentrating on the effort.

Deer Haven? Not Portugal? Not New Zealand? Really?

"I can't imagine a place better than this," he continued. "I have my own business, my boat. I get to watch the sun rise and set over the water every single day. I have this little house. What else could a person want?"

"Maybe you're the kind of person who's happy wherever he is," she offered, deciding to be generous even as she felt a dull sense of disappointment at the lack of adventure in his answer.

"Maybe. Or maybe I'm just in the perfect place," Ben said, his eyes glinting in the low light. "I left for a year, once, remember?"

"Right. Denver," she replied, hoping that he'd swung open the door to the larger story. "And?"

"I hated it," he shrugged. "Everyone was always in a hurry. And no ocean."

"You know there are other cities, right?" she teased. "Some that are actually located by the ocean?"

"I think I've heard that," he chuckled. "But I don't know. It's just not for me. The smells alone."

"Worse than the fish cannery?" she demanded, recalling the stench that had greeted her when she'd first arrived at the ferry terminal in Craftsport.

"I guess I'm just used to that," he shrugged.

Chloe nodded, unsure of how to convince him that there was more.

Was that the depth of her arrogance? That desire to talk him out of his sense of contentment because she *knew better*? Her cheeks flushed with shame, and she tried to tamp the impulse down but found herself unable to stop thinking the same thought.

Your life is too small for me.

Suddenly, she envisioned Charlie starring in that travel show he'd been offered. She pictured him hanging out the side of a helicopter, his eyes bright, hair blowing from his face. He'd be scuba diving off the coast of Australia, riding a camel in Dubai, participating in those Scottish games in which beefy men throw giant logs around, having the time of his life while the cameras rolled. He'd dart from location to location, never settling down, grinning that devastating grin and flashing that damn dimple across the globe. Could she imagine Ben doing any of that?

She softly shook her head to reset her thoughts.

"The steak is perfect," she blurted, brushing her bangs from her eyes and looking up to find him staring at her.

"I was nervous."

"You shouldn't be. You're a really good cook."

Ben got up to flip the record, Billie Holiday's mournful voice filling the air again. He held out his hand, an invitation to dance as if they were in a black-and-white movie, and her knees were about to go weak. Embarrassed, she accepted, allowing him to pull her close, her hand clutched in his, her chest pressed against his chest. They swayed slowly to the music, and she laid her cheek on his shoulder, breathing him in, reveling in the utter corniness of the moment, never wanting it to end. She wondered if being a part of this big man's small life could eventually fill her up, if it could always feel like this, if it could be enough.

He leaned down to kiss her, and she opened her mouth to him, to his tongue, to the teeth that softly drew in her bottom lip. He moved his mouth to her neck, his hands buried in the back pockets of her jeans, where his gentle squeeze reminded her of junior high dances spent in darkened gymnasiums, when the air was thick with hormones, and Chloe suspected that her appetites were more than what boys her age could handle, even back then. Ben seemed more than up to the challenge as he guided her to the dining table and backed her up against it, his lips still on hers. She wrapped her legs around his waist to draw him closer, and took her time unbuttoning his shirt, finally pushing it from his shoulders, revealing the octopus made of lines and shadows that moved when he moved.

"You're so beautiful," she whispered, running her fingertips across his clavicle, down his bare belly to where that perfect little trail disappeared.

His smile had the effect of a shrug, like he was brushing it off, like it didn't matter. When he pulled her sweater over her head and murmured that she was the sexiest woman he'd ever met, she accepted it as gospel, arching her back and pressing her breasts into his bare chest. She felt jittery with desire, trembling and poised to scream out her pleasure the second he touched her.

"Are you cold?" he asked softly, running his palms down her shins, around her calves, up the fronts of her shaky thighs.

"No," she murmured. "I just want you."

He leaned over her to kiss her throat, the feeling of his scratchy stubble against her skin nearly enough to push her over the edge. He brought his lips to her ear, drawing her earlobe gently into his mouth before whispering her name. She thought of their phone calls in Vermont, their voices hushed and breathless in the dark.

The record had stopped playing, and the ragged hum of Ben's breathing was the only sound in the room. He eased himself into her with a low groan, elevating her hips to meet him while she writhed beneath him on the cool wood. She watched his face as he found his rhythm, and his hair fell across his eyes. His shoulders tensed and relaxed, the muscles lean and strong, golden even in the winter from a lifetime in the sun.

"Don't stop," she breathed.

Don't stop, Charlie, she nearly said, squeezing her eyes shut to will away that name and the image of *his* chest, *his* mouth, the curves and planes of *his* body. She gripped his arms and bit her own lip so she wouldn't say his name. Ben cried out and collapsed against her, his cheek on her chest as he worked to catch his breath, completely unaware of her near mistake.

Getting ready for bed together didn't feel the way Chloe feared it might when she was packing her toothbrush and racking her brain to try to remember the last time she'd spent the night at a man's house. Like with the dancing and the sex, she and Ben moved gracefully around each other, making room at the sink and pulling down the top of the quilt to slide between the sheets without ever discussing who would sleep on which side.

It was as if they had performed the ritual hundreds of times before, and when he leaned over to kiss her, his minty toothpaste mingling with hers, it all felt so natural, so completely normal. He opened his arms to her, and she lay across his chest, her ear pressed against the steady beating of his heart. His fingertips lightly ran up and down the soft, worn cotton of her T-shirt. She slung her bare leg over his and felt her eyes grow heavy as she drifted toward sleep.

"You should stay," he said softly.

"I am staying. I'm in your bed, not wearing any pants."

"No, I mean, stay here. On Deer Haven."

Chloe lifted her head to meet his eyes, which looked so bright and hopeful, even in the low light of his bedroom.

"Stay here? But I live in Chicago. My whole life is there."

And we just met, Chloe thought. *And I like you. A lot. But I almost just screamed another man's name while we were having sex on your table, and you're still clinging to a stack of love letters from an old girlfriend, and I haven't told you about Lila yet, and all of these secrets are just piling up between us, and this all just feels like a little too much.*

"I know it's soon. But I ... I want to know you."

His words hung between them while she considered her response. She allowed herself to envision a life on Deer Haven, days devoted to exploring the water's edges and weekends spent cooking in Ben's small kitchen. She imagined a sweet little second-floor apartment with polished wood floors and a view of the sea, a space that was twice as big and cost a tenth as much as her place in the city.

She thought about how the water that surrounded them would gleam during the summer months, how she could have a small garden full of raspberries and cucumbers, tendrils of spring peas that would climb up a sun-dappled trellis. She thought of Ben's bread baking in the oven, sex on the kitchen floor, and curling up together in front of the wood stove at night. And despite her best efforts, she thought about Charlie, and how it would feel to know that he was coming and going to and from the island while she was living a whole life on the other side of the trees. Would she still cook for him? What work could she possibly find on a tiny rock in the middle of the ocean?

"I don't know what I would do for a job."

Ben ran his finger around the outer edge of her ear, which would have lulled her to sleep had her mind been quiet. "I think you're smart and resourceful and you'd figure it out," he replied. "Maybe just think about it."

She took a moment to fantasize about opening a restaurant on the island, wondering if, other than the market with their daily breakfast sandwiches, any place could survive year-round. She considered farm-to-table concepts ranging from fine dining to tacos, worrying about the logistics of even being able to get ingredients that weren't produced right on Deer Haven. She thought about a supper club model, a restaurant where diners could share family-style meals based on the catch of the day. She imagined a small Italian place, a gourmet sandwich shop and butchery, a brunch restaurant with ten varieties of mimosas and live music every Sunday, but quickly dismissed them all, concluding that they were stupid, far-fetched, unsustainable for an island of three hundred.

When Ben murmured, "Just think about it," again, she answered with a quiet, noncommittal "Mmmm." She continued to stare into the darkness for the next hour, considering the words of the beautiful man sleeping beneath her, thinking of all the ways it could go so right, and all the ways it could go so, so wrong.

Chapter Seventeen

She woke up tangled in sheets, her hair plastered to one side, the smell of coffee drifting up through the floorboards. She stretched drowsily as Jasper shifted beside her, his wet nose pressed against her arm beneath the quilt.

"Really?" she asked him, scratching his belly as his back legs twitched, running races in his dog dreams.

In the shower, she replayed her conversation with Ben from last night, his words echoing in her ears as she rinsed away his coconut shampoo.

I think you should stay.

Downstairs, he seemed to be making his case, mixing batter for pancakes and using a fork to flip bacon in that old cast-iron skillet. He kissed her good morning, his own hair still damp from the shower, and Chloe found herself powerless to resist tucking that rogue tendril behind his ear. He handed her a cup of coffee, and she curled up in the worn armchair at the edge of the living room, savoring the way the morning sun was washing it in a beam of light, bleaching the faded upholstery even further.

She hoped he wouldn't bring up the idea of her staying—or anything related to what came after this weekend. She needed to tell him about the offer from Lila and was just considering a way to share the news without puncturing their blissful little bubble, when he suggested a morning hike around the island.

"A hike?" she repeated. "I don't know if I brought the right clothes and shoes for that." What she wanted most was to get back into bed with him, to have sex, watch old movies, and eat dry cereal out of the box, their legs intertwined beneath the quilt, to take a shower together and make pasta and do it all again the next day.

"Well, here's the thing," he teased, pretending to look around as if someone might be listening. "A hike is just a walk."

She laughed and agreed, admiring the clear, sapphire sky outside the cottage window and hoping they'd be back in bed by early afternoon.

They left their breakfast dishes in the sink and dressed in layers, Chloe in a cropped hoodie, down coat, and a slouchy red beanie, Ben in his work boots and hunter jacket, the dark green wool turning the greenest parts of his eyes into exclamation points. They headed down the steep and rocky path toward the shore's edge, where the ocean glittered in the sunlight.

The tide was out as they ambled across rocks and over the exposed roots of pines that had dared to grow too close to the shoreline. Jasper led the way, wagging his tail and slapping a paw into an icy tidepool, barking at a duo of seagulls that swooped too low, ever spry despite his old age. Ben held out his hand, and she hesitated for a moment before taking it, realizing that he wasn't offering her stability in her footing. He just wanted to hold it. They walked around the curves of coves while he pointed out his favorite houses perched on the cliffs above them—gable-roofed manors and a few smaller houses like his own, clad in weathered shingles and featuring stout porches with rocking chairs. He led her down the rocky coastline to the beach below a newly-constructed modern home nestled against the trees, its angled geometry featuring wide stretches of glass and black cedar siding. He explained how everyone said they hated the house, claiming that it was an assault on the architectural traditions of the island, but he counted it as one of his very favorites.

"None of these people mind that we're just walking on their beaches? On their property?"

"None of them are here this time of year. Most people who have water views aren't really interested in winter."

"Except for you," Chloe said. *And Charlie.*

"I love it here in the cold months," Ben said. "It makes Islanders feel like the place belongs to them again."

"But where does everyone work? When all the tourists are gone?"

"The ocean doesn't freeze over, you know," he replied, squeezing her hand as they navigated the rocks. "The ferry still runs, people still fish, they still go to school, charter boats, shop at the market, and eat. Our world doesn't stop."

"But so many places close up for the season," she pointed out, remembering the galleries, the ice cream shop, and this alleged bar that he told her about.

"And the people who own those places are lucky. They get to use the off-season to rest, to travel if they want to, or to explore a new thing right here."

"Huh," she said, barely able to consider the concept of an off-season, entire months reserved for "exploring a new thing."

The air was still, and the clear sky inspired them to walk for another hour. Chloe tipped her face to the sun while Ben explained the history of each place they passed, obviously proud to show her around his island. They reached a small peninsula with a lighthouse and a modest cottage attached, the white paint weathered and wind-worn, completely bare in some places from the salty air and sea spray. Chloe found herself wondering if anyone still lived there, if there was a person whose job it was to maintain the property, to beckon to travelers through the fog, to change the bulb.

They stopped to rest, laughing together as Jasper pranced along the water's edge, a giant snarl of seaweed hanging from his mouth. Chloe settled into Ben as they sat on a massive piece of driftwood—an entire length of tree trunk that had been worn velvety smooth and now lived permanently on its side where the large rocks met the smaller ones.

"This is my favorite spot," he sighed. "This place has a great story."

She let her head rest on his shoulder and squinted toward the lighthouse, at the small waves that lapped against the break wall.

"Tell me."

"Well, two sisters grew up here with their parents, who were the caretakers of the lighthouse. One of the sisters fell in love with a fisherman and they got engaged. The fisherman would go out for days at a time, pulling traps, fishing for cod and haddock, and he always told his fiancée that if he was ever lost, he would just look for the light in the lighthouse and he would find his way back to her. Then his boat just disappears. He doesn't come back for three days, five days, a week—"

"Shit, is this a ghost story?"

"No. No ghosts." He chuckled. "So, every night the woman goes up to the top of the lighthouse and moves the light to help him find his way home. Night after night, she does this for weeks. Then, one night she makes her way up the stairs and finds her sister already up there, doing the same thing! The fisherman was in love with both of them, and he had made them both promises, told them both to wait for him, to shine the light like a signal."

"Bastard! Did he ever come back?"

"He never did. And the sisters lived there for the rest of their lives, long after their parents died. And they maintained the lighthouse for fifty years, shining the light every night for their lost fisherman. Never marrying or having families of their own, just living there until they grew too old to care for it anymore, too old to get up all those stairs."

"Ben."

"Mmmm?" He kissed the top of her head through her hat in reply.

"That is the worst story I've ever heard! Why would they just wait like that, for a man who couldn't choose? Who was cheating on them both?"

"Because they were in love with him. And they wanted him to come home."

"But he was probably just shacking up with someone on the mainland or something! He probably had all these different lives he was living."

"Cynic," Ben laughed, pulling her even closer, stretching his long legs in front of him and letting out another contented sigh, as if he truly had all the time in the world.

They spent most of the remaining weekend in bed and on the way to bed. At one point, they were halfway up the stairs when Ben reached for her hip, and she turned to kiss him, which naturally led to Chloe's lower back being pressed into the lip of the sixth step. She loved the feeling of his big hands lathering her hair in the shower, the suds streaming down her belly while he pressed against her back. She whispered his name, always his name, the reality of Charlie feeling more and more distant as the days progressed.

On Saturday afternoon, she was in the kitchen, wearing only his soft, grey T-shirt, when Lila's assistant called. In a hushed tone, Chloe confirmed a meeting in Chicago in two weeks, whispering her cordial appreciation and hastily committing it to the calendar on her phone.

When Ben called to her from his bedroom, she took the stairs two at a time, anxious to return to him, to the warmth of his bed, to her cold feet tucked between his calves. He was sitting up, shirtless and beautiful, the sun just beginning to set outside the window behind him. She slid easily into his hold, his arms around her back, her cheek against his chest. She could smell his shampoo, and as he breathed in the top of her tousled hair, she knew she smelled of coconut too. She didn't want to waste a single minute of the weekend away from his arms.

"I like you," she murmured into his shoulder, her lips grazing his skin as she formed her mouth around the words. She knew it wasn't much, but it was the most she'd ever given to anyone.

"I like you too."

I like you, she repeated to herself, nervous and a little proud.

When they finally tore themselves from his sheets, Ben pulled out a dusty Atlas pasta machine, and Chloe taught him how to mix the dough. They marveled at the almost orange egg yolks from the farm just down the road, reverently separating them from the whites and adding them to the well in the center of their flour mixture. They cut long, flat ribbons of tagliatelle that they topped with ground venison simmered in San Marzano tomatoes and garlic. She told him about recognizing her love of food in Italy, how it was the first place that had validated everything she'd learned from her life on the farm. She described how both her host mother and her own mother had celebrated the simplicity and beauty of quality ingredients, how they would close their eyes and press their noses against the skin of a tomato, inhaling its perfume before pronouncing it to be perfect.

"Maybe we can go there together someday," Ben said, savoring a forkful of his pasta and following it with the Prosecco that Chloe had brought.

"I'd love that," she replied, still wondering how there could possibly be a "we" beyond the edges of Deer Haven.

She marveled again at how easy everything felt, but she worried it was just because they were in a very specific kind of bubble, their secrets unspoken. She didn't have that relentless lure of work, that pull that she always felt was more powerful than exploring the possibilities of a relationship. She didn't have Saturday dinner service or two a.m. cocktails with Steph, stolen smirking glances with David, or the endless, endless task of planning and replanning every plated detail. She didn't have Charlie and his stupid hands in his ridiculous hair, posing in the frame of every doorway in the house, calling to her without saying anything.

For now, it was just Chloe and Ben living their best weekend life, and each night before she fell asleep in his bed, he whispered the word "stay" before pressing his mouth to hers.

She found herself imagining that maybe she could.

On the last night, they were cuddled up atop a quilt on the floor by the wood stove, their clothes in piles around them. As they caught their breath together, Ben ran his fingertips over her back, tracing her spine and the soft curves of her waist.

"These freckles make me crazy," he growled, kissing her bare shoulder, brushing that lower lip across her skin.

She was lying on his chest, her cheek pressed against the rise and fall of his breathing, her leg slung across his legs. The fire cast a golden glow as she studied the profile of his face, the straight angles of his nose and jaw, the blond stubble on his cheek. She brought her fingers to the crinkles around his eye, and he smiled, deepening the lines beneath her touch.

She slowly inhaled, preparing to dive in.

"Has anyone ever broken your heart?" she asked, holding her breath as she waited to see if sadness, anger, or regret made an appearance in his expression.

"Once," he replied without hesitation, gently touching her hip with his knuckles.

"Tell me," she whispered.

"Lauren. We were together here for a couple of years and in Colorado for just over a year," he said softly. "Like I said, I wasn't happy there. I knew I wanted to come back to the island. I convinced her to come back with me."

"What happened?"

He swallowed so hard it made a tiny sound deep in his throat before he answered. "She cheated on me," he admitted. "First with some guy she met in Australia. Then with the stern man on my boat."

"But you fish alone," Chloe pointed out.

"Yeah, now I do."

She closed her eyes, listening to the crackle of the wood in the fire and the calm and even rhythm of Ben's breath.

"I guess they're still together," he continued. "They travel all over the place now. Together."

"Did you ever stay in touch? With either of them?"

"I never spoke to him again. She wrote to me for a while..."

But you never wrote back, even though you kept all her letters. You asked her to marry you, and she said yes and then backed out. Her dog is your dog now.

"I guess even after she left that last time, I was still waiting for her to come back. To come to her senses and come home," he confessed, his voice thick. "For a while, anyway."

"I'm sorry that happened to you."

He shifted slightly beneath her to look at her face. "Has that ever happened to you?" he asked tenderly, brushing her bangs from her eyes.

No, because I'm the Lauren Chase. I'm always the Lauren Chase, she thought as David and then Charlie flashed through her mind.

"When I left Chicago...when I left my restaurant..." she began, unsure of how to go on at first, how to tell her story without Ben associating her with the woman who betrayed him.

She drew a deep breath and released the words in a rush, before she could reconsider. "I left my restaurant because I got caught in an affair with a married man."

"And that married man was my boss—well, actually, his wife was my real boss, and it was stupid, and I'm still not really even sure why I did it, you know? I hate that I did that to another woman. I just... maybe I was different there? Or, I don't know, maybe I wasn't."

She wondered if it was the right time to confess that she'd had sex with Charlie, that she'd once again made a stupid, impulsive choice only because it had felt amazing in the moment. Maybe she wouldn't use the word amazing. She'd tell him about Lila and Chicago, and that she had her career to think about, so she was likely leaving earlier than she'd planned. She opened her mouth to speak, then closed it again, the words catching in her throat.

Ben's silence felt like it would last longer than the fire in the wood stove, like it might stretch on until the sun rose over the harbor outside the cottage. She felt like she'd blown it.

Swallowing the secret of her night with Charlie, she decided the only way forward was to try to forget it had ever happened. She wasn't even sure if Ben would see it as an actual betrayal, and she didn't want to find out. His silence about David wasn't exactly confidence-inspiring.

Then he said, "That must have felt terrible. Losing everything like that."

"It did," she replied with an exhale, tears springing to her eyes, threatening to trail down her cheeks and pool onto his chest. She blinked quickly to make them dissolve. "Do you ever still wish Lauren would come back? I mean, do you still think about her a lot?"

"Honestly, I haven't even thought about her since you...for a while," Ben answered, stretching his arm above his head and affording Chloe a view of the soft underside of the octopus's tentacles. "There comes a point where you need to know when to look forward. Always forward."

She nodded and rolled atop him so her body was stretched the entire length of his as he wrapped his arms around her.

Always forward.

"If I stayed..." Chloe began softly, prompting Ben to shift underneath her so that they were looking at each other again. "If I stayed, what would that look like?"

She was surprised to find herself seeking assurances. Beyond her contracts for work, she'd never asked anyone to really make a commitment to her before. Outside of her restaurants, she had never been willing to make a promise in return.

"It would look like you living on the island. Getting to wake up to the ocean every day. Teaching me how to make more pasta." Ben pulled her against him and brought his cheek to the top of her hair. "And we would be together."

He said it so simply, like it was the easiest thing in the world, and Chloe found herself wondering if it was. She considered her apartment in Chicago, the huge windows that looked down onto the park below and the way the light would greet her in the morning. For just a minute it felt like it was on another planet, way too far from the salty air.

"I'd have to figure out what I would do for work," she said, imagining the misery of private cheffing in the large homes of other rich people, knowing the ins and outs of their family lives, getting a too-close view of their marriages, their personal business. What if she met another Charlie? Or possibly worse yet, what if she continued to work for Charlie when he was on island?

"I think you'd figure it out," Ben replied, a hint of pride at the edge of his voice. "I think you know exactly how to figure things out."

"How about you? With your work. Do you ever think about growing it?"

Ben pressed a kiss to the top of her head and offered a small shrug. "I feel like I'm in the sweet spot right where I am," he said, his voice low and sleepy.

"Do you ever want more?"

"More what?" he murmured, slowly brushing her bangs from her forehead with the side of his thumb.

When she realized that his question was also his answer, she nestled into his side, pressing her body against this man who always wanted her, who'd made his desires completely plain since the day he'd handed her his card at the market. She closed her eyes and drifted toward sleep, the fire warm on her back and shoulders. Ben folded the quilt over her bare skin, covering them both. She hadn't slept on a floor since college, but right now, it felt like the only place she ever wanted to be.

"Mmmm...stay," he whispered, pulling her closer.

She settled further into him and breathed, "Maybe."

Chapter Eighteen

Back at the house the next morning, Chloe watched Emma measure almond butter, oat milk, and some kind of beige powder into Charlie's rocket ship of a blender. The actress was dewy from her workout, her lavender leggings and matching sports bra displaying every toned angle of her slim physique. Emma watched, incredulous, as Chloe slathered a thick slice of bread with butter and raspberry jam.

"You just go for it, don't you?" she asked. "Just eat whatever you want?"

Chloe smiled sympathetically at the other woman, at her flat, sunken stomach and her wide-eyed expression. "I eat when I'm hungry. And I eat what I'm hungry for."

Emma shook her head in amazement before returning her attention to the powder that had grown cakey on the underside of the blender's lid.

"I could never," she said coolly.

"You could if you wanted to. If there was something you wanted enough."

"Not if I hope to ever work again."

Chloe shrugged. "I think of this as my work." She bit into her bread, the jam and butter turning the entire thing into a slice of heaven.

Charlie walked in, towel around his neck, red-cheeked from his workout. Emma handed him a smoothie, and Chloe frowned as he scooped a heaping portion of gray weight-gain powder into the swampy-looking drink.

"Can I make you two something?" Chloe offered. "Eggs? French toast? I have some beautiful berries in the fridge."

"We're good," Emma answered for them both, her voice clipped.

Chloe watched as the actress stood on her toes to plant a kiss on Charlie's lips before bouncing out of the room, a blur of taut and perky lavender.

He smiled apologetically and cleared his throat. He looked nervous. "She's leaving today," he said softly, casting his eyes to the floor.

"Charlie. It's OK."

He just shrugged and sipped his smoothie, wincing as the chalky sludge hit his tongue.

"Let me make you some real food," she insisted.

"Nah, I really am good." He wiped his mouth delicately on the back of his hand. "Maybe a big dinner, though? I need to talk to you about something."

"OK," she replied, swallowing hard and trying to sound more casual than bewildered.

Charlie focused his attention on his phone, tapping out a text while a crease formed between his furrowed eyebrows.

"So, good. Dinner then," he stated absently, tucking his phone into his back pocket and smiling weakly as he strode from the kitchen and stomped up the stairs, sounding as if he was taking the steps three at a time.

She texted her sister.

I think I'm about to get fired.

Why do you think that?

Charlie is acting weird. Emma is still here. Everything is weird.

Don't worry about it. You have a contract for three months. Want me to check with his biz manager?

No, I'll just keep you posted.

How was the weekend with the sexy lobsterman? 🦞🔥

Kind of perfect.

Tell me.

He wants me to stay.

STAY??? OUT THERE?

Chloe smiled, hearing her sister's disbelieving shriek as if they were in the same room. She imagined that Julia had already told Beth, spilled the beans before Chloe even had a chance to respond.

Yes, out here. I don't know…

Are you thinking about it????

Maybe.

She promised to call later to talk about details and possibilities. She'd tell Julia about the offer from Lila, once she'd had time to brace herself for her sister's inevitable warning sirens. It felt strange to keep something so huge from her, and as Chloe continued not to speak of the opportunity that had been laid at her feet, something about offer started to feel a little more off. Julia would surely tell her that Lila's motivations were sinister, and it would be hard to disagree, but she felt she had to at least get a better sense of what she was being offered.

Desperate for something to do, she ran the water for a bath but found herself hesitant to rinse away the scent of Ben's shampoo.

Perched at the edge of the tub, waiting for the water to get hot, she impulsively texted him.

I miss you.

She tossed her phone through the doorway and onto her bed, not waiting for a response, but feeling uncharacteristically giddy about just firing a feeling into the ether like that.

In the bath, she considered her future and ran through potential scenarios.

She could return to Chicago, back to the city that she really did miss, back to her life, back to the restaurant scene she knew. She would start something new, something more rustic and simpler. She could recapture that thrill of building something from the ground up—her food, her vision, everything just as she wanted it. Her experience had taught her that professional scenarios rarely worked out that way, that there were always investors to please, but from the bathtub, she silently asserted that in her next job, she would call the shots. All of them.

Or she could stay on the island and see where this thing with Ben went. There'd be great sex on demand, and they could be happy together, couldn't they? She really liked him—she'd even said it out loud!—but there was something still holding her back, some itchy little rash of uncertainty that gave her pause when she tried to imagine a future for them. She couldn't quite name it, but it had something to do with what she viewed as his overall lack of drive, that absence of desire to accomplish more, to see more, to do more. A weekend at his cottage was one thing, but she wondered again if it could always feel that good.

And then there was the ghost of Lauren Chase. Chloe wasn't sure if Ben's wounds had really healed, and if she stayed, would she continue to open that desk drawer, reaching her fingers to the back until they found that well-worn stack of envelopes bound in a rubber band? Would she pull out that photo again, smoothing that little wrinkle at the corner and squinting at the way his arm draped across her tanned shoulder? If one day they did disappear, would she assume he'd just found a new place for them, or would she decide that he'd most definitely tossed them into the fire of the wood stove? And what would it all say about her if she continued to search for them? She didn't want to carry the baggage of all that doubt.

She drained the tub and saw that he'd texted back, her worries receding.

I miss you too…a lot. Is tomorrow too soon to see you?

Chloe brought her fingertips to her lips and found them smiling, a blush slowly rising in her cheeks. She tried correcting her face into a neutral expression, but then she thought about the way it had felt to breathe, "I like you," into his shoulder a day ago, and decided to try giving herself over to the giddiness, at least for a little bit.

Dinner that night with Charlie was a quiet affair. Janey had picked up Emma and shuttled her to the charter plane earlier in the afternoon, and the actress had delivered quite a performance, singing out, "Janey!" as if she and the caretaker were long-lost friends. Chloe had to hide her snicker when she saw the old woman's tight smile and tense shoulders as Emma air-kissed each of her cheeks.

Now, across the banquette table, Charlie was digging into his second helping of chicken and biscuits, spooning the thick gravy of peas, carrots, and tender thigh meat onto his plate while she picked at her arugula salad.

"This is so good," he said. "It's exactly why, I mean, it's kind of what I wanted to talk to you about."

"Biscuits?"

"No," he laughed, meeting her gaze, his smile appearing tentative, almost nervous. "Coming with me back to L.A."

Chloe set down her fork and leaned back, inviting him to

continue, even though she was tempted to shout, "Oh, for fuck's sake!" and run from the room. It felt like everyone was proposing to her—first Lila, then Ben with his whispered pleas of "stay," and now Charlie, who looked disarmingly sweet as he leaned forward over his plate.

"So, I'm headed back sooner than I expected. The studio wants me for rehearsals next week. I know you planned on being out here for a bit longer, and so did I, but I have to go where the work is, right? And I was thinking, maybe you could keep working for me in L.A. I still have to focus on gaining some weight, and beyond that, I know you can cook pretty much anything. Maybe you could just keep doing what you do so well, and you could do it out there. For me, I mean... with me," he explained in a rush. "We can work out all the details, but we wouldn't live together out there like this, obviously."

"Obviously," Chloe replied, stunned at his overture.

"You could, though. Live there. If you wanted. I have a guest house in the back," he offered. "But I wanted to see what you thought. You know. About working together some more."

She blinked at him, at a complete loss for words. It was hard to imagine that only last month she'd felt she was out of options, that she'd so dramatically needed to regroup that she'd come to this big house in the middle of the sea to figure out her life. And then she met Ben, and then Charlie, and she remembered what it felt like to cook for a person rather than in service to a concept. But she didn't want to be Charlie's personal chef. She didn't want to be anyone's personal chef. She wanted to create something of her own.

When she closed her eyes at night, whether she was restlessly tossing in her bed at Charlie's place or warm and still beneath the pile of quilts at Ben's, she saw a restaurant. She'd sift through menu concepts and names before she drifted off, imagining how she'd design the kitchen, even picking out place settings for the dining room. She imagined a small wine cellar, a trusted sous chef, a roster of dishes that reflected the growing season. And it was all hers. She wondered if she could ever find a way to attain that sense of ownership with Lila's money. As she looked into Charlie's hopeful blue eyes, she also feared that she couldn't possibly achieve it *without* Lila's money.

"Or I'm sure Julia could help you get set up there with a great place because she knows everyone, and we could figure this out in a way that really works for you," he hurriedly explained, his voice soft. "I think we could figure it out."

"Charlie, look," she began.

"It's OK." He smiled sadly across the table. "I didn't think you'd go for it."

"It's not that I'm not flattered. I am. I just need to think about getting back to my career, you know?"

And I desperately need to get outside of your orbit because I'm afraid I won't stop making bad decisions as long as I'm around you.

He looked crestfallen, his shoulders low. "Is that a definite no then?"

"It's a definite *I need some time to think*," she explained, her head spinning.

"I get it. I do," he replied, fiddling with his phone, turning it over again and again in his hands.

"And I'm...I'm sorry you're leaving early," Chloe said quietly, thinking about how she had just started to get settled in the house, how she had finally gotten used to the clanging of the pipes when the shower first turned on, how she now felt at home in the kitchen. "But you don't really even need a chef here. Do you think you'll really need one in L.A.?"

He shrugged before looking directly at her with those turquoise eyes, nearly knocking her from her seat with what he said next.

"I just really like you."

He gave her a small smile as his dimple showed itself, and she forgot to breathe for a moment. When he reached out and softly brushed her bangs to the side, she hoped he didn't notice her sharp and sudden intake of breath.

"I like you a lot," he continued. "And I trust you. And I think we could be great together."

As what? She wanted to shout, unnerved by the cryptic words that he was trying to pass off as directness. *As friends? As employer and employee? As more?*

"And if you worked for me—"

"Charlie, you don't need to put me on the payroll to be your friend, you know," she interrupted.

"I'm not saying that," he replied, looking wounded.

"Well, I don't know what you're saying. You're distracting me from what I really need to be focusing on right now," she said, not sure if she meant Ben, her career, or both. "I just...I can't put myself in a position where I always need to talk myself out of you."

But there was something inside of her that couldn't be denied, a small part of her that wanted to just say yes, to agree to everything he was offering just to see what would happen next, despite Ben's repeated pleas of *stay* and every other opportunity that still hung in the air. She was starting to feel like she was living multiple lives, in one mode when she was in the comforting embrace of the lobsterman's cottage, in another when she imagined a return to her real life in Chicago, and slipping back into yet another when she was on Pine Point Road, involved in whatever the hell this was.

"I didn't ask Emma to come, remember?"

"It's not about Emma," Chloe explained, her tone softening. "I just have a lot to think about."

She still didn't mention Ben or the fact that she was considering Deer Haven, but she did tell him about the call with Lila Harris, the meeting they had planned, and how she would have the chance to build a brand-new place, trusting that she and Lila were on board with each other's terms. As she described the concepts that she'd begun toying with, outlining how she would present them to the management group when they met in Chicago, it wasn't lost on her that Charlie was now the only other person who knew.

"But you already built a restaurant," he said, sullenly helping himself to a chocolate walnut brownie from the plate she had set in front of him. "Even with everything that happened, you don't want to try to get Redbud back?"

"It's not mine anymore," she explained. "I gave up on it."

"But you made it what it was."

"I just don't think I want to cook that kind of food right now," she said, swallowing the lump in her throat, picturing her past self using tweezers to move a single flake of salt atop the thread of a microgreen. "Or maybe ever again."

As she asserted it with confidence, she realized it was feeling closer to being true.

Charlie nodded, a brownie crumb clinging to his lower lip. She began to reach out her fingers to brush it away but stopped herself. She pictured California with Charlie—where they might have sex again, where she'd fall in love with the farmers' markets and vow to never return to a climate that didn't have a twelve-month growing season. She pictured jetting off with him when he flitted around the globe to shoot the travel show, being by his side as they hiked into volcanoes, learned to scuba dive, tasted hundred-year-old eggs in Hong Kong and jackfruit in India. She could see her sister anytime she wanted, be the devoted auntie that she knew she could be. Would she join Soul Cycle? Would any of it make her happy? Would she think of Ben, of his golden hair and crinkly eyes, remembering how it had felt when she finally let him take her hand as they walked along the rocky shoreline?

"I just think we could...have fun together," Charlie said with an almost shy smile, that dimple nearly undoing her.

"Charlie. I think my iPod is older than you. You don't know what you want yet."

"But what if I do?"

She cast her eyes toward the window to avoid his gaze, fearing that she'd fall into some kind of trance if she looked at him.

"You could stay, you know. If you don't come with me," he finally acquiesced.

"Stay here? In the house?"

"Yeah, I mean, I won't be back until summer, but you could stay here as long as you want to, as long as you need, until you figure out your next thing. Janey could check in on you. I'll obviously still be paying you through April like we planned," he explained.

It felt uncomfortable to be discussing money again, somehow wrong to be starkly reminded that theirs was designed to be a professional arrangement, and nothing more. Suddenly, she desperately wanted to be with Ben, settled in the crook of his arm by the wood stove, winding that lock of hair around her finger, matching her breathing to his like a meditation.

"I think it would feel weird to stay here," she eventually replied.

"It wouldn't have to."

"But it would."

"I understand," he said before rising from the table with his hands buried in his pockets, leaving his dirty dishes behind for Chloe to clean up.

Chapter Nineteen

Janey had insisted on making good on her dinner invitation, demanding that Chloe bring Ben. As the two of them bounced down the winding road to the boatyard in the cab of his truck, he turned up the radio and squeezed her knee through her jeans, the sound of Van Morrison filling the air between them. He was beautiful in the dim light of dusk, when the sun had sunk behind the pine trees, and shadows were cast across his softly stubbled face.

"You know where they live?"

"I do," he answered with a smile.

"Right. Island."

The elderly man who greeted them at the door was older than Janey, easily in his eighties, with kind blue eyes that could only be described as "twinkling" set in his weathered and wrinkled face. He walked with a crooked gait that reminded Chloe of her father, that same telltale lumber that was equally spry and limping, a sure sign that he had spent his life doing physical labor.

"Hey, Bob," Ben said, gripping the old man's hand with equal strength.

"Bob Higgins." He extended his leathery palm to Chloe. "You must be the chef!"

Chloe shook his hand as Bob invited them into their modest,

immaculate farmhouse. Every room was a lesson in tidiness, each surface polished to a mirrored sheen. Chloe took in the antique lamps, the braided rugs, the bounty of doilies, and realized it was like stepping into the dollhouse of her childhood dreams.

"Hello, hello!" Janey called, emerging from the kitchen as she wiped her hands on her floral apron. "I'm so happy you both came!"

She gave Chloe a big, warm hug and delivered the same to Ben, adding a kiss to his cheek. Chloe handed her a bottle of wine along with a loaf of ciabatta, freshly baked by Ben that morning.

"It smells amazing in here, Janey. Can I help?"

"Oh my gosh, no. Give yourself a night off!" Janey exclaimed. "It's beef stew in the crockpot. Nothing fancy, but it's Bob's favorite."

Ben and Bob disappeared in the basement so that the old man could show off the new deep-sea fishing reel he had built, leaving the chef and the caretaker alone in the kitchen.

"So, how's it going there with Charlie?" Janey poured them each a small glass of wine, and they sat down at the doily-topped dining table.

"It's been...surprising."

"We know he's leaving earlier than planned, right?"

"He talked to me about it last night. That part wasn't that surprising, I guess."

Janey sipped her wine and touched Chloe's hand. "It really is OK if you stay in the house, you know," she said, obviously aware of at least one of the offers that Charlie had made.

"I know. It just doesn't feel right, being there alone. You know, if I'm not working or anything."

Janey nodded and rose to her feet, pulling bowls from a cabinet and worn cotton napkins from a drawer, handing them to Chloe to place around the table.

"It was really good for him to have you there, you know. To have someone to talk to. To make sure he ate," Janey said.

"I hope so," she replied softly, trying her best to thwart the blush that she could feel rising to her cheeks.

"It hasn't been easy for him. Losing his parents. Attaching himself to some not great people," the caretaker continued. "And everyone always wanting something from him, like that awful woman."

Chloe bit back a smile, remembering how Janey had gone rigid when Emma leaned in for that overly familiar hug.

"He struggles when he's alone," Janey continued. "I think it's easier now, but in the beginning, it was so hard. He would call me in the middle of the night. He would have these nightmares, and I would just talk to him until he calmed down enough to go back to sleep. He didn't have anyone else to call. He was just a kid."

Chloe took in Janey's misty eyes and swallowed the lump that had formed in her own throat. She thought again about Charlie's moods, how they could swing from aloof to needy, searching to distant within seconds. She considered the moments in which he'd trusted her enough to give her a tiny peek at his wounds. She refused Janey's offer of more wine out of fear that she was getting too weepy, just as the men clomped back up the basement stairs.

"Are you fellas ready for some supper?" Janey asked, ladling stew into bowls before they had a chance to answer. She had warmed and sliced Ben's beautiful bread and presented it in the middle of the table in a linen-lined basket.

Everyone complimented Janey on the food, especially Bob, who confessed how lucky he felt to have married such a good cook almost fifty years ago. Janey beamed and praised her husband, who had grown the potatoes, onions, and carrots in his garden. Chloe was just starting to tell the Higginses about her own family's farm when a knock sounded from the front door. Bob got up from the table and returned with Charlie in tow, his hair tousled and his perfect face appearing freshly scrubbed.

"I'm sorry I'm so late. And you're already eating! I hope I'm not being rude." Charlie hugged Janey and then Bob, who slapped him on the back affectionately.

"No, no! There's plenty, and it's all still hot," Janey assured him. "You know us, we're not formal here."

"Oh. Hey, man." Charlie held out his hand as if noticing Ben for the first time.

Ben stood halfway and shook it, displaying a certain set of his jaw that was so subtly tense, she likely wouldn't have noticed it had she not been deliberately looking. She gave Charlie an awkward little wave as he greeted her with a corny, "Long time, no see." She was annoyed that he had obviously driven her rental car to get there, which was ridiculous considering that he'd been paying for the hatchback since she picked it up at the airport in Portland weeks ago.

Janey served Charlie a bowl of stew, and he echoed everyone's sentiments about its deliciousness before proclaiming, "How lucky am I to have such great cooks feeding me?" which visibly delighted the caretaker. She put her arm around his shoulders and pulled him in for a sideways hug.

"Ben made the bread!" Chloe blurted out. "It's amazing."

"You're kind of a renaissance man, aren't you?" Charlie said as his eyes met Ben's across the table. "Lobsters, bread, what can't you do?"

Ben responded by offering a tight smile, the rigidity in his jaw deepening as he pressed his leg against Chloe's under the table. She reached for his big hand and squeezed.

"Where did you learn how to do that? Is there a baking school here on Deer Haven?" Charlie pressed, selecting a small piece of Ben's bread and setting it against his soup bowl.

"Just books, and online, I suppose," he said as he leaned back in his chair and met Charlie's gaze.

"I'm more of a 'learn by doing' kind of guy myself," Charlie asserted with an ill-timed wink in Chloe's general direction. "I mean, I wish acting was just as simple as reading a book."

"I'll bet you do," Ben replied evenly, his signature composure unruffled.

"So, back to California, huh, kiddo?" Bob asked, seemingly unfazed by the low-level frictions between his dinner guests.

"Yeah, back to work, but I'm excited," Charlie replied, pouring himself some water from a rooster-shaped pitcher and sending a pointed look toward Chloe. "I just hope I can convince this one to come with me."

He went on to tell Bob and Janey all about his HBO series, how he hoped it was going to be the project that changed everything for him, and Chloe could *feel* Ben's gaze on the side of her face as she clutched his hand a little harder under the table. She hadn't said a word to him about Charlie's offer, simply adding it to her arsenal of secrets, and she certainly hadn't wanted the subject to come up this way.

The topic shifted to island politics, and Charlie locked eyes with Chloe, smirking in a way she found irritatingly mischievous. She shot him a stern look, and he grinned, prompting her to concentrate on buttering her bread as if it were a complex puzzle to be solved. Charlie hadn't touched his own bread, but he asked for seconds and then thirds on dessert. Chloe tried to help Janey with the dishes before she was affectionately shooed away with a dishtowel.

When they expressed their thanks and bid their farewells, she felt very much part of a unit as Ben handed her coat to her. As she slid her arms into the sleeves, she tried to catch his eye, but he was busy accepting a container of leftovers from Janey. She wondered if they would talk about everything on the way back to the cottage, if they would have their first argument, or if it would all just dissipate into the apple crisp-scented air of Janey's house, undiscussed and left behind.

Hugs and handshakes were exchanged, and as Janey pulled her into one of her wonderful embraces, she spoke softly into Chloe's ear.

"Hold onto him, honey. He's a really good one," the kindly woman whispered, leaving Chloe hoping that it was indeed Ben she was talking about.

In the truck, they were barely out of the driveway when Ben's agitation finally spilled over. "Ugh, what an asshole."

"Bob?" Chloe joked, a futile attempt at lightening his dark mood.

"Charlie." They rode in silence for a few minutes before he said softly, "You didn't tell me he asked you to go with him."

"It was nothing. I didn't even really consider it."

Lie.

"Not even with your sister out there and everything?"

"No."

Lie.

"Why not?" He asked as he squinted at the road, obviously needing something, wanting to hear something.

"Because I don't want to be someone's personal chef," she shrugged, every other transgression, every ounce of uncertainty and hope and desire settling like a stone at the back of her throat.

Ben nodded thoughtfully, his jaw tension nearly gone. "Yeah, I think you know you can do a lot better."

"Exactly."

Back at the cottage, he lit a fire and poured them each a bourbon. She winced as the liquid burned its way down her throat, but she found herself enjoying how it settled with warmth in the pit of her belly. They turned on a movie, something stupid that didn't capture her attention, and she focused instead on Ben's arm around her shoulder, her legs across his lap, the dog snoring by the woodstove, that octopus that revealed itself from the edge of his sleeve.

Later, they fell asleep with their arms around each other beneath the quilt on his bed. As Chloe matched her breathing to his and waited for her feet to warm against his bare calves, she thought about Janey's words and how holding onto someone wasn't so bad.

Chapter Twenty

Ben insisted on picking Chloe up the next afternoon, proclaiming that he wanted to take her somewhere to show her "something special."

"You're not going to blindfold me or anything, are you?" she teased.

"Maybe later," he shot back, moving his hand to her inner thigh and making her squirm beside him.

As always, she was happy to be back in the cab of his truck, cocooned in his gorgeous Ben scent. They passed an oil delivery truck headed in the opposite direction, and as he waved to the elderly man behind the wheel, Chloe noticed a silver-haired woman pressed against the driver, a serene smile on her face.

"That's Jim and Nancy Bowen," Ben explained. "She's been riding with him on his delivery route for...geez, I dunno, as long as I've been alive."

"She just goes with him every day?" Chloe asked, smiling at the sweet notion that an eighty-year-old woman might not have anything better to do, but soon frowning at the realization that a forty-year-old woman likely had. "And she always sits next to him like that? All cuddled up?"

Chloe decided to try it out, unbuckling her seat belt and closing the gap between the two of them. She pressed the side of her leg against his and fastened the lap belt in the center of the old truck's bench seat. She leaned her head on his shoulder, and he wrapped his free arm around her, pulling her closer while he drove. She looked up at his face, at the way the sun made the hair curling from his winter hat look like spun gold. She kissed his cheek, and he smiled like Nancy Bowen all the way to their top-secret destination, a ramshackle little building in the center of town, right across from the ferry dock. The faded lettering on the wooden sign spelled out "Fresh Fish" in a color she guessed had once been red, and the worn gray shingled siding looked weathered nearly to the point of disintegration.

"Here we are!" Ben cheerfully announced.

"At the haunted fish market?"

"Just keep an open mind," he laughed, leading her by the hand.

She shot him a bewildered look as he pushed through the unlocked door like he owned the place, holding it open with his long arm so she could enter behind him.

"Are we supposed to be in here?"

"I had Ginny Brown unlock it for us. She's the realtor."

Chloe hesitated at the threshold for a few beats before entering the empty space, her wet boots marking the dusty wood floor. The sun streamed in through the large windows, and she squinted at Ben through the particles that floated between them, illuminated by the afternoon light.

"What are we doing here? I mean, what is this?"

"It's just...a possibility," he said, a little shy. "It's to show you that maybe there *is* something for you out here. That you could build something for yourself."

"In here?" she asked, taking in the dingy ceiling and the ancient, chipping Formica counter. She didn't even want to know what was lurking in the back, where the plaster ceiling appeared to be collapsing into the shadows. She pointed at the front window, wondering if Ben had noticed the four-foot crack that ran across it.

"Broken things can be fixed, you know," he reminded her, lifting a corner of battered linoleum in the entryway and finding that it covered the same beautiful wood floor that ran throughout the rest of the space.

"This is just...a lot."

"I'm not proposing marriage, Chloe. I just think you can do anything."

She opened her mouth to protest and then closed it again as she continued to look around. It was just one big room with the counter and case that ran across the back and a large area behind the wall for storage...or for a kitchen. The natural light was ample, and the shiplap walls and black farmhouse pendants were already starting to win her over.

She ran her hand along the vintage fish case, admiring its retro light blue enamel and tracing its curves. She smiled at Ben, and all at once she could see it—the floors refinished to a honeyed sheen, a scattering of small wood tables and metal bistro chairs, the fish case restored to its former glory and filled with pastries. Diners would reach the front door by a stone path lined with blooming lavender, echinacea, and large mounds of mint. There would be lobster rolls on fresh brioche buns, oyster chowder made golden from a pinch of saffron, and fritters of mussels and fresh herbs. And there would be pie—strawberry rhubarb early in the summer, blueberry lime in July, and peach when the precious Amish produce made its way up to New England. She could almost taste it all.

Ben's green eyes continued to sparkle. "It's been empty for a few years. Ginny told me that it would sell for practically nothing. I mean, you'd have to put some money into it, but this spot gets busy in the summer with everyone getting off the ferry."

"But..." she began, unsure of how her sentence would end.

"And she gave me a rough estimate, but I could even do some of the work for you. I could strip these old floors, and I could help you get set up with some vendors."

"So, it would be *ours?*"

"No, it would be yours," he asserted as he smiled and spread his arms, gesturing to the space. "And you could do it without an investor. Maintain total control. I mean, I'm sure you have tons of offers coming in by now, but are you thinking about something else?"

"No," she replied, dismayed by how easy it felt to withhold the truth. "I don't...I don't know what to say."

"Just say you'll think about it."

He wrapped his arms around her, and she was reminded of that day on his boat, when he shielded her from the wind as she struggled to find her footing. She was already so used to the feeling of their bodies leaning against each other, of his chin resting on the top of her head. As she lifted her face for his kiss, she promised him she would think about all of it.

On the short drive to his cottage, he pulled off the main road and navigated his truck down a barely plowed path. Before Chloe could ask where they were going, the narrow road opened into a wide view of the ocean. He stopped the truck at the edge of a small cliff, keeping the engine running for heat as they gazed at the glittering water beneath the sinking sun.

They grinned at each other and unbuckled their seatbelts. In less than three seconds, Chloe was straddling his lap, the seams of her jeans grinding against his as the steering wheel pressed into the small of her back. His mouth was on her mouth, on her throat, and when he unzipped her jacket and reached his hand under her sweater, she giddily felt like she was in high school again, breaking curfew to drive around with the boy she liked. As they rocked against each other, giggling at the bulk of their coats and making out like teenagers, all wet tongues and bitten lips, she wondered if it could always be like this.

She leaned against him, and when he said, "Chloe, I think —," she cut him off, silencing his beginning with her mouth on top of his, somewhat certain of what he was about to say, but still too scared to find out for sure.

Chapter Twenty-One

Everything started to melt a few days later when a warm front elbowed its way through winter and brought unseasonably mild temperatures to the island. Chloe was in Ben's bed when she bolted upright at two a.m., worried that the roof was leaking after hearing the rhythmic dripping in her dreams. She quickly realized it was just the snow turning to water atop the cottage. "Spring thaw," he mumbled into his pillow, tugging her back toward him. She was more than happy to settle her bare back against the warmth of his chest and fall asleep for another few hours.

Chloe had fallen into a new rhythm on Deer Haven. She would wake up early at Ben's and then head to Charlie's to prepare his breakfast and plan for dinner while the lobsterman was out on the water. She baked cinnamon bread and challah, buttery loaves that she twisted and braided before cloaking them with a dishtowel to proof, slapping Charlie's hand like a mom when he passed through the kitchen and dared to peek underneath. She enticed him with polenta topped with a lamb ragu, lobster pot pie, and a seared scallop and risotto dish that he confidently declared was the best thing she'd ever made. She watched as his face started to fill out, his angles becoming softer, his chest and shoulders growing noticeably bulkier because of the extra calories and his altered workout regimen.

Outside of meals, they barely saw each other. Once at lunchtime, when she was pureeing sweet potato soup in that ridiculous blender, and Charlie commented on the fact that she wasn't around very much anymore, she pretended she couldn't hear him over the deafening whir of the motor. She spent most of the day in the kitchen, and he was consumed with his scripts, preparing for rehearsals with a focus that she hadn't known he was capable of. He did ask her to run lines with him once, and after he laughingly told her to "stop doing a voice," she found that it was actually fun to watch him work.

"Remember when you said that cooking was a lot like acting?" she asked. "This feels a lot like cooking. The repetition, the fine-tuning. Do you know how many oysters I had to shuck, how many chickens I needed to debone, repeating the movements over and over until it all just became muscle memory?"

"How many?" he asked, his aqua eyes dancing.

"Well, I don't have an exact count or anything. But a lot."

Their eyes met, and she swore she could hear him even though neither of them had spoken.

You get me, his expression said.

I know, she wordlessly replied with resignation.

When they were together, his offer to join him in L.A. hung between them, just like the subject of the old fish market did when she was with Ben. Though she couldn't stop thinking about that sun-drenched, empty space, she worried that if she built something on Deer Haven, people wouldn't come, that they would dismiss her as just another city person looking to disrupt life on the island. She wondered if chefs had arrived before her and tried the very same thing, failing when summer tourism led to the lean months of winter. She knew she could cook anything, anywhere, but she'd never owned a place before, and as much as she craved the autonomy, she found herself wondering if she could do it, if she would actually like it. There were questions unanswered, and she did her best to stuff down the angst of how unsettled everything felt, all while counting down the days until the meeting with Lila.

After she made dinner for Charlie every evening, she headed back to Ben's house, where he was always waiting for her with his hair still damp from the shower and dinner for two underway. He was working his way through the tattered Jacques Pepin cookbook he'd checked out of the library and confessed was overdue by two weeks. He made her a flawless French omelet and followed it up with an apple galette —he had overworked the pastry, though she had no plans to tell him, as it was still delicious.

Her meeting with Lila was fast approaching, and Chloe knew she had to find the right moment to be honest with Charlie about his job offer. Between the unknowns in Chicago and the possibilities on island, she couldn't devote any more bandwidth to the ridiculous idea of giving it a go with a movie star in L.A.

Then, over breakfast burritos, Charlie confessed that he and Emma were going to "give things another try," and that he had plans to move into her Malibu house when he returned to the West Coast.

"Wow, I'm surprised," Chloe blurted out, irritated as she watched him douse his breakfast with hot sauce.

Have you forgotten that you offered me something? she wanted to demand. *And true, I might not be really considering it, but I haven't officially said no yet, even though all signs are obviously pointing to no.*

He shrugged and took a bite. "It just seems like the natural step."

"Does it?"

"Well, we always find our way back to each other in the end. And she knows where I come from, because she's from the same place, you know?"

But you're not a wolf like her, Chloe wanted to say. *You're a little bit broken, and she'll swallow you whole if you let her.*

"Well, it sounds like you have it all figured out," she managed instead, the tightness of her smile making her cheek twitch.

"And you have your big meeting in Chicago."

The truth was, Chloe still hadn't determined whether it would be a one-way or a round-trip ticket. She'd confirmed her meeting details again with Lila's assistant, but she hadn't been able to bring herself to decide what would happen after that. Especially since she hadn't told Ben, or even Julia, yet.

She'd always thought of herself as someone who was perpetually quick on her feet. The way she could pivot a plan, rethink a dish, and make a quick decision based on instinct was one of her superpowers in every kitchen she had ever run. But something about all the options on the table had her feeling paralyzed now, unable to act beyond the food she was preparing for Charlie every day. And she couldn't stop considering the fantasy of the old fish market, of what she could build there. She hadn't even had a chance to see how that beautiful natural light would look in the summer.

"I knew you couldn't come with me," Charlie said softly, letting her off the hook. "It's OK."

"A part of me really wanted to."

He lifted his shoulders in a slow shrug, and Chloe met his eyes across the table. She studied his dark lashes, his thick brows, and the faint and tiny line of a scar at his temple that she had never noticed before. They smiled at each other again, Chloe's grin hesitant and close-lipped, Charlie's wide enough to activate his dimple.

"It was a long shot. I knew it was," he said. "You want more."

Chloe nodded, surprised at the lump in her throat, at the pinpricks of impending tears behind her eyelids. She got up to pull a dish of ratatouille from the oven and cleared her throat to cover the sniffle that escaped her.

Charlie had asked, Chloe had hesitated, and he had made plans outside of her rather than deal with the rejection. She asked herself if she could have saved him from the She-Wolf and quickly dismissed the idea. It wasn't her job to save Charlie Davis from anything.

But she couldn't stop wondering why the moment felt so much like a breakup.

She walked down the rocky path to the beach and called her sister. As she waited for Julia to pick up, she took a moment to marvel at how dramatically the landscape had changed in the past week. The snow was completely gone—it was like the storm had never even happened. Dark mosses had appeared on some of the rocks, and as she began her descent toward the water, she spotted a few brave crocuses peeking out of the ground as if they'd been there all along.

Chloe told her sister about Lila and the Chicago meeting. She described the old fish market, outlining exactly what she would do with the space, practically reciting the menu that she'd already designed. And she explained the situation with Charlie, how he'd asked her to come back with him to L.A., how he was now planning on moving in with Emma.

"Jesus Christ, Chlo. You could've ended up working for the She-Wolf!" Julia bellowed.

After they joked about the prospect of the chef becoming a professional kale massager and an expert on gluten-free breads, Chloe attempted to explain the progression of events with Charlie.

"I don't know," she began, "he asked me to work for him out there, but it was like he already knew I would say no, and then a few days later he tells me that he's going to live with Emma in Malibu, like maybe that plan was already in motion."

"Like he just had to take his shot with you first. Before committing to her."

Chloe zipped her jacket against the wind and shook her head. "No, I don't...it was just a job offer."

"Was it?"

In the distance, the ferry chugged across the harbor, and she watched three seagulls glide across the now cloudy sky, wondering if Charlie did have feelings for her. It seemed impossible. She'd successfully pulled away from him in the last week, focusing her attention on her food, on Ben, on the actually viable options that continued to swirl inside her head. Charlie was and would always be just a shiny distraction from her real life, and even though she'd declined his offer, she hated that little tremble of thrill she still felt at the idea that she'd somehow been chosen by him.

"I'm just...I guess I'm just surprised by the way he asked. And his reaction. He seemed sad."

"And what about you? Are you sad about it?"

"I don't know. Maybe a little? *I don't know.* I guess I could have imagined myself out there. For like a minute."

"Chloe? Did you catch feelings for Charlie Davis?"

The chef made a scoffing sound that sounded less than convincing.

"Did you?" Julia demanded.

"No!" She insisted. "No. He just...he just wasn't what I expected. Or I don't know, maybe he was exactly what I expected."

She thought about the sparks that crackled whenever Charlie was in the room, how she became almost overcharged, buzzing with electricity when he stood too close. She remembered how he'd remained distant even as he was pulling her closer, recalling all the times he disappeared when she found herself wanting more, even while she held out her arm to assert her own requirements for distance. She realized that was part of the appeal—that space, the boundaries, the utter lack of strings.

And then she thought about Ben, how he was always offering himself to her, forever generous in how much he was willing to give, in how much he had already given. She pushed away the nagging voice that insisted it was all too easy, that it was all too much. Even as they were exploring the old fish market, their wet boots charting every step on the dusty floor, she was well aware of the subtext that hung in the stale air between them: *If I let myself fall in love with this, I let myself fall in love with you.* It felt like he was asking her to commit—not just to the place, but to him—and she still wasn't sure she could.

"And how about The Lobsterman? Is he pressuring you to stay?"

"No, not really," Chloe replied. "He's just showing me that there could be something for me out here if I choose to stay. But I have a chance to set everything right again in Chicago. I ran before I could even sort things out."

"Look. You know I care about your career. But I want you to be happy."

"I know it's weird. Working with Lila sounds crazy. But she and David have split, and I think—"

"I'm not talking about Lila and David. I'm talking about you.

Going back to the city and picking up right where you left off, working those long days, not leaving any time for anything else. It's not healthy."

"Hey, you work crazy hours too," she protested, heading back up the path toward her car.

"Yeah, and I have a hot wife and a baby on the way. And we go to parties and yoga retreats, and we have dinner with friends, and we have a whole life outside of work."

"So, I need to have a partner to have my life in order, according to your standards?"

"Of course not, but you have to make room for something," Julia insisted. "Even if that something you make room for is yourself."

Chloe exhaled slowly and looked up at the sky, at the sun that was now setting and turning the pine trees into black silhouettes. She glanced at the house, where it appeared that Charlie had left every single light on, even though he was probably in the dark basement watching a movie.

"I hate when you know you're right," Chloe grumbled. "You're like the smug therapist I never wanted,"

"Well, let me know when you figure out where I should send my bill."

Driving to Ben's cottage, Chloe attempted to quiet the chaos in her head, reminding herself that she didn't need to decide today, that she could just enjoy Ben's company tonight.

Inside, he was making shrimp tacos, and when he opened the door, he kissed her like they hadn't kissed in weeks, like he'd been waiting to kiss her all day. His arms wrapped around her back, always pulling her closer.

"Hi," he said softly, cupping his hands around her freckled cheeks and kissing her again.

When they finally pulled apart, she was flushed and breathless, and he was still smiling. He tucked that stray curl behind his ear and offered her a beer, leaning into the refrigerator to grab one for each of them.

"I made these for you," she said to Jasper, who had perked up and creaked over to her as soon as she'd walked through the door. She handed him a dog treat.

"You baked cookies for my dog?" Ben asked incredulously as Jasper held the biscuit between his front teeth like a cigar before carrying it to his bed.

"It was nothing," Chloe answered with a shrug. "Just peanut butter, some almond flour, and a few egg whites. I discovered that the secret to perfect texture is baking them twice like biscotti."

"Well, it doesn't sound like nothing. And Jasper definitely approves." He gestured to the old dog, who was currently licking the underside of his paw, surrounded by a snowstorm of crumbs.

She studied Ben's knife skills while he prepped avocado, pineapple, cilantro, and red onion for a salsa. He was very slow, but his cuts were careful, deliberate, and he was just so earnest about it, the way he tucked his hair back and moved his knife through the ingredients. As he warmed a stack of tortillas and sautéed the shrimp, she sipped her beer and continued to watch, not even remotely compelled to give him any tips or make a gesture to help.

"I like watching you."

"Don't make me nervous!" he teased.

She crossed the small kitchen and pressed her body against his back while he tended to the cooktop. Sliding both hands into the front pockets of his jeans, she whispered huskily, "Does this make you nervous?"

"It makes me something, but not nervous."

She rested her cheek between his shoulders, and she wondered how she could possibly give any of this up—the cottage, the dog, the food, the fire in the wood stove, and the beautiful man who always wanted to know her more, who seemed genuinely invested in her happiness, in her pleasure.

She pulled her phone from her pocket and texted her sister, looking to confirm that everything had gone well at Beth's doctor's appointment. Julia responded with an ultrasound photo, a gray and grainy assembly of shapes that could have been anything.

MEET STELLA! she announced in all caps, prompting Chloe to squint at the image again, desperate to see something.

"Oh wow," Ben declared, delivering Chloe a perfectly ripe piece of pineapple and catching a glimpse of her screen. "Is that from your sister?"

"It's their first ultrasound."

Chloe's lips grazed Ben's fingers as she accepted the fruit, her eyes meeting his as she swiped at the juice that dripped down her chin.

"What do you think about all that?"

"It's hard to tell what I'm even looking at," she replied, turning the phone in her hand. "Just some blobs and blurry lines."

"I mean, kids," he chuckled. "What do you think about all *that*?"

She tried not to look for an exit like a burglar caught mid-heist. It was the second time Ben had mentioned his desire for children. Chloe was working overtime, trying to play it cool, trying not to worry about the shrimp that was sizzling in the pan and likely overcooking, trying not to pull the neck of her sweater from her skin in that universal holy-shit-it's-too-hot-in-here gesture.

Couldn't a dog be enough? she wanted to plead. She wondered if this was how Lauren Chase had felt when Ben had proposed, like her clothes were shrinking around her body, threatening to suffocate her.

"Um, I don't really. Think about it, I mean," she confessed, straining to keep her tone even as she drew a slow sip from her beer bottle in a way that she hoped projected an inner calm. She wondered if her cheeks looked as hot as they felt as Ben pressed on.

"You've never pictured a little one by your side in the kitchen? Teaching them how to whisk the pancake batter or baste the turkey?"

"I would never baste my turkey. I brine my turkey," she replied playfully, hoping to shift the topic to something less panic-inducing, like the year she'd cooked Thanksgiving dinner for her entire staff of thirty.

"I just mean you've never even imagined it?"

Chloe shook her head and shrugged, searching Ben's eyes for signs of judgment or disappointment, but they just looked as sweet and green as always, crinkled at the corners and locked onto her own. He turned to squeeze some lime onto the shrimp as she studied the broad plane of his back, attempting to gauge what was going through his head simply by assessing the set of his shoulders.

I care about what this man thinks of me, Chloe realized, surprised by the newness of the feeling. *Just not enough to change my mind.*

Ben assembled their tacos while Chloe gently set "Born to Run" by Bruce Springsteen onto the record player. As Bruce's hoarse drawl delivered stories of the American dream, Ben delivered dinner and fresh beers to the table. The tacos were spicy and delicious, and as Chloe slowly sipped her drink and ran her toes up Ben's calf, up to his inner thigh, and finally into his lap, she felt pure, warm contentment. He rubbed her foot while she closed her eyes, humming with pleasure as she tipped back her head.

When she crossed to his side of the table, sitting sideways on his lap and pressing her lips against his, he tasted like pineapples and beer. She kissed him slowly and softly, pausing to lean her face into the side of his neck as he wrapped his arms around her. This was the part that made *her* nervous—not yet knowing if this was the end of something or just the beginning.

Chapter Twenty-Two

The afternoon that Charlie Davis left Deer Haven was sunny and clear, a "perfect day for a ride on a plane," according to Janey Higgins, who had just appeared at the house to shuttle him to the airfield. Spring had continued to insist on arriving early on the island, and Chloe could feel the still-cold air from the ground rising to meet the warmer temperatures. Practically overnight, daffodils had boldly sprouted up all around the house, their yellow and white bell-shaped blossoms seemingly unafraid of the frosty nights that were still inevitable.

As she helped the caretaker load suitcases into the back of the truck, Chloe couldn't recall Charlie showing up with so many bags. Then she remembered that she hadn't exactly seen him arrive at all, had only heard him climb the creaky stairs as she hid in her bed with the blankets pulled over her head. It all felt like forever ago.

In the house, Charlie was doing a quick scan of the rooms, retrieving phone chargers and script pages with the casual indifference of someone who knew he'd be back eventually. He was wearing slim-cut black sweats, a dark gray hoodie, and her red beanie. Over the last few weeks, all their winter gear had started to co-mingle in the bins of hats and gloves in the mudroom, overturned and mixed up. She liked the way it looked on him.

While Janey waited in the truck, the two of them awkwardly faced each other in the kitchen. He had his hands in his pockets, and she didn't quite know what to do with her arms.

"Well, I guess this is it, Chef," he said, his smile more habit than heart.

Chloe smiled back at him. *My fun mistake*, she thought fondly.

"You know the offer still stands," he said, pulling a pair of Ray-Bans from his pocket and setting them on his face, going full Hollywood on her again. "You're welcome to stay here in the house for as long as you'd like."

"I'm good," she replied. "But thank you."

"So, what's next?" he asked, crossing his arms across his chest and pressing his fingers into his biceps.

"I'm headed to Chicago for meetings, and I'll start to figure things out when I'm there."

She didn't mention Ben or the old fish market at all. Something inside of her felt protective of the prospect of staying on Deer Haven with her lobsterman.

Abruptly and stiffly at first, Charlie leaned in for a hug. His stubble was rough against her cheek, but she didn't mind. She wrapped her arms around his neck, as he tightened his grip across her back, and she breathed him in one last time, inhaling the notes of his Charlie Davis soap that just a few weeks ago was enough to drive her crazy.

They pulled back from each other, and she lifted his sunglasses so she could see his eyes, pausing to marvel over how cool and blue they were, thinking about how in the past month she'd seen every version of them—icy and flat with indifference, sparkling with curious excitement, and flashing with wild lust. She pressed her mouth softly against his dimple, and he kissed her cheek back, not the searching, hungry, savage kind of kiss they'd shared before, but something that felt like a resigned goodbye.

"Thanks for feeding me," he said, smiling broadly now.

"Thanks for letting me cook for you."

"Will you come and say hi when you visit Julia?"

"Sure," she said, and for half a second, she even meant it. "Good luck with...everything," she added. "With the series, with Emma, all of it."

He just smiled and kissed her again at the corner of her mouth, a warm, chaste little kiss, before pushing his sunglasses back onto his face and closing the door behind him. She watched Janey's truck head down the driveway and fought the urge to wave from the kitchen window like a weirdo until they disappeared around the bend.

Just like her Deer Haven adventure had begun, Chloe was once again alone in the big house. She slid onto the bench on what had become her side of the table and gazed out at the glittering harbor. She would miss eating across from Charlie, would miss watching as he moaned with pleasure over buttermilk biscuits and seafood chowder.

Her phone vibrated with a text from Ben.

Still OK to come over?

Yes! It's just me, come over any time.

She'd invited him to stay for her last night at the house. She would sleep at his place the following night and drive to the airport in Portland the morning after that. She still hadn't told him about Chicago.

As the sun started to sink behind the trees, she ran mental lists of everything she needed to do to close up the kitchen. She would clean out the refrigerator and cupboards, using what she could so that it wouldn't go to waste. She would make bread pudding out of the remaining challah and deliver it to Janey and sweet-toothed Bob. She would layer the leftover polenta with lamb ragu and top it with torn pieces of fresh mozzarella, bake it all together for a lovely little dinner to enjoy with Ben. She would scrub the stove, because even though a cleaning crew would work their way through the whole house the following week, she could never leave a kitchen anything less than shining.

She considered all the ways her life had changed since she'd agreed to come to this little rock thirteen miles off the coast. She'd arrived antsy and angry, cursing the circumstances that had sent her packing. She thought about how, in the beginning, it had felt like a penance for her sins in the city—a perfect cocktail of her lack of options and a means to punish herself—yet the universe had still rewarded her with Ben, and in a weird way, Charlie. Would anything have changed at all if that lock on the office door had worked correctly? She could still be working eighty-hour weeks, still sneaking around with David, still barely tasting the food she tortured onto artfully composed plates at Redbud.

Propping her chin on her fist and watching the ferry inch across the water below, she realized she'd really settled into this house even when she knew it was always designed to be temporary. And now it was her last night here, and Ben would soon be sitting in Charlie's seat for dinner.

The headlights of his truck shone through the kitchen window, and she jumped up to greet her lobsterman at the door. Jasper cautiously stepped into the kitchen, hanging his head low and taking in his new surroundings before sidling up to Chloe and giving her a tender lick on the wrist.

"Hi, buddy," she murmured softly, laying her hand on top of his head.

She leaned into Ben, her cheek resting against his chest. She tilted her head, and he pressed his lips against hers.

"Hi."

"Hi," she hoarsely replied.

"I'm at the movie star's house," he declared as he followed her into the kitchen in his wool socks. "Is that weird?"

Yes.

"Of course not," she insisted. "It's not weird at all."

"Are you glad he's gone?"

Chloe watched Ben coax the cork from the bottle of Prosecco he'd been thoughtful enough to bring.

"I'm glad it's just us," she finally replied.

She busied herself with checking on the baking polenta and mixing the vinaigrette for the Brussels sprouts as Ben padded from room to room, snooping his way through the house's layout just as Chloe had done when she'd first arrived.

"This place is huge!" he called from the formal dining room.

She watched as he ran his hand reverently over the intricate woodwork on the fireplace mantle. He was admiring the craftsmanship of the house, and she smiled as she guessed what he was likely thinking: *they just don't build them like this anymore.*

"All these rooms for just one guy?" he scoffed. "Seems a bit much, doesn't it?"

"Well, it wasn't always just him."

Chloe wondered where Charlie was, if he'd landed in Portland already, if he'd boarded his cross-country flight and was currently in his seat, hoodie pulled up, scrolling on his phone and waiting to take off. She wondered if he was thinking about her.

She wanted Charlie back. She wanted Ben. She wanted L.A., Chicago, Deer Haven, Lila, all of it. She wanted all of it and none of it.

Ben bent to kiss the back of her neck as she placed their dinner on the table, the mozzarella perfectly golden and blistered.

"Ben."

"Chloe," he replied softly.

She took a deep breath, forcing the words out before she could reconsider. "I have a meeting in Chicago. In two days. It's with someone who's made me an offer to build a new restaurant with her."

She closed her eyes and waited for him to say something.

"Don't go."

She felt her cheeks grow hot as she turned to face him. "What do you mean, don't go? I have to go."

"Do you?" he asked, his green eyes pleading.

"Yes, I do. This meeting is huge. It could be a way back for me, you know that."

"A way back to what?" he replied softly. "Were you even happy there?"

"It's not just about being happy," she stammered. "It was my whole life."

"This could be your whole life. Out here. Working like you did in the city, that's not a life."

"It was *my* life. Coming out here...this was something I did when I didn't have any other choices."

Oof. Reel it in, Chloe. This is getting away from you.

"But Deer Haven could be really great for you," he insisted, reaching for her hand.

"Ben," she began, extracting her hand from his. "You've only known me for a few weeks. And I've been thinking about my next move since the second I got here. I always knew I wouldn't stay."

"Did you know when we spent the weekend together? After the storm? Did you already know there was no chance when I brought you to the fish market?"

She opened her mouth and closed it again, clueless as to how to respond.

"What are we even doing here, Chloe?"

"I don't...I'm still trying to figure everything out. I've never...I've never wanted more than one thing before," she stammered, her eyes begging with him to understand. "I've always known exactly what I wanted in my life. And I don't...I still don't know if I can trust—"

"You don't know if you can trust me?" Ben whispered, his dark green eyes wide. "You're the one who has been keeping your plans a secret for who knows how long. What have I done to make *you* not trust *me*?"

Lauren's letters in the back of the drawer. Your easy, unwavering goodness. The fact that you even like me this much doesn't exactly inspire me to trust your judgment, she thought.

She felt overheated, like the oven had been on all day rather than just the forty minutes it had taken to cook their dinner. She swiped the back of her hand across her brow and wanted nothing more than to run outside, to gulp giant mouthfuls of the cool evening air that was blowing in from the water. She darted her eyes around the room, looking everywhere but Ben's sweet face, searching for an escape hatch.

"You could really build something here. You know you could. The old fish market or something else," he continued. "We could really build something. Together."

"This wasn't supposed to be *anything*, Ben. This thing between us. I always knew I was only going to be on Deer Haven for a short time, and you knew it too. From the beginning."

"I know, but then things—"

"And I hate that you're asking me to give everything up," Chloe interrupted, the venom in her voice rising with each unfiltered word. "It's different for me than it is for you. I'm not just living in my parents' house, fishing from my dad's boat. I built something real in Chicago."

"This is real," he insisted. "*I'm* real."

"This is just moving too fast for me," she said, pressing the heels of her palms into her eyes so she still wouldn't have to look at him, wouldn't be tempted to reach out to tuck that one lock of hair behind his ear. "I just...I'm worried I don't want the things that you want."

"I'm in love with you."

"Ben."

"I love you. And I know we're great together. And I think you know it too."

Chloe met his eyes in helpless silence. She thought about all the ways a person could be generous, ways that extended far beyond making dinner, opening doors, having unselfish sex, letting her pick the record. In the short time they'd spent together, Ben was constantly curious about her story, forever asking her questions, leaving her the space to answer or not answer them. Everything she wanted to tell him —how she loved the way he made her feel like the most fascinating woman in the world, how she noticed the way he constantly praised her strength and independence, how she thought about his kisses, his green eyes and his bread for hours after they said goodbye—it all formed a tight little knot stuck deep in the back of her throat.

"Can you not imagine a life for us here? Together?" he asked, reaching out his fingertips to touch her freckled cheek.

"I'm just..."

"What?"

"I'm scared I'm going to fuck it all up," she whispered.

"Chloe," he laughed, not mockingly, but the innocent laugh of someone who had no idea what she was capable of. "There's something real here for you."

She took in Ben's sweetly hopeful expression, and the same words echoed in her head like a heartbeat. *Don't, Chloe. Don't.*

"Ben—"

"And my parents are coming next week for a visit. I thought if you stuck around—"

"I slept with Charlie," she blurted, the escape hatch finally found.

Ben pulled back his hand as if he'd been burned, and for the first time since they'd met, his face didn't project that signature golden glow. He looked pale, tired, and unbelievably sad, his eye crinkles nowhere in sight. He didn't demand, "When?" or ask her why, forcing her to admit that she had no idea why she did most of the things she did when it came to men. He didn't ask if it had meant something to her or if it had happened more than once. He didn't say anything. He just called to Jasper and walked out the door, closing it softly behind him with a quiet little click.

It was the worst sound Chloe had ever heard.

His taillights disappeared at the bend in the driveway, casting the pines in a sinister wash of red until she was staring into only shadows.

Sitting in the darkening house completely alone, she realized that the night with Charlie was a weapon she'd been concealing, and that a part of her had always been poised to slide it from its sheath and strike when she felt cornered. Throughout her whispered confessions with Ben, the daydreams of the fish market, even when she was feeling her safest and warmest wrapped up in his arms, a part of her had remained sadly aware that she would be compelled to reach for her quiver at some point. It was the realization of that inevitability that crushed her more than anything.

Collapsing onto the banquette seat, she regarded their untouched dinner with a mixture of heartbreak and nausea. As if in a trance, she used the side of her forearm to slowly push the baking dish toward the side of the table, inching the steaming mixture closer and closer to the edge until it finally fell, smashing upon impact on the slate floor. Shards of ceramic, spatters of sauce, and rubbery globs of cooled cheese were everywhere, but Chloe couldn't bring herself to look at the mess she'd made.

She just continued to gaze out the window at the harbor below, where everything looked darker than ever, not a beacon in sight.

Chapter Twenty-Three

Janey Higgins was clearing branches from her yard when Chloe pulled into the driveway. The mostly melted snow had revealed everything the trees had shed during the big storm, and the caretaker was piling pine debris into a heap, her cheeks especially rosy in the morning sunshine.

"Hi, sweetheart!" she greeted Chloe, pulling her in for a hug.

Chloe leaned on the old woman for just a minute, allowing the weight of her sleep-deprived head to rest on her shoulder. She'd been awake all night after her blowout with Ben, fitfully drifting off just before the sun came up, her phone clutched in her hand in case he decided to return any of her many texts.

I'm sorry, Ben.

So, so sorry.

Are you awake?

Can we talk about this?

I hate thinking this is it.

Are you up?

I'm sorry I screwed this up.

Can I come over?

Ben.

I'm sorry.

She never heard back.

"You OK, honey?" Janey asked, assessing Chloe's cowlicked hair and the dark circles that ringed her eyes.

"I'm just really tired...and I'm leaving today. Back to Chicago," she said quietly. "Earlier than I thought, and I didn't want to go without saying goodbye."

"Well, I'm going to miss you, but you'll be back, right? To see Ben Libby or to cook for Charlie the next time he comes out?"

Her throat caught when she said, "I don't think so, Janey."

"Oh, hon, what is it?"

Chloe didn't know if it was the exhaustion, her impending departure, or the fact that she had somehow managed to lose both Charlie and Ben in the same day. Maybe it was just the familiar warmth of Janey's hug, so much like her mom's embrace, that prompted her to burst into tears in the caretaker's arms. Janey just held onto her, petting her hair and assuring her that it would all be OK as Chloe's body silently shook with sobs. It was pouring out of her at once—all the heartbreaks, big and small, that she'd both suffered and caused over the past several weeks. She was like that saucepan of cream—boiling over and making a mess of everything.

She sniffled loudly and wiped her eyes with the cuff of her jacket. "I'm sorry, Janey. I don't...I don't know what's wrong with me."

"Oh, honey, there's nothing wrong with you," the old woman assured her, pulling a crisp, lace-trimmed handkerchief from her coat pocket. "You're going to go to Chicago and get things sorted out. And you'll be back here, I know it. This place is tough to shake. It sticks with you. You'll see."

All Chloe could do was nod as she gave Janey one last hug, thanking her for everything as she returned to her car. She resisted looking in the rearview mirror as the caretaker waved sadly from the foot of her driveway.

She texted Ben again while she was waiting for her flight.

I left early for Chicago. Can we talk soon?

Nothing.

When she looked up with bleary eyes, she thought she saw him making his way down the concourse, his gait so familiar, a duffel bag slung over his flannel-clad shoulder. She stood abruptly, knocking her terrible airport salad to the floor, wondering if it was too much to run to him and throw herself into his waiting arms. But it was just some other tall, blond man with a face that didn't look like Ben's at all.

Please, she texted, before finally dropping her phone into her leather tote in defeat.

She knew it. She knew she was capable of blowing everything up, that even on a tiny island in the middle of the sea, she would find a way to make the most impulsive choices possible until everything around her was just piles of black, smoking rubble. She couldn't stop seeing Ben's face and the look of utter heartbreak in his eyes. In the moment of her confession, she had just wanted to break everything, had wanted to show him how awful she could be, how she was capable of destroying him.

Now that he wasn't responding to her, Chloe only felt regret. For all of it. She should have just said goodnight to Charlie and gone to bed the night of the storm. She should have been willing to give just a little bit more of herself to Ben. She should have felt more honored and lovestruck and chosen when he gave himself to her. Or maybe she should have stood her ground when Julia offered her the position cooking for someone who wasn't Harrison Ford.

Every time she closed her eyes on the plane, the deafening buzz of her remorse overpowered her fatigue, and she found herself wondering if she would ever sleep again. She could still hear Ben's voice, whispering her name in the dark, like an echo she couldn't shake. It resounded in her ears when the plane touched down at O'Hare, sounding its refrain when her Uber sped toward her building as she barely noticed the Hancock Building jutting up from her beloved skyline.

She was immune to the bustle of downtown traffic and the choppy shadows of the lake. Leaning her head against the backseat, all she saw was the Atlantic, remembering how it had glittered silver in the morning sun and reflected streaks of hot pink toward the sky at dusk. She thought about the *Andrea May*, how Ben had trusted her to drive the boat back to the dock as he used his own body to block the wind that swept up from the water. She saw him piling lobster traps in his yard, swinging them into stacks like they were weightless, using those same perfect arms to pull her closer. She pictured his octopus, an inked premonition for Chloe herself—the ultimate escape artist.

Climbing the three flights to her apartment, she kept expecting to be hit by a wave of nostalgia or a flutter of excitement about returning to the home she'd spent so much time missing, but it never came. Her mood was just as flat when she walked in, grimacing at the stale air and seeing the plant she'd forgotten, sitting brown and dead in the center of her dining table.

She opened all the windows to welcome in the freshness of spring and winced when the stench of garbage rose from the alleyway below. She thought of Jasper when she heard two dogs barking down the block and shook her head in irritation when her thin walls began to vibrate with the thumping bass from her neighbor's place. They were playing an old Britney song on repeat, and Chloe scowled, wondering if they'd always been so annoying and she'd just never been home enough to notice.

She flopped onto the couch and hit FaceTime.

"Whoa, you look like shit," her sister declared as soon as their connection stabilized.

"Gee, thanks," Chloe muttered.

"Wait, is that your apartment? Are you back in Chicago already?" Julia demanded, squinting at Chloe's backdrop.

"I came back early. Changed my flight."

"To prep for your meeting with Lila?"

"I fucked it all up, Jules."

"Tell me."

In a breathless rush, Chloe confessed everything—how she'd felt cornered, trapped by how much Ben was asking of her, how his face had looked when she'd dropped the bomb about her night with Charlie, how he'd reacted by not reacting and was now serving up nothing but silence, how her heart felt like it was breaking apart in her chest.

"He told me he loves me," she said softly.

"And what did you say?"

"I panicked! It was all too much. It's only been a few weeks."

"You know that doesn't matter, Chlo," Julia said. "And I'm almost afraid to ask, but how about Charlie? Did you sort all of that out?"

"Charlie and I are fine. I've barely thought of him since I left the island."

As she said it, she realized it was true and felt as if the real estate in her mind had tripled since she'd evicted all thoughts of the actor. She just wished all that extra space would give her a better sense of clarity.

She pressed her fingers against her temples, the depth of her exhaustion truly hitting her. "I'm here to get my real life back, right?" she croaked.

"You're there to take a meeting with a potential investor. That's it. But you have choices," Julia adamantly declared. "You always have choices. And your life is *real,* no matter what. No matter where you are."

"After everything I did, everything her shitty husband did...she's still willing to give me a shot."

"She knows who you are and how hard you work," Julia assured her. "But I need you to remember that she's just giving you *a* shot. She's not giving you your *only* shot. And I need you to be careful."

Chloe flopped onto her back with a sigh, staring up at a brownish water stain on the ceiling, wondering if it was new. She exhaled hard, wishing she could crawl out of her own head for just five minutes.

"How are *you*?" she remembered to ask. "And how's Beth feeling?"

"We're great. Headed to a spa weekend in Tahoe tomorrow. She told me that I'm not allowed to bring my phone," Julia said with genuine horror in her voice.

"I believe in you," Chloe teased, struggling to imagine her sister not logged on to at least three devices at any given moment.

"Well, we'll see if I survive it," Julia said wryly.

Chloe promised to update her after the meeting with Lila, and Julia dispensed a rapid-fire pep talk about "holding your ground" and "being firm," asserting that investors need talent as much as talent needs them.

"Thank you, Jules," she said, her voice growing thick.

"For what?"

"For everything. This whole time."

Julia joked that she would send her bill to Charlie's office, which was almost funny.

They said their goodbyes, and Chloe immediately called her favorite Thai noodle place, where they still remembered her regular soup order and confirmed her longstanding preference for extra herbs and extra chilis. She curled into the couch, saw that the Irish Lady Detective Show had a new season, and accepted the small win. She pressed a throw pillow over her face, wondering if the streetlights outside her window had always been so aggressively bright, just as the Britney song began for the ten thousandth time.

Tired of fighting the weight of her eyelids, she started to drift off, suspecting that Deer Haven and everything that had happened there had just been one long dream. But before she gave in to sleep, she saw the cab of Ben's truck, the two of them bouncing over island roads with Jasper between them while the ocean revealed itself in flashes through the pine trees, and all she could think was, *I wish I could have given myself to you.*

Chapter Twenty-Four

Chloe saw the UNKNOWN CALLER alert while walking to her meeting with Lila. Fumbling to answer it, she nearly dropped her phone into a puddle, frantic that it might somehow be Ben calling from a different number, ready to talk. Ready to forgive her.

"Chloe Foster!" Jenna Moran greeted her. "You're back in the city! What did I tell you about getting out for a bit?"

"Here I am," Chloe replied flatly, annoyed that it wasn't her lobsterman after all. She was still holding a grudge after her ill-fated lunch with Jenna, when the powerhouse chef had tough-loved her over tapas.

"I know you're meeting with Lila this morning," Jenna began, the rapid rhythm of her chef's knife audible in the background. "And I know things got weird between you two, but I just wanted to encourage you to keep an open mind."

"I was having an affair with her husband, so I'm not sure 'weird' is the right word, but OK."

"Right, but she still really wants you for this new project. Despite all that ancient shit."

"I'm walking there now, so sure—my mind's open," she said, even though she wanted to scream, *Ancient? It was less than six weeks ago!*

"Lila's backing my new place," Jenna continued. "Craft cocktails and classic Portuguese dishes. Polvo à Lagareiro, Arroz de pato, custard tarts. I've been dreaming of it for years. I pitched the concept, and she basically handed me a blank check."

Chloe tried not to let Jenna's description of her own vision cloud the pitch she'd been practicing for the last twenty-four hours. She was going to present a French fine-dining-meets-street-food concept. She'd fuse everything she'd tasted in her travels throughout France with the pedigree she'd earned working in some of the best kitchens in the world. The menu would be simple, but pristine. She'd source all the best local and French ingredients for an elevated take on merguez frites, jambon beurre, and socca, the flatbread she'd adored when she traveled to Nice back in culinary school. She'd never cooked anything like this menu, but she planned to speak with total assurance when she described the food, even though the plans hadn't completely gelled in her mind quite yet.

The truth was, as much as she'd always loved brainstorming restaurant concepts, she was feeling blocked. She'd been struggling to connect with any of the ideas she'd scribbled into her little notebook, finding herself thinking only of the Deer Haven Library's collection of "The Downeast Homemaker's Cookbook," which was no help at all.

If this was going to work, she needed to push herself toward something brand new. Jenna Moran certainly understood that, and Chloe needed to understand it too.

"That sounds great for you, Jenna," she finally replied, wondering if the chef had called just to discuss how amazing things were going for *her*.

"It's great for *us*. She's committing to only financing woman-run restaurants from now on. Said it's time to break up this boy's club that's dominated the city for so long."

"And using her family's money to do it."

"Lucky us!" Jenna exclaimed with a low chuckle.

"Lucky us," Chloe echoed dryly, a part of her still convinced that Lila was somehow setting her up.

"So anyway, just putting it out there. I'd love to work with you someday, Chloe, to collaborate on something. And I think Lila would love to make that happen, too. The history is complicated, but just think about it, OK? You know you're not done with Chicago yet."

Chloe promised she would think about it and said goodbye, letting the chef get back to her empire. She reflected on the profound strangeness of the call. It was weird that Jenna was acting as a hype woman for Lila Harris. And Lila working with only female chefs? Chloe adored the concept but wondered if it had only come to pass now that David was officially off the Harris payroll.

A large delivery van was blocking the side street where Chloe needed to cross, and it was only when she scowled and walked around it that she noticed the giant red lobster decal on the side, under the words "Mazzo Bros Fresh Fish and Maine Lobster." Her eyes filled with tears, her head full of Ben. She was a mess.

Take a breath, dummy, she silently commanded as she walked the remaining block to her meeting. *In five minutes, you'll be auditioning for Lila Harris. Time to pull it together and sing for your supper.*

Lila was wearing a sharp black suit and dismissing a designer's tile samples with a flick of her manicured hand when Chloe arrived. Her impeccable auburn blow-out gleamed under the makeshift lighting that had been strung throughout the construction zone.

"Chloe Foster."

Of course you came, Lila's tone suggested. *Even after everything, you'd be a fool not to.*

"Lila," Chloe replied. "Thank you for setting this up."

"What do you think?" Lila asked, gesturing to the cavernous shell of a space.

"It's...big."

"Well, we can build it out to your specifications. Open kitchen, closed kitchen, whatever you'd prefer. You'd work with our design team to select everything down to the soap dispensers in the washrooms."

"And the menu?" Chloe asked, waiting for the other shoe to drop, for Lila to tell her she would be carrying out the Harris brand's vision of more tweezer food, that she would return to a life of arranging a single fennel seed atop a meticulously composed, tiny portion in the center of an absurdly large white plate.

"That would still be up to you as well. You'd assemble your own team, and the concept is yours to design."

Chloe looked around the empty restaurant, trying to visualize it without the plumbers and electricians that were currently retrofitting the space, running wires, and cutting pipes. Like a computer rendering on one of those house flipping shows that Julia loved so much, everything came together in her mind—the weathered wood floors, the vintage schoolhouse light fixtures, the charmingly mismatched tables and chairs.

"What is your menu concept then?" Lila asked in her clipped tone, obviously ready for the pitch portion of the meeting to commence.

"Modern New England comfort food," Chloe said before even realizing it. Then, she just kept going. "Seafood chowder. Lobster popovers. Venison stew. Chicken and biscuits. Blueberry pie. The classics, just elevated. But still rustic."

She was breathless by the time she was done, poised for Lila's response, unsure if she was going to receive adoring applause or an exclamation of *Venison stew? You've got to be fucking kidding me."*

"Fine," Lila said curtly. "We'll work on the budget and details. My business team will be in touch with an offer for salary and scope."

"Wait, what?"

"Was I not clear? I'm going to finance your restaurant."

"But that's it?" Chloe asked in disbelief. "After...everything?"

Lila waved her hand like she was reviewing more tile samples—the shooing of an unwelcome gnat. "If I let the bad behavior of men hold me back, I wouldn't be here," she said matter-of-factly.

Chloe let her words sink in, for the first time seeing this formidable woman as something more than just a giant bank account in killer heels. Lila had a drive and dreams of her own, just like she did.

She swallowed hard before speaking the long-overdue words. "Lila. I'm sorry about everything. It wasn't just David,' Chloe admitted, clearing her throat nervously but maintaining unwavering eye contact. "I wish none of it had happened."

"It's done. Behind us," Lila asserted as her expertly Botoxed cheek betrayed her by twitching ever-so-slightly. "And I like to be in business with the best, so consider it forgotten."

Chloe blinked, still in shock that Lila would want anything to do with her. It seemed that her punishment had ended and now, as Jenna had boasted, she was being offered a blank check.

"So, my business department will be in touch with a formal offer," Lila repeated with a single crisp nod, the implication of *we're done here* registering loud and clear with the chef.

They shook hands and Chloe walked out in an absolute daze, wondering what on earth had just happened. She'd barely described her concept, and it seemed like Lila was prepared to agree with whatever she said, before the words "blueberry pie" had even left her mouth.

I like to be in business with the best.

Lila's declaration echoed in her ears. Two months ago, it would have meant everything to her. The knowledge that Lila was stacking the bench with the top chefs in the city, Chloe among them, would have filled her ego to the brim, increasing her drive to be the *very* best among the best. Now it just felt like...nothing.

She found herself distracted, absently looking for that van with the lobster on it when she crossed the street. Ducking into her old favorite wine bar, she decided that a celebratory glass of Shiraz was in order. She claimed a seat at the end of the nearly empty bar, far away from the two hipsters who were sharing a bottle of pinot, their heads bent together in conversation.

As soon as she took a sip, she was brought back to Ben's kitchen, to the night of the steak dinner, when he'd held out his hand and asked her to dance. All the embarrassment about the utter corniness of the moment had dissolved, and now she only felt a deep and hollow sadness for everything she'd lost.

She fiddled with her phone and checked her email, where an offer from Lila had already arrived. The salary proposal was enough to make her gasp—almost twice what she'd been paid at Redbud—and the contract was standard Harris Group legal jargon, identical to the one she'd signed before.

Gently swirling the wine in her glass, she called Julia, who answered on the first ring.

"I thought you weren't supposed to have your phone," Chloe teased, already knowing her sister would answer anyway.

"We haven't left yet," she said with a nearly audible eye roll. "But I still think I can sneak it into my bag when I pack the car. Hey, how did it go?"

"It went well. Really well," Chloe confessed. "She offered me my own place. Her money, my concept."

"Wow, Chlo. That's amazing."

"I can design everything. The space, the menu, the staff, all of it."

"That's a big deal. Especially after everything." Julia paused. "But why don't you sound more excited about it?"

She had been asking herself the same question since she'd shaken Lila's hand, wondering if that *nothing* feeling would eventually become *something*. She wondered why she wasn't currently scribbling her opening night menu on a napkin, sketching out concepts with more detail as she considered the best way to feature Wellfleet oysters during their winter season. Why wasn't her mind whirring with every possibility now that she'd be able to design her own kitchen for the first time? She hadn't even begun to consider where she would source her lobster. Why wasn't she weighing the pros and cons of Maine versus Massachusetts, contemplating the difference in the water between southern and northern New England? Why did it all feel so flat?

"I don't know what I want," Chloe said softly.

"Yes, you do."

"I don't, Jules. I feel completely lost, and I don't know why. This is everything I've ever dreamt of. My own place in the city. Endless budget. Food that I feel excited about cooking. Full control. It's what I've been working for my whole life. It should be easy to say yes."

"You know what you want, Chlo. You're just afraid to say it."

Feeling that telltale lump in the back of her throat again, Chloe attempted to wash it down with her last gulp of wine.

"I don't—"

"Yes, you do, sister. You do."

"It's just...why does the world expect me to give something up? Why can't I have everything?"

"You can," Julia answered matter-of-factly.

"I mean all at once."

"You will. As soon as you drop the bullshit and admit to yourself what you really want your life to be."

Chloe indulged in a little sniffle before drawing her shoulders back and hopping from her stool. She left a twenty on the bar and cast a small wave to the bartender, who told her he'd see her soon.

"I have to go. I love you, Jules. Have a fun weekend away."

"I love you," Julia vowed. "And Chlo? You've got this. You're Chloe Fucking Foster."

She silently repeated the affirmation as she headed toward her apartment, tipping her face to the sun and noticing that the trees lining her street were covered in tiny buds, a barely green promise of what was to come. Several of her neighborhood restaurants had tempted fate and set up their outdoor dining tables, a brash move considering every Chicagoan knew what March could deliver in terms of weather. It was a leap of faith, that unapologetic embrace of spring.

Inside, Chloe still felt wrapped in the layers of winter, bundled and tense, waiting for a cold wind to sweep through and finish knocking her over. She scowled and kicked a small rock down the sidewalk, nearly hitting the two men in Cubs hats who approached from the opposite direction. They glared at her in unison as she shrugged and mumbled a halfhearted apology.

She didn't want to go back to her apartment. She didn't want to go home. Didn't want to be alone. But who was left to call? Steph would be deep into dinner prep by now, and who knew if she would even want to hang out anyway. A brief scroll on her phone presented the bitter realization that most of her contacts were former Redbud employees and suppliers, which left her feeling completely pitiful, like she didn't have a single friend in the entire city.

This is the problem with letting people in, she thought. *They convince you to make space, and then all that you notice is the stupid hole they leave when they're gone.*

Her mind flashed to Ben, and she could almost feel his soft stubble brushing against her cheek, his hands on her back, his whisper in her ear. She'd cracked the door just wide enough for him to slip inside and then had promptly pushed him out, breaking everything, fleeing the island, fleeing him. And she considered Deer Haven itself, how she'd so quickly made herself at home in the frigid and salty air, how the old fish market was still sitting empty, dusty and sealed, just waiting for someone.

Her phone pinged with a text from Janey.

Did you make it back ok?

It wasn't lost on her that the caretaker hadn't used the word *home.*

Made it back.

Then, desperate for something, anything, that she could cling to, she asked,

Have you seen Ben around?

Janey's three dots flickered and then reappeared before disappearing again. Finally, she responded,

Lois told me he's the new stern man on Bud Weymouth's boat. They're headed up to Nova Scotia next week for a month.

"That can't be right," Chloe mumbled. Ben leaving Deer Haven? Working on the crew of someone else's fishing boat and spending a month away from his library books, his records, and his wood stove?

Who would pull his traps or feed his sourdough starter? Who would take care of Jasper? She didn't know what to say. She had left, and Ben had put a plan into motion that didn't include her in any way, just as she had done when she'd bought a one-way return ticket to the mainland.

He'll be back, honey.

Janey assured her.

I promise.

Chloe felt dizzy—Lila's offer and that big, empty space in Logan Square feeling hazier than ever.

Desperate for a place to sit down, she ducked into a cineplex for a matinee, deciding that's what sad people did in the middle of the day—sat in the dark alone. She told the teenager working the counter that she wanted a ticket for whatever was starting right now, it didn't matter what, and she bought the most massive bucket of popcorn they sold, extra butter and salt, of course.

As her eyes adjusted to the barely lit theater, she realized she was the only one there. Feeling like the most pathetic person in Chicago, she plunked into a seat and paid half attention to the opening credits, googling a map of Canada and tracing her fingertip up to Nova Scotia. She wondered what Ben had been thinking when he'd accepted that job. She wondered if it was her fault.

A voice she'd heard before blared in surround sound, and she looked up to find Emma Marcone's face filling the entire movie screen. Her glossy black hair was slicked back into a high ponytail, and she was wearing some sort of futuristic leather catsuit. She looked powerful and confident, deservedly full of herself.

"Jesus Christ, does this woman have a single pore?" Chloe muttered as the shot centered on her flawless cheek.

She threw a handful of popcorn at the screen and booed rudely, offending no one in the empty theater. When she physically couldn't roll her eyes anymore without inducing a migraine, she slumped in her seat and spent the next two hours watching the She-Wolf save some post-apocalyptic dust world from further doom. As she studied the actress's eyes as they narrowed and sparkled, looking fierce as she battled enemies with her quick wits and fight training, Chloe had to admit she was good. Really good. Emma was magnetic, stealing every scene, the mesmerizing center of all the action in an otherwise terrible script.

When the lights went up, and she drew a noisy last sip from her cherry Coke, she sat blinking in the half-dark, allowing the last two hours to settle inside of her. Emma Marcone allowed the distraction of men like Charlie Davis, that British director, and whoever else, but she still did her work. She put on her catsuit and high-kicked everything and everyone who got in her way without a single partner on that bleak desert planet, and she'd leapt, physically leapt, off a cliff's edge onto an enemy ship to save herself.

Flinching from the abrupt sunniness of the sky outside the theater, Chloe snapped back into her own former She-Wolf self.

"Just leap," she murmured.

Then, before doubt could catch up, she pulled out her phone and texted Lila.

I'm in.

Chapter Twenty-Five

Building a restaurant with Lila's money was much easier the second time around.

Chloe worked closely with the Harris Group's architects and designers, all of whom had been told she had carte blanche on any decisions related to equipment, finishes, and setup. Whether it was the black slate shipped from a quarry in northern Maine, the hand-glazed tile from the Portland potter who'd been featured in Dwell Magazine, or the fleet of Vulcan ten-burner gas ranges that all arrived on the same rainy Wednesday morning, not an eye was blinked. Chloe requested, suggested, and demanded, and everything just appeared: the orders placed, the checks signed swiftly from behind the scenes.

This is fun! she told herself. *I love making decisions, running the show, and being assured that I'm important and successful.*

But it wasn't filling her up in the way she'd hoped, not even when $8,000 worth of copper cookware arrived, express shipped from France. She'd ordered it all just to see if she could get away with it. And the answer, again and again, was yes. The thrill of seeing the space start to come together still wasn't enough to distract her from thoughts of the Atlantic, of the *Andrea May*'s bow cutting through the choppy cove, of Ben wrapping his long arms around her.

The lobsterman was surely in Nova Scotia by now, spending days at a time out at sea, those same long arms hauling nets and traps in all varieties of weather. Chloe wondered if he was happy, if he'd found a sense of satisfaction in the adventure of it all. She wondered if he was staying warm at night, wondered what he was eating when the crew retired to the belly of the boat for meals. She wondered if he missed her.

When she slogged home through the cold rain, she asked herself how she could have been so stupid, so careless, so mean. Replaying their fight over and over, she considered how stingy she'd been with offering any sort of assurances, how she could only focus on the too-muchness of Ben's big feelings in the moment.

She texted him over noodles and Netflix, pleading with him to talk to her, to understand, to forgive. He still didn't text back, and she chose to believe it wasn't a result of his remote location.

Sometimes his silence made her angry, and she questioned what right he had to act like she owed him anything. They had barely known each other after all, and she hadn't even needed to confess about her night with Charlie. It wasn't like she'd stepped out on a marriage or something. Then she remembered how he'd said that he loved her, and how her immediate response was to show him how stupid he'd been to even dare.

Plans for her brand-new yet-to-be-named restaurant marched forward. When she started interviewing line cooks and sous chefs, she was astonished by how arrogant and driven they all were. They were so hungry, singing their own praises, reciting their training and pedigrees, dropping names every chance they got. Chloe couldn't remember if she had sounded the same way out of culinary school, fresh from her prestigious internship, if she'd displayed that much focus and swagger, been so quick to declare herself the very best at this or that. But she recognized that it was her own hubris that had not only helped launch her career but had continued to keep her relevant in a world where she was often the only woman in the room. She was gifted and hardworking, almost to a fault, but the fact that she'd displayed the fearlessness to demand more, more, more had kept her working in some of the top kitchens in the world over the years.

Now she found it all just a little obnoxious, and she hoped to discover a team of cooks who could just let the food speak to their talents.

She missed Ben and the slow ease with which he made his way through the world. She missed that careful, deliberate pace that had once unnerved her. It was confidence without flash, the opposite of the young chef who boasted about his ambidextrous knife skills while Chloe arched her brow and asked him to stick to highlighting his actual resume.

"They all suck," she lamented to Julia as she kicked off her shoes and sank into her sofa, moaning at the sheer ecstasy of sitting down for the first time in twelve hours.

"I'm sure they don't all suck. They just all want to work with the Great Chloe Foster, so they're showing off," her sister replied absently.

"Is this a bad time?" Chloe asked, almost too exhausted to pour herself a glass of wine. Almost.

"No, I just have to drive all the way out to Malibu to meet with this pinhead client," she complained. "She still doesn't understand that drunk tweeting her ill-informed impressions of serious world events is just a little beyond her pay grade. Or mental capacity."

"That sounds like fun," Chloe said, stifling her yawn, realizing she hadn't gotten more than a four-hour night's sleep since she'd started work on the new restaurant three weeks ago.

"Whatever. She's the worst. I want to hear more about you! What's the name of the new place?"

Chloe stretched out and flexed her stiff ankles and toes, struck with the nagging feeling that her sister was making a concerted effort to sound excited for her.

"I actually don't know," she confessed. "I can't think of anything I like."

"Well, clear your mind and shut your eyes. What do you see on the sign?"

Chloe indulged Julia and allowed her eyes to close. She tried to envision a modern black awning with crisp white lettering. She waited, but the awning remained blank. All she could see was that charmingly faded "Fresh Fish" sign on the front of the old seafood market, its letters wind-worn and sun bleached.

Her eyes snapped open. "Jules?" Her voice caught in the back of her throat. "Have I made a huge mistake?"

Julia exhaled slowly—like she was letting go of something heavy. "If you were my client, I'd tell you that this is a massive move for you. The right move," she finally replied. "But you're my sister..."

"And?"

"And I don't think you sound happy. At all."

Chloe's eyes welled up, and she swiped roughly at her wet cheeks, annoyed by her own tears.

"And I think you were starting to sound happy, out there. On the island," Julia continued. "And it really freaked you out. Because that was never part of the plan."

"Right, because *this* is the plan," Chloe shot back. "*This* is the plan. Building my own place, getting paid what I deserve, and being offered no-strings financing. Creating a restaurant of this scale. This was always the plan."

"First, stop assuming there are no strings. There are always strings. You know that. Second, if you want to back out, it's not too late. You know that too."

"Actually, it's quite literally too late. The contracts were signed weeks ago."

And the tile for the kitchen just arrived, and it's the perfect shade of forest green, the exact color of the pine trees I saw from the ferry that first day, and I had to go through about thirty samples before I found the right one.

"Please. We can get you out of that if we need to. My firm's attorneys—"

"No," Chloe interrupted, her voice firm. "I'm sure I just have cold feet. Because I'm so tired, you know? I'm sure that's what it is."

"Do you even want any of this anymore?" Julia asked, her own voice low and gentle.

"It's just cold feet."

"Chloe."

"Hey, I have to go. I'm meeting friends for drinks in a few minutes," she lied. "Talk soon, OK?"

"Oh. Please keep me posted. On...everything. OK?"

"I will."

"Promise?"

"Yes, elder sister. I promise."

After they hung up, Chloe stretched out on her side and reached for the throw blanket that was draped across the back of the couch. Instead of the soft, snuggly effect it usually had, it suddenly felt itchy, heavy, and too warm. In a huff, she kicked it off, scowling and curling her body into itself, the idea of eating dinner never even dawning on her.

"Chef? Did you hear me?" her contractor asked at their daily meeting. "What do you think about keeping these columns exposed?"

Chloe snapped to attention, realizing she'd been staring into space for a full five minutes, locking and unlocking the lid atop her travel mug and listening to zero percent of the conversation. Everyone was looking at her expectantly—the architect, the designers, the lead carpenter, plumber, electrician, and Lila herself, who appeared less than impressed with Chloe's lack of engagement.

"Uh, yes. Keep them exposed. Natural wood. Yes," she answered quickly, catching Lila's icy expression across the table.

"Can you excuse me for just a minute?" she asked, making a beeline for the bathroom and feeling the arctic burn of Lila's gaze on her back.

She closed herself in and exhaled slowly. She was having serious reservations about the space, realizing that it was all too big with its impossibly high ceilings and designer light fixtures that were only made to *look* vintage. She wondered if she could ever achieve a sense of intimacy, of coziness, in such a posh cavern. Worst of all, she was worried about her menu, terrified that none of the food made sense outside of that little island in the middle of the Atlantic.

"What are you doing?" she whispered. "You're fucking this up."

She leaned against the wall and closed her eyes, picturing the *Andrea May*, remembering how its dark blue bow had looked carving through the choppy grey-green harbor. She tried to snap herself back into the present, to pull herself together, to get her game face on, but it felt impossible. All she knew was her finger trailing through the cold salt water, the smell of Ben's neck, the taste of lemon tea from his thermos.

Why don't you want this anymore? she asked herself, closing her eyes against the sound of the kitchen of her dreams being built outside the door.

Julia's voice echoed in her ears. *You know what you want, you're just afraid to say it.*

Chloe shook her head and straightened her shoulders. As she tucked her chambray shirt neatly into her jeans, she couldn't help but recall that last night at Redbud when, hands trembling, she'd smoothed her chef coat and returned to service.

"You're Chloe Fucking Foster," she murmured, consciously arranging her face into a serene smile as she strode across the massive space to rejoin Lila and the others.

She focused on trying to look alert, engaged, and *alive* as the meeting wrapped up, final decisions locked down, and committed to a team of laptops. As soon as they broke for coffee, Lila wrapped her long fingers around Chloe's arm and led her to a back corner, her glossy burgundy manicure digging through the chef's shirt.

"Are you with us here?" she hissed. "Because you seem like you're somewhere else."

"Yes," Chloe asserted. "Yes, yes of course I am."

She felt humiliated, having a weak performance called out like that, by Lila of all people. She needed to get her head in the game, especially by the afternoon, when she would present her menus to the business team. She reminded herself that this part would eventually be over, that they would choose an opening date, that she would be cooking again at some point. But for now, she made assurances, promising she was on track, that she had it all under control.

"I'm here, Lila. I'm totally here," she swore, not remotely believing it as she said it, tempted to just drop her shoulders and confess the truth—that she was really, really sad. That she was worried that none of this would succeed in lighting her up ever again.

"Well, then stop fucking around and get serious. You should be practically living here at this point. And until the kitchen is finished, you should be refining your costs, working on your socials."

"My socials?"

"Yes, your socials," Lila huffed. "You want to be relevant again? You have to do some of the work to make that happen. Did you connect with Liz in digital marketing like I asked you to? She'll tell you exactly what to do, and she'll even take over your feeds for you. It was Liz who leaked to Natter after I gave her the green light."

"Wait, what?" Chloe gasped, feeling as if she'd been slapped by Lila's clawed hand.

"The Natter piece? About your misconduct?" she replied, barely looking up as her fingernails rapidly tapped a message on her phone.

"You contacted Natter? *You* were the leak?" She said in disbelief, the pieces still not completely coming together in her mind. "But... why?"

"Because you fucked my husband," she replied matter-of-factly, finally meeting Chloe's eyes with her cold gaze. "And I was furious, but I saw an opportunity."

"An opportunity."

"To create some buzz before announcing our big launch here. To make sure you stayed relevant while you were being punished. I knew you'd come back to the city, and I needed to be sure that people were still talking about you when you did."

"You got me canceled," Chloe hissed, her numb incredulity tipping toward rage. "You tried to ruin me."

"And look, now I'm bringing you back to life," Lila declared, her eyes flashing. "And don't try to tell me that you wouldn't have done the same if you'd thought of it. We're exactly alike, Chloe."

"No. No, we're not. I don't use people like that. I don't—"

"You'll see," Lila interrupted, ignoring the chef's protestations. "All of this will actually turn out to be good for the brand."

"What brand?"

"Your brand. *My* brand," she replied, gesturing toward the lavish space behind her. "So now that you're in again, I expect you to be *all* in."

Lila turned on her Louboutin heel, dismissing the chef with a toss of her impeccable blowout, leaving Chloe to stare, dazed, at the half-built restaurant that surrounded her. Her gut had been correct when she'd questioned Lila's motives, when she'd wondered if she was being set up. Yes, the chef had been handed a blank check, but she'd unwittingly become a pawn in the process. Lila didn't care about her or even about the food. She'd barely listened when Chloe had pitched her menu. As Chloe watched the tile being painstakingly laid in the open kitchen and the row of faux vintage chandeliers being installed over the bar, she realized that all of it was nothing more than a product to Lila. And Chloe had allowed Lila to buy her, sell her, and then buy her back again, as if she were merely a product herself.

She felt sick as she considered the deal that she'd struck, full of heartache for everything she'd left behind. And she felt like a total fool, for trusting, for believing in any of it.

I'll never be in charge here, she admitted to herself as she headed toward the exit, ignoring the electrician who needed her thoughts on pendant heights, along with an incoming call from Lila, who was already summoning her from her town car. She silenced her phone and stepped into the blinding midday light, startled at the sunshine on the other side of the door.

What am I doing? she asked herself, unsure if she was referring to the deal she'd made with the devil, or the fact that she was currently walking away from it. All the old Redbud feelings had come back—the tightness in her chest, the manic mindset, the nearly crippling exhaustion. They were the feelings that had felt like home until she'd left them behind for the island, shedding them like layers before the spring thaw.

She considered all the times she'd forgotten to eat in the last several weeks, forgoing meals for the little antacid tablets she'd begun to keep in the back pocket of her pants. She'd chew them up, three at a time, as her stomach burned while she walked into that ridiculous soon-to-be restaurant, crushing them between her teeth as she assessed the progress of the build-out, taking in the details that felt all wrong, even though she'd chosen the finishes herself. She'd started keeping a package of them on her bedside table, reaching for them when she tossed and turned, willing sleep to arrive, unable to think about anything but the old fish market.

You want a different outcome? Make a different choice.

Chloe quickened her pace as she walked past the small gardens in front of her favorite row of brownstones, where redbud trees boasted showy fuchsia petals and tulips grew in every shade of pink. The city was in full bloom, and springtime in Chicago was bold, unapologetic, almost obscene in its showiness. She'd always loved that audacity after the long, cold season that came before it.

But it no longer felt like home.

She abruptly stopped in her tracks on the sidewalk, right outside her old coffee shop, the sweet little place she'd visited every morning for years, where they practically had her cortado waiting when she arrived. It suddenly looked like a place she'd never been.

What am I doing? she asked herself again, thinking only of Ben, of his halo of blond hair and those perfect, perfect crinkles that framed his eyes. She remembered grilled cheese in his kitchen, her legs bare under his flannel shirt. She thought of him gracefully chopping chilis, how he was thoughtful enough to ask permission before making her plate extra spicy. She pictured the smooth tan of his back, the strength in his arms when he held himself over her. She considered the way she would run her fingertips down his spine as she breathlessly awaited his kiss, the lust evidenced on his face when she gently pushed him back onto the bed.

"What am I doing?" she said out loud to no one right before she started to run.

She dodged people walking dogs and toddlers on bikes as she

sprinted toward her apartment, cursing her creaky knees as she ran as fast as she could down the cracked sidewalk. Her lungs were on fire as she pushed away the nagging voice telling her that she really needed to exercise more. She groaned, desperately winded, when she recognized it as Julia's voice.

She couldn't get her keys into the door quickly enough, couldn't be bothered to really worry about what she was haphazardly tossing into an old leather duffel bag. Her unpacked suitcases still sat in the corner of her living room, stuffed with dirty laundry, so she threw her duffel aside, reaching for the closest roller bag without a care as to what it held.

As she zipped her jacket with fumbling hands, she asked herself how she could have been so stupid to just run from the island like she had. A few texts and calls didn't count as fighting for someone. She should have shown up on his doorstep with a lasagna or a three-tiered coconut cake that said I'M SORRY in a swooping script made of lemon icing. She should have been Lloyd Dobler with the trench coat and the boom box, blasting "You're the One" by The Black Keys until he came to the window.

She should have told him that she just wasn't ready for him when they met, but that she wanted to be ready for him now.

She needed to get back to Deer Haven, even if she had to steal a ship and sail it there herself. She'd find someone who knew where Bud Weymouth's boat was, and she'd swim to Nova Scotia if she had to.

With no time to indulge in sentimental last looks at her apartment, Chloe tore open the door and found herself facing Ben Libby, looking impossibly tall in her hallway, his knuckles raised mid-knock.

He glowed golden even in the dim light of the stairwell. He was wearing a navy Henley and dark pants, his weathered barn coat clutched in one big hand, and when he tucked that stray lock of hair behind his ears, Chloe had to grab the doorknob for support.

"How did you..." she breathed, feeling wobbly.

"Janey tracked down your address and offered to take care of

Jasper. I just got on the ferry and drove to the airport. I didn't even pack a bag."

"But I thought you were on a boat...someone else's boat. I thought...I thought you wanted to get farther away from me."

"I didn't go. I couldn't do it," he continued, his words coming in a rush. It was the only time she'd ever seen him hurry to do anything. "I was out on the water, watching your ferry leave, and all I could think was that I blew it. I totally blew it. So, no, I don't want to get farther away from you. I just want to know you."

She stared at beautiful Ben in her hallway as he twisted his coat in his hands, pleading with her. She imagined him on the deck of the *Andrea May*, watching her ferry cut through the harbor, getting smaller and smaller until it disappeared completely. All the while, she was staring back at the island, searching for his cottage on the shoreline until Deer Haven eventually vanished around the bend.

"The thing with Charlie was a big mistake. I make those sometimes," she confessed. "Actually, I make them a lot."

"It doesn't matter. He doesn't matter at all."

"I just...I got scared. About all of it, about the way you felt about me. About the way I was starting to feel about you. It was all just so fast and...I found the letters from Lauren in your desk, and I think they messed with my head a little. Or, I don't know, maybe I was just using them as an excuse," she admitted, the weight of her pent-up confession rising from her shoulders and making her feel an instant sense of relief.

"We can start again."

Chloe nodded, hoping he meant it.

"I should have talked to you. Before you left. And after," he continued. "And Lauren is...Lauren is my past. We both have one of those, right?"

"Ben," she said, suddenly aware of the threshold that stood between them. "I don't know if I can give you everything you want."

"I just want you," he replied. "Just you."

Chloe blinked, stunned to find that her mind wasn't racing with all her characteristic questions about logistics and "what ifs." She didn't fret about the fact that she'd just exposed the softest parts of her underbelly, and she didn't even consider the halfway-built restaurant that was currently covered in her fingerprints just a few blocks away. She just saw Ben at her door, offering himself to her again. Everything with Lila and Jenna, David and Charlie faded into the furthest reaches of her mind, and all she could hear was her sister's voice echoing in her ears.

You know what you want. You're just afraid to say it.

She wanted to be able to say it.

Just then, Ben noticed the suitcase at her side, and his face fell. "Oh. Were you going somewhere?"

"I was on my way back to the island," Chloe whispered. "To find you."

Before another word passed, they were in each other's arms, holding on like she was the one who had returned from being lost at sea and he was the beacon at the top of the lighthouse. She leaned into his chest and let him hold on tighter, resting her cheek against the softness of his shirt, inhaling his perfect Ben scent and feeling relieved that it was the same lemon and wood smoke, even in Chicago.

"I missed you," she murmured, pressing her lips against his. "I really, *really* missed you."

"Me too."

He brought his mouth to the side of her neck, and she closed her eyes and buried her fingers in his hair, feeling his smile as he kissed her. When their eyes met, she smiled back, opened the door, and finally invited him in.

Chapter Twenty-Six

SIX MONTHS LATER

Chloe was in the midst of her busiest lunch service since she'd opened the doors only a month earlier. Plates flew out with satisfying speed, but the tickets were stacking like a game of Jenga. She craned her neck and noted a line out the door where waiting diners chatted and snapped photos of themselves, creating Instagram fodder that would be hashtagged with phrases like "#WEMADEIT!" "#DESTINATIONDINING" and "#CHEFCHLOEFOSTER." The food was all hers, but the marketing frenzy could only be credited to Julia, who had insisted on treating her sister like her most important client even while working extra hours to prepare for the maternity leave that was only weeks away.

"Order up, table three, table five, refill on table one," Chloe recited in her signature medium-volume expediting voice, this time as a call for her servers, two young women home from college for the summer who had already more than proven themselves with their reliability and hustle. She gave the plate a quick swipe with her kitchen towel before setting it on the pass, allowing herself a half second to admire the simple presentation of a salmon sandwich on a glossy brioche roll with lemon caper aioli and a tangle of microgreens on the side. She checked her station and realized that they were likely going to run out of lobster chowder for the third day in a row. It seemed that, however much she made, it was always gone halfway through service.

"Maybe triple rather than double for tomorrow?" suggested her sous chef, Rachel Higgins, Janey's granddaughter, who Chloe had hired on the spot after learning she had graduated from Johnson and Wales the spring before. She was relentlessly steady and hardworking, just like Janey herself, and after only a few weeks, Chloe couldn't imagine working without her by her side.

The chef nodded and focused on her plates of lobster rolls, crab salads, and the little fritters of bay shrimp and sweet corn that would grace the social media channels of so many of the people waiting in line. She glanced out at the dining room and was happy to see a healthy number of islanders enjoying their food as well. If anyone had been skeptical of the city girl taking over the old fish market, she had long since won them over with her chowder and pie.

The restaurant had turned out just as beautiful as she'd imagined it could. The faded *Fresh Fish* sign had remained on the façade, announcing the space's past and present in a weathered script that made Chloe swell with pride every time she saw it. The worn pine floors had been brought back to life and now gleamed beneath her diners' feet, and the original farmhouse pendants had been restored. Even the retro fish counter was working again, living its best life, housing an assortment of pies, despite the pleas of three different electricians who had examined the vintage wiring and implored her to just have it hauled away. But the true star of the place was still the natural light, which streamed into the space in soft beams, greeting Chloe every morning when she came in to start the prep and baking.

Passing her server two plates of arugula salad with pickled peaches and island-made feta, she glanced up to see Ben through the large front window. He was framed by the stenciled logo in a way that always made her laugh, her restaurant's name—The Catch—floating like a thought bubble over his head. He stopped to greet Jasper, who was right where he always was, curled up and smiling dopily under one of the outdoor tables, shamelessly hoping for a head pet or a fallen piece of food.

The crowd at the door parted to let her lobsterman through, and Chloe noticed more than one visitor perform a double take at the extraordinarily tall, beautiful, golden man who was there to see her. Ben made his way to the counter, stopping to chat a couple of times and clapping the backs of a few old fishermen who frequently came in together for lunch. He sat at his regular seat at the end, on the stool that she kept open every day just for him. She'd grown almost superstitious about what that seat symbolized—that she had made room for him, for them.

She leaned over and gave him a soft kiss, wiping her hands on her apron.

"Hi," he greeted her, his summer skin a deep and salty tan.

"Hi," she hummed. "You smell like the ocean."

"Funny how that works."

She thought back to the expression on his face six months ago, after they'd spent their entire first day in Chicago in bed, when she'd finally dared to admit that she wanted to cook her food on Deer Haven. She would develop the menu she'd pitched to Lila, but it would all be rooted to the Island, to its history, and to the ocean itself. She would start small, secure a business loan, and scrape her savings account. She'd be stretched thin, but the only one investing would be *her*. As she laid out her plans, Ben looked like he'd just won the lottery, grinning like he simply couldn't believe his luck. That last wavering piece inside of Chloe had just kind of clicked into place. She wanted to try being someone's jackpot.

For that entire weekend, she was almost embarrassed by how happy it all made her, even as she was leading him on a farewell tour of her city. She took him to Lost Larson for cardamom buns and Tiztal's for an oatmeal shake. She gave in to his insistence that he needed to see what all the deep-dish pizza fuss was about, then laughed when his ultimate verdict was, "Meh, too much sauce." They went to Girl and the Goat for an early dinner and then to The Publican for a late second dinner, where they shared the best roast chicken either of them had ever eaten.

She pointed out Redbud as they walked by, but she had no desire to go in, even though she knew that Steph was likely inside prepping for dinner service and sharing a family meal with the staff. After her last conversation with her old sous chef, she'd been forced to admit to herself that some friendships simply spanned a contained era, that like relationships, not everyone gets to be a forever person—and that's OK. Also, Chloe had no desire to risk running into Lila, not after she'd backed out of the new restaurant despite assurances from both Jenna and the mogul herself that she was making a "huge mistake," and that her career was officially over.

For the most part, Lila had taken the news like the cold-hearted pro that she was, promising the chef that there were twenty other "cooks" lined up to take her place. Chloe didn't bother asking what had happened to only wanting to work with the very best, and when Lila told her that she'd handle her contract and would consider the previous weeks of work a "consultancy arrangement gone wrong," Chloe felt like she was getting away with something—and a little like she was being fired all over again.

And now she was on the island, serving Ben the last bowl of chowder with two buttermilk biscuits on the side as they chatted about seeing each other that evening. It was his turn to come to her place, a sweet, high-ceilinged two-bedroom over the post office that Ginny Brown had rented to her after Chloe signed the papers for the old fish market. She still watched the ferry each night from her kitchen window, now from a different angle—and it never got old.

She was hard at work doing something she loved, something she'd built herself from the ground up, and they were happy. Chloe had her space, Ben had his, and it all worked, despite that one time that he offered her half of his dresser, and she'd felt a powerful sense of panic rise from her belly and into her throat. The topic of marriage, of children, still sat between them, unresolved, and she hoped they could somehow just continue, not talking about it at all. In her mind, things were perfect the way they were, and she found herself wondering how she could have ever felt that it wouldn't be enough, that Deer Haven, Ben and Jasper, the light glinting off the bay, the chowder and biscuits, wouldn't be enough. Together, it was everything.

She hadn't even felt compelled to search for Lauren's old letters again, to confirm that the bundle still existed, or to check if any new envelopes had been added to the stack. She wanted Ben to have his past, his story, just like she had hers. She realized that the ghost of Lauren had never been a threat to her at all, not really.

And they were planning a trip to Spain and Portugal in the off-season, when the restaurant would close for six weeks, and the fishing slowed down. Ben had already proven himself an ideal travel partner when they drove from Chicago after cleaning out her old apartment. He was predictably easygoing and agreeable on the road, up for anything from driving twenty-five miles out of the way in Ohio to find a pie stand that she'd heard about to checking into a motel in the middle of the afternoon because the space between them in the car suddenly felt way too far.

When Ben finished his lunch, he helped himself to a piece of peach pie from the case, packing it into a to-go box so he could enjoy it on the boat that afternoon while he was weaving in and out of coves and pulling his traps. He kissed her goodbye and whispered something salacious into her ear, prompting Chloe to emit a mock-scandalized gasp. She smiled wryly as she watched him walk out the door, crafting the exact words she would say to him later in bed.

Lunch service came to a close, and by late afternoon, Chloe had sent both Rachel and the dishwasher home for the day. She poured herself a seltzer and sat down for the first time since she'd gotten out of bed that morning. Stretching her tight back muscles and scrawling notes in the margins of her grocery list, she reminded herself to ask her produce supplier about fennel and yellow plums. She was deep in the research rabbit hole, examining recipes for sour cherry clafoutis, when the door opened, letting in a warm gust of sea air. The words, "Sorry, we're closed," had barely escaped her mouth when she looked up to see Charlie Davis standing in her restaurant.

He wore all black, an odd decision for a sunny day on the coast, but an ideal choice for his slimmed physique, his dark jeans and faded T-shirt proudly displaying every taut curve and angle.

"Well, look at you," Chloe said, lowering the pen from her lips when she realized that she'd been caught chewing on its end.

"Look at *you*," he replied, removing his sunglasses and tucking them into his back pocket.

She stood and hugged him, another one of those awkward embraces where neither person is sure about the acceptable arrangement of their own arms. He smelled the same.

"You stayed. Is this your place?" he asked, looking around, his eyes bright, his dimple engaged.

"It is," she answered, smiling to herself because she knew that Charlie had asked Julia about her at least twice, and he was fully aware she'd come back to Deer Haven. "How long are you here for?"

"Just a week. Just a little break before my next job."

Chloe nodded and offered him a coffee, a soda, or an iced tea. He agreed to an iced tea, and she was relieved to have something to do with her hands, even if slicing the lemon would only take about ten seconds.

"You're skinny again!" she said, handing him his drink and jokingly shaking her head. "After all my hard work fattening you up."

He smiled and shrugged, explaining that his HBO job had wrapped, and he'd just been cast in a new superhero movie, some franchise that Chloe had heard of but had never been compelled to see. She found that she wasn't remotely dazzled by the hints at his glamorous life, and wasn't compelled to ask a single follow-up question. He shrugged again, looking a bit lost.

"How's everything out here?" he asked, leaning back in his chair and letting the afternoon sun cast a beam across his shoulder and chest.

"Things are great. I'm finally cooking what I want to eat, and people seem to like it, so that's a plus."

He glanced around at the ship-lapped walls, the vintage counter case. "This place feels like you," he said softly,

"What, old?"

"No," he chuckled. "Real."

"How's Emma?"

"Emma moved to France. About a month after I got back to L.A."

Chloe had already heard that little nugget of gossip from Julia, but she still needed to bite back a smile at the idea of the actress trying to survive in the motherland of dairy and carbs.

"How's... Ben, is it?"

You know his name, Chloe wanted to reply, but instead assured him that Ben was just fine, that the two of them were happy, that they were making travel plans.

She brushed her shaggy bangs from her eyes and studied his face—same long, dark lashes, same angular jaw and flawless skin, same flushed lips that were currently curved impishly at the corners. She inhaled and waited for that dizzy, flushed feeling that she'd started to grow used to when they lived together, but it never came.

She watched him drain the glass, skipping the straw, letting the ice knock against his lips like always. "Can I make you something to eat?" she offered. "You know, old time's sake and all?"

"Nah, I'm good. Thanks." He rose from his chair and smiled his signature Charlie Davis smile as if that dimple just couldn't help itself. "I just wanted to say hi. I should get going, let you get back to it."

"It was nice seeing you," she said, meaning it even in the absence of that old flutter in her chest. "Next time you should stay for lunch."

He headed to the door, turning toward her just before he left, the sun shining onto his face as if it had been placed in the sky just for him.

"See you around, Chloe."

"See you around, Charlie," she echoed, watching him stroll down the herb-lined path before eventually returning to her work.

Thank you for reading! Did you enjoy? Please add your review because nothing helps an author more and encourages readers to take a chance on a book than a review.

And don't miss more from Jess Turner coming soon. Until then read THE ROMANCE LOOP by City Owl Author, Mary Shotwell. Turn the page for a sneak peek!

You can also sign up for the City Owl Press newsletter to receive notice of all book releases!

Sneak Peek of The Romance Loop

BY MARY SHOTWELL

Lacy Travers blinked at the two-star average rating on the phone the young woman held over the table.

"That's the book you're signing, right?" the forty-something woman asked.

Lacy sat at the table in the broad center aisle of Books & Bean, her gaze switching between the sad pair of yellow stars on the screen and the pathetic line of three, no, two people, led by the phone holder. The third person asked what the line was for and decided it wasn't for her.

But hey, at least enough people trickled into the suburban Boston indie bookstore to keep her from having huge gaps of staring off at the *Halloween Sale! Spooky Savings!* poster.

"Yes. Would you like me to sign a copy?" *Please.* She'd already been warned that if she didn't start selling out at signings, the tour may be a farewell one. Lacy signed the book with the two tennis players on the cover, their tennis rackets in the shapes of hearts. *Thirty Love*. Her thirteenth romance—the number not proving so lucky.

MAY YOU FIND YOUR PERFECT LOVE MATCH.

"There you go." *Take it.*

"Is it like *Heartbeats of a Drum*? That one wrecked me."

"Same author," Lacy said. "Less wreckage, more kissing."

"*Just be.*" The woman sighed, clutching the new book to her chest. "The best."

Lacy took a breath. It wasn't that she was unappreciative of her fans. On the contrary, she wouldn't be in such a position with her publisher, in the middle of a three-book deal over the next two years, were it not for the very people still putting forth the effort to meet her and read her work. Granted, she originally pitched a five-book series, but the publisher wanted to see 'how things panned out.'

But creeping into hour two, she found her cheeks sore from having to smile, trying to lure other customers over to her signing during periodic lulls. The store announced it every ten minutes or so, as if no one could see her table smack in the middle of the store, in plain view of everyone walking in.

The next woman up completed the end of the sorry line. She had curly blonde hair and wore a bright orange sweater.

Lacy's eyes watered from tiredness. It didn't help that her bangs were getting long enough to meet her eyelashes, tickling with every blink. *Sell another one, buy another coffee.* She grabbed a fresh copy of the book off the embarrassingly large stack—a monument of expectations versus reality—and flipped it open to the title page to sign.

"I just adored *Prognosis Love.* What Doctor Luke did for Maya. And the ending at the aquarium with the pearls and the sandwich." The lady sighed deeply, cradling the newest crime thriller hardback by the author who need not be named—the one who could slap his moniker on a plain notebook and people would buy it—at her chest.

So, you're the one fan, she almost said. It wasn't that extreme. Not yet.

She caught the unmistakable feeling of being watched and glanced to her ten o'clock , and a head ducked behind a shelf in the nonfiction section. It happened so fast; she questioned whether she was seeing things.

She handed the fan the signed copy. "I'm glad you enjoyed it. Thank you for coming out today."

The woman nodded with glee and stepped away from the table.

Lacy glanced at the bookshelf again, this time catching the coffee brown hair of the spy before another vanishing act. Or was she so caffeine-deprived she was seeing coffee everywhere?

Another woman emerged from behind the fan.

Funny. She could've sworn the line was over. Lacy held up a hand. "Sorry, can you hold on just one moment?"

Lacy stood, the blood rushing to her head creating a second of dizziness before focusing again. Someday her body would pay her back for her early twenties, but she didn't expect it at thirty.

"Elliott?"

The man popped his head around the side of the bookshelf. He looked around as if Lacy had meant some other random person named Elliott in the store, before he left the security of his hiding spot.

"Lacy?" Elliott stood taller than she remembered. Then again, she hadn't seen her ex in...had it been six years? He wore dark jeans and a gray sweater and held a book upside down in his hand.

"I didn't realize—you're here signing books?" He stepped over to the table, grabbing a copy of *Thirty Love* with his free hand, glancing at the cover then back cover copy, flipping it around a few times. "That's great." He put it down on the stack haphazardly, correcting it to sit exactly on top of the one beneath it. As he stepped away, his foot kicked the table leg. The stack of books wobbled. He fumbled to catch them but knocked over the next stack in the process.

"I'm so sorry." He bent down, picking up the books.

"Don't worry about it." She joined him, helping to stack them back on the table. "They were a little heavy on the book ordering." She cleared her throat. "Lots of books on the table." Her voice faded off with the creeping embarrassment.

"Oh, they knew the famous Lacy Travers was coming." He met her gaze, green eyes lighter, corners of his eyes a little wrinklier. Six years had served him well. Damn men and their aging. "People will snatch these up. I mean, heart-shaped rackets? I bet they serve aces."

Her face flushed with boiling heat. She bit her lip, the sight of him triggering a mix of nostalgia and heart-wrenching memories from their shattered relationship. She stood and tugged her red plaid dress; the waistline having crept up from the crouching.

Elliott winced as he rose, using the table for support.

"How's the knee you swore didn't need a brace?" She recalled he used to have pain in one of his knees, something to do with an injury in high school.

"It's funny. Instead of healing itself as I've aged, it's gotten worse." He smirked, his way of downplaying the subject.

"Well, thanks for helping with the books."

"No problem. I'm the one who knocked them over in the first place."

"What brings you out here? Are you visiting from New York?" She straightened her bangs out of habit, wishing her hair was down instead of in a ponytail to hide her reddening ears.

Elliott relaxed a bit, loosely holding his selected book. "I actually moved back a few months ago. Fenway area."

"No kidding? That's where I'm at."

"Yeah, I'm teaching now at Northeastern, so it just made sense."

"Teaching. Wow. Good for you." She meant it in a genuine way, hoping it didn't sound patronizing. The career in publishing must not have gone to plan. Sure, at first, she had hoped it wouldn't. For selfish reasons. But that was years ago, and she had moved on from that phase of her life.

"Thanks." The ensuing seconds of silence rolled along painfully. "Anyway, I stopped by here on my way to my niece's birthday. You remember Sasha? She's turning thirteen."

"Oh, that's right. Your brother..." She clicked her fingers.

"James."

"Yes, James. I guess he still lives out this way." She shook her head. "I can't believe little Sasha is thirteen."

"It's crazy. She's already past my shoulders."

"What did you pick out for her? Maybe I can help."

"Nah, that's okay."

"I'd like to think I'm in the know. Got my favorites, of course, from when I was a teen."

"It's nothing. I'll probably get something else."

"Come on. What is it?"

"Well, I um—" He reluctantly lifted the book in the air, showing the title.

"*Putting the Me in Menopause*," she read. "Interesting." She covered her smirk.

He stared at it. "Yeah…That's exactly…What better way to empower women than with knowledge? Even if it's decades away."

"You picked the closest book on the shelf when I saw you, didn't you?"

He broke into a chuckle. "I may have panicked, a little bit." He hadn't lost his honesty. Or the lock of hair that stubbornly stuck slightly out of place over his forehead in defiance.

"So, are you not writing science fiction anymore?" Writing had been their common ground. He poked fun of her writing romance when they started dating, which led to back and forth jibes about the genres. Over the years, she'd scan the new sci-fi and fantasy releases, expecting to one day see the name Elliott Stephens on the cover.

"You know, I try to keep at it. Hard with the classes and—"

"Sorry to interrupt, but I've been waiting, and I don't know how much time I have." The woman shoved her copy of *Bakery on Sweet Street* into Lacy's hands. The silhouette of the heroine and hero faced each other, the heroine in an apron, the hero in a business suit. "This is drivel."

Her hair was pulled back into a loose bun, gray hairs sprouting from the frame of her face as if she had rubbed a balloon through it before leaving the house. "I'm familiar with all your books, from *Heartbeats of a Drum* to *Range of Attraction*. And they've gotten worse. They set unrealistic expectations for single people trying to find love out in the real world. Everything you write is too perfect."

Lacy swallowed, the lump in her throat almost not going down. "I'm sorry you feel that way. I write these books as fun reads. A way to help people escape reality, give them hope."

"You don't understand," her voice escalated. "There's only so much time, or else—"

"Hey, now." Elliott stepped to the woman, the menopause book still in hand. "Calm down."

The lady leaned away from him, her long skirt and beaded shirt with a cat pin on the chest rattling like a shade on a scooted lamp. She broke a slight smile, yet her eyes read sadness. There was an awful familiarity to her face. "You'll help her, right?"

"How about I help you find something else to read? Perhaps you'd like the newest from Janet Rostren? It's a great work of nonfiction that really resonates." He eyed Lacy, his mouth wincing in uncertainty.

She had to hand it to him for trying.

"Fine." She pointed at *Bakery on Sweet Street*, still locked in Lacy's hands. "You can have that back." She reluctantly followed Elliott. He turned around with a look of victory.

"Thank you," Lacy mouthed.

Elliott quickstepped from the woman back to the desk. "She's terrifying. Is every book signing like this?"

Lacy shook her head.

"I don't know what you're doing after this, but if you could use a beer, you should stop by James's house. I'm sure the family would love to see you."

Her instinct was to say no. She didn't have the bandwidth for seeing her ex and his extended family in the same day. But he did help her out, and a cold drink didn't sound so bad after the day she was having. "We'll see."

"It was good to see you, either way."

He jumped back next to the lady, guiding her towards the front of the store, away from the signing table.

Already she had encountered her ex-boyfriend and the rudest reader she'd ever met, and there was still time left on the signing clock.

"Can't wait to see what's next."

Don't stop now. Keep reading with your copy of THE ROMANCE LOOP.

Don't miss more from Jess Turner coming soon and discover all the details at jessturnerwrites.com

Until then, discover THE ROMANCE LOOP by City Owl Author, Mary Shotwell.

What if your love story rewrote you?

Romance author Lacy Travers's career is flatter than the champagne at her last pity party. So when a disgruntled fan accuses her of "ruining love" at a sad little book signing—and her ex-boyfriend Elliott swoops in like a knight in polyester armor—it's just another weird chapter in her life.

But things take a surreal turn when a party invite lands her not in Elliott's apartment... but in an *operating room.* As the surgeon. In a world straight out of one of her books.

Trapped in her own romance novel—with no clue how to escape—Lacy must survive cringey tropes, steam-soaked plot twists, and the very clichés she once mocked. When Elliott gets pulled into the chaos too, the two must navigate vampire seductions, cowboy duels, and more than a few forced proximity scenes.

The real kicker? The more they rewrite the story, the more the story rewrites them.

With every sizzling page turned, Lacy begins to question the love she's always written off—and the nerdy sci-fi writer who's been beside her all along.

The Romance Loop is a laugh-out-loud, genre-hopping romantic comedy—a story about messy hearts, meta love, and the unexpected magic of a story you never saw coming.

Please sign up for the City Owl Press newsletter for chances to win special subscriber-only contests and giveaways as well as receiving information on upcoming releases and special excerpts.

All reviews are **welcome** and **appreciated**. Please consider leaving one on your favorite social media and book buying sites.

Escape Your World. Get Lost in Ours! City Owl Press at www.cityowlpress.com.

Acknowledgments

When my family moved to a remote island off the coast of Maine in the mid-nineties, I knew I would write a book about it someday. Thank you, North Haven, for inspiring the landscape, the romance, and the "utterly marooned" vibes of this story.

Tremendous thanks to my earliest readers: Amanda, Mo, Beth, Steph, Jenn, Andrea, and Eden—beloved and powerful friends who remind me every day that women should run the world. Thank you to Aron Gaudet, fellow Mainer, fellow writer, and forever AG to me. I love that you still want to read my work even after those terrible stories I showed you when we were in our twenties. Thank you to Kristen Simmons, whose talent and grit inspires me to keep writing. Meeting you at a retreat at a weird Scandinavian tiny house in Midcoast Maine was truly a gift from the universe. And to fellow Scone Campers Cory McCarthy and A.R. Capetta, I'll never forget the wisdom you shared with me over fancy cocktails and while floating in the megapool. The two of you gave me the courage to try. Thank you to Amy Bishop-Wycisk, who helped me believe that people other than my friends might read this book someday, and who worked tirelessly to help shape my first drafts.

I owe so much to the team at City Owl Press. Thank you to Tina Moss, Yelena Casale, Caroline Trussell, and Tee Tate for championing this book. Tee, you are the editor of my dreams! Your insight, passion, brainstorming powers, and your disdain for excessive adverbs are what helped me to fully realize this story. Working with you has been beyond delightful and I could not have done this without you.

Huge shout-out to my fellow writers in the trenches, especially those of you in your mid-life era. Remember this: you're not too old and it's not too late. Please prioritize your dreams and keep going, because the only people who definitely don't make it are the ones who stop. My old English professor once told me that writing is its own reward, and I think of her words every day. Never stop writing, never stop rewarding yourself.

I was raised on a small farm by parents who love reading, and even when money was tight, there were always books (hooray for Mr. Paperback in Dover-Foxcroft, ME). Today, trading books with my father is one of the great joys of my life. That being said, if you want to skip certain passages in this book, I think that would be best for both of us, Dad! Thank you to my parents for expecting me to read, encouraging me to write, and for always being up for a trip to the library.

To Josh, who knew me back in 1995 when I had purple hair and wrote scathing college newspaper articles under the name Nora Quinn, thank you for always believing I could do this, and for understanding that often I need to put on headphones and shut the door on you to get it done. Thank you for driving me crazy and making me laugh for all of these many years, and for reminding me that love at first sight isn't just a fictional trope.

Finally, thank you to my Lily, who consistently asked if "romance was brewing" as I wrote this book, and who delivers chaos, humor and happiness to every single day. You are my biggest dream come true and I am so lucky to be your mom.

About the Author

JESS TURNER began her career as a journalist and spent several years working for newspapers and magazines before realizing that she only wanted to write romantic stories. A New Englander to the core, she grew up in Maine and currently lives in Vermont, where she hatches schemes, pretends she's the mayor, and does not ski. She loves to bake cakes, read about powerful women, listen to trashy celebrity podcasts and make hideous crafts with her daughter.

jessturnerwrites.com

instagram.com/jessturnerwrites
pinterest.com/jessturnerwrites
threads.com/jessturnerwrites

About the Publisher

City Owl Press is a cutting edge indie publishing company, bringing the world of romance and speculative fiction to discerning readers.

Escape Your World. Get Lost in Ours!

www.cityowlpress.com

facebook.com/CityOwlPress
x.com/cityowlpress
instagram.com/cityowlbooks
pinterest.com/cityowlpress
tiktok.com/@cityowlpress

www.ingramcontent.com/pod-product-compliance
Lightning Source LLC
LaVergne TN
LVHW091107080826
845145LV00008B/1842

* 9 7 8 1 6 4 8 9 8 5 3 9 3 *